HUNTING
OF MEN

Blue Mysteries

HUNTING OF MEN

A Johnny Till Detective Novel

*Danny,
Thanks for your
support!
Enjoy the
hunt!*

LANCE J. LORUSSO

LANIER
PRESS

LANIER PRESS *an Imprint of BookLogix*

Alpharetta, GA

ISBN: 978-1-63183-610-7 - Paperback
eISBN: 978-1-63183-611-4 - ePub
eISBN: 978-1-63183-612-1 - mobi

Library of Congress Control Number: 2019918061

Printed in the United States of America   1 1 2 5 1 9

⊚This paper meets the requirements of ANSI/NISO Z39.48-1992 (Permanence of Paper)

Glock® is a registered trademark and brand of Glock, Inc.

Kevlar® is a registered trademark of E.I. du Pont de Nemours and Company.

Kramer® is a registered trademark of Kramer Handgun Leather.

TASER and Axon are trademarks of Axon Enterprise, Inc., some of which are registered in the US and other countries. For more information, visit http://www.axon.com/legal. All rights reserved © 2018 Axon Enterprise, Inc.

This book is dedicated to my wife, Barbara, who supports me in every venture, keeps a "big picture" focus, and always knows when to jump in to help me reach the finish line.

This book is also dedicated to the elite men and women in law enforcement who hold the title of homicide detective. Thank you for being the voice of the victims who can no longer speak for themselves.

There is no hunting like the hunting of man, and those who have hunted armed men long enough and liked it, never care for anything else thereafter.

—Ernest Hemingway

INTRODUCTION

For the courts, there is a resolution to every murder case brought before them. Whether by conviction, plea, or acquittal, there is closure of each file stored on the shelves and computers in the offices and archives of court clerks around the world. For the victim's loved ones, the files are the memories of the decedent that live on, along with the horror of their death and the uncertainty of life without them.

Cold cases are different. The crimes remain unsolved. There is no file before the courts, no trials to commence, and no resolution for the justice every victim deserves. For those left behind to carry on after the death of the victim, there is a special emptiness—a hole with no known floor. It is a story with an unwritten chapter that has no ending. Until the cold case is solved, the victim's story is both unfinished and untold, and there can be no rest.

For the detectives assigned to Homicide, every victim deserves justice. Cold cases are especially frustrating. Once the media has lost interest, the public stops asking questions, and after significant time has passed, only the victim's loved ones and the homicide detectives keep lit the hope of justice.

Cold case; noun

. . . Any case whose probative investigative leads
have been exhausted.
—National Institute of Justice

. . . An unsolved criminal investigation that has stopped
being actively pursued because of a lack of evidence.
—Merriam-Webster Dictionary

. . . A case forgotten by all but the victims' families and the
officers who cannot and will not let it go.
—Lance J. LoRusso

PROLOGUE

T he dampness made the forty-degree weather seem colder. The rain had finally let up after a week, and people were willing to walk in any weather if they could stay dry. Officer Mike Dunlap stood in a dark, quiet area at the back of the football stadium. There were no lights in there, so it was the perfect place to meet her. He checked his pager again and saw the number.

God, I hope she shows up. Not sure what I'll do if she doesn't. I can't take too much time here. Someone will notice that I'm missing.

The pager showed a number and a code: #3400 930. The stadium was known in the school as building 3400 on the campus map, and "930" made sense to Officer Dunlap, as he knew the number that paged him was the pay phone in the cafeteria. The football game would be over, the crowd would be thinning, and they could be alone at 9:30 p.m.

They had to be alone.

As Dunlap checked his watch again, he heard someone approaching. He looked up as the person moved slowly toward him, hunched over and wearing the same hat and coat he'd seen her wearing at the game.

Dunlap smiled as he saw the fog from her breath rise. As dangerous as it was to meet her, it warmed him inside. A few feet closer, and they could whisper without anyone hearing them.

Come on. Come closer, and trust me.

Two steps later, Officer Dunlap saw movement as both hands came out of her coat pockets. It was quicker than he expected and hard to see clearly in the low light. He was still smiling when the first shot hit him.

Oh, God! No! What's happening?

The next shots came quickly, without hesitation. The figure never stopped moving toward him. Dunlap watched in horror as the flashes of light from the barrels blinded him. As he began to fall, his mind searched for an explanation and his hand searched for his Smith & Wesson Model 686.

No! Why?

Intense, searing pain wracked his body, and he felt weak. His gun hand couldn't function as he tried to draw his revolver—a movement he'd performed hundreds of times in training and once on the street to shoot an armed robber who'd nearly killed him and his partner. On the ground now, looking up, Dunlap watched as the figure got closer. The final flash of light passed into his eyes and through his mind as his thoughts seemed to slow to a stop.

Fight! Breathe! Can't see anything!

As the last of Officer Michael Dunlap's life ran out onto the concrete, his killer put the guns out of sight in the coat pockets and walked slowly away. It was done.

CHAPTER 1

"Officer Till, do you see the driver of the pickup truck that you arrested in this courtroom?"

"Yes, ma'am. I do."

"Please point to him and describe his clothing for the jury."

There is an uneasy silence during every trial when the courtroom is poised for the next fact to be revealed, or the next stage of the proceedings to bring a resolution closer. This case was no exception. The prosecution had worked hard to focus the jury on these facts and this exact testimony. The tension was palpable.

Officer Johnny Till raised his right hand from his lap and pointed his finger at Randy Laymen, a sixty-year-old white male sitting at the defense table. "He is seated at the defense table. He is a white male in his sixties wearing a blue sport coat, a white shirt, and a blue-striped tie with a diamond tie clasp."

The prosecutor stood a bit straighter, turned toward the defendant, then toward the jury. "Let the record reflect, Your Honor, that the witness has identified the defendant, Randy Laymen." Ana Liss was a tall, attractive, smart, and focused young prosecutor whom

Johnny guessed to be just shy of thirty years old. A bunch of cops thought she was too young, and it did not help that she could pass for nineteen. However, Johnny always enjoyed having her on his cases because he was impressed by her skills and admired her fierce dedication to the job. As for her looks, he thought it probably played well with a jury, and her youthful appearance likely disarmed a lot of criminal-defense attorneys who learned too late that she was fearless in the courtroom.

"The record shall so reflect," Judge Whitlow said. It was a formality, and the judge's comments were not legally required. It was more of a tradition, really, but Judge Whitlow was very much in favor of tradition and formality. She also loved to watch a good scrap in the courtroom. It reminded her of her twenty years as a trial attorney before taking the bench. This case was not disappointing her.

"Your witness, counselor." Ana returned to her seat, picked up a pen, and prepared for battle as her opponent tried to challenge the testimony of Officer Till.

At six foot five and three hundred pounds, defense attorney Ronald Pressman was a presence in the court-room. As a former professional football player, his voice alone was intimidating, but his seemingly inside knowledge of the police department was uncanny. Many times, he had taken a witness off his feet by asking about a fact, as inconsequential as it may have been, that only someone working in the PD would know. Today was no exception. After hours of cross-examination on skid marks, paint transfer, and forensic evidence, his efforts to produce a reasonable doubt for his client in this hit-and-run and vehicular-homicide case were dwindling. So he decided to pull out the only other card he had: distraction.

It was a game he played well, and truth be known, he enjoyed it. As for the fairness of it, in his mind, a win was a win.

"Officer Till, you have been a fatality traffic investigator for three years, correct?"

"Yes, sir."

"And you are appearing today in your uniform?"

Johnny Till made a point to look down at his badge before turning to the jury, smiling, and answering, "Yes, sir." Several jurors smiled.

"Did I make you smile, Officer?"

"A little, sir. I looked down to make sure I hadn't forgotten to put on my badge or something. I thought you had me there for a minute!" Several jurors chuckled at this comment. Judge Whitlow put her head down so the jury could not see her smile.

"But you are no longer a fatality accident investigator, isn't that right?"

"Yes, sir. That's correct." The courtroom—and the jury—were quiet.

"Yet you came here today, appearing before this jury, giving them the appearance that you are something you are not. In fact, you have been '*invited*' to leave the Fatality Accident Unit, when most officers work in that unit their entire careers, isn't that correct? Was that due to your lack of experience in fatality accident investigation or to errors made in this and other high-profile cases?"

Johnny Till smiled, as did the prosecutor. Then he turned toward the jury. "Well, sir, I appreciate that you used the correct term, 'invited,' although I think using air quotes with your fingers was a bit much." Johnny paused as a few jurors started laughing, and the judge admonished everyone to maintain order. When the courtroom was quiet, Johnny Till continued, "I was invited to leave the Fatality Accident Unit by the chief of police. Today, assuming I leave the courtroom before five o'clock," he looked back toward the defense attorney, then returned his eyes to the jury, "I will become the first officer to leave the Fatality Accident Unit and go straight to the Homicide Unit. I'm honored and looking forward to it. You are correct, sir. Most officers spend their careers as fatality traffic investigators. However, I will be the youngest officer ever assigned to the Homicide Unit in terms of both age and time in service."

Flustered, Pressman tried to find something else to say. When he faltered for a minute or two while shuffling his papers in his large hands and dropping one, Judge Whitlow spoke. "Anything else, counselor?"

"Nothing further, Your Honor." The walk to the defense table no doubt seemed longer than the approach to the witness stand.

Judge Whitlow looked at Ana Liss. "Anything further from the prosecution?"

Ana stood, looked at the defense counsel, smiled at the jury, then spoke in a calm voice. "Nothing further from the State, Your Honor. May Detective, excuse me, *Officer* Till be excused?"

Judge Whitlow looked down. "Yes." She glanced at Johnny. "Officer Till, you may step down." Judge Whitlow seemed to be holding back a smile.

Johnny returned to his seat and saw a note Ana had written on the legal pad sitting in front of his seat: *Where does he get his information?* The judge began speaking about the schedule for closing arguments that would begin after lunch as Johnny scribbled a response: *Not sure, but he won't try that again anytime soon!*

As Johnny stood to leave, he heard Pressman ask the judge for a brief recess. As the judge presumed the purpose was to gather his thoughts, or lick his wounds, a ten-minute break commenced. Johnny was walking into the men's room when Pressman caught up with him out of breath.

"Till, wait a second."

Johnny allowed the restroom door to close and stood there in the hallway waiting for Pressman to close the short gap between them. As he approached, Johnny saw the open palms facing up, the conciliatory look on Pressman's face, and the slight smile of a man working to disarm his adversary for the next battle.

"What's so important that you sprinted over here?" Johnny's face showed little emotion.

"Well, I just wanted you to know that nothing I said in there is personal. It's a role lawyers play, like on a stage."

"A stage?" Johnny was fighting to keep the anger down in his belly. Johnny recalled the crime scene and the thick pool of blood where a little girl's future shortened to a few minutes.

"Yes. The jury expects some theatrics. You can't deny that. They see trials on television and in the movies. They're pulled from their jobs and their homes to sit in the strange courtroom environment. We have to keep them entertained to some degree."

"Interesting perspective." Johnny replied.

"So you see, my questions attacking your integrity weren't personal. No, in no sense were they personal. They were simply part of the script, a distraction, to attempt to get the jury to focus on some semblance of doubt in favor of my client." Pressman had caught his breath and was smiling now.

Johnny was certain the first three responses in his head would've ended in his termination, so he went with the fourth. "So, I have a different perspective, counselor. You attempted to paint me as a liar."

Pressman put his hands up in mock surrender. "Perhaps a man who would bend the truth to appear in a better light, but I never called you a liar." The last words were spoken in time with his finger pointed at Johnny's face.

After a quick look to see that several people were approaching but were still too far away to hear, Johnny locked eyes with Pressman and quietly said, "The courtroom is your stage. The rest of the world is mine. If you plan to call me a liar again in any theater, I suggest you start hitting the gym, Pressman."

All the mock collegiality ran quickly from Pressman's face. He now looked like a man who felt a threat to his authority. He leaned over and attempted to use his size to intimidate Johnny. "Are you threatening me, Till?"

"If, dumbass. If. That makes anything I say a conditional threat at best. But, if you do, that knee replacement you were discussing with your client will come sooner than expected and your jaw will likely be wired shut during your rehab." Johnny smiled. "Now, a dozen witnesses are watching you lean toward me all red-faced and angry, and every one of them will swear I was smiling with my hands at my sides the entire time." Johnny stared intently at Pressman. "Are we done here or are you feeling like a tough guy?"

Pressman stared at Johnny for a moment, then leaned back and quickly walked away.

Johnny returned to headquarters after the lawyers finished their closing arguments. Ana promised to call him if the jury had any questions or when they reached a verdict.

Johnny always wanted to be there, good or bad, when the jury returned with their verdict. For him, it was closure. In this case, this was especially true. The defendant had driven around a stopped school bus and killed a little girl who was attempting to board the bus for elementary school. He barely missed her mother, who had just let go of her hand. A few paint chips from a mailbox he hit when leaving the scene were all the evidence Johnny had, because the camera on the side of the bus malfunctioned and everyone involved was too shaken up to remember anything about the driver. It took three weeks to find him, and receipts in his car showed he'd consumed fourteen drinks the night before.

Johnny walked into the Homicide Unit and looked around for his new desk. He had his personal items in a box in the back of his assigned marked car, but somehow thought it was pretentious to walk into a new unit with his hands full—especially this unit. The Lawler County Homicide Unit was well-known throughout the Southeast. They'd solved some of the worst "whodunits" in history, and the detectives had been featured on crime TV stories and national news shows many times. There were two movies made about the crimes they solved. It was a big deal to be part of this team, and he knew he had to put his game in overdrive to keep up.

As he walked in, he saw a couple of detectives sitting at their desks. It was day shift, so most of the detectives who were on duty were chasing leads and finding witnesses. He remembered a statement one of his buddies in another department once made to a micromanaging boss who questioned why he was never in the office.

"Well, sir, yesterday I spent all day looking around the office. I looked in the closets, under the desks, and in the trash cans, but I didn't find a single bad guy! So I thought I'd change tactics and get outside and look!" The answer got him a write-up for being a smartass, but he was right. Good detectives are out working unless they can use the phone or the internet to work a lead. Johnny believed in the acronym GOYAKOD: Get Off Your Ass and Knock on Doors.

Johnny found the major's office and knocked. The man behind the desk looked up and smiled. He stood up, walked around the desk, and shook Johnny's hand. "Glad to have you on the team, Till."

"Thank you, sir. It's an honor to get the nod to work here."

"We've done some great work here, but I look at it differently. We're fortunate to have you." The words struck Johnny in an awkward way, and he had no response. Sensing his uneasiness, the major spoke. "We're busy, Johnny, and every case here is critical. This team is made up of smart folks, but there are plenty of smart folks in the department. Many of them have more experience and more gray hair than you." He smiled at Johnny. "You are here because we had an opening, and you've demon-strated your ability and a drive to dig deep to solve a case. That horrible hit-and-run in the paper today, I followed that case. That was some damn good police work. More than that, you never gave up. Your sergeant told me he had to order you to go home more than once."

"Thank you, sir." He paused. "Giving up is overrated." Johnny smiled. "Besides, I couldn't look those parents in the face again until I did everything I could to find the man who killed their daughter."

The major nodded. "All right, enough with the niceties. Let's get you to a desk. You'll have some admin stuff to do, swapping out your car for an unmarked and such. Put your stuff on your desk and get settled, then come see me. I want to show you something. It's a ritual around here."

"Will do, sir." Johnny walked out, and then went back to his car. After he'd placed all of the items in and around the desk the major showed him and made arrangements to exchange his marked unit for a detective car, he walked into the major's office again.

"All set up, sir. I'll swap cars in the a.m. on the way in. You wanted me to check with you about something before I left for the day?"

The major got up and walked past Johnny. "Yep. Follow me."

The two men walked down the hall to an area of the Homicide Unit Johnny had never seen before. They walked to the end of a long hallway and stood in front of a door. Major Bill Worth turned the key in the deadbolt, and then stepped away.

"Your turn in the barrel." As Johnny stepped forward, he turned to the major, who spoke as he looked directly into Johnny's eyes. "Every homicide detective in this department has walked into this room. It's a rite of passage. I make sure every detective steps in on their first day in the Homicide Unit. It's a reminder that once they take their last breaths, the victims only have us to fight for them. Others will miss them and grieve their loss, but only homicide detectives remain in the fight to allow the victims to have their day in court."

Johnny looked at the seasoned veteran who was well-known for his sense of humor. He'd first met the major when he started as a recruit visiting every unit in the department. For the first time, he saw the lines around his eyes and the weight of the crimes he investigated. Johnny knew in that instant he wanted to make him proud. In a sentence, the major told him to up his game, to be better than anyone ever expected, and to be worthy of the immense trust placed in him. That was the mark of a true leader. No further words needed to be spoken to convince Johnny that letting the major and his new team down was never an option.

Officer Johnny Till walked into the Homicide Unit that afternoon. Now Detective Johnny Till opened the door to the file room that was both hated and revered by every homicide detective. The sign on the door was as ominous as it was inviting: COLD CASE FILES.

The ritual in the Lawler County Police Homicide Unit was simple. Every new homicide detective was tasked with pulling a case file out of the cold case file room. From that point forward, that became their case file. It was a tradition started many years ago by Worth, who was somewhat of a legend in homicide circles, and not just within Lawler County or the state of Georgia. He had served in Homicide longer than most officers wore the badge: twenty-five years. He believed that every new homicide detective had the potential to be the next best detective, and he wanted to get them on the toughest cases as soon as possible. It was a mark on the horizon, a goal to reach while working all the other fresh cases. It was also a reminder that solving homicide cases quickly was the best opportunity to obtain justice for the victim.

The young detective turned on the light and looked around. The room was lit by two fluorescent fixtures in the ceiling. Across the back wall was a row of floor-to-ceiling shelves filled with three-ring binders. Across the spine of each was a name and case number. The first two digits of the case number corresponded to the year of the incident, and the remaining numbers were specific to the case. The oldest file bore the amazing beginning digits of "15." The yellowed label made it clear this case was about a homicide committed during World War I.

"Damn," Johnny said out loud. "That's a long time to wait for justice."

"Yes, it is," Major Worth said behind him. "I'll leave you here to pick a case. Send me an email and let me know which one you have. Then set a time for us to discuss it after you've reviewed the file. Pull the door closed when you're done, and lock the deadbolt." The major handed him a set of keys, gesturing. "This one is the back door, this is the evidence drop box, this one is for your desk and credenza, and this is the cold case file room. This is your set."

"Thanks," he said as he took the keys and studied them a moment.

"One more thing." Worth reached into his front left pocket. He pulled out something and then held out his hand. In it, face up, was a Lawler County Police badge with the word DETECTIVE engraved in the banner at the top. The badge was worn, and as Johnny took it, he looked at it carefully.

"Sergeant Bastin in Supply will give you a new, shiny one for your uniform and another for your waist. This one belonged to an old homicide detective I knew. It will remind you that you are now part of a tradition. Make him proud."

"Will do." Johnny watched as the major turned and left the room.

His mind thought about the fact that a file from 1915 would read more like a historical novel than a case file. The victim was, of course, dead. But by now, so was everyone else: the perpetrator, the detectives, the spouse, and probably the victim's kids, as well. He knew, however, why the case file still remained an active case file. It was an unwritten rule among homicide detectives: Justice never dies. As long as there is a victim, there is reason to pursue the case. Although the chances of ever solving a case that old were remote, if it happened, the answers would mean something to someone, even if it was a grandchild.

Some of the labels were yellowed. Others were in worse shape, and the ink on the labels was starting to fade. He made a note that he should probably recommend that the admin print a new label for these older cases. However, they would never remove the handwritten paper on the spine. That was forbidden. Every file in that room belonged to the homicide detective who originally drew the case, either because they were on call or they had a specialty in that area. The original work of the detective was sacred. The new labels would be affixed with care and respect but would never replace the originals.

The binders had one thing in common: they were all blue—or, nearly all of them. Johnny looked around and estimated that there were over a hundred binders, but many of them had the same case number. The biggest cases looked to have four or five, while a few had only one. Each represented not only the loss of a life and a person who drew their last breath prematurely, they also represented the blood and sweat of dedicated professionals. Some probably evidenced hundreds—and perhaps thousands—of hours tracking leads, while others showed the only leads that ultimately proved to be dead ends.

His eyes focused on the odd red binders. There were only a few files in red binders, and maybe that was why they caught his eye. He stepped forward and walked to his left toward the older cases. He thought about starting with a more recent case, but he knew his heart would never let him do that.

"Go big or go home, right?" he said as he stepped forward and pulled three red binders from the shelf. The spine of each read "98-17862." He piled the binders on the small desk in the corner and turned on the reading lamp.

Johnny unclipped his tie and unbuttoned his uniform shirt. He sat down and took a deep breath. The stale air in the cold case room was familiar and eerie. It reminded him of visiting his grandparents and helping them clean out their attic or searching a house that had long been abandoned. In the latter case, he was usually looking for a bad guy or a victim. It was strange how an odor could bring back such a rush of memories. He recalled that there was scientific support for this. The sense of smell was tied closest to memory.

As he sat down, he pushed the two binders marked "2 of 3" and "3 of 3" aside. In front of him was the first binder of the case. As he opened the binder, he saw a picture of the victim in a yellowed plastic sleeve on the inside of the cover. It was a man in a Lawler Police uniform. Johnny had pulled the cold case file of an officer murdered in the line of duty. The thought caused him to stare at the picture in front of him for more than a minute. The picture looked familiar to Johnny.

The first page of the binder contained a fact sheet. The officer's name was Michael Dunlap. He was thirty-five years old when he died on Friday, November 4, 1998. He was shot by an unidentified assailant or assailants and was pronounced dead on the scene due to obvious, lethal wounds. He had been assigned to the Public Relations Unit.

That's when it hit Johnny. He knew this man. Officer Michael Dunlap had come to Johnny's elementary school and spoken to the students. He remembered being in awe of his presence, his shiny badge, his pressed uniform, and his patrol car. "What could be cooler?" he had said to his best friend Ronnie. "You get to drive fast and catch bad guys!" Ronnie had been more impressed with the free food and donuts cops were rumored to get.

Johnny was back for a moment in his small desk, listening intently to the advice of "Officer Mike," as he had called himself. He was touched by the visit of Officer Mike. Although Johnny did not understand it at the time, each visit to a school had probably touched Officer Michael Dunlap, as well. No one could have predicted the turn of events that led to this moment, when the student became the sheepdog tracking the wolf who killed the teacher.

As Johnny stared at the page, the weight of the task before him fell full force upon his shoulders. But never once did he think about putting the binders back and choosing another case, even though he was alone and no one would know if he did.

Mike Dunlap was a murder victim in some ways like any other, with a family who missed him every day, but he was also a murder victim like no other. It's not that his life was any more important than the other victims; the reason was deeper than that.

The murder of a cop was an attack on society itself. In the United States, unlike other countries, the military was not involved in civilian law enforcement. So the officer on the street was the highest level of protection present in society from criminals and people that meant to do harm. When a cop was killed, there was a logical understanding that the perpetrator would kill anyone if they would kill a cop. For that reason, the resources of every law enforcement agency focused like a laser on apprehending the perpetrator. That was standard practice. This explained why there were only two or three sets of red binders among all of the cold case files, and most were much older.

That's also why Johnny was puzzled as to why this case remained unsolved. The older cases could be explained by a lack of forensic techniques, like DNA and blood-type matching, or even advanced crime-scene-processing techniques. But in 1998, the detectives and the department had a lot of tools in the toolbox.

The next few pages contained a synopsis of the investigation written by the last detective who worked on the case. The synopsis was short. It was intended as a roadmap for the next detective who picked up the case file. The documents behind the synopsis in this binder and the other two provided more details.

As Johnny read the synopsis, he gained a sense of the tremendous amount of frustration faced by the Homicide Unit. There was reference to hundreds of interviews of citizens, cops, and criminals, as well as reviews of the physical evidence available at the scene. They had visited every type of location, from businesses to schools, homes to prisons. Finally, there was a list of homicide detectives who worked on the case. It was long; Johnny counted twenty-four names. He made a mental note to speak or meet with each of them. He knew they would all remember the case, and perhaps the years since their involvement—which for some extended into retirement—had allowed them to formulate opinions or theories that might help him.

He imagined the frustration and sense of defeat of each detective as they removed the binders from their desks and returned them to the cold case file room. Johnny figured that he would start with the most recent detective to work the case. As he reached the end of the synopsis, he saw the initials and the name: J. B. Lettieri.

Johnny looked at his watch and realized he had not heard back from the prosecutor on the trial. He also realized it was nearly 6:00 p.m., and he had been up for thirteen hours. He had worked out prior to coming to court this morning at 7:00 a.m., and he was tired. He would take the binders to his desk and lock them in his file cabinet, formally sign out the binders with the major, then head home. He had a lot on his mind and wanted to review the media reports of the murder of Officer Mike.

Without realizing it, he had personalized his victim. It was something every homicide detective did. It felt at once comforting and daunting.

CHAPTER 2

J ohnny placed the three binders into the file cabinet behind his desk. He locked it, then headed to the major's office to tell him what file he pulled. When he walked in, the major was on the phone. The major waved him into his office, and Johnny stepped through the doorway. Instead of sitting down in one of the chairs in front of Worth's desk, Johnny remained standing and walked around the office looking at the decorations and plaques on the walls.

By Johnny's quick count, Bill Worth had been recognized by every federal agency with a presence in Lawler County. Plaques from the FBI, DEA, ATF, Secret Service, and United States Marshals all mentioned his commitment to the mission and professionalism. More impressive was the fact that the plaques virtually tracked Worth's career, reflecting his rank as a detective, sergeant, lieutenant, captain, and major. Even though he was in different units ranging from Homicide to Intelligence, Narcotics to Uniform Patrol, Worth excelled in every assignment. Johnny was beginning to see the true person behind the legend the recruits learned about in the police academy.

As he looked around, he also saw a large bookshelf. A lot of the books were about homicide investigation, and others were about specific law enforcement topics like hostage negotiation, crime-scene processing, and DNA analysis. The rest were a mix of books about serial killers, biographies of a few famous folks, a copy of *The Federalist Papers*, and a copy of a book about officer-involved shootings titled *When Cops Kill: The Aftermath of a Critical Incident*.

Next to the bookshelf on a small table was a form titled BOOK SIGN-OUT. Johnny could see that several detectives had borrowed the major's books. As Johnny pulled a book from the shelf titled *Criminal Investigation* by Charles R. Swanson and Leonard Territo, he noticed that the book was signed by the authors. A random check of a few other books revealed that they were all signed. Johnny thought about a commander who would loan out signed books to anyone who asked to read them.

As Johnny continued to look around the office, he was trying to piece together the other side of the phone call. The major passed Johnny a clipboard and a pen. The top of the paper attached to it read COLD CASE FILE ASSIGNMENTS. Johnny filled in the name of the victim, the case number, his name, and the date. He then handed the clipboard back to the major, who was finishing his call. He hung up the phone with an audible sigh.

"Tough call?" Johnny asked.

"Part of the job. Dealing with politics. Sergeant Thomas caught a suicide last week and has been working it hard, but the family is convinced it was the murder of the century. 'There's no way he would have killed himself!' I've heard it a million times. It doesn't help matters when they don't leave a note."

"Denial?"

"Denial is one thing, but suicides can make some folks downright ornery!" He picked up a pen on his desk and began tapping it on the edge. "Who said a person who is so distraught, in so much pain living their everyday life that they see death as the only way out, *must* take time to write a note? There's no manual. Sometimes I wish they'd write a novella—like, thirty pages—to answer the questions of all the friends and family they leave behind." He looked at Johnny. "Ask any veteran homicide detective, and they'd rather work a true whodunit than a suicide."

"Why is that?"

"You can't win, no matter what you do! If you solve the case, you tell the family and friends left behind the one thing they do not want to hear and will never accept." The major put the pen into a cup on his desk that held a lot of others. He paused and looked up at Johnny. "I understand it, though. The people left behind have only two things facing them: grief and questions. They torture themselves so much with the what-ifs and 'Did I miss some sign or cry for help?' that some never get past believing that the person must have been murdered. It allows for a simple answer to those questions—it wasn't suicide. Then they blame the police for botching the investigation, and the conspiracy goes on. I really feel for them." He sat back in his chair and took a deep breath. "It's something that the public never seems to understand but every homicide detective sees firsthand. The families of murder victims often get closure, but the families of people who commit suicide rarely do."

The words were as much an observation as a mentoring moment. Johnny let them sink in. "So I guess you spend a lot of time trying to keep the family off the detectives' backs so they can work the case."

Worth smiled. "Very perceptive, Detective, and not just the family. I hear from the pastors, rabbis, politicians, reporters, coworkers, bosses, kindergarten teachers, you name it! Remember that when you're hip deep in a tough one and I'm stuck here in my office half the day." He took a long sip from his coffee cup. The hot beverage that seemed to make a homicide detective's world go around was not fresh, and he winced a bit as he swallowed. Worth put the cup down and shook his head.

Worth picked up the clipboard and looked at Johnny's entry. "Well, you'll never make it in Homicide. I can read your writing!"

Johnny smiled. "The nuns drilled it into my head."

"It's a good thing. Most of the guys around here—and a few of the ladies—write like a chicken on meth! Good thing for them we type everything now." Worth put down the clipboard and settled back in his chair. "Mike Dunlap. Well, you do like a challenge."

"Yes, sir. Well, I didn't know it was a murder of a cop when I pulled it off the shelf."

Major Worth was a stocky man with big arms and a barrel chest. He put his hands behind his head and leaned back in his chair. He looked at Johnny with an intensity he had not seen before. "No one was in there when you pulled it. You could've put it back and pulled another." He focused on Johnny.

"If it was easy, sir, everyone would do it. Go big or go home."

Worth nodded. "Where do you plan to start?"

"I thought I'd start with the media reports tonight. That's something I can do from home. I want to get a sense of what was happening around here then. After all, I was in grade school then." Johnny smiled and the major rolled his eyes. It was a respectful recognition of the large age gap between them. When the moment passed, Johnny continued, "Then I'll finish reviewing the file and speak with as many of the detectives who worked the case as I can. They may have some ideas. I want to get a good foundation in the case before I interview family or friends. Then," Johnny paused, "I'll see where that leads me."

Worth nodded. "That's a good plan. I always prefer getting the lay of the land first on a cold case. It helps avoid duplication of effort and makes you more efficient when you do speak with witnesses and potential suspects. That's the tough part of a cold case—the suspect is likely sitting right under your nose, and the family and friends will get pissed if you don't know the facts." He leaned his chair forward. "Let me know when you're ready for my interview."

Johnny looked surprised. "Sir?"

"You'll find my name in the original list of officers who responded. I was new on the street." Worth looked up as he sat back in his chair. "It's a night I'll never forget." He shook his head. "What a waste." He took another sip of his coffee and winced again. Johnny noticed the mug was marked with his name. Based upon the inscription, it was a gift from the Homicide Unit. He made a note of that. He also wondered how the major and the unit would react to his aversion to coffee in favor of green tea.

"I wondered why you never worked on the case. You were a witness!"

"I guess, but not a witness to much. We heard shots, responded, and found Mike dead on the ground. No one around. It was just as weird as it was heartbreaking."

"Okay, then I'll set up an interview when I'm ready in about a week."

"That'll work." Worth pointed his index finger at Johnny and motioned for him to close the office door. After Johnny did so, he continued, "One thing to remember, and it's a bit sticky."

"Sir?"

Major Worth sat up and leaned over his desk. In an instant he became serious, and his eyes locked with Johnny's. Johnny could instantly understand why he was so successful as a detective. His look was one of severe intensity that demanded attention and focus. "Mike's death rattled this department. The theories rivaled the JFK assassination, and when it went unsolved . . ." His voice trailed off and he paused. "Well, there was a lot of anger directed toward Homicide. In fact, somewhere in that file, you'll find a letter from the chief approving the case for cold case status. Highly unusual, but that's what it took to gain acceptance of the situation. There were no more leads to run down. It was the right call, but not an easy one."

Johnny looked down for a moment, and then looked up. "I'm not trying to ruffle feathers, but going to cold case doesn't mean that people didn't work to solve it. I'm sure everyone wanted to catch the perp."

"Oh, absolutely. But you've been here long enough to know that a police department is a lot like a family."

"I get that. No one wanted to give up," Johnny said.

"Absolutely, but every family has critics." He sat back a bit, turning off the intensity. It was as if he could sense that Johnny had enough of a taste to get his point across. He took another sip of coffee to create a pause. "Every family has the negative person who sees only failure. As a family, everyone wanted the case solved because it was one of our own, and when it wasn't, the anger some folks felt toward the perp or perps turned inward. It was nothing personal, really, just human nature . . . but it got ugly at times."

"Understood. Even though you're a witness, I hope I can lean on you for guidance. You've solved more cold cases than anyone in the state."

Worth smiled. "A detective who does his homework. Well, we can't have that around here! Of course I'll help. You get the bastard who killed him, and I'll buy you a steak!" As Johnny smiled, Worth closed his eyes for a second, then spoke again. "You'll also help a lot of people close an open wound. It would be a good thing."

"Well, I can't retire for another twenty-six years, so I've got time!" Johnny smiled.

Worth did, too. He recognized the instincts of the young detective putting a witness at ease. Johnny's actions encouraged him. "That's the way to look at it. Time is always on your side as a detective if you stay on the trail. Remember, those files in the cold case file room are not there because they can't be solved. They land there because the leads have gone cold, a detective retires, or we know who did it, but the proof isn't there— or at least, not yet."

Johnny looked intently at Worth. "Is that this situation here? We know who did it but can't prove it?"

The major looked at him dead in the eye. The intensity was back. "No, Johnny. No such luck for you. This is a real whodunit."

"Roger that." Johnny got up to walk out, and the major stopped him.

"One thing, Till."

Johnny turned. "Yes, sir?"

"Until you get on a trail, keep your investigation on a low profile. Folks have had enough false hopes in this case. It's hard on the victims, and in the case of a murdered cop . . ." He paused, and Johnny thought he suddenly looked very sad. "There are a lot of victims."

"Got it. See you in the a.m."

Johnny clocked out on his computer and walked out to his patrol car. The words echoed in his head: *There are a lot of victims.* He felt his phone vibrate and checked for a message. It was Ana Liss. The text read: `Guilty—all five counts. Sentencing next week. Join us. I'll send the time and date. Thanks for your help. Great job!` Johnny responded thanking Ana for her efforts.

As he got into his car, he called the mother of the child who was killed. He'd gotten to know the family well. He knew that justice was done, but tomorrow morning they would still wake up missing their little girl. Nothing could fill that hole in their lives. They were very wealthy, but nothing they could buy and no money they spent could change what happened. The loss of their child was worse than any fate they could have imagined. It carried with them a sense of helplessness and futility—an overwhelming feeling that the world was cruel, and no amount of goodwill and effort could dull the blade of evil.

Johnny knew the parents and the surviving siblings by name. He knew their neighbors and many members of their extended family. He had made the death notification, as well as let them know that the perpetrator was in custody. Come hell or high water, Johnny would be at that sentencing.

It was a fine line for every cop with every victim. You had to become close enough to learn about the person who lost something at the hands of another human being, whether it was a television or a loved one. But you also had to remain distant enough to be objective. Often, that was the hardest part.

Johnny dialed the number to the home of Ronald and Rhonda Emerson. They recognized the number on their caller ID.

"Oh, Johnny, we were just about to call you! You got him!" Rhonda Emerson broke out in tears. "We'll never get Sadie back"—the phone was silent except for a short gasp—"but you got him. You did it, Johnny!"

Johnny heard the phone switch to speaker mode.

"We are eternally grateful, Johnny," Ronald Emerson said as he choked back tears. "The offer stands. If you ever need help, you call us, and we'll come running."

It was tough for Johnny to hear the sadness in their voices. He knew the trial was like pulling the skin from a deep scar. The experts say that the trial of a case brings closure for the family, but like every healing process, there was more pain included in the process. They were good people whose lives were changed forever in an instant by someone who had no respect for human life.

"Thanks, y'all. I'm so proud of both of you for attending the trial. I know how hard that was, but I know nothing could have kept you away. The sentencing will be hard, as well."

"I know," Rhonda said, "but you know we will be there."

"I have no doubt," Johnny replied.

"If they let me, I'm going to read a poem Sadie wrote a few days before . . ." She paused. It had been three years, and Johnny had never once heard Rhonda refer to the day of the wreck as the day her daughter died. Perhaps she would never be able to do so. "The poem is about the people in her life—her family, her friends, her teachers, even the sweet man at the grocery store who bags our groceries. He's about forty and he has a lot of disabilities. She was always so kind to him, and he smiled when he saw her walk into the store." Johnny thought she said something else, but her voice became faint.

"You will have a chance to make a victim impact statement. Just remind the prosecutor that you want to read the poem."

"We'll see you there then," Ronald said. "We're sorry about not sending a card about your promotion. We're very proud of you—the entire family. You're a good man, Johnny. You will make a great homicide detective—maybe even a great chief one day."

"Thanks, Ron. That means a lot. I will be at the sentencing. The prosecutor wants to introduce a few statements that were excluded from the trial because they may have inflamed the jury. The judge will allow them in during the sentencing phase because he's already been found guilty. The judge has heard them already, but he can consider them during this phase."

"Johnny," Rhonda said, her voice shaking, "we will always love you for never forgetting Sadie. I wish you could have known her."

The conversation ended, and Johnny took a minute to think about a little girl who took the time to write about the people in her life. So many people are focused on the things around them that they miss the rest. The world truly lost a special person the day Sadie Emerson left this earth. He couldn't do anything about that, but he did the

28

best with the job and responsibility entrusted to him. Maybe that was all he had in the way of closure for himself. It would have to be enough.

As he pulled his car out of the parking lot, his cell phone rang. It was Sanderson "Sands" Banks, a reporter with the *Lawler Monitor*. Johnny took a second for a deep breath, then answered. Although he was tired, he would never forget the assistance Sands gave him with the Sadie Emerson case: running progress reports of how the police were looking for people with information, running stories to keep the public interest alive, and finally reporting on the safety of children at school bus stops when the department announced the arrest of Randy Laymen. Banks was a decent guy, about Johnny's age. Perhaps that was why Johnny didn't mind speaking with him.

"Hey, Sands. Let me guess why you're calling."

"You'd have to be under a rock to not know about the verdict." Banks paused. "You saw me there every day."

"Yep. You were there every day for the trial." Johnny paused. "Did you get to speak with any of the jurors?"

"Only two of them. Both are fans of the paper. One was hoping I would introduce him to a reporter at WNIZ. I guess he thinks we all eat dinner together." He laughed into the phone.

"Of course," Johnny replied. "One big, happy family, right?"

"Sure. You just keep thinking that." Sands spoke again and his voice changed. He was back to business. "Any reaction to the verdict that I can post in my story tomorrow morning?"

"Well, that depends. Will I be above the fold?" Johnny smiled. He couldn't resist teasing Sands.

"Of course, Detective Till! The story is big news, and with a quote from the new 'Wonder Boy of Homicide,' the story will likely be national within twenty-four hours." His sarcasm was showing through, but it made Johnny feel comfortable. "You know I can't promise anything, but my editor is pretty interested in the story."

"You're such a smooth talker." He continued, "Okay, here it is. 'I cannot imagine the horror Sadie's parents live every day, but I'm glad we were able to catch the man responsible.'"

Johnny could hear Banks typing in the background. "Rather vanilla, but it'll do."

"You know the drill, Sands. More than that and you have to go through the department's public information office."

"I already have their press release. Your simple sentence speaks volumes more." He typed for a few more seconds. "Congrats on the promotion, Till. Your exchange with Pressman nearly made me laugh out loud."

Johnny smiled. "It was . . ." He fought for an appropriate word in case Sands decided to publish his response. "It was interesting."

"Interesting. I'll bet Pressman has a different description."

"I'm sure he does." The phone was quiet. "Tomorrow's paper? I'd like to get a copy."

"Yes. Morning edition. If you're nice to me, I'll drop a copy at your new, high-rent district office, Detective."

"That would be awesome." Johnny paused. "Please tell me you're leaving Sadie's family alone, at least tonight."

"Their family attorney put out a press release. I'll

email it to you. It essentially thanks you and the department, and requests privacy for the family. Bottom line: no questions, no answers, and no statements forthcoming."

"As I suspected. Don't take it personally. They've been through a lot."

"I never do. My dad convinced me that was never appropriate. He used to say, 'A newsman should never be about the news.' I believe that."

"Then you'll always be successful. Have a great evening, Sands."

"You, too, Detective." There was a long pause. "You know, my phone will ring if you call the number. Keep me in mind with any fresh stories in the future."

You know I will, Johnny thought. He instantly thought he needed to contact Worth about how to respond to the media when cases were breaking quickly. There was probably a protocol in the Homicide Unit.

CHAPTER 3

J ohnny arrived at his house and got out of his uniform. He set out his sport coat, shirt, and pants for the morning. He would drop off his car on the way in and pick up his unmarked. It would be the first time in his career that he would go to work without putting on his uniform. He looked at the weathered detective badge and put it next to his keys. Then he went to the kitchen to get something to eat.

It was about 8:30 when Johnny was able to sit on his back deck in the screened porch with his laptop. He opened his favorite search engine, typed "Michael Dunlap Lawler Police Department," then hit search. The response was both immediate and massive.

Like most internet searches regarding police cases, there were several spam sites and a bunch of anticop sites. Sadly, Johnny had become numb to the venom on the internet concerning cops. Once he pushed past the nonsense, he got to media coverage of the search for the person who murdered a uniformed cop on a beautiful November night.

There were a lot of follow-up media reports as recent as last year with reporters asking questions. Some were genuinely trying to keep the search alive and assist the police. Others were criticizing the police for not being able to find the killer, as well as blaming the Lawler Police Department for every other ill in the county. Oddly, Johnny also read the reports detailing the progress of the investigation. He was surprised that the department shared so much with the media. Perhaps at some point, the media blitz appeal became the last hope for a resolution, or at least a new thread they could pull that might lead to the killer.

Johnny read the reports late into the night. He was comforted that at least some of the reports mentioned the work Officer Mike did in the schools. Johnny wondered how many children benefitted from seeing a uniformed law enforcement officer in a positive light through Officer Mike's visits. One report really caught his attention. A local attorney named Joe Amorini donated money to create a scholarship at the Lawler County Community College for the criminal justice program in the name of Officer Mike. He also contributed to the $100,000 reward that had yet to be claimed. Was it even still available? *Need to check.*

Johnny knew Joe Amorini. He represented a lot of cops in the county and the state. His actions had a strange effect on Johnny that he did not expect. He made a note to speak with Amorini. *No stone left unturned.*

After several hours, Johnny knew he had to get some sleep. He wondered how long it would take him to get through the cold case file if a quick search of the internet took several hours. However, he'd learned that you can't complete an investigation without adequate sleep. Sometimes "adequate" was a relative term, and you only got a couple of hours, but he could not stay up all night. Besides, he was in a new unit with a new boss and a big day ahead of him. For the first time in his career, he would be the homicide detective in the room on call when a suspected murder came out on the radio. That challenge alone mandated some rest.

* * *

As predicted, 6:00 a.m. came around quickly. Johnny did a quick workout in the spare bedroom filled with weights. Then he showered, shaved, and dressed in his coat and tie. He drove his marked unit to the county garage to swap for his assigned unmarked car. All of his personal and issued gear that would no longer be needed now occupied a place in his basement. The rest would be transferred to his new police car. He pulled into the garage and was back on the road in about an hour. He was thankful that day for the advice of his field training officer, who had told him to make friends at the county garage. The process was smooth and pleasant.

Johnny's next stop was the Lawler County Police Supply Unit. He took a few minutes to make small talk with the supply clerk, who provided him two detective badges. He also received an allowance to buy plain clothes. Perhaps Johnny was an anomaly, but he always enjoyed buying dress clothes on his own. He committed himself to using the clothing allowance for a few top-shelf purchases. He had to look like a professional in court, even though his everyday jackets and pants had to be expendable. Homicide detectives often searched wooded areas and nasty crime scenes; both locations were hard on clothing.

The next part of the supply visit was, as expected, the most difficult. Johnny was speaking with the supply sergeant, Ralph Bastin. He was a persnickety man who seemed to act like his unit was guided by two principles. First, the rules of the Supply Unit were the forgotten verses of the Bible. Second, the money spent on equipment would be dispensed as if Sergeant Bastin himself had to purchase it by pulling the money out of his own retirement savings. It was easy to see how he earned his predictable nickname, and his given name, Bastin, made it seem almost too easy.

"All right, Detective Till. We need to trade your full-sized Glock 22 for a smaller Glock 23."

"Thank you, sir, but I've decided to keep the full-sized model. I have my own holsters to wear with plain clothes."

The sergeant stared at him and spoke slowly. "All detectives must switch their full-sized handgun for a smaller model. That's the rule."

"Actually, sir, I checked the regs. It's my choice."

"Why would you want to carry that bigger gun when you don't have to anymore?"

"It's all in the holster, sir." Johnny pulled his jacket back. "Kramer gun leather—best in the business. Besides, I find it strange that when I was on the street, the chances of me running into a murderer were pretty slim. However, now that I'm assigned to Homicide and my job is to find them, someone wants to give me a gun that holds fewer bullets."

Sergeant Bastin scowled and wrote REFUSED in big letters on the form. Johnny thanked him, as he always did, and left. While he was walking to his car, he had to smile. *Why would he care what size gun I carry?*

Johnny got into his unmarked car and drove the short distance to headquarters. He parked in a spot marked DETECTIVE VEHICLES ONLY and walked inside. It was his first full day as a homicide detective, and he was looking forward to it.

CHAPTER 4

In a small hotel room in South Florida, Hannah Trover blinked her eyes, trying to clear the fog that seemed to dull her every sense. She was lying on a bed, but her head was spinning, and it was hard to tell which way was up.

She reached around to see if she was back in the hotel room with her girlfriends. The four of them were sharing a cheap room with two beds. Maybe they were just as hungover as she was, and her best friend Nicole would be sleeping next to her. She was wearing the T-shirt she had on last night at the party and a pair of panties, but her bra was gone. *Did we pass out when we got home?* Her arms reached and felt nothing, and her reaching turned into a frantic motion.

My phone. I'll check my GPS and see where I am. Hannah leaned over to reach to the nightstand that was now coming into view. Her purse wasn't there. There was nothing on the nightstand. She rolled to the other side of the bed. *If I'm in a hotel, there will be a phone.* Her hands felt the nightstand on the other side of the bed: no phone, just a lamp. *That will help. Maybe I can find my purse.* Hannah reached to find the switch for the lamp and felt something on her ankle. She found the switch and turned on the lamp.

The room was bare. There were two folding chairs, a dresser with a mirror, and a tripod. The window was covered with a dark curtain and some kind of plastic. As she moved around, she felt something on her leg again. She tried to pick her left leg up to see what it was, but she couldn't. When she reached down with her left hand to see if her foot was caught in the covers, the horror swept over her like ice water. *What the fuck?*

Hannah started crying, but knew she had to keep her head together. The handcuff on her left ankle was cold and barely allowed her to move around, but there was nothing on her shaking hands, so she could get up. *I have to stay calm. People will be looking for me.* She took a deep breath and listened. She heard nothing but faint music. *If there's music and I'm in a hotel, there have to be people around.*

That's when the idea hit her. *Get to the window, see where you are, and get someone to call 911!*

Hannah carefully moved to the side of the bed, cautious about how far the handcuff on her ankle would let her go. She managed to get off the bed and stand. *So far, so good. I just have to stay calm, and get to the window.*

Her left leg stopped about three feet from the bed. She considered that, then shifted so she could step as far as possible with her right foot. As she did, the metal edge of the handcuff caught the top of her ankle bone. *Crap, that hurt!* Hannah made no noise, though. She was smart and tough. Fourteen years of soccer and eight of Krav Maga had taught her some skills, but refusing to give up and staying calm were the most useful right now.

She reached the window and pulled up the curtain

and the plastic. Behind them was another thick curtain that was pressed against the window. She pulled it back, only to see darkness with a few lights of the city. *Am I still in Florida?* She wondered where her friends were. *Stay calm. People will be looking for me.*

As she stood at the window, she turned her mind to escape and self-defense. It was too far up to jump, even if she could get this handcuff off her ankle. *WHEN I get this thing off my leg!*

The room was barren, but her Krav Maga instructor's words were in the forefront of her thoughts: *There's always a weapon available. Fight, then run!*

Hannah saw sheets that could be used to strangle someone, or perhaps as a rope to lower herself; a pillow to smother someone. The tripod would make a good weapon. The lamp was bolted down—no luck there. First, this damn shackle on her leg had to go.

Hannah was strong, but slim; however, there was no way to squeeze out of the handcuff. She was able to see it, but not very well. When she tried to pull on it, it got tighter. *That's my way out!* Her dad had told her how he learned in the police academy that the handcuffs had to be double-locked so they wouldn't keep closing tighter. When she saw the teeth of the hasp appear, she gathered some of the sheet in her hand and started wedging it into the back side of the handcuff. She wedged it in as tightly as she could, then she started closing the cuff slowly, forcing the sheet into the top of the handcuff on top of the teeth. *I hope I can get it open before it closes too tightly on my ankle.*

Hannah closed the cuff, click by click, until the first muffled click told her the sheet was getting into the ratchet. A few more clicks and she would be free. It was hard to squeeze the handcuff now, and the angle was terrible, but she could take the pain if freedom was the reward. A deep breath and a hard squeeze, and the sheet was imbedded into the ratchet. She felt the handcuff close tightly on her ankle. *Not a moment too soon.*

Hannah saw the tip of the sheet appear on the other side of the hasp and pulled on it to keep it tight. Then she slowly opened the handcuff and set herself free. *Deep breaths, Hannah. Think three steps ahead, and escape!*

She looked around for her clothes and again for her purse. Nothing. The closet was filled with raunchy lingerie. *Don't think about it. I have to get away!* She looked to the window again. *Four stories up. No way to lower myself down. No balconies to jump to.* Hannah looked to the door. *I only have one way out.*

Hannah folded the tripod and held it in her hands. It would be a formidable weapon. She remembered what her dad said: "It's a weapon if you wouldn't want to get hit with it!" The thought caused her to smile and feel confident that she would get out of here. Were her friends here, too, in other rooms? *I need to get out of here first.*

She tried the door and realized that hotel room locks can't keep anyone in. They were designed to keep people out. She pressed her ear against the door. *That damn music. Someone must be here.* She went back to the bed and turned out the light. If it was dark in the hall, the light would alert anyone who was watching. With the tripod in her right hand, she slowly pulled down on the handle to open the door. As she did, the door hit her in the forehead with enough force to knock her back to the bed.

As she tried to get her balance, she swung hard with the tripod and hit her mark.

"Motherfucker, that hurt! Grab her!"

It was dark in the room, and the light from the hallway was dim. She dropped the tripod and grabbed the hands on her arm. Her left hand slid up the arm to find the man's face. She put her left thumb into his right eye, and he let go as he screamed.

The blow to her head nearly put her out. She fought unconsciousness as she was put onto the floor. She heard a woman's voice: "No! Don't mark up her face! She's beautiful. I'll get an extra thousand for that face alone."

Why is a woman hurting me? The voice was familiar. *She was in the bar and in the bathroom with me! She's the one with the scar on her chin who went on about my "beautiful mocha skin."*

As she struggled to stay awake, she felt them pressing her to the floor. She rolled out from under them once, using her hips for leverage, then she felt another blow to the side of her head. Her vision was closing in now, like when she got kicked in the head last year in the championship game against Yarborough High School. She could hear the three people in the room talking. What scared her was that they weren't whispering. *They don't care who hears them!* Hannah's strength was running out.

When she was pinned the second time, there was a lot of cursing, and someone wrapped something around her right bicep. Then, she felt a sharp sting in her right arm. A hot rush hit her blood as weakness spread over her body. *No! What is this? Why can't I feel anything?* Horror mixed with the dull sense of nothing took over. She felt herself being lifted up and placed on the bed. Then the hands were off her.

"How the fuck did she get out of these cuffs?"

Hannah was in a fog, but happy that she had pulled the sheet free from the handcuff to keep anyone from knowing how she did it. *I have to stay awake! Listen!*

Hannah heard them talking as they set up the tripod. She could see more now that they had turned the light back on. She watched the one guy holding his eye. *Good for you, motherfucker. I hope it hurts!* She tried to speak, but nothing came out. Her efforts to move were useless. Her body felt like it weighed a thousand pounds. She could see someone putting a camera onto the tripod.

Then she heard the woman speak again as she leaned into Hannah's ear. Her voice was low—not like a whisper, but closer to an effort to be kind. "Listen, honey. If you fight, you die, and it won't be quick, either. I'm all that's keeping you alive and free from a beatdown. I don't want them to hurt this pretty face. Stop fighting the drugs. They'll make it easier." She patted Hannah's forehead in a grotesque gesture that seemed almost nurturing. Hannah looked up at her. "You'll learn to love the drugs."

Hannah was fully unable to move but was angered by what she heard. *Drugs! I'll kill this bitch!* Those were her thoughts, but she could not do or say anything. She was a prisoner inside her own mind.

The heroin was taking over. She saw brighter lights come on that nearly blinded her. Her left hand started to move to cover her eyes, but it was easily moved away. She heard the woman speak again, but her voice was harder to understand as Hannah felt her body rise and her T-shirt come over her head and off her hands. She fell back down on the bed and felt her hips rise as her panties came off: slid down her legs and passed over her feet.

In a bar three miles away, Hannah's purse sat under the back of a toilet. Her phone was buzzing over and over as Nicole called her again and again. It was 5:00 a.m.

Nicole wanted to call 911 right now. "We haven't seen her for six hours! Something's wrong!"

"She probably hooked up with somebody. The place was packed. Maybe she went back to his room." Janie was just as scared but was hoping there was a good explanation for why they couldn't find Hannah.

"She knew the rules. 'No one hooks up without telling us.' I want to call the police."

"And tell them what? That we used fake IDs to get into a bar, were smoking weed, got drunk with some college guys, and now we can't find our friend?"

They all looked at each other.

Megan was crying. "Hannah wasn't smoking weed!"

"She was drunk, though, just like all of us." Janie was looking down at the bed.

Megan caught her breath. "If we don't call now, we definitely call at noon. I don't think she'd hook up without telling us, but if she did, we'll definitely hear from her by noon."

They all shook their heads as Nicole tried Hannah's phone again. Then she sent another text: C'mon, Hannah. This isn't funny anymore. Where are you? She activated her location app again and saw that Hannah was still near the bar. They had looked until the bar closed at four in the morning, then had to leave.

No one would find Hannah's purse until the cleaning crew came in at 11:00 a.m., twelve hours after the girls last spoke with Hannah.

By then, she would be out of Florida.

CHAPTER 5

When Johnny arrived in the Homicide Unit, a lot of desks were empty, and Major Worth's door was shut. He could tell through the partially opened blinds that there were two people in the chairs in front of the major's desk. While he couldn't make out the words, the conversation seemed a bit tense. Johnny figured it didn't concern him, so he went to his desk, then grabbed a cup of green tea.

Behind the major's door, the conversation was getting animated. The two chairs were occupied by Lieutenant Danny Paschal of the Intelligence Unit and Captain Roger Stills of the Evidence Unit. The three men were of roughly the same age and tenure in the department. Their careers followed similar paths, but Worth had made rank quicker.

In the case of Dan Paschal, the reason was clear. He was often gone for eighteen months at a time on reserve duty with the United States Army. While lots of folks told him to push for promotion through the courts, Paschal was of a different mindset. As a US Special Forces soldier, he was honored to hold rank in the department. He recognized the hardship a deployment would place on the department if he rose higher than lieutenant, so he was content to continue in this rank until he retired from the military.

Roger Stills was a different person altogether. Stills scored a few points below Worth on the captain's exam but was promoted a year and a half after Worth on the eve of the list expiring. That was five years ago. The rank of major was an appointed position, and there was no testing for the position. Stills was never in contention for any of the major slots, while Bill Worth was promoted to major after one year. The two men were colleagues, but they were not friends.

Worth knew that Stills wanted to work in Homicide but had refused two chances to transfer, stating he would never work in the unit as long as Worth was in charge. For Worth, this was more unproductive drama that he did not have time for.

"Look," the major said, "I just wanted both of you to know that Detective Till is working on the Dunlap murder, and he might be calling you. He's new to my unit, and I wanted to personally ask you to help him in any way possible."

"New to your unit, my ass!" Stills spat out. "He's damn near a recruit! He's got no business in Homicide to start with, and definitely no business working a cold case on a dead cop!"

"Major, if I may," Paschal said quietly, "he will have my full cooperation. Respectfully, sir, you know that would have been the case even if you did not call this meeting." He looked at Stills and shook his head.

"I truly appreciate that. For you," Worth paused and looked at Paschal, "this meeting was a formality." Both men knew Paschal was there, in part, as a witness.

"Captain Stills, before you go shooting your piehole off even further, let me tell you something about that detective you call a recruit. He's solved twelve hit-and-run homicides in the past two years. He found one of the perps in Ohio six months after the wreck. He found another who killed a trooper by driving around the area for a month, even on his off days, checking every car that fit the crappy description given by a witness and based on the blur from the trooper's dash and body cameras. He's been to nine homicide schools, including the FBI profiler school in Quantico, and completed every class on blood spatter, DNA evidence, interviews and interrogations, and internet investigations offered in the state. So while he may be new to Homicide, he's far from a recruit!"

"How could he have attended all those courses? He's only been here about seven years!"

"Well, for an unknown officer, you sure know a lot about him, Captain!"

Stills got red-faced and sat back hard in his chair. Paschal smiled and put his hand over his face.

"He's been using his vacation time and attending these schools at his own expense since he got on with the department. He came to the academy with several of these classes that he took in college. He graduated from Kennesaw State with a 4.0 average with a joint degree in criminal justice and psychology—largest CJ program in the state. So maybe, just maybe, he can bring something to the table. What do you think, Roger?"

Roger Stills was quiet. Two things were obvious. First, he had nothing to say, and second, the major's request for a response was a mere formality.

When the silence became uncomfortable, Worth spoke

again. "Aside from that, he's in my unit and therefore one of mine. When he asks for cooperation, consider it the same as a direct request from me. Is that clear?"

"Yes, sir." Paschal's response was in a respectful and even tone.

Stills' simple "Understood" was as close to insubordination as one could get while acknowledging an order from a superior officer. Worth let it slide. He was reminded of a favorite saying: "Never try to teach a pig to sing. It wastes your time and annoys the pig."

After he let the silence sink into the room, Worth spoke. "I responded the night Dunlap was killed. Both of you did, too. We all want this guy caught. It's been nearly twenty years. This guy is one of the brightest cops I've ever met. He chose this file at random out of the cold case room. When he realized what it was, he hung on to it. 'Go big or go home,' he said when he told me which one he pulled. He was alone in the cold case room. No one would've known if he put it back and picked another."

Paschal sat up in his chair. "That's pretty stout. I look forward to meeting him."

"Indeed," Worth said. "In that vein of cooperation," he stared at Stills, "I'd like to bring him in here and introduce you to him to ease the process." Worth continued staring at Stills, who was looking up now but was clearly unhappy, appearing like a child going to see his favorite dentist.

"As long as we're here," was all Stills could muster.

Paschal looked at Worth and winked. Nothing more needed to be said. Worth reached for the phone on his desk and punched a button.

The phone on Johnny's desk chirped. It was different from the normal ring he had received a few minutes ago when someone called for his predecessor, who had retired the week before. "Detective Till."

"Major Worth, Johnny. Can you step into my office for a minute?"

"Yes, sir. On my way." Johnny was at the door knocking in less than a minute.

Major Worth came out from behind his desk to open the door. "Come in, Detective Till. This is Captain Stills and Lieutenant Paschal."

Johnny stepped forward and shook their hands. The use of his title had not escaped him. This was a business meeting.

"Captain Stills is over—"

"Evidence, sir. Sorry to interrupt, but I looked through the department directory last night to see who was assigned to the units I'd need to contact on a regular basis. I knew there were some moves recently, and I wanted to be on top of them. Great to meet you, sir. Your folks sure made my life a breeze when I was in hit-and-run!"

Stills was clearly uncomfortable. "Well, as you pointed out, I'm new to the unit, so they were not 'my folks.'"

"True, sir. I meant they're yours now. They always had my evidence ready for court, and I appreciated that. I look forward to working with you and them."

Paschal leaned forward. "Pleased to meet you, Detective. Here's my card with my cell. Anything you need, just let me know."

"Thank you, sir. Intelligence, I saw that on the directory. If you don't mind, sir, I believe my dad served with you. He was Special Forces during the first Iraq War."

Paschal looked at Johnny and studied his face. "You're Max Till's son?"

"Yes, sir. I don't remember much about him, but I've seen his medals and his certificates from all the schools he attended. I just heard that y'all were in the same unit."

"Damn straight, we were. Your dad was a great soldier, Detective. Any time you want to hear more about him, we'll get dinner." He paused and looked at Johnny, then he looked at Major Worth. "I had no idea."

"Yes, sir. I wanted to enlist, especially after 9/11, but my mom made me promise her I wouldn't. After what happened to my dad, you know. It was really hard on her. So I had to find another way to serve."

"I completely understand. Your dad was a good man, and I was honored to serve with him. I'd be happy to review those medals with you. Each one tells a story you may not fully understand from his service record."

"Thank you, sir. I look forward to working with you and maybe learning more about his life in the army. My mom and I are very proud of him."

The conversation broke the tension in the room, and Major Worth spoke up. "Detective Till, as you move through the Dunlap case, you will eventually want to look at all of the evidence personally. Captain Stills can arrange that. There is a room reserved for Homicide in the Evidence Unit for that purpose. You'll need to reserve it in advance."

"Yes, sir," Johnny responded.

"As to the Intelligence Unit, you'll find they are the best in the state, or in the Southeast, in my humble opinion. Lieutenant Paschal and his folks can help you screen out the backgrounds on a bunch of folks and also help connect the dots on a few, as well. It's a huge time-saver."

"Great. I like to be efficient. Not enough hours in the day."

"If it's okay, Major, I've got a meeting in ten with the

chief about a misunderstood citizen of the highest circles of Lawler society." Paschal smiled.

"Not a problem, Danny. Thanks for taking the time to drop in." The two men shook hands.

"I'd better be going, too." Stills got up and waved as he left. He stopped in the door as a perfunctory gesture. "Unless there's something else, Major?" The word *major* was just a bit overemphasized, but not enough to justify any ire or discipline.

"Nope," Worth said, smiling. "Thanks for stopping by. Always a pleasure."

Johnny sat down as the two men left the Homicide Unit. He waited for the major to speak.

"You handled that well, Johnny. Sorry about the formalities."

"I heard 'Detective Till' and thought I was in trouble already on my first full day in the unit!"

"Not at all. I knew you would need their assistance, and I wanted to smooth out any rough spots." He paused. "I had no idea of the connection with Paschal and your dad. He's been on the interview board for years! I'm surprised he didn't know."

"Well, there's a lot of Tills, sir. Besides, my dad cut his own path. I owe it to him to do the same."

"Admirable. That way you'll be beholden to no one. Not everyone can say that." He paused. "At any rate, I'm glad we got you." He sat at his desk. "Get anywhere on the Dunlap file last night?"

Johnny knew from speaking with other detectives that you did not joke with the major about solving cases. To him, it was serious business. Everything else, however, was fair game. "There was a lot on the internet about it. That was a good thing. I met him, you know."

"Dunlap? Did he come to your school?"

Johnny was not surprised that Worth had figured it out. "Yes, at least once. Nice guy. Very good with the kids. Thinking back on it now, it must have been hard to have all those kids pawing at your uniform all day. I don't like to even have people stand close to me when I'm in uniform."

Worth laughed. "He had a knack for it. I think it came naturally to him. He and his wife had three kids. They're grown now. His wife still lives in the area—Farington, I believe. It's in the county but closer to Atlanta, a nice area down along the Chattahoochee River. You should go talk with her when you finish the file. Not a bad person to start with. She will understand that you are getting up to speed and appreciate that you picked up the file."

"Well, sir, the logical person to start with is you. You were first on the scene, you have a knack for recalling details, and—"

"And I'm here," Worth interrupted.

"You are the most logical starting point for several reasons."

"Agreed. Just let me know when you're ready. Have you met with Holly Forrester yet? I've assigned you two as partners."

"No, sir. I went around the office and introduced myself to everyone. She must have been out on something."

Worth checked the schedule on his desk. "Dentist appointment and errands. She'll be out today. So make yourself at home, and get started."

"Yes, sir. I'm looking forward to going through the Dunlap file. I expect that I'll get through with the former detectives assigned to the file by the end of next week. Should we set a time to meet to avoid any conflicts?"

The organization and plan impressed Bill Worth, as did the desire to avoid wasting time without an appointment. "Get with Charlotte. She'll put something on my schedule. Ask her to block an hour. It'll only take about twenty minutes to tell you what I know, but we can use the rest of the time to go over what you've learned by then. I can also help with any questions or help provide any direction, if you need any."

"Much appreciated. I'm sure I'll be in a good spot for some direction at that point. Right now, I'm chomping at the bit to get into that file."

"Well, chomp away, and again, welcome to the unit. Just don't expect us to be nice to you every day. Being the new guy wears off pretty quickly." Worth smiled.

"Then I'll feel right at home." Johnny laughed.

Johnny started to walk out of the office when the major stopped him.

"I hear you had a dustup with Sergeant Bastard— that's Bastin to you—earlier."

Johnny paused in the doorway and turned. "Nothing unusual, sir. I was very respectful."

"I loved it! 'Why would they give me a gun with fewer bullets when I'm getting paid to find murderers?' That's classic!" He smiled and laughed.

"I hope I didn't cause any problems for you."

"Are you kidding? He's not happy unless he's complaining about something! You made his day. He asked me to speak with you about it, so now I have. That's the end of it, as far as I'm concerned."

"Thanks."

Worth leaned back in his chair. "Bastin was a helluva detective in his day. He worked Homicide. Back then, they carried five-shot revolvers, so you can understand his 'confusion' with your request."

Johnny blushed a bit. He understood that Worth recognized that Bastin's statement about the gun was clearly not a request and could have been handled better. However, it was evident that no further discussion was required on that point. "I had no idea he was a homicide detective."

"Yep. He was a terror back then. If he got on a suspect, he would trail them to the ends of the earth. He once drove all night to catch a guy when he got off a bus on the run from Bastin and his partner! I wish we had video then. The look on that guy's face must have been priceless when he saw Bastin standing outside the bus in another city! Legend has it, he saw Bastin, then turned around and put his hands behind his back! No fuss at all. The US Marshals had to convince Bastin to let them drive his unmarked back to Lawler County because he was too tired. He told them the perp was going back right then in the back of Bastin's car! It was obvious that Bastin wasn't likely to take no for an answer, so they made some accommodations and let him ride in the passenger seat while one marshal drove and another followed them back." Worth laughed. "He was something else!"

"What made him go to Supply? Who would want that job? That's why I'm always respectful to him. That job would drive me nuts!"

"Well, Bastin got promoted and convinced the chief to let him stay in Homicide. That was highly unusual even then, but he was a bulldog and could be quite convincing. Then he and his partner went into a convenience store, and while they were at the back coolers, an armed robber decided to hold up the place."

"Bad timing."

"Agreed. The guy was so stoned out of his mind that he walked right past the unmarked car parked out front with the police radio talking. Bastin and his partner were great cops. They always monitored the local uniformed division channels in case someone needed help and they were close by."

"What happened?"

"The perp saw Bastin's partner—I think it was Mark Alonza." He thought for a minute. "Well, I'm not sure who it was. He left the department and law enforcement after this. The perp saw a reflection of Alonza's badge on his belt in the concave mirror in the corner and panicked. He shot and hit Alonza in the back. Fortunately, he was wearing body armor, as they had just been interviewing a potential perp who turned out to be only a witness. Body armor was very heavy in those days and did not feel good under a dress shirt." Worth took a sip of his coffee that had no doubt been neglected during his previous meeting.

"So anyway, Bastin and his partner were about five steps apart, so the perp couldn't see Bastin when he shot. Bastin heard the shot, of course, and saw Alonza go down. He ran up a side aisle and got behind the perp. The perp was advancing toward Alonza, who was crawling out of the line of fire and trying to draw his gun at the same time. The perp kept shooting, but he only hit the cooler above Alonza. He fired a bunch of rounds at Alonza. Bastin ran toward the perp and shot him five times in the back. He didn't even take the time to reload and grabbed his backup off his ankle, ready to shoot him again, but the perp was dead. Alonza survived, but he was never the same. He had enough years to retire. I think he's living out west somewhere." He paused for a second.

Johnny just let him talk. He had questions but didn't want to interrupt.

After a few minutes, Worth started again. "They gave Bastin a medal of valor. It was a big deal. The company that owned the stop-and-rob made a huge donation that actually seeded the funds to start our current Canine Unit. I understand there is still money in the foundation they created."

After an extended pause, Johnny spoke up. "Was the clerk injured? Any other customers shot?"

"No. The clerk was shaken up, but just fine. He only had the gun pointed at him for a couple of seconds before the perp turned his attention to Alonza. There were no other customers in the store."

"Did the department get sued?"

"Not sure, but probably. You can count on that."

"So what happened? Why did Bastin leave Homicide?"

Worth got serious. His face showed an emotion Johnny had not yet seen from him: intense empathy. He tilted his chin down for a second, and then he looked back up when he responded. "The perp was fourteen years old." The two men were silent. "He was wearing a ball cap, sunglasses, and a hoodie. No one knew how old he was until they removed everything at the scene. After Bastin handcuffed him and secured the gun, he and Alonza and the clerk did CPR on him until EMS arrived. It was mostly the clerk and Bastin, as Alonza could barely move his arms. EMS pulled everything off his head to secure a cervical collar on him, and that's when they saw his face.

"It was some kind of a gang initiation, if I remember correctly. The Intelligence Unit locked up a bunch of the gang members after the shooting as accessories. One stole the gun, another gave it to the perp, and others planned the robbery. The media never got past the fact that the perp was a kid who was shot in the back. The parents were very vocal. Several groups threatened Bastin, and rumors were there was a contract out on him. He got concerned that any future work he did in Homicide would dredge up the shooting, and he feared that his presence on the street would make it more dangerous for any partner who worked with him. So he asked for a transfer to Supply. It's a secure unit in a locked building with no public contact. He's been there ever since." Worth stopped and drank his coffee. "Truth is, I suspect that he never got over the fact that he killed a kid."

Johnny let the information sink in. After a moment, he spoke. "I'm glad he didn't quit the department. That would have been the easy choice."

Worth looked at Johnny, impressed with his analysis. "Much easier, but Bastin was never one to quit anything. He also never forgot that he is still a peace officer. Look on his left ankle if you don't see a gun on his right hip. He's always armed—on and off duty. He still prefers that little five-shot revolver. He may have called me to complain, but you gained his respect. My guess is that your dealings with him will be far more pleasant in the future . . . or as pleasant as Sergeant Bastin is capable of being." Worth smiled.

"Everyone has a story, Major."

"Remember that, Johnny. Know their stories, and you'll understand what makes them tick." He then looked back down at his desk. Johnny took the cue that the conversation was over. As he crossed the threshold of the door, Worth called to him. When Johnny turned to face him, he saw the major looking down, reading. "Congrats on the guilty verdict. Let me know what happens in the sentencing. Make sure you're there, if at all possible."

"Yes, sir." Johnny paused. "How did you know?"

Worth pointed to the morning edition of the *Lawler Monitor* on the table between the two guest chairs in his office. "My job to know. Keep it." He paused. "One more thing. Admin stuff bites us in the ass here, just like everything else. That trial put you over hours for the pay period. Take the next two days off. The two days after that are your regular off days. Got to keep the OT down."

Johnny was surprised. "Okay. Got it."

"If you're working an active case, chasing a lead, or finding a suspect, we can get by with the overtime. You're new to the unit, so it won't fly." Worth paused. "Enjoy the break. You've been busting it. Besides, you won't get many in this unit."

"Thank you, sir."

Worth was now deep into what he was reading and didn't look up.

Johnny went to his desk and took out his laptop. It was secure and scanned by the department. All detectives were issued one, and he had received his as a hit-and-run fatality investigator. That was another fight with Sergeant Bastin, until the chief called down and ordered him to issue a laptop to Johnny. It was funny now, but not then when the entire supply staff disappeared during the exchange. Thinking back to it, Johnny had to laugh. Knowing more about Bastin, he knew it was just part of his game: an initiation of sorts.

Four days off. It's been a while since I had that! Heck of a way to start in a new unit. Sitting still during the trial was boring me out of my mind.

Johnny resigned himself to being as productive as possible under the circumstances, getting a feel for the cases assigned to him, and then taking the Dunlap file home with him.

Everybody's got to have a hobby.

Johnny opened the file cabinet and took out the red binder marked "1 of 3." He put the binder into his backpack and placed it on the ground. He spent the rest of the shift knee-deep in paperwork and catching up on email.

CHAPTER 6

J ohnny went for a run when he woke, then cooked breakfast. After some stretching, he grabbed a cup of hot green tea and took his backpack and laptop onto the back deck. The air was crisp and clean. Without his fleece, it would've been uncomfortable, but the sun made up for the cool breeze. He decided to dive into the Dunlap file here, at least for a few hours.

If I never put it on my timecard, they'll never know.

Johnny opened the binder he pulled from his backpack and flipped to a divider with the words CRIME SCENE PHOTOS. Johnny took a deep breath. He knew he was about to see pictures of a dead police officer in uniform. His heart was racing a bit, and he took a deep breath before turning the page. *You can't help him if you can't get inside the perp's head.* With a confident motion, Johnny turned the page and saw the first photo. He knew he would never be the same again.

Officer Dunlap was lying on his side wearing the dark-blue uniform of the Lawler County Police Department. The patches on his shoulders were the older style, as the current chief redesigned them in 2002 after 9/11. His badge number was low, and Johnny noted that he had likely known a lot of older officers who would know more about him. Any source of information was a possible link to the killer.

There was blood on the ground—a lot of it. As he looked at the photos from all angles, he understood why Dunlap's body stayed at the scene and was not transported to the hospital. One of the shots had struck Officer Dunlap in the neck. It passed through both carotid arteries and jugular veins, and then severed his spine. From the looks of the wound, he was probably dead within a minute or two. Johnny started to wonder how long he was conscious of what was going on around him. If the brain can survive without oxygen for about four to six minutes, he must have had some conscious thoughts. Johnny understood that line of thinking wouldn't be productive right now, and he focused on the blood spatter.

The blood spatter was hard to see, because Dunlap fell quickly and was standing in the open. Therefore, there was little around him to "catch" the blood from the gunshot wound. However, Dunlap must have had his left hand and arm up for some reason when he was shot, because there was evidence of some blood spatter on his sleeve. From the looks of what he could see, the blood spatter was high velocity, but did not look like it came from a rifle. Johnny made a note to check the evidence log to see if any shell casings were found at the scene.

As Johnny made his way through the photographs, he had to take a deep breath. When the medical examiner moved the body, he saw a second bullet hole behind Dunlap's right ear. There was no way the bullet came from the same weapon that was used to shoot him in the neck, because it would have ruptured his skull.

Two weapons and a shot behind the ear . . . that's personal or professional—no overkill, Johnny thought. He made a note to explore those angles and moved on.

The rest of the photographs were pretty bad. They contained the autopsy photographs and pictures of the projectile recovered from Dunlap's head. Johnny was convinced he was right, as the projectile was a 9mm or .380. Even at close range, a 9mm or .380 would not have done that much damage to Dunlap's neck.

Johnny checked the evidence log next and learned that no shell casings were found at the scene. In fact, little evidence at all was found. Dunlap was shot while standing on asphalt, so there were no footprints around the body. The projectile fired into Dunlap's neck was never recovered. That was not unusual given the through-and-through nature of the injury and the lack of objects around him to stop the bullet after it left his neck. With the paucity of evidence, Johnny understood the frustration of the detectives who'd worked the case, and that of the entire department.

Johnny had three theories about solving cold cases. He'd read a bunch about them and heard from detectives who cracked them in his classes. Sometimes the detective on a cold case was able to employ techniques or methods unavailable at the time of the murder, like DNA analysis. Sometimes, the fresh set of eyes saw something the previous investigators had missed. Although that was a favorite Hollywood theme, it was always a rarity, as cold cases were usually reviewed by experienced detectives before they were designated as such. That seemed especially true in this case with a murdered cop.

The third theory was not appealing to Johnny: pure luck. A tip came in, a person wanted to get something off his chest, or a perp with something else to lose, like his life on a death sentence, agreed to come clean in exchange for leniency. Johnny didn't like the luck angle. He'd worked his whole life and his career to avoid relying on luck to get ahead. That's why he never played the lottery. However, he remembered the words of a crusty old Chicago homicide detective who taught a class he took several years earlier: "It's amazing how lucky you get when you work your ass off!" When the class stopped laughing, he finished the thought with the other part of the equation: "But sometimes, it's better to be lucky than good!"

Johnny would take any mojo that went his way, but he was becoming more akin to a dog with a new bone about this case than a new homicide detective with a file. He felt the adrenaline rise as he read the file, and his brain was working hard for connections as he put the case file into his head.

Johnny believed in actively manipulating information, and for him, that meant creating lists. While in hit-and-run, he had made lists of possible tag numbers, colors of vehicles, approach and escape routes—any information that needed to be digested in his mind. He even installed a whiteboard in his basement to keep the information on his mind when he woke and before he went to bed. *If it worked in hit-and-run, it will work with a homicide.* Johnny took out his laptop and began writing some theories.

What could all those detectives have missed? Be the new set of eyes. They were probably smarter with more experience. You've got to work harder!

He remembered what he heard so many times in classes on homicide, victim patterning, suspect behavior, and case studies of successful resolutions of cold cases. *There must be a connection to the killer. There's no way this was random.*

Johnny started a spreadsheet marked IT'S NOT RANDOM. *Maybe I'll convince myself it is. Gotta run down that road to see where it leads.* He knew he would likely also write a list titled IT WAS RANDOM at some point.

His first list encompassed all of the facts in the case that pointed away from a random killing.

- *Dunlap was a cop.*
- *Dunlap could defend himself—poor victim selection.*
- *Dunlap was not transient, unlike most random victims of opportunity.*
- *Dunlap would have been aware of his surroundings.*
- *Dunlap knew the area he was in—not surprised in a bad area of town.*
- *Dunlap was not robbed or disarmed after he was killed.*
- *Dunlap's gun was in the holster. He was not expecting an attack, and likely knew or recognized his attacker.*
- *The location of the murder was public—potential for a lot of witnesses.*
- *Dunlap was in full uniform—no chance of a mistaken identity.*
- *The location of the murder was not a high-crime area.*
- *The manner of death was methodical (few shots, all deadly)—nothing random.*
- *No one heard any arguing or loud commands. An armed or suspicious stranger would've evoked both from Dunlap.*

An hour later, Johnny was looking at the list he'd

created. *No way it was random. Got to keep my eyes open, though.*

The morning came and went. At 1:00 p.m., Johnny's stomach could be ignored no longer. He thought about making something that would make for good leftovers. However, as he got up and started to walk to the kitchen, he looked back at the Dunlap file. He then walked to the kitchen, made a protein shake, and grabbed the power cord for his laptop.

A couple of hours, my ass. Johnny plugged in his laptop to make the annoying red battery symbol disappear, then dove back into the case.

CHAPTER 7

H annah's nostrils filled with the smell of cinnamon and gingerbread. She was sitting at her grandmother's small kitchen table, the one reserved for her "special helpers." As the smell grew to intoxicating levels, Hannah's mouth started to water as her tongue anticipated the warm, light goodness that was her Maw Maw's ginger loafs.

Her grandmother placed a fresh slice of the holiday treat in front of Hannah on a plate adorned with holly leaves and red berries. On the right side of the plate, a cake fork sat waiting to pull off a chunk of the treat and deliver it to Hannah's mouth.

As Hannah reached for the fork, she faltered and tried again. Her efforts seemed to move her whole body as her grandmother watched and waited for Hannah to give her seal of approval. Hannah tried again and grew more and more frustrated. Her grandmother looked sad. There were no words passed between them, but Hannah felt a need to apologize. She tried, but her words remained inside her head. As her frustration turned to panic, Hannah's grandmother started to fade.

The rhythm of the roadway woke her up. *Thunk,*

thunk, thunk, thunk. Hannah concentrated. She recognized the sound and took note of the rhythm. It felt to her like she was riding down the road quickly in a big vehicle, because there was a lot of space between the axles and the tires making the sounds. Hannah shifted slowly, afraid to move. She was sweating buckets and felt horrible. Every part of her body either ached or was numb, and her left leg was asleep.

As she tried to move, her dream started to make sense. Her hands were bound with some kind of cloth. Her head ached. She thought back to the past day. *Was it a day?* The last things she remembered were the bright lights, the feeling of being unable to move, then the sensation of weight on her body. *Was I raped? Oh, my God! Will I ever know what all has happened to me?*

Hannah never did drugs, and she didn't have any prior experience with the feeling of being disassociated from her body, like she felt after a warm rush hit her bloodstream.

Was the moisture she now felt on her body from sweat, or was some of it from blood?

As she moved her knees, she found her feet were tied, as well. Whatever it was didn't feel like the handcuff from before. *Rope? It's hard to tell.*

Hannah felt helpless to stop the tears that began streaming down her face. After a minute or so, she knew she had to calm down and forced herself to stop crying. *No telling who's watching me or listening.* She slowly tested the tightness of the bindings on her wrists and ankles. *These are loose enough for me to get out. I'll save that for later.*

It was so dark, like she was in a closet. *Even a truck would have cracks for light to come through—sunlight, head-lights.* Hannah blew out a puff of air and confirmed what she felt. There was a hood over her face and head. *So it could be light enough for someone to see me move, if someone is watching.* She stayed still, breathing slowly. *Listen. Learn what's going on—wherever I am.*

The truck slowed and stopped. When it started with a jolt, Hannah heard a couple of voices grunt near her. It was like they were surprised by the movement of the truck. *They must be blindfolded or wearing a hood, like me. Listen!*

When the truck made a few more turns, Hannah heard traffic—more than a couple of cars. Realizing there was no way to tell how long she'd been out, she thought, *I could be anywhere.* Even though she tried to remain rational about her ability to get home from any big city like New York, L.A., or Dallas, her blood ran cold with a thought: *What if I'm in another country?* She decided to keep breathing slowly until she could learn more. *I can't do anything while I'm locked in a truck, tied up with a damn bag over my head. I have to be ready if there's an opportunity.*

The truck came to a stop, and Hannah heard a mechanical door opening. *Warehouse? This truck sounds too big for a garage at a house, and that didn't sound like the garage door on a house. Maybe a parking garage?*

Then she heard someone outside of the truck say something in English. *Okay. Maybe I'm still in the United States. I know my fingerprints and retina scans are on file with the airlines since I signed up for the new fast lane at the airport. I can prove who I am even without a driver's license.*

The truck moved into the building and the mechanical door closed. Hannah heard a couple of voices that sounded muffled. *Girls. They must have hoods on, too.* Then the truck engine stopped, and she heard more voices outside the truck. They were garbled, but they were speaking loudly. *Another group that doesn't care who hears them. Great. Nowhere to run to here, either.*

A few minutes later, she heard the sound of a lock coming undone, then a lot of loud clicks as the mechanism on the truck door unlatched. *Damn! They really had us locked in here. Who are these people?* The door opened—slowly at first, then faster as it rose. The light outside the truck was bright enough to let some of it come into the hood—probably more than her captors expected.

Hannah moved her head a bit as she felt movement around her. She heard a voice and felt the truck rock side to side as people stepped into it.

"Don't fucking scream. No one is here to help you. Do exactly what we say, and you won't get hurt. Try anything stupid and you will be hurt . . . a lot. The men moving around will untie your legs so you can walk. Then, they'll lead you to the bathroom."

None of the girls said a word. Hannah heard a couple of grunts as the men untied or cut the cloth that bound the ankles of the girls around her and eventually her ankles, as well. As the girls were pulled to their feet, Hannah tried to count the number of male voices and the number of people in the truck. *Five men, plus the guy talking . . . bad odds for trying anything, especially when I'm blind.* She lost count of the number of girls at ten.

The truck was high, and the girls were handed down to men who put them onto the ground. The air outside smelled a lot better. Hannah was convinced that someone in the truck had thrown up, or worse. Her hands were still bound, but she started to get her balance. She was led by the arm, but if she stared hard, she could see shadows through the hood. *Act like you can't see, Hannah.*

Let them believe you're helpless. As she was led across a hard, frigid, concrete floor, her bare feet started to get cold. Finally, she was near a room with a bad smell. *Got to be the bathroom.* Hannah was pushed against a wall.

"Stand here. Don't move." She felt him release her arm. The voice was not the same as the man who had given instructions at the truck. This guy was younger, had a slight accent, and a higher tone. As his hand grabbed her arm again, he spoke. "You're next. I'll take you to a stall." Then he untied her hands for a brief moment and retied them in front of her. It gave her enough flexibility to move around. *Maybe I can get this hood up enough to see.*

Hannah was guided to a stall without a door. *Perverts probably want to watch. Good luck in here. It's darker than the area around the truck.* She felt her waist and figured out she was wearing sweatpants. Then she touched her waist and chest—a sweatshirt. *That's why it was so damn hot in that truck.*

Well, no sense in playing around. No telling when you'll get another chance. Hannah relieved herself and felt more comfortable. She also quickly felt for any injuries. *I don't have any cuts.* When she finished, she put her head down and tried to pretend that she wasn't done. Her hands moved to the bottom of the hood, and she smelled the hands she had run over her body. They smelled like sweat but didn't have the metallic scent of blood. *Well, they haven't hurt me too badly . . . yet.* The thought started the tears again.

Hannah pulled the hood up a few inches. With her head down, she was able to see without raising the hood too much. *Tile floor. Industrial looking.* She moved her head to the side a bit. *Green paint and mold. One window.*

Three sinks. Hannah pulled the hood down when she heard a scream.

"I told you not to try to take off the hood!"

Hannah recognized the voice. It was the first man from near the truck. She heard a hard slap and another girl scream.

Oh, my God! . . . Hannah, turn off the fear and listen. How many people? Any doors opening?

The man spoke again to the girl he had just hit. "You listen, you live easily. You fuck up, you feel pain. Lucas!"

Hannah heard someone close to her walking away and toward the man's voice. "Yeah."

"You and Raul take her into the office. She's yours for thirty minutes." The girl let out a scream, and Hannah heard another slap. "You'll learn."

Hannah heard the girl yell and call for help as she was pulled away. A minute later, she heard a door slam. Hannah tried to focus. *No reaction to her screaming. They know no one can hear her. Not the time or the place for an escape. Will there ever be?*

She pulled up her sweatpants and stood motionless. *Got to let them think I'm not the problem.* As she thought this, she moved her wrists a bit, confident she could get the binding off if she had the opportunity to do so. *If they think I'm not a threat, they may leave my hands in front.*

Someone took Hannah's right arm and led her back into the warehouse. "Stand here. Don't fucking move."

Hannah stood for a while as the men around her brought other girls to stand in the same area. Then she heard them reading something. She could make out names, or possibly labels, for the girls and associated addresses. *Oh, no. It sounds like a list of orders!* Hannah's tears welled up and she let out an involuntary moan.

Why do they have names for some of us? Do they know my name?

Someone put a hand on her left arm, and then moved something attached to her sweatshirt. "Daytona. This is her."

"Okay. Daytona goes to . . . 191 Durango. Put her into the blue pickup. Then hit her with it."

Hannah was jerked by her arm and stumbled about twenty steps to her right, then stopped by the force of the hand on her arm. She didn't want to get hit again with anything. *If they start hitting me, I've got to fight back. They nearly knocked me out last time with the second blow. I'm not going to give them another chance to do that.*

She stood still as her feet were tied again. She was pushed slowly backward until her butt hit what felt like a tailgate.

"Sit."

She pushed her feet off the ground so she could get up onto the tailgate. Then she was pushed back across the metal until the back of her head hit something. *There must be a camper shell on the pickup truck. At least they left my hands in front of me.*

Then she felt it: a sharp prick to her right arm. Her head dropped, and she was caught before she fell off the tailgate. *No! Not again!* The drug took over more quickly this time. *This is different. Oh, my God! What's happening?* Hannah felt her body being moved, but she had no ability to tell up from down. When her body stopped moving, she felt another person being pushed next to her. Then she heard the door to the camper shell close and a padlock snap.

As she tried to slow down her breathing, she saw something. *I have a hood on. I can't see anything!* But

Hannah did see. The creature coming toward her was chasing something. It was difficult to tell exactly what it was.

As she felt her breathing and heart rate increase, she also felt her legs trying to move to escape the monster closing in on her! The bindings at her ankles made her panic. *No escape! No, no, this can't be real! This isn't real! I'm in the back of a truck! Focus!* Her sense of smell and hearing sharpened. Every sound seemed amplified, while every faint smell of gasoline, exhaust, and the dampness of the warehouse flooded her like a waterfall. She was immersed in them, drowning.

The truck started and moved forward. Every squeak of the truck frame was etched in her memory. She heard the clicks of the large door to the building as it opened again; each click echoed like a gunshot in a cave. In the distance, the screams of the girl who had been dragged to the office intensified Hannah's hallucination. *Fight it! I have to fight it! Stay focused!*

Hannah was strong. But in the end, the ketamine was stronger.

CHAPTER 8

hree days later, Johnny was sitting at his desk looking at the preliminary report of a shooting that took place the night before when he heard a voice behind him. He had no idea how long he'd been reading and flipping pages.

"Officer homicide for your first cold case! I guess the new guy isn't afraid of anything!"

Johnny turned to see a brunette woman behind him. She was about five feet, nine inches tall and slim, but muscular. She was carrying her jacket in her left hand, and her sleeveless blouse told the tale of many hours in the gym. He saw her pistol on her right side and was pleased to see that she carried her jacket in her off hand. Perhaps it was a coincidence, but he hoped it meant she hadn't forgotten her street tactics: always keep your gun hand clear.

"News travels fast," Johnny replied.

"You were out for a few days, and," she paused, "you work in a unit with a bunch of people who get nosy for a living. Holly Forrester. You must be Till." She extended her right hand and gave Johnny a firm handshake.

"Johnny or Till is fine. After years in hit-and-run, anything is better than my previous nickname."

Holly smiled and her head turned slightly to the side. "I hadn't heard it. Do tell."

"'Bumper Car Cop.' I know, childish, but it stuck after I found a guy who hit about twelve cars on his way out of a bar parking lot."

"Impressive driving! I thought you only worked fatalities."

Johnny was impressed that she had checked up on him. He couldn't blame her. No one wants to get stuck with the Fucking New Guy. "There were three unique things about that case. First, he had a two-hundred-dollar bar tab, and he was alone, but wait for it . . ." Johnny paused for effect. "He was drinking beer."

"Damn! I'm just an amateur!"

"Second, one of the cars he hit belonged to the wife of a city council member visiting her sister from Waseca near Minneapolis. It seems the council member attended a training class with one of the Lawler commissioners."

"Well, that's enough! What was the third thing?" She was leaning forward now. Johnny took note of that. She was a true detective, always wanting the last details.

"He hit a valet parker on the way out who tried to make him stop. The body flipped into the bed of his pickup truck, and he bled out while the drunk was at home sleeping it off."

"That's cold. Did he know the body was in the truck?"

"Hard to tell. He was a .18 when we found him the next day, nine hours later. He's doing fifteen to serve fifteen."

"Probably making his own booze in the joint and selling it."

"Probably. He might as well stay there. The family of the dead valet hired a lawyer, who got a five-million-dollar judgment against him and another two-million-dollar judgment against the bar! Seems the perp was an architect with plenty of bucks, and the lawyer was a former cop. If he lives long enough to get out of prison, he'll be living on the street."

"Breaks my heart." Holly touched her right hand to her chest and closed her eyes. "I'm gonna lay asleep thinking about him all night. Sorry piece of shit."

"Yep. At least in Homicide you have motives! Solving vehicular homicides was like chasing the same damn perp all the time. No motives, really, just pure, unadulterated stupidity."

"Motives we got! Most are the same, though when you get down to it, love or money in one form or another. Both of them make the world go around. For some, it seems like it makes their world stop."

"Good to know." Johnny laughed.

"Looks like you're getting settled pretty well. At least you found the most important thing on the Homicide Unit . . ."

"What's that?" Johnny smiled.

"The coffee pot! By the way, we have a tradition of taking the new guy to lunch at Mazzi's. Until then, I'm going to work on a John Doe from last week. Unless something comes in, we should have a quiet morning."

Johnny didn't want to tell her yet that he didn't drink coffee. Best not to look like an alien the first day with your new partner. "Got it. I haven't had lunch at Mazzi's since I was a recruit."

"It hasn't changed much. Maybe that's a good thing." Holly smiled and noticed something strange about her new partner: he didn't stare at her. The thought was comforting. Maybe he would be one of the few guys in the department who didn't try to hit on her.

Holly walked to her desk, hung up her jacket, and sat down in front of her computer. Her desk was just a few feet away in a cube in front of Johnny's.

Johnny took a big sip of tea. Having finished the preliminary report from Lawler's most recent homicide, he turned his attention back to the Dunlap file, going to the witness tab. This contained not just potential eyewitnesses, but also anyone who was interviewed in connection with the case. The list was about forty pages long. It contained the name and address of each witness, along with any other contact information. The later witnesses had email addresses and social media names and handles. Below each name was a one-sentence summary of the person's background and the reason why they were believed to have a link to the case. Finally, there was a notation by the detective as to whether they were a suspect, eyewitness to any related event or transaction, if they were cooperative, and if they warranted further scrutiny. Later pages contained transcriptions or detailed notes of their interviews.

Three things struck Johnny almost immediately. First, the list was long. He was not surprised. He imagined that the case was worked aggressively by any and all detectives for several months, and then by whomever was available when the leads began to dry up. Second, there had not been many new people interviewed in the past ten years. That was not encouraging. Most of the new "leads" came from news stories on the case on the anniversary of Dunlap's death or from inmates who were looking to get immunity for their crimes. Finally, several witnesses were interviewed more than once. While that spoke to the diligence of the detectives, it did not give Johnny a warm, fuzzy feeling.

As he flipped through the hundreds of pages of witness statements, Johnny realized that he could not possibly re-interview every one of them in less than several months, especially with a workload in the Homicide Unit. He also thought about the classes he'd taken and the articles he'd read on cold cases and was convinced that re-interviewing every witness would not be the way to attack a case like this. He decided to look at the evidence list first and see if there was anything obtained that could be tested with new technology or retested with improved technology. Next, he would comb the witness list and pick the top twenty people with whom he would speak. When creating that list, he had an advantage. He would include the long list of detectives who had the case. They were seasoned professionals, and he could shortcut a lot of the paper by staying at the ten-thousand-foot level and out of the minutiae to get a fresh perspective. He also believed it would help him to visit the crime scene. He wanted to see it during the daylight and the night, as the original detectives and witnesses saw it.

Johnny opened his computer and found the electronic version of the Dunlap file. The entire file had been entered into the electronic database in 2008 but was only available to senior command staff and the detective assigned to the case. He was encouraged that Major Worth had already ensured that he had access.

Johnny opened a tab under his name and created a to-do list with bullet points. Next he created a spreadsheet for the names of the people he would interview with columns for a summary, updated contact information, and notes for any follow-up that he felt was necessary. His final creation was another spreadsheet with a list of evidence in the case. Nothing was too small to note. He would note what was gathered, what was preserved, what testing was done with specific limitations on the tests at the time, the results of any testing, any tests that were not done and why, and what new technology was available to take the forensic analysis to the next level. Some of the limitations were not known to the detectives who worked on the case in the past, so that was somewhat encouraging. He also noted if any evidence was stored outside the walls of the Lawler PD. For example, the medical examiner at the state crime lab still had tissue samples and the projectiles recovered from Dunlap's body as well as the objects picked up from the area.

As Johnny began filling in the to-do list, his mind started racing. This was his opportunity to bring all his training and experience to bear for this victim and his family. A part of him wanted to be the one who solved *the* big case. That was part of every good detective's goal, but somehow Johnny could feel a fire burning within him about the murder of Officer Michael T. Dunlap. While he couldn't quite put his finger on it, something was nagging at him. Johnny chalked it up to the pressure to "swim with the big fish," and forced himself to focus on filling in the documents he'd created. When he looked up, three hours had gone by, and Holly was standing next to him, tapping her foot. Behind her were five other detectives, the lieutenant, and the sergeant.

"FNGs! When will they learn? Hard work will only get you so far. You gotta eat lunch!" Sergeant Vladimir Rostavic, a.k.a. Vinnie, said. The comment drew an audible laugh from the group, and Johnny turned a bit red despite his best efforts to avoid it.

"C'mon, kid. No need to burn your nose off on the grindstone during your first shift. We need to start you off right in Homicide." Lieutenant Jeff Biggers was a short man with a slight build. He was also well-respected within the department. Johnny was there the day he shot an armed robber outside of the First Fidelity Credit Union. The media was up in arms about it for over a year because he shot the man with a patrol rifle from across the street, and the armed robber, it turned out, was armed with a fake gun. Lost in the media stories and comments from so-called experts was the fact that the police couldn't tell the gun was a replica. The experts said he would be able to tell through the rifle scope that the gun was not real. Johnny found the ignorance entertaining for several reasons, not the least of which was the fact that Biggers made the shot at fifty-two yards with open sights. Besides, it certainly looked real enough to the teller the robber stood in front of. She was nearly paralyzed with fear when the officers got to her. Johnny heard that she never worked in a bank again. Like most victims, her life changed forever.

Lunch at Mazzi's was great. The detectives welcomed Johnny offering help any time of the day or night. Every offer had the same theme: There's no one way to do this job, so don't hesitate to ask for a second set of eyes or hands. It was great for Johnny to hear that. While he always had help when he needed it in the Fatality Accident Unit, lots of officers didn't like working them. It was an odd clash of cultures, as the Fatality Accident Unit was part of the uniformed division, and most of the folks in that division loved to be out on the street. Hit-and-run fatalities, however, required a lot of desk time, especially with all of the databases available. So even though he was never refused when he needed assistance, the acceptance of a request was usually less than exuberant.

Johnny also got to meet Mazzi for the first time. The owner knew the first names of every homicide detective, as well as the names of their wives and children. Mazzi had been serving cops for years and catered the annual holiday dinners at several precincts, as well as a few detective units. No one really knew his connection or the reason for his allegiance to the police officers who served his community. However, Johnny came to realize this was not uncommon. A guy like Mazzi probably just respected the job they did.

When they returned to the Homicide Unit, Holly walked Johnny around and showed him the evidence room and procedures, the on-call rotation, and the white-board known unofficially as the "murder board." On it were the active cases being worked within the Homicide Unit and the detectives assigned to the case. Each case had a primary and secondary detective in the event that follow-up was needed while the primary was off, out on vacation, or tied up on a homicide scene. Currently, the Lawler County Police Department was working forty-three homicides. The ages of the victims ranged from a six-month-old child to an eighty-five-year-old man who was brutally beaten to death in his home during an apparent home-invasion robbery. His daughter had, just a week prior, removed all of his guns from the house, saying it just made her "feel better." The case was on the news and disgusted Johnny. The poor man was defenseless.

Johnny's name was already on the board. He was assigned as a secondary to all cases Holly had on the board, except for one. On that case, Sergeant Rostavic was the secondary.

"Why is Sergeant Rostavic on this one with you?" Johnny asked.

"Ramirez. Tough case. Rostavic responded to the scene first because he was in the area. He's also very helpful during interviews and meetings. Don't let that light, creamy complexion and those baby blues fool you. Rostavic is fluent in Spanish and several other languages. I can hold my own with Spanish, but he is a master. While I'm stumbling to speak with someone, he's able to listen to everyone in the area and call bullshit on a perp in a heartbeat! It's great to see their faces, especially when the perp is locked up. They never see it coming!" Holly laughed.

"So where are the files for the cases I'm on with you?"

"All on computer. Anything in hard copy will be in the lateral cabinet behind me. The online system is pretty good at tracking everything. We use a running log of notes and a record-management system developed specifically for homicide cases. It's easy to work, and you'll get up to speed quickly. Just be sure to enter everything you do to avoid any duplication."

"What about court appearances? What do we bring with us?"

"That's when Charlotte will be your best friend. She's been the unit secretary for years. She'll print out the latest from the file and put it into a three-ring binder for you. When you get back, you give it to her, and she'll hold it for the next appearance."

"That's pretty efficient."

"Yep. It also keeps us from having to manage a pile of binders behind our desks. At the end of the case, if there is a trial, Charlotte prepares the case file to go to the DA. It's that simple."

"Sounds like it. It'll keep us from spending more time managing the file than working the case!"

"And that can happen pretty easily. What are you planning for the rest of the day?"

"I'm going to take a quick look at the facts of each of our cases. Then I want to start scheduling interviews in the cold case."

"Okay. Let me know if you want a second pair of ears and eyes on the interviews."

"Will do. A lot of them are internal—cops who worked the case or were there that night. I'm comfortable with those, but I'll get you on board with any others."

"Are you planning to speak with family members?"

"Yes, but I want to get with the previous investigators first."

"Good idea. Get a feel for the case first."

"That, and I want to make sure I'm all over the facts before I sit down with any of them. I figure I owe them that." Johnny pointed to the Dunlap file that was slowly taking over his desk.

"I understand. They'll have a lot of questions . . . better to be able to answer them right away." Holly nodded.

"That's my thought," Johnny said, then took a sip of his tea.

As she walked away, Holly stopped. "You know, Johnny, it took a lot of guts to pull that case. Everyone in this unit will help you find Dunlap's killer. Remember that. We'd love nothing more than to put him away on our watch."

The words hit Johnny in a pleasant way and also

emphasized the responsibility he had taken on. "Thanks. I pulled it by accident, really. I didn't know what the red binders were."

Holly laughed. "Well, that means you're either unlucky or weren't smart enough to put it back before anyone knew you had it!" She smiled at Johnny then walked back to her desk.

Johnny took a few minutes to call the last three detectives who worked on the Dunlap file. He started with John Benedict "J. B." Lettieri. *A guy named after a pope. That's a first,* Johnny thought. He called the number for his home, and it rang a few times before someone answered. Johnny was getting ready to leave a voicemail when J. B. picked up the phone.

"Hello." The male voice was flat.

"I'm looking for John, excuse me, J. B. Lettieri." Johnny had made his first mistake. The voice on the other end, a newly retired homicide detective, was not interested in giving out any personal information on the phone to someone he did not know.

"Well, we're all looking for someone. Who are you?"

Johnny instantly realized he should have identified himself immediately before asking for Lettieri. He would not make that mistake again and instantly worked to get a rapport going before Lettieri hung up. He had no obligation to speak with Johnny. "Sorry about that. I'm Johnny Till, a detective with Lawler PD."

"Sure. What unit?"

"Homicide."

"Homicide? You sound like you're twelve! Okay, Detective Till. If you're in Homicide, what was my badge number?"

Johnny quickly pulled up the first page of the Dunlap

file, as he remembered seeing Lettieri's badge number next to his signature on the final summary. "One, two, seven, five."

"Okay. What's your badge number?"

"One, seven, nine, one."

"Jesus! How many people have they hired over there? Okay. Tell me the name of the day-shift sergeant, and I'll stay on the phone."

"Sergeant Vladimir Rostavic." Johnny paused. "Do you want to speak with Vinnie? We just came back from lunch at Mazzi's." Johnny knew that should have been enough to soften the crust. He listened in silence until Lettieri spoke.

"Sorry about the third degree, but I get tired of hearing from reporters. I also expect that one day one of the wackos I put away will get rehabilitated and released. Hopefully by then I'll be too old and not worth a bullet." He laughed a bit to himself. "What's up, Till? I'm too old and fat to come back to the department, so you must be calling about a case. Or does Stills miss me now that he's in Evidence?"

Johnny made a note to ask someone about the reference to Stills. He suspected it had something to do with Lettieri's time with the Dunlap case.

"Don't know about Stills, but I'll make sure I ask him. He's usually pretty cooperative and pleasant." Johnny heard the laughter on the other end of the phone. He was happy he had made it past the test. Now he looked forward to meeting Lettieri.

"That's a good one, kid. Stills wouldn't know how to cooperate with a guy selling cold water in the desert! It's in his nature to be a pain in the ass." He cracked himself up with that one and laughed a bit more.

Johnny was glad he had read that correctly. It could have ended badly if the two men were friends, but playing the odds, he got lucky.

"So why are you calling an old homicide detective? Need some rosebushes planted? It seems that's all I do these days. That, and whatever honey-do's my wife has been holding for me for the past forty years."

"Well, sir, I'm working a case, and you were assigned to it for a while."

Lettieri cut him off. "I'm no sir, but I appreciate the effort. J. B. will do."

"Sorry, but anyone who catches a serial rapist of fourteen women deserves a lot of respect."

The phone went silent. Johnny had made it a point to learn something about everyone he intended to call, especially the homicide detectives, but a lot of cops knew about J. B.

"That was a horrible set of crimes." Lettieri's voice was low and emotionless. "I'm very proud that we caught that guy. He mutilated the first twelve, then he started killing. He never would have stopped. Well done, kid. Well played." More silence. "Okay, you have my attention. I admire your diligence. Did you look that info up before calling me?"

"No, I studied the case three times. The first was in college, and then we did case studies on it in two classes I took—one in Chicago and a sex-crimes-specific course in Seattle."

"Walter Bartholomew Baglin. What a piece of crap he was. A true sociopath. Cared about as much about cutting a woman as carving an apple. He's dead, you know."

"Yep. He was raped, shanked, then hung at Garrard State Pen. Didn't last a week."

"Ain't pretrial publicity a bitch?" Lettieri chuckled. "Of course, it also didn't help that the brother of one of his victims was in the same cellblock. No one knew. He was adopted with a different last name. I heard the state paid Baglin's mother some money, though, in a civil suit. Anyway, I guess I don't need to worry about him getting out and coming for me."

"No one does, thanks to you."

"Very kind of you to say that."

Johnny allowed the silence to progress before speaking. It was healthy, and he suspected that like most cops, Lettieri was unaccustomed to true gratitude. "You know the tradition in Homicide—new guy picks a cold case. Well, I pulled one that you worked on."

"Hmm. There were a few. I was fortunate that all of the cases closed when I was primary, and secondary, too, now that I think about it. I worked on several cold cases during my time in Homicide. Is it Rester or Havlin?"

"No. I pulled the Dunlap file."

Another long silence passed between them. "Okay, kid. In person or on the phone? Your choice."

"In person, if that's okay."

"That's the sign of a good detective. Always sit down with them and watch them while you talk. Name the time and place, and I'll be there. Bring someone with you. My advice is to bring someone with you to every interview and when you track down any lead in this case. And don't expect everyone to welcome you with open arms. A lot of people were sore about this case going to cold case and even madder when we couldn't make an arrest."

"I appreciate the advice. I've been forewarned."

"Probably by Bill Worth. He knows more about

homicide than anyone I've ever met. Listen to him, and you'll learn a lot. Okay, here's something else to be warned about. You listening?"

"Yep."

"I never gave a rat's ass about politics, so I spoke my mind. Now that I'm retired, I've lost my filter, as my kids say. I'll answer any question you want, and I won't hold back. I only ask one thing, and it's non-negotiable."

"What's that?"

"When you catch the son of a bitch who killed Dunlap, you personally call me and every detective who's still alive. I don't want to learn about it when I read about it in the paper. Deal?"

"Absolutely. You have my word." Johnny paused. "And for the record, I understand why."

The two men made plans to meet at Young's Sports Bar and Eatery near Kennesaw State. The background noise of the thirty or so televisions made it an ideal public place for a private conversation. It was a strange name, but it got around Lawler County ordinance concerning Sunday hours for bars. Eateries were neither mentioned nor regulated by the ordinance. Pretty clever. Johnny was not surprised when Lettieri mentioned it, as the owner was a retired New York City firefighter. They would be able to get a booth in a closed section to talk in private. It was just a bonus that the food was good. The menu always included some fairly healthful choices, and any first responder was free to order any specialty item to conform to their diet du jour.

They were set for Thursday at noon. Johnny made a note and put it on his calendar and Holly's calendar, as well. Sadly, they were not able to meet for two days, because Lettieri had doctor appointments both days. He made a joke of it—"The old parts are falling off the frame"—but Johnny sensed it was something more serious.

Johnny told Holly about the appointment, then set up three more for that week and the next. That brought the Dunlap file back twelve years. He figured that was enough time to get a feel for the case and the instincts and hunches of the detectives who plowed the ground before him. If the classes and books were correct, these detectives had been stewing over the details of the Dunlap case since they put the file back into the cold case file room. It would be a bone of contention with them. Hopefully, they had reached a point where they just wanted somebody to solve the damn thing. There was a measure of pride that was a delicate balance. Too much, and they would be reluctant to provide information, afraid that someone would see something they too easily missed. Too little, and they lost hope that it would ever be solved.

The three other detectives were available in the next two days and seemed eager to meet. All but one also seemed eager to join Johnny for a meal. They were meals for which the department would not reimburse him, but he was proud to get the checks. He looked forward to speaking with those who came before him.

Holly was a champ and rearranged her interviews to go with him. She was especially looking forward to the lunch with Lettieri, who was featured on a true-crime-type show a few years back in reference to the Baglin arrest. Word was that Lettieri participated in the writing of a screenplay but donated the check the company gave him to the rape crisis center. Johnny hoped that both of them wouldn't be too starstruck to ask the right questions.

He spent the rest of the day getting up to speed on the cases he shared with Holly by reading the summaries online. He made suggestions in a couple that seemed to make sense to Holly. He was glad to see that a new opinion was welcome. They made plans to re-interview two witnesses that week after checking with the crime lab on a new test Johnny had read about.

At 5:30 p.m., he was heading for the elevators in his workout gear when he ran into Holly. She was heading to the gym in the building, as well, and he held the elevator for her.

"A fellow gym rat, I see. Thanks for holding the elevator." Holly was dressed in an oversized T-shirt and leggings. Johnny suspected that she was making a concerted effort to avoid any unnecessary attention.

"Yep. I don't see how folks survive without working out. To me, sitting at a desk every day is harder on you than moving around, working patrol. I feel like a coiled spring all day. If I don't work out, I'll go nuts." Johnny stretched his arms over his head as he spoke.

"And you'd feel like crap. At least I do when I miss a workout. What's on the menu today? Weights? Cardio?"

"Cardio. Don't laugh, but I also started doing yoga." Johnny watched her face and waited for the expected comment or laughter.

Holly smiled and turned her head to the side a bit. "Really?" Holly found the comment adorable. The thought of a six-foot-two, two-hundred-twenty-pound man doing yoga with housewives and senior citizens nearly did make her laugh. "Where do you go?"

"The gym near my house has a class in the evenings. It's taught by a woman in her fifties who looks twenty-five and is more flexible than anyone I've ever seen."

"So how have you evaluated the flexibility of this hot woman who is nearly twice your age?" She winked at him.

"Purely from a distance." Johnny smiled. "Seriously though, weights will affect your flexibility. The yoga is awesome for keeping you from getting bound up. It took a bit to get used to, but now I look forward to it."

The elevator stopped and opened on the basement level. They walked to the left and into the gym.

"I may have to give that a try. Enjoy your workout."

"You, too. See you in the a.m."

CHAPTER 9

J ohnny and Holly sat in Sally's Biscuit House waiting for retired Detective Anthony Tucci to arrive. He had worked on the Dunlap file a while ago and held on to the file for about three years. He was about ten minutes late, forcing Johnny to explain his green tea habit to Holly. He could only hope that the confidentiality between partners would save him from the inevitable ribbing he faced if the unit discovered his secret: "No coffee? That's un-American!" or watching everyone drink coffee around him with their pinky fingers held away from their cups. In a way, it was inevitable and part of being on a team. *Qui te t'aquine bien, t'aime bien*, his French grandmother would say. "We tease the ones we love, Johnny." He smiled when he thought of her.

Tucci walked in dressed in a pair of tan khaki pants and a freshly pressed button-down shirt. He was older, in his seventies, and he moved slowly. It was more indicative of caution than disability.

Johnny and Holly stood as he entered. They recognized him from his retired identification photo that they had pulled up. Johnny noted that he had a full head of hair, and although it was gray, it gave him a somewhat more youthful look. He was slim, about five foot seven, and looked serious. His hair was neatly parted, and he wore wire-framed glasses. Johnny guessed they were progressive lenses and not bifocals, as he didn't shift his head when navigating the step down to the back section of the restaurant. He looked like he had dressed for the occasion. That was encouraging. Johnny expected every one of these detectives to take this case seriously.

Tucci had a big smile on his face as he made his way toward the back of the restaurant.

"Holly Forrester," she said as she extended her hand.

Tucci took her hand and shook it. He looked at Holly silently for a moment—perhaps a moment longer than was expected or comfortable for the three of them. "Well, the detectives were never this lovely when I wore the badge. If they were, I might never have retired!" He turned to his right as Holly smiled. "And you must be Till."

Johnny extended his hand. "Johnny Till, yes, sir. It's a pleasure to meet you." Tucci looked unsteady on his feet. Johnny pulled out a chair. "Please, have a seat."

Tucci sat down, and the waitress walked up. She handed Tucci a menu. He took a moment and stared at her. She was in her early twenties, tall, and blonde. Her long hair was pulled back away from her face, and she smiled as she approached.

"Did anyone ever tell you that you look like a movie star?" The waitress blushed. "Tessa, is it?" he said after an almost imperceptible glance at her name tag. "I'd like black coffee, two eggs over easy, grits, and wheat toast."

Tessa scribbled on an order ticket, then looked at Holly and Johnny. They ordered quickly and watched Tessa walk away, a little lighter on her feet. Tucci looked at Johnny and spoke in a stage whisper that anyone within fifteen feet would have heard. "Never miss a chance to make a woman smile, son."

Holly looked at Johnny, and the two of them smiled. Without saying a word, they decided that Holly would start the conversation. Holly looked at Tucci, who was looking around the restaurant. "So, Detective Tucci, thank you for meeting with us today."

His face brightened, and he sat up a bit higher in his chair. Using his title made a difference. "Oh, it's no problem at all. I don't get out much anymore. My wife passed a few years ago. Normally, I sit at home and make my own breakfast, so this is a treat for me." He looked at Holly and his face dropped a bit. "I hope I did not offend you, but I guess I just say what's on my mind these days . . . and you are a beautiful woman."

Holly blushed a little. Tucci had reached that age where he was harmless, and his comments were just cute. "Nothing to worry about. No offense taken. I thought your comment was sweet."

Tucci looked at Johnny. "You hear that, Till? Sweet is just another word for harmless." He let out a sigh. "Well, I'll take it." Tucci sat back in his chair as Tessa brought his coffee.

"Your food will be out in a few minutes." She smiled at Tucci then at Johnny. She was definitely standing a bit taller following Tucci's comment. As she walked away, Johnny watched Tucci turn toward Holly.

"So what brings you here to talk with an old detective? The food is decent, but it can't be the cuisine or the ambiance." He waved his hands around as he said "cuisine" and "ambiance," and watched Holly's face to see if he made her smile again. He did.

"Johnny called because he's working on a case you had for a while." She motioned to Johnny.

Johnny piped in, "I thought it would be a good idea to start with the most recent few detectives to get their impressions."

"Well, I always took good notes and wrote long reports. I'm sure it's all there in the file." It was clear that he was fishing for more information.

"You definitely documented the file well," Johnny said, "but I wanted to get any impressions you might have had since you left the department."

Tucci laughed a bit. "Since I left the department, I haven't done much. I read a lot and visit my grandchildren occasionally. It's been quiet since my wife died, but I try not to think much about the cases I worked. I probably won't even remember the facts without looking at the file, but you can give it a shot. What case do you want to ask me about?"

"The Mike Dunlap case," Johnny said.

Tucci's smile faded. He looked away, then down at his coffee. He took a long sip, then he looked at Johnny. A silence settled over the table as Tucci took a deep breath and exhaled audibly. Then he spoke in a different tone. It was flat, calculated, and sounded like a man defeated. "Officer Michael Dunlap, murdered on November 4, 1998. Shot multiple times—probably two weapons. No witnesses. Left behind a wife and kids. He was assigned to public relations. No recent arrests to make anyone mad. Frustrating case." He paused and looked directly at Johnny. "It never really made sense."

"We know you worked it hard, but weren't able to develop any new leads," Holly said.

Johnny chimed in as Tucci just shook his head. "I'm most interested in your impressions, your gut . . . anything that you didn't put into the file for any reason. I'd really appreciate anything you can tell us."

Tucci took another sip of his coffee. "I'll help any way I can." Just then Tessa appeared. She put the food down, looked at Johnny again, then walked away. When she was about fifteen feet away, Tucci put his left hand on Johnny's shoulder. "She's sweet on you, son. That's the second time she stared a second too long at your dark hair and baby blues. Probably a student at the university working a part-time job. You're single. Ask her out."

"Why do you think she's a student?" Holly said. Even though many cops didn't wear wedding rings on duty, detectives most often did, so she didn't bother to ask Tucci how he knew Johnny was single.

Tucci smiled. A chance to show off. He realized Holly had done it intentionally, but he didn't care. He sat back up in his chair and began speaking. "She's wearing a high school ring and graduated two years ago, yet her left hand has paint stains on it. Art major likely, but it could be ink, and she could be an architecture major. Definitely some type of artistic course of study, no doubt. She's working the breakfast shift, which does not bring in the big bucks, and her shoes are relatively new. They are also more modern than the typical uniform shoes worn by professional waitresses that they often order from catalogues dropped off by uniform vendors. Comfortable, but not particularly stylish. We'll test my theory when we leave. At any rate, you should ask her out. Life's short, son. Don't waste time."

Holly and Johnny were smiling. Tucci was good and had not lost his edge. Johnny broke the silence. "I'm glad you remember the case, but I'm not surprised."

"Well, I am. When I worked that case, we had a helluva case load. There was a gang war of sorts going on. It seemed we worked more homicides in the years I had that file than in the prior ten years." Tucci picked up a piece of bread and broke an egg yolk with one corner. He sprinkled some pepper on the yellow coating on his bread, then took a big bite. "After a while, I realized there was nothing new, and I put the case back into the cold-file racks." He took another bite of toast. Then he looked up at Johnny, then Holly. His eyes looked sad. "It's a terrible thing, you know—not being able to solve a murder with a dead cop. We did everything we could. I solved ten cold cases while I was in Homicide, and I'm very proud of that." He looked toward the wall and stared for a moment. "But that was the craziest case."

"How so?" Holly said.

"That file was one of the most thorough I'd ever seen. The original detectives explored every lead, every angle that made sense. Family, friends, neighbors, relatives, and nothing led to the perp. No leads at all. It was like an alien came down and killed him, then left the galaxy." Tucci then went back to his breakfast. "Eat up before it gets cold. We can talk after."

Tucci's frustration was clear. Holly and Johnny decided to leave it alone and eat, as well.

After they finished, Tessa cleared off the plates. As Tucci sipped his coffee, he started again. "Sorry to seem dramatic, but it's frustrating. We had a great homicide crew. We solved some of the toughest cases in record time. We found perps all over the United States. Hell, Smith even extradited one from Alaska!" He paused. "But you can't solve one when there's nothing to work with."

"Nothing in writing, nothing official, but what's your gut?" Johnny said.

Tucci thought about it for a few minutes. "You're right, both of you. I've thought about that case a lot since

I retired. When you retire, you will think about the victims and the families, but there are some cases that stick with you. I think about the perps we locked up when I was convinced it was not the first time they took a life. Just a hunch sometimes, but they were too cavalier about watching the life run out of someone or hearing them take their last breath. I shot a perp, and thirty years later I still think about hearing his last breath. Then there are the people who never got past the tragedy of having a loved one murdered—divorce, alcohol, suicide. Murder nearly always leaves a wasteland in its wake."

Holly and Johnny just listened.

Tucci switched from his coffee to the glass of water Janie poured for each of them without a request. "But Dunlap's case, I think about the way I felt when I put the folders back into the cold case file room. I think about how I felt when I signed the log relinquishing the file back to cold case status, and I think about the way I felt when I called Dunlap's widow to tell her I was not able to find her husband's killer." Tucci put his head down for a moment, then he looked at Holly, then Johnny. His face was serious and focused. "If I had the chance to start over, if I was twenty years younger, I'd look past the normal motives and suspects. There was something missed in the first few hours, some connection that slipped by the original detectives. It must be there. It's always there. We all missed it. There must have been a connection to his killer, or some connection to the motive." Tucci ate the last of his second triangle of toast, then took another sip of his water. "There always is. My advice to you? Widen the net."

Holly and Johnny looked at the man, who suddenly seemed much older. Tucci drank more water, then looked up at both of them. Johnny spoke first. "Any insights would help. Widen it to include who?"

"Back then, kids didn't kill people like they do today, especially cops. At least, not in Lawler County. Look at the kids. I know that seems crazy, but that's the only group that hasn't been explored. At the time, it seemed like a crazy theory to look for a cop killer in a high school. Now though . . . perhaps your killer was ahead of his time—or her time." The last comment seemed to have an effect on Tucci, like a recognition that there was no good in the world anymore.

The comment wasn't lost on Johnny or Holly. Statistically, cop killers were overwhelmingly young and male. It made sense to consider this as a theory. However, both of them felt bad that Tucci seemed to have lost a bit more faith in humanity with his observation.

"Did you get the impression there were any inappropriate relationships between Dunlap and any of the kids?" The question hurt Holly, but she had to ask.

"No," Tucci said. "I never thought it was anything like that. I say that for two reasons. First, like I said, no one has ever looked in that direction for a killer, but they did consider a passion murder. Nothing turned up. Second, if it's not one of the kids, then it was a true random act. The FBI never turned up anything similar involving a cop anywhere in the United States, so there's no pattern to rely on. If this is a truly random crime, a crime of opportunity, then it may never be solved. But as you know, those are very rare, even if it appears that way at the outset."

The three of them sat quietly for a few minutes. In a near act of clairvoyance and mercy, Janie came by and delivered the checks. Johnny took the three checks from her hand. "I've got this one." He passed the bills to Tessa, along with the checks. "No change. Thanks for taking care of us."

As Tessa turned, Tucci spoke to her. "Good luck in school, Tessa. What are you studying?"

"Thank you. Art history. It may be a useless degree, but I love all types of art." She smiled at Tucci, then at Johnny. "Come by and see us again." Then she turned and walked away.

Tucci smiled at Holly, then at Johnny. He stood up, and Johnny and Holly followed suit. "Thanks for the breakfast. I enjoyed meeting with you. I wish I could have helped."

Holly took his hand. "You did help, Anthony. We really appreciate that you took some time to meet with us."

"Of course." Tucci looked at Johnny, then back at Holly. "What else have I got to do?" He smiled, then shook Johnny's hand tightly. "Thanks for making me feel useful today."

Holly put her hand on Tucci's left shoulder. "You're always useful, Anthony. You've got a lot of experience." Holly's eyes showed her empathy and kindness. There was something about the image of a man rattling around an empty house that touched her.

There was a comfortable moment between the three of them, and Johnny hoped he would speak with Tucci again. Tucci turned and pushed in his chair. Then he leaned on the back and stared at the table. Speaking to neither of them and both at the same time, he spoke, and his words were calm, measured, and fierce. "You catch this son of a bitch, and you let me know when you do. I want to be there to put my eyes on that murderer."

Tucci turned without looking at them again. Holly and Johnny watched Tucci walk out of the restaurant and wondered if he was tearing up.

"One down and three to go, Johnny."

"Yep. He's a smart guy. That advice is kind of scary."

"I hope I'm still that sharp at his age. I asked around about him last evening. He retired from the navy before he started with the PD." She shook her head. "It's sad that those cases still torture him."

"At least we have something to look forward to." Johnny smiled at her.

"There's some good news." She chuckled. "Anyway, don't get discouraged. The good thing is those students were at least twenty years younger than Dunlap. It won't be too hard to track them down and see if he's right. If he's wrong, at least we'll be shutting down another avenue of inquiry. We'll figure it out. Let's get back to the office. I've got an interview with a doctor on a natural death at nine."

"Need a witness?"

"Nope. About as vanilla as you can get. Ninety-five-year-old white male with a history of heart disease and strokes died in his sleep in an assisted-living facility. No signs of petechial hemorrhage, and the tox screen came back normal. No signs of trauma at all. Just need to get an interview and a signature on the death certificate to let the family have the body."

"Why did you get the call?"

"The legislature amended the Death Investigation Act about three years ago requiring a police report on every death that occurs in a personal-care home, assisted-living facility . . . any facility that is providing long-term care. The only exception is a hospital if the death occurs more than twenty-four hours after admission. It came after a string of suspicious deaths in unlicensed facilities. Nice idea, but I guess the folks at the capitol thought we would double the number of homicide detectives when they passed the law."

"Dying peacefully in your sleep. Not a bad damn way to go."

"Compared to what we see? Absolutely!" As they reached the car, Holly stopped Johnny. "Hey! You forgot something."

The urgency in her voice made his blood run cold for a second. New to the unit, and he already missed a key question during an important interview. He thought quickly. "What did I miss?"

"You forgot to get Tessa's number!" She grinned at Johnny. She got him.

Johnny opened the door to his car. "Shit, I didn't forget. I have a no-drama rule when it comes to dating. Art history student at Wymouth dating a cop? Think of all the insightful conversations about police work I could have with her friends."

Holly got into her car that was parked next to Johnny's. "Wymouth?"

"She was getting something out of her purse when we walked out. Her student ID was attached to her keys that she put on the counter. I saw the logo."

Holly started the car, then rolled down the driver's window. She smiled as she put on her seatbelt. "Not bad. Maybe you'll make a good hit-and-run investigator someday."

Johnny laughed and pulled away from the curb.

CHAPTER 10

They drove separately to the Homicide Unit, just as they had met at the restaurant. Johnny started thinking about the evidence list in the file. He didn't recall seeing a yearbook from West Lawler High School. He decided to take a detour and stop by the school. He would ask for a yearbook from 1988, then scan it so it could be returned. He was also hoping to get a student roster but figured he would need a grand jury subpoena for that. Yearbooks are public, in a way, so principals were more willing to part with them as long as you brought them back. It didn't hurt to ask, though. If he got a firm "no," he would check online yearbook databases or the library at the police department. They often ordered high school yearbooks when they could to help secure identifications or get information about associations. Social media made the latter reason less important, but in 1998, that was the way it was done.

He pulled into the parking lot of West Lawler High School about fifteen minutes later. The school had undergone renovations in the past five years, and Johnny had not been there since he graduated. He pressed the intercom and identified himself, as he had called ahead. The electronic lock clicked, and he opened the front door.

It was a weird feeling, entering the front door of your high school as a cop. There are certain sights, sounds, and odors that trigger memories in all of us. Schools are no exception. Johnny wondered what it was, but he had this overwhelming feeling that he was late for class. It made him smile. This would be the first willing trip he took to the principal's office.

Johnny made his way to the front office. Apparently, the renovations were more focused on adding classroom space than a true remodel, as the administration office and the principal's office were in the same place. In fact, they looked like they only rated a fresh coat of paint and a new desk or two.

He walked through the double doors and approached the counter. "Good morning. I'm Detective Till with the Lawler Police. I called earlier."

An older woman in her midsixties stood from behind a desk and approached the opposite side of the counter. She carried her glasses around her neck, having taken off another pair of glasses at her desk. As she approached the counter, she said, almost to herself but loud enough for Johnny to hear, "Detective Till?" She pulled on the chain around her neck and brought the glasses to her face. She looked at Johnny and smiled. "Oh, Detective Till, my dear! Come hug me, Johnny Till!" She walked to a break in the counter and pulled up the top. When she met Johnny on the other side, she hugged him tight. "It's so good to see you, Johnny!"

"It's good to see you, too, Ms. Winters. You haven't changed a bit!"

She stepped back from him and held both his hands.

"That's very sweet, but just a very polite way of saying that I've looked old for a long time! Let me look at you. We've followed your career in the paper and on TV. We're very proud of you, you know!"

"Thanks! That means a lot. How is everyone here?"

"The same, just older. Ms. James retired last year. Forty years! Can you believe it? A few folks have moved, and you know Mr. Renner, who taught Spanish, passed away."

"I know. I was at his funeral. It was very sad. He was so young."

"Yes, he was." She paused, almost seeming to honor his memory. "Come with me. You wanted to see the principal . . . and she will want to see you!" Holding Johnny's hand, Elizabeth Winters walked Johnny down the other side of the counter into a hall that led to the administrative offices. Along the way, they stopped at every desk, and Johnny heard the repetitive chorus of "You remember Johnny Till?" and "Oh, yes, of course I do!" Several people asked about his mom, and he told them she was well. At last they arrived at the office door of Dr. Lena J. Sullivan, who had been principal of West Lawler High School for close to twenty years. Ms. Winters knocked on the door and entered.

As they entered the office, Lena Sullivan stood from her desk and walked around to greet them. She was a stunning woman, impeccably dressed, and looked more like a CEO of a Fortune 100 company than a high school principal. She was tall, and her heels only added to the impressive impact she made. Her features were unique, due to an Irish father and a Thai mother. She truly loved children and served with a vitality that endeared her to the community, the parents, and the children most of the time.

"Johnny Till! Look at you. You've grown up on us!" She stepped forward and hugged Johnny. "Please, sit." She motioned to the two chairs in front of her desk. When Johnny settled into a seat, she sat behind her desk.

"I've got a lot of paperwork to catch up on. Is there anything else, Dr. Sullivan?"

"No, Elizabeth. Thank you so much."

Ms. Winters closed the door behind her, then walked back to her desk. She was still smiling when she sat down. After thirty years in the school system, she enjoyed seeing students succeed.

"So," Dr. Sullivan began, "to what do I owe the honor of a visit from a famous alumnus?" She raised a copy of the *Lawler Monitor* from the corner of her desk that contained a photo of the man convicted of killing Sadie Emerson alongside a photograph of the little girl. The paper had a yellow sticky attached asking her staff to add the information to the alumni newsletter.

"You are too kind. I was just doing my job, just like every other officer."

"Of course, but some do a better job than others."

"And some just work on high-profile cases that end up in the newspaper," Johnny offered.

She laughed. "Humility. You came by it honestly. You were that way in your freshman year here when you won the JV All-County Wrestling Championship. The coaches still talk about you coming across the mat to shake hands with the prior year's winner, who was knocked out of the finals." She put the paper back on her desk and leaned her elbows on the desk. "So, I'll assume your mom is well. Based upon the message I received from the receptionist, you are here on police business."

"Yes, I am. Mom is fine, by the way. She'll be thrilled

that you asked about her." Johnny paused and leaned forward. "I need to borrow some old yearbooks. We can scan them and return them in a day or so." Johnny knew it was best to get right to the point with Dr. Sullivan. She was all business, but he wasn't sure how well she could keep a secret. He also wasn't sure if she would be required to report any police contact with her school to her chain of command. He was ready to deflect attention away from the Dunlap case, though. He thought of that on the way over. The last thing he needed was for this visit to appear in the alumni newsletter.

"Of course. Depending on the year, it will be fairly simple. If they are too old, they might be archived. I recall an effort by the central office to scan all of the books to preserve them, but I believe the originals were kept somewhere." She picked up a pad with her left hand, then placed it in front of her. Her right hand reached for a pen. Johnny noticed that it was a very nice pen and recalled that her husband was a serial entrepreneur. Some people criticized Lena about it, and Johnny remembered hearing the snide comments. Johnny and his mom always thought it said a lot about her that she continued working in the school system when she did not have to work.

"Okay, Detective." She smiled at him. "What yearbooks do you need to borrow?"

Johnny had rehearsed this part on the way over. He needed to be smooth and avoid any emphasis on his real target: 1998.

"I would like to borrow the yearbooks for the following years." He made a show of getting out his notepad. He read the years off the paper in front of him, which he had jotted down in the car when he parked.

"1988 thorough 2000." There was a method to his selection. Sometimes people miss their high school annual photograph, so he would need the years surrounding 1998, as well. In addition, ten or so years of annuals would give a good deal of cover if she or anyone else started snooping on the internet. Any more than that would seem excessive, and his request might lose some aura of credibility.

Lena Sullivan wrote down the years. "Okay. Those would be recent, and they are all on site. I don't want to waste any of your time if you have to come back, so why don't we get you the yearbooks from 1985 through 2005 inclusive. I'll also check to see if we have any of them scanned. If so, we can put them on a thumb drive for you. Would that help?"

Johnny knew she was offering a favor in exchange for information about the case he was working. He expected this. "That would be great. I can wait for a bit and take what you have, if that would be convenient."

"Of course. I'll ask Mr. Fander to bring them to the front office. He is the unofficial registrar when he is not coaching soccer or baseball. That will save you some time." She picked up her phone and called Mr. Fander on the intercom. He agreed to have a student bring the yearbooks to the front office immediately and agreed to check on the scanned copies, as well.

"I really appreciate it. I have another question about records," Johnny said.

"Fire away."

"I noticed that the school system started using a new records-management software a few years back. I remember there was a lot of debate about the cost in the paper." Johnny knew this would distract her a bit, as he believed

she was about to ask the name of the student he was looking for.

"Oh, yes. What a mess. You'd think people would be
happy if we wrote on stone tablets and hired monks to
make copies!" She laughed to herself. Johnny smiled.
"Our new system, Records and Attendance Data System,
RADS for short, or that's what everyone calls it, went
online three years ago. Why do you ask?"

"Well, we may have a need to retrieve some student
enrollment and attendance records, as well."

Lena Sullivan made a note on her pad, then her face
showed some concern. "Well, you may or may not be
aware that those documents are confidential educational
records. They are protected by state and federal law."
Johnny could see she was using a rehearsed line no doubt
given to her at a seminar or conference and used to
successfully dissuade the faint of heart from seeking
records, even if they had a lawful need for them.

"Of course. I'm aware of the privileges. I thought you
might be able to assist in explaining how the older
records are maintained and in what form they are
available so that I can secure a grand jury subpoena for
them." Johnny worked hard to ensure that his face and
body posture did not change. He wanted to appear just
as friendly and collegial as when he walked into her
office. He was successful; Lena Sullivan was not. The
change in her demeanor and body language was
undeniable.

"While we would be happy to help the police department in any way possible, any subpoenas would have to
go through the attorneys for the school system. I have the
firm name and number."

"That's okay. I have it. Unfortunately, I've had to get

records in the past about students in the last several years while investigating hit-and-run cases." He looked down for a moment, then back up for effect. "It is sad that we have children committing crimes like DUI and felony hit-and-run. Don't you agree?"

Johnny's planned speech worked like a charm. Dr. Sullivan sat up and her face changed from a look of cautious concern to one of empathy. "Indeed, it is. I know we can only do so much, but when I see or hear about a student in handcuffs, it just breaks my heart."

Johnny raised the pen in his right hand and asked her a specific question. "So if we had to follow up to retrieve records for the years corresponding to the yearbooks, would those records be on an old system, archived somewhere, or were they imported into the RADS system?"

Lena Sullivan began thinking. "I know there was an effort to incorporate the records into the new system, but there was much discussion about how far back we could go. I mean, it did not make sense to take up storage space with records that would not likely be needed. I mean, why would anyone want the attendance records of a student from 1985?" She looked at Johnny—another fishing expedition. At least she was focused, intentionally or not, on the wrong year.

"That makes sense. I guess you create a lot of documentation around here." Johnny focused her on the work the school system did and the immense burden of keeping seemingly endless records. She took the cue and went on for several minutes about the amount of staff and the cost of simply keeping records that no one ever reviewed or used for any purpose, even though some of that data might answer some questions about the state of education today.

Eventually, she got back to the question. "The original data is kept electronically at the headquarters of the school system in Winder. The old servers were all collected from the individual schools, and as far as I know, they are still there."

"Great. What was the name of the old system?"

"It was known as EDIS to all of us. Let me think. You cannot put 'the EDIS system' on a subpoena. That would not look very professional. I believe it was the Education Database Indexing System. Yes, that's it."

"Do you have the contact information for the person at the system headquarters who is in charge of the EDIS data?"

"Let me see, I should." She typed on her computer, then wrote down the name, email, and phone number of the chief information officer for the system. When she handed the paper to Johnny, he could see that she was still being cautious. She no doubt knew the exact person who had access to the data. She had been there too long to go through layers of bureaucracy. Johnny understood that. She had to protect herself.

"Thank you very much. That will save me a great deal of time. I'm not even sure we will need the records, but this will help."

As he finished speaking, the principal's phone rang. She picked it up and spoke with someone at the front desk. She hung up, then stood. "The yearbooks are at the front counter, along with a thumb drive. We have a document for you to sign. I hope you don't mind, but these are originals and, in many cases, the only copies we have." She began walking toward the door, obviously anxious to avoid any further discussions about student records. Johnny guessed that she would be on the phone with her superior before he left the parking lot to advise them of his inquiry.

As she opened the door, Johnny took her invitation to walk past her down the hall. They approached the front counter to see a large box of yearbooks sitting on the counter. A staff member was standing by them with a form in front of her. She appeared to be guarding the crown jewels, but Johnny understood. This was a big deal and he suspected it would be big news around the school by the end of the day.

As Johnny signed for the books, the staff person set the books on the counter to confirm the years represented by the collection. Lena Sullivan looked on, observing the process. "How long will you need the books, Detective?"

Johnny heard the title and at first was concerned that this would further lend an air of intrigue to his request. Then he realized that everyone in the front office already knew he was there. "One week should do it. We'll have them back safe and sound. Is that okay?"

"Of course. Anything we can do to help."

Johnny asked for a copy of the form he signed for his records, hefted the box of yearbooks, and began the long walk to his car. The goodbyes and well-wishes followed him as he left the office. Johnny smiled as he walked away from the main office. He had successfully distracted Lena Sullivan from asking why he wanted the yearbooks or what years were particularly important to him. He imagined that she was likely sitting at her desk, frustrated with herself for not getting that information.

CHAPTER 11

J ohnny began walking from the main office through the familiar hallways to the exit. He thought about some of his friends who had walked those halls with him. Some lost touch with him soon after high school; many lost touch intentionally when he became a cop.

He recalled running into a friend, Michael Jones, at a gas station shortly after graduating from college. They shook hands and did the "guy hug" thing. Mike invited Johnny to a party at his house that weekend for the Fourth of July. Johnny accepted and was excited, as it was the first Fourth that he wasn't working. The two men discussed who was coming and everyone's new occupations. When Johnny shared that he was a cop, Mike turned pale. Then he just nodded when Johnny asked if Mike and his guests might be more comfortable if Johnny did not show up. This was how cops wound up having only cops for friends, with a few firefighters thrown in to keep it interesting.

Johnny paused as he passed the library. The display windows on either side of the main doors contained collections of old and new books. Edgar Allan Poe's *The Murders in the Rue Morgue* and *The Night Thoreau Spent in*

Jail by Lee and Lawrence caught his eye. *One scared the hell out of me, and one helped me understand who I wanted to be.*

As Johnny stood there a moment, the main door opened and Mrs. Violet Sanders, the head librarian, appeared. She smiled at Johnny, looked both ways down the hall as if they were both under surveillance, then waved to him. "Detective Till! Please come into my office a moment." She spoke in a stage whisper.

Johnny instinctively had begun checking the hall, as well, and had to stop himself. "You can call me Johnny, Mrs. Sanders. You've known me forever."

"No, sir! Titles are there for a reason, and we show respect here." One more check of the hallway apparently convinced her their conversation was free from observation by the Russians or British double-naught spies. Johnny had to smile. She was known to be a bit odd and quite likely the biggest scandalmonger on the faculty.

"Sure, Mrs. Sanders. Let's go into your office where it's private." *Why not? It could be something, or perhaps I forgot to return a book my junior year! A minute or two couldn't hurt.* Johnny held the door open as she turned to walk quickly toward her office. She seemed to walk with a purpose, occasionally nodding to the parent volunteers and students they passed.

When they reached her office, she closed the door behind Johnny and took a seat. Johnny took the other seat in front of her desk, placing the box of yearbooks beside his chair. He'd sat there once as a freshman receiving the "Libraries are for learning; let the words come from the pages in your hands, not the lips on your mouth" speech. He smiled as he recalled the memory. He looked up at Mrs. Sanders.

She was not smiling. "I know why you're here."

News travels fast. She probably got a call as soon as I entered the main office. "Do you have a collection of yearbooks? I know you take excellent care of the items entrusted to you," Johnny observed.

"You're not here about yearbooks, Detective Till."

"I'm not?" Johnny fought the urge to smile.

"No. You're here about the murder of that officer, Dunlap."

No title. Interesting. "Why do you say that, Mrs. Sanders?"

"Well, it's never been solved, and you're the first detective to come here in a long time asking questions. The detectives who come by always want to speak to a specific teacher or student. You wanted to speak with the principal and no one else." She turned her head again to look out the office windows. Apparently spotting no one with a drinking glass up to the windows straining to listen to their conversation, she continued. Her eyes focused, and she looked directly at Johnny. "I know who killed him."

Johnny paid attention to his body language to make certain he gave away nothing. Violet Sanders was known to have an opinion about everything and everybody she met or even heard of. This was serious, though. This was not a personal theory of who was getting divorced or having an affair on the PTA board. He made a conscious effort to focus his voice. She was eccentric, but not crazy.

Johnny moved his hand to his phone and feigned putting it on vibrate while he started a recorder. "Who, Mrs. Sanders? Who do you think killed Officer Michael Dunlap?" He leaned forward to encourage her to speak.

"Listen, Detective," she said as she also leaned in, making Johnny very happy knowing the microphone would pick up every word, "I didn't say I *thought* I knew. I know exactly who killed that officer." After one more check of the windows, she leaned in even further. "It was Melanie Rast."

Johnny's mind searched his mental picture of the case file suspect list. Melanie Rast did not appear in his mind, and he was pretty certain that name appeared nowhere in the entire file. Johnny took out his notepad and looked at Mrs. Sanders. "You don't mind if I take some notes?"

"Of course not, Detective Till. I know you detectives write everything down. Just promise me you'll keep my name out of this, if at all possible."

"Rast?" Sanders nodded her head. "I appreciate your confidence, Mrs. Sanders. I will do my best." *If I find out you've kept the name of a cop killer silent for all these years, I'm going to make you fucking famous.* "Please tell me how you know Melanie Rast murdered Officer Dunlap." *Let's see if she balks at my use of the title.*

"I've been here at West Lawler High School for forty years, Detective Till. Some officers who are assigned to the schools get far too cozy with the students . . . but that's none of my business. However, Dunlap was one of *those*." Johnny noticed how she drew the word "those" out for effect. She continued after a long pause. "He was always speaking with them in the hallways, talking with them at school events after hours, and," she paused again, "I even saw him at a couple of dances when I volunteered to chaperone."

I remember when you prevented me from kissing Cathy Reynolds while we were standing at the lockers.

"None of my business really, but he was far too close with one of the girls in particular—a junior named Melanie Rast."

Johnny wrote quickly to distract her from being recorded. "Did you catch them in a compromising position?" He looked directly at her. *Time to fish or cut bait. Let's see if she stands up to a full-on stare.*

Sanders looked away from Johnny. *Dammit. I knew it. She's full of it. What a waste of damn time!*

"Did you see her actually shoot Officer Dunlap?" Johnny put a heavy emphasis on "officer" to see her reaction.

"Of course not! I would have reported that to the police immediately!" Sanders adjusted her sweater as if the mere suggestion of her inaction was a grievous injury.

How horrible of me. You've just told no one about this instead.

"Well, Mrs. Sanders, help me out here as I sum this up. You never caught the two of them in a compromising position, you didn't see Melanie Rast harm Officer Dunlap in any way, and you didn't see anyone kill Officer Dunlap. So how is it that you know that Melanie Rast killed Officer Dunlap?"

After a few more adjustments to the same pieces of her sweater, Sanders spoke. "I'm not blind, Detective Till. There was something going on between them. They always walked off together and alone, and she disappeared when he died."

"Disappeared." Interesting choice of words. "What do you mean by 'disappeared'?"

"Gone, vanished without a trace. We simply never saw her again. She never graduated, never attended another class. No one has seen her since."

"You seem pretty certain of this." Johnny stopped writing and looked directly at her again.

"She was in my library science class. The next day,

after Dunlap died, she was absent. I checked with the office. No note, no call. When she didn't appear in my class the next week, I checked with the front office again. She hadn't come back since he was murdered. She was eventually listed as withdrawn. The administration told me her neighbor, the one who took Melanie in after her mother died, said she'd run away."

Now Johnny was interested. It wasn't much, but it was more than he had an hour ago. He continued scribbling, hoping he was successful in his earlier blind attempt to start his recorder. He had no way to confirm that he was actually recording the conversation. "Have you ever told anyone about this before? The possible connection between Officer Dunlap and Melanie Rast?" *Just because it's not in the file doesn't mean she didn't tell anyone. Maybe they dismissed her as a nut at the time, but that may have been before Melanie Rast pulled a Houdini. Her rapid exit puts things in a different light.*

"I spoke with a homicide detective. His name was Little . . . Herman Little. Tall man, skinny. He was quite rude to me when we spoke."

"When was this?"

"A few days after Dunlap was killed. The detectives spoke with all of the teachers." More sweater adjustments interrupted her. "I think they nearly forgot about me here in the library."

"Did Detective Little take notes when he spoke with you?"

"Yes. Just like you are now."

If she only knew. "And no one ever asked you about this again?"

"No. Detective Little stormed out and told me to have a good day," she huffed.

"Why didn't you tell anyone when Melanie Rast dropped out of school? You must've seen the news stories in the paper and on television. You knew the case was still unsolved." *I can't wait to hear this.*

"Detective Till, I did my civic duty and provided the information that I knew. I'm not one to stick my nose where it doesn't belong. Besides, there is a price for preying on children."

Johnny took a deep breath. *Every busybody I ever met would swear on a stack of Bibles in the Vatican that they minded their own business.* He closed his notebook, took out his business card, and handed it to her. "If you think of anything else, please let me know."

She took the card and studied it. "This looks different from the cards of the other detectives who come in here about students."

"I had them made up myself. I'm new to the unit. Do you like them?" Johnny was trying to rebuild a rapport with her. She probably felt he was hard on her, and he might have to speak with her again about this case or another.

"They're very impressive. So are you, Detective Till. I prayed for you and your mother after your father was killed in the war. I'm so happy you, you know, turned out okay."

Another deep breath. "Thanks, Mrs. Sanders. I did. I was proud to wear the same uniform as Officer Michael Dunlap. He was murdered in that uniform." He stood up, then paused on his way to her office door. "After Officer Dunlap died, the detectives looked through his personal life, as well as every other lead possible. No one found a single shred of evidence of any impropriety—not even a single affair or improper advance. You know, Mrs.

Sanders, you may be right about Officer Dunlap. Then again, you may be wrong. I give you my word that I will look into it. But consider this: If you are wrong, you may be making a horrible accusation against a man who died defending your school and your students. Perhaps you should keep this information between you and me for now, just in case."

Violet Sanders looked at him. Her eyes welled up with tears. She suddenly looked down. "You'll let me know, won't you? If I am wrong, I have some amends to make to Officer Dunlap's family."

"I will, Mrs. Sanders. I will."

When Johnny got into his car, he let out a deep breath he seemed to have been holding since the first time Violet Sanders mentioned Melanie Rast. He couldn't go back and ask for Melanie Rast's information now. It was best to do his own background check. She was a junior in high school, so she probably had a driver's license or at least a learner's permit. If her mom was a problem and her dad wasn't in the picture, perhaps she didn't.

Johnny made a couple of notes. He'd check for information on Rast and get as far as he could. He would re-check the Dunlap file to make sure, but he was certain her name did not appear anywhere. Then, he would take Holly and visit with Detective Herman Little. Leaving information out of a homicide investigation, especially the murder of a cop, was a big deal. He had a lot of explaining to do. Johnny decided to give Major Worth a heads-up before that interview to see if he had any guidance, insight, or suggestions. Only after he interviewed Little would he use a grand jury subpoena to get Rast's file.

That damn school is an information sieve. Ten minutes after

I serve the subpoena, the whole county will know I am looking into Rast. He wasn't worried about the whole county; he was worried about Anna Dunlap.

He put the car into gear, drove out of the parking lot, and headed back to the Homicide Unit. He had a couple of hours left before his next meeting with retired detective Lieutenant Rick House.

CHAPTER 12

J ohnny got back to the office anxious for answers. *Sanders has always been a bit of a nut, but she did see a lot. Every kid in that school came through the library at some point.* He grabbed a cup of tea and ran Melanie Rast on the National Crime Information Center (NCIC) using her expected year of birth, 1972. Nothing came up. He then used 1971. Perhaps she was one of the kids who had a birthday in December and started school a year earlier than her classmates. *Bingo! Got you!*

The information came up about Melanie Renee Rast, born December 10, 1981. She got her first driver's license at sixteen. The license expired two years later, as all so-called junior licenses did. It was not renewed. Beyond that, all he learned from NCIC was that there were no existing warrants, probation, or BOLOs for her. *Strange. What eighteen-year-old doesn't renew her driver's license?*

Johnny pulled up the records management system (RMS) for the Lawler PD. This was the logical next step. If Rast ever appeared on a police report, got a ticket, was arrested, or was the subject of an investigation, her name would pop up. *Having her DOB will make every other search more accurate.*

The computer screen populated with four case numbers. Three pertained to juvenile runaway reports. All were cleared when she either returned to her home or was found by the Lawler PD. The fourth, however, was disturbing. It was an investigation regarding the death of Rast's mother, Jennifer Leigh Rast, at age thirty-four. About two months before Melanie turned seventeen, her mother committed suicide. Melanie was listed as a next of kin and a witness.

Johnny pulled up the case narrative. The records had been imported from an old version of RMS, so it was difficult to retrieve everything in one search. After some digging, it appeared that Melanie came home one evening from a part-time job at the Freeze Out ice cream store and found her mother dead. She was hanging from the railing leading down the stairs in their home. Lawler PD had investigated the case and determined there was no foul play. Her mother was blind drunk when she made the decision to end her life. The detective's notes documented a blood-alcohol content of .45, about four times the DUI limit.

The detective's narrative stated that Melanie stayed with a neighbor that night who had a daughter who went to school with Melanie. That's where the report ended, and that made sense. This was a homicide investigation, not a case study. The crime was solved, the involved parties were all accounted for, and the case was appropriately closed.

Finally, Johnny checked a commercial database for Melanie Rast and found nothing. Social media—nothing. Court records—nothing. She just disappeared. *How does an almost eighteen-year-old disappear?*

Johnny sat back a moment and thought. Sipping his

tea, he went through the Dunlap case in his mind again. *Melanie Renee Rast is not in there.* Just to be certain, he opened the spreadsheet he created with all the players and ran her name—nothing. His spreadsheet contained the name of everyone mentioned in the report. Johnny made the database to help him search the huge file, to put every name into his head, and to help the next detective who had the case file, if he was unable to solve it. He added Rast's name, then he thought for a moment. He recalled that Detective Little was listed as an assisting detective, but so was everyone else in the unit and several other departments in the state. Johnny searched for Little's name in the main case file and found his notes. He had, in fact, interviewed Violet Sanders on Thursday, November 10, 1998.

Little's notes contained a list of the teachers and staff he interviewed, and there were a bunch. Johnny surmised that Little was designated that group of individuals, and he probably spent a lot of time at the school. He noted Little's badge number and ran it on the personnel database. He was now a captain in Zone Six—a deputy precinct commander in one of the busiest zones in the department.

As Johnny wrote down Little's work, cell, and home numbers, he remembered Major Worth's warning that Dunlap's death and status as a cold case was a very sore spot for folks in the department. *Better get his insight before I speak with him.* Johnny looked up and saw Major Worth was in his office. He sent a computer message: *Got ten, boss?*

The reply was quick: *Just about that. Come in.*

Johnny picked up his notes and started walking. *I want his insights, but at some point, Little is going to tell me why the hell he left that information out of a homicide file.*

CHAPTER 13

J
ohnny walked into Major Worth's office and closed the door. Worth looked up and smiled as Johnny walked in. "One of *those* conversations, huh?" He grabbed a big glass of water from his desk and leaned back in his chair. "Okay. How bad is it?"

Johnny smiled. "Why do you think it's bad? You encourage us to close your door when we discuss cases."

Worth decided to play along for a minute. "Well, let's just say you look more focused than usual."

"Good to know. I hope I always look focused on something."

"You do, Johnny, but I'm guessing this is about Mike Dunlap's case."

Damn. He's good. "How did you know?"

"You look focused every time I see you at work. When you're working on Dunlap, you look like a dog with a bone—focused, determined, and not to be messed with."

Johnny thought about that for a moment and decided he was fine if that's how he appeared.

"Besides, Lena Sullivan called me this morning and tried pumping me for information about what case you were working on. Seems she saw you walk into the library before you left the building." Worth was smiling now.

"So less Yoda and more good detective work on your part." Johnny had to smile.

"It's good to have a bit of both. What's up?"

"You encouraged me to get with you if I thought the Dunlap investigation would ruffle any feathers."

Worth looked at Johnny. "Don't you mean *your* Dunlap investigation?"

Johnny looked Worth square in the eyes. "The investigation belongs to Homicide. It will be mine if I solve it."

Worth nodded. "Okay. Fair enough. I figured you'd be in here sooner rather than later. What did you find?"

"According to the librarian, Violet Sanders, she told then Detective, now Captain Herman Little that she believed Mike Dunlap was having an inappropriate relationship with a West Lawler High School student named Melanie Renee Rast." Johnny watched as Worth took in the information. He showed no surprise. *Interesting.* "I've been through the case file a dozen times, including a database I created with every contact and name in the file to make it easier to manipulate the information. Little notes that he spoke with Sanders, but Rast's name does not appear anywhere."

"I saw the database when I checked on your progress last week. Impressive."

"That sort of tool helps me. If I don't solve the case, it will hopefully help the next detective."

"Well," he sat forward, "my money is on you. Besides, I don't foresee you ever putting the Dunlap case back into the cold case room."

Johnny nodded. "Giving up is overrated."

"Indeed."

"A homicide detective leaves out a name. Pretty serious. It begs two questions. First, why did he leave out Rast's name, and second, what else did he leave out?"

Worth nodded as he looked down at his desk. "I can answer one of those questions and give you my suspicions about the other." He leaned back, running his hand down to smooth his tie. "The rumor wasn't true. It was thoroughly investigated and left out of the report to keep the media from running with it if—I mean *when*—the case is solved."

"And the second? What else—"

Worth cut Johnny off for the first time ever. "We'll have to ask him."

"'We' doesn't sound good."

"Little is a bit thorny. Good cop and a nice guy, but he seemed to be born with a concern that the whole world was after him. Not rising to the level of paranoia, he's a great supervisor and manager, but he's the type to start sucking down antacid pills every time he believes the chief is cutting orders. My presence will make it go much smoother."

"I take it that you will be more present than involved."

"Your case, your questions, Johnny. Just like Internal Affairs, perhaps more so, Homicide gets paid to ask the tough questions. Besides, I'm a person with knowledge." Worth smiled at Johnny. "Call and set up breakfast. He's an early riser. Make it 0700 at Molly's on the South Side near the river. He will meet us on the way in from his house."

"Will do. It helps to have your insight."

"I'm not insightful, Till." Worth went back to his computer. "I'm just old."

Johnny gathered his items and walked out of Worth's office, leaving the door open. He walked back to his desk, checked his calendar, and sent an email to Captain Herman Little. *An email will look less formal than a call and inquiry from the Homicide Unit and will avoid any follow-up questions from Little.*

Little responded before Johnny could scan the new material he had into the Dunlap case. Given Worth's insight, Johnny put all references to Melanie Renee Rast and all the information he found into the confidential section on the computer. As he was wrapping up and checking his email for subpoenas, he saw Little's reply: *Thursday works for me. See you there, and tell your major he's buying this time.*

CHAPTER 14

J ohnny checked in with Holly to confirm her meeting with the physician went well. He checked the murder board and found nothing outstanding. His email inbox was nearly full with messages from the county Human Resources Department, information about the pending change in health benefits, and the schedule for annual training. It struck Johnny that every member of the department, from recruit to chief, had to sift through these emails every day. He wondered what it would be like when he had ten homicides as the lead and still had to keep up with email from HR. *They never talk about things like this in detective novels.*

As noon approached, Johnny rounded up Holly and headed to their lunch appointment. Rick House had selected a steakhouse just outside of Lawler County, where country clubs replaced the subdivisions and shopping malls were seen everywhere else. Johnny wasn't sure why, but it struck him as strange: three people, two of them detectives and one a retired detective lieutenant with over twenty-five years of service, meeting outside of the jurisdiction. He discussed it with Holly, and she was at a loss, as well. In typical Holly fashion, she came up with her own theory: "Maybe he's trying to protect his current reputation and not be seen with the cops." Johnny was starting to wonder if he and Holly were cut from the same cloth.

They drove out to the east end of Lawler County on State Route 120, driving past the vanishing expanses of farms, over the river, to the dense housing developments started ten years ago. With lots in the one-third-acre size, the houses seemed out of place and were intermingled with the two- and three-acre estates of the residents who built thirty or more years earlier. They had refused to sell their land, even at the height of the market. Johnny wondered if they would ever sell. Some people would rather live out their days surrounded by familiar sights than have money.

"What did you make of Tucci this morning?" Holly was staring out the side window, clearly running the meeting over in her head.

"Pretty sharp. Clearly, he's still frustrated about the Dunlap case. His body language changed when you mentioned it. I think he was hoping you wanted to talk about another case . . . really, any other case."

"You're right about that. You can't underestimate his hunch, though." She looked at Johnny. "You're new to Homicide, but you know what it's like to have cases working inside your head twenty-four hours a day. Sometimes you just crave some time away, disconnected from everything, to just think."

"I agree completely."

"Well, that's how I see these old guys. They aren't consumed with emails, texts from victims, departmental politics, and all of the other cases we are working. They can have downtime, *real* downtime, and think about the cases that they want to focus on. Tucci and the other retired folks have probably spent hours thinking about what they saw in that file. Maybe it was five minutes at a time or a day at a time, but hours, nonetheless. I say you should trust their instincts and give careful thought to any direction they give you."

"Except for the alien-from-outer-space theory." Johnny smiled.

"Yeah, I think that one can be ruled out." She started laughing. "I actually thought that was pretty funny. It was good to see he still has a sense of humor. Poor guy. It's sad that he's all alone."

Johnny took the opportunity to poke at her. "He doesn't have to be . . . alone, that is. He clearly finds you attractive." Johnny looked forward for a minute until he was certain Holly was staring at him with a look that could kill. Then he laughed out loud. "Payback, Holly. It's a bitch." After a few minutes, Johnny spoke. "What are the odds this is a true stranger crime of opportunity with no connection to track between Dunlap and the killer?"

Holly thought for a while. "If he wasn't a cop in uniform, I would think it was possible, and random murders are extremely rare with anyone. No, my friend, it would be highly unlikely that a person would choose a uniformed cop as a random victim. Armed victims fight back. That alone makes it not even worth considering. Besides, if that's the case, Tucci's right, and no one may ever solve it unless the killer cracks."

Johnny turned left onto Highway 9 at a small intersection with a feed store on one corner and a hardware store on the other. It was a sure sign of a change in the community. He listened to the prompts from his GPS. He rarely traveled to this area and did not want to be late.

"What do you know about Rick House?" Johnny asked. "He retired before I joined the department, but I think you had a year of two of overlap with him."

Holly was looking out the window again. "I met him once. He was a lieutenant on the road when I started as a recruit, then he went back to Homicide. He was a homicide detective for about five years before he made sergeant. Word was that he begged the chief to send him back before he retired. I think he was only back in the unit for a couple of years before he left the department.

"He signed out the Dunlap case as a sergeant and a lieutenant, so he must have rotated back in, as well, after his promotion."

"Not surprising. As you know, any promotion comes with a transfer, usually to uniform patrol, but supervisors move around, especially if they do well and play their cards right. Two of my narc supervisors were in Narcs before they got promoted, but they had to do some time in uniform with every new rank."

"It's not a bad idea, when you think about it. But it would be tough to leave Homicide." Holly was clearly thinking about something.

"That's why a lot of detectives never take the promotion exams," Johnny replied.

"We're nearly there. Any new theories on why we're meeting way out here?" Holly was looking at the GPS.

"Not a clue. I checked the utility records, and he still lives in Lawler County, on the west side of the county about a mile or two from the precinct, in fact," Johnny explained. "You got me, but at least we'll get a good meal out of it."

"Easy for you to say. You're not paying!"

Johnny knew no one would ever reimburse him for these meals, but human nature makes a conversation over a meal somehow less formal. "I know. A steak always tastes better when you don't see the check."

Holly smiled at him.

Johnny spotted the restaurant and pulled in. He drove up to the valet, who graciously offered to park Johnny's unmarked car. When Johnny declined, the valet parker seemed perturbed until he saw the police radio. He then directed Johnny to a lot off to the side.

Holly and Johnny entered the restaurant about ten minutes early. They wanted a table toward the back that would give them some privacy. As expected, the hostess refused to seat them "until the party was complete," so they waited in the entrance area for House to arrive. They joked about sitting at the bar but decided the paperwork would be tremendous.

Rick House walked in and took off his sunglasses. The hostess greeted him by name, and he looked around as she pointed toward Holly and Johnny. House put his sunglasses into the pocket of his sport coat and thanked the hostess. Then he put on a big smile and walked toward the two detectives.

Rick House was a tall man in his sixties and appeared to be in great shape. His left wrist sported a five-thousand-dollar watch, and his clothes were top shelf. Johnny was thinking that whatever transpired today, this meeting would not be boring. Something told Johnny the inevitable question—"What have you been doing since retiring?"—would not yield the same old responses of "yard work" or "whatever my wife tells me to do."

"Rick House," he said as he extended a large, tan hand.

Holly reached out first and gave his hand a firm shake. "Holly Forrester. Thanks for meeting with us." Holly made eye contact with House, who locked eyes for a moment before releasing her hand and looking at Johnny.

"You're Till. I saw your picture in the paper a few times." House reached out his hand and Johnny shook it. "Doing some good work in hit-and-run. I worked that unit, you know. A real pain in the ass. Most of the cases are just drunks or housewives shopping at the mall who are driving cars the size of yachts." He laughed to himself. Johnny and Holly smiled.

The hostess, a woman in her forties with shoulder-length, dark hair pulled back in a tight ponytail, walked up with three menus in her hands. "Mr. Till? Your table is ready if your party is complete."

"That would be great," Johnny responded.

"Please, follow me," the hostess said. The three of them followed her to the rear of the restaurant, noting how many people were in the restaurant, their body language, and whether or not they seemed out of place or agitated. It was automatic. As she led them past the occupied tables to a closed section of the restaurant, Johnny and Holly felt comfortable that they would be able to speak without the fear of eavesdroppers. "I understand that you want some privacy. I hope this table is suitable."

"Perfect," Johnny said. "Just to let you know, we may be here a while."

"No problem. Your waiter will be Zack. He will come by in a moment to take your drink and appetizer orders."

House allowed them to sit facing the door. It was a foregone conclusion that they would, so he made a gesture waving his arm toward the two seats on the far side of the table. Holly took the seat closest to the wall, and Johnny sat in the seat with the most room to put his legs out. House kept his jacket on and pulled his chair out for himself. He made a pronounced assessment of the leg room afforded by the chair and table. It was clear he would likely be more comfortable putting his legs out to the side, but he made a good showing of the analysis.

"I know y'all will be watching the door, so no one will come in and steal my steak!" He seemed to crack himself up with the comment. "I was so focused on watching the door when I was still working. Glad that's over with."

The bus boy brought a basket of fresh, warm bread and a plate with a medallion of butter in the shape of the restaurant logo. Next, he filled up the water glasses, smiled at them, then left. In typical detective fashion, all talk, no matter the topic, ceased when the staff was at the table. Johnny noticed that House did it automatically. He found it amusing in a way that the habit stuck with him.

House picked up the breadbasket and motioned to Holly, who waved her hand toward it. House did the same to Johnny and received a similar response. "I bet neither one of you eats donuts, either!" With that, he unwrapped the bread from the white towel, enthusiastically grabbed the loaf, and broke off a large piece. Johnny saw a brief wisp of steam escape and was starting to reconsider his decision. It smelled like heaven.

As House spread a thick coat of butter on the bread, he spoke as he stared in awe at his creation. "Yep. Amazing what fitness nuts the department has been hiring over the past twenty years. I've always been a runner and never stopped, but good food is enjoyment for the soul! That's why I brought both of you here, and by the way, this lunch is on me. One of you grabs for the check, I'll scream, 'Police brutality!' That will give the lunch crowd something to tell their friends this afternoon." He bit into the bread, smiled as he chewed, and nearly let out a sigh.

"Thanks for the lunch," Johnny said. "I'm sure the department would reimburse us."

"Not for the lunch we're going to have! Listen, Till. Do you know what I've been doing since I retired?"

"No, sir."

"Sir! That's a laugh! How about you, Holly? Any of your sources let you know what I've been up to?"

Holly finished taking a sip of her water. "Nope. Folks were kind of tight-lipped about it. A few said they didn't have a clue, and others said they hadn't seen you in years. Apparently, you do not attend the quarterly retiree lunches." Holly knew he wanted to build up the mystique of his pending announcement. She decided to help him have his moment.

"No retirement lunches for me. Oh, I might go one day just to catch up and let folks know I'm still this side of the dirt, but I only keep in touch with a few folks from the department. It's funny. Nothing against the others, but I was close to a core group of folks. We seemed to go through everything together. Other folks were more professional colleagues than friends. So after retirement, it probably does appear that I faded into the wind." House took a gulp of water and then attacked the last piece of bread on his plate. When he finished chewing, he leaned back in his chair. "Enough of the small talk. Whatever it is, you both must be hurting for ideas or information if you reached out to an old warhorse like me. What's up?"

At that moment, Zack, the waiter, arrived. He reviewed the specials, and with each description two things occurred. First, House provided audible approval with an occasional question to clarify preparation methods or ingredients. Second, Johnny was getting ready to pounce on the bread. He was really hungry, and what began as a stress-filled lunch hoping House didn't exceed the amount Lawler County bean counters would consider reasonable was shaping into a pleasurable—and cheap—experience.

"Zack, normally we would let the lady order first, but I know these two. They will order a salad or some other stupid choice, so I'm going to set the example . . . and please bring the check to me." House went on to order a Caesar salad, a bone-in filet, and a side of lobster mac and cheese. His order nearly made Johnny salivate. After Holly and Johnny ordered, Zack disappeared, promising to have the three salads out quickly.

Johnny knew House was dying to tell them what he had been doing since retirement. Despite his attempts to fly under the radar, it was obvious he wanted everyone at the department to know. Somewhat afraid of what he might hear, Johnny asked, "So what have you been up to, sir?"

"House. Just House will do. Lighten up, both of you. I would have killed for a break like this from fast food when I was in Homicide."

"Okay, House. What's been keeping you busy?" Johnny could tell House instantly became even more relaxed. He was now in his element and ready to talk. Johnny hoped that willingness continued when they got to the unsolved homicide of a cop. He watched House take a sip of his water, then lean back in his chair.

"Well, a long time ago, I worked a part-time job directing traffic at the home of this guy in the hills. Fancy dinner party, and he not only wanted some help with the traffic, but also with security. He told me point blank on the phone that he had some extremely wealthy guests attending, and he wanted to keep the place safe. So I got together a group of about four Lawler cops, and we worked the party. I went in the house from time to time to check on the party and ensure that everyone was okay. I had my portable radio on, of course, and heard some commotion about a car chase with a pair of armed robbers. As I listened, they were heading toward the house. Then they wrecked, of course, about two blocks from the party on a dead-end street and were out on foot. Fortunately, when the homeowner told me about the heavy hitters in attendance, I did some leg work to look at the area. I was more worried about getting an ambulance there if someone's heart gave out, but nonetheless, I had a good map of the area in my head.

"As I listened to the radio traffic, I could tell they were heading straight for the backyard. *Great*, I thought. A full complement of street cops and a K9 were about to burst into the middle of this party! Anyway, I left two guys on the street to watch the cars, and the rest of us got into the backyard. I told the homeowner to get everyone inside, and the last person hit the door as the armed robbers came sailing over his short fence. We had both of them on the ground at gunpoint when the troops came over the fence. As they were cuffed, I looked up and saw the entire party, about one hundred and fifty guests, glued to the windows, watching. It was the craziest thing I'd ever seen, but not the craziest that night. As we got the perps up off the ground and took their guns, the party guests came back outside and gave the whole group of us a standing ovation! Man, I never thought I'd ever see that!"

Johnny and Holly were watching him gesture and swing his arms. His face was red with excitement as he told the story. As House pulled off and buttered another piece of bread with the same precision as before, he started again.

"The guy thought I hung the moon. He wrote a glowing letter to the chief and the newspaper commending all of us for our fine work. He harped on me to retire early for years, and I worked parties at his house and his friends' houses from that day forward. Anyway, come the day I told him I was retiring, he made me the chief of security for his company. Very little travel, even though they are all over the US. He just trusts me and wants my input. I was in no position to say no. He's a great guy, and the money is definitely sweet! So I do my thing, take time off with the wife to travel when I want to, and enjoy taking homicide detectives to lunch at nice restaurants when I can!"

Holly laughed at that. "Well, good for you! It's great to see someone land in a pot of money when they retire. So many folks either take piddly little jobs here and there or go to a small town and police."

"Or work as a school resource officer," Johnny chimed in. "Great for them, but that would drive me nuts."

"Yep," said House, "I'm very lucky. My advice to both of you is start a plan now for retirement. You cannot just hope to land in the sweet spot like me."

As he finished, Zack brought their salads and conducted the ritual of passing the pepper grinder over them. When he walked away, House started in again.

"So what's the topic du jour? Did I mislabel some

evidence in a case that is now front and center? I tell you, that's what I worry about, not bad guys coming after me. It's funny. Maybe I should worry about that more, with all the perps I arrested and so few of them doing life anymore."

"We wanted your impressions on a cold case. You signed it out as a sergeant and then as a lieutenant. I'm working it now, and I wanted to start with the last few detectives who had the file. You know, get their impressions and hunches. You've had a lot of time to think without being distracted by a case load and email."

Holly kicked Johnny under the table and put her head down as she took a sip of her water.

"I worked several cold cases, solved three. Two were just luck with a break from the evidence or a perp turning talkative. One, though, was just good, old-fashioned police work. I left three unsolved. The Turner case was solved three years after I retired by a death-row confession and statement about the location of the murder weapon. The Mirazh case was solved by a detective finding a witness who had been in prison for five years. Damndest thing, the perp confessed. So that leaves only one case . . . the Dunlap case."

Johnny suspected that the jovial and carefree nature of their visit was a façade. He also was not surprised that House was still sharp as a tack. "Yep. I pulled the Dunlap case. I knew him, you know. He came to my school. It may take me the rest of my career, but I really want to solve this one."

Holly piped in, "What he's not telling you is he picked it up by blind luck. When he realized what he pulled, he never faltered, though. He may just crack it."

Johnny had never heard that from Holly before. He

was humbled by her statement. She did not pass out compliments like hot dogs at a church picnic.

"Well," House began, "that case was, and is, a pain in my side. You look nationally—hell, around the world—at the number of unsolved cases involving a murdered cop, and you'll find only a handful." He took a sip of water, then looked down at the table. "We took a lot of heat for not being able to close that case. I met with Dunlap's wife, Anna, several times. Finally, I apologized to her and put the file back into the cold case room. That was a bad day at the office."

Johnny looked at House. Gone was the vivacious man who greeted them in the lobby. He smiled as he looked up at Holly then back at Johnny, but he was sitting a bit lower in his chair, his cheeks not quite as flushed and his eyes not as bright.

"What do you want to know?" House spoke slowly. "Not sure I can help, but I'll do anything I can."

Johnny continued, "We respect your work on the case and your experience. You were also working at the department when the media frenzy was in full swing when Dunlap was murdered. That's insight we can't get from black-and-white pages in the file. Anything you can tell us will help. Everyone talks about the benefits of a fresh pair of eyes, but I also don't want to plow old ground."

House shook his head as they looked at him. Holly was watching him carefully. The remorse was real, and she saw something else. It was a look of helplessness, defeat. She instantly felt sorry for the man who a few moments ago beamed with pride at his accomplishments while acknowledging the role luck had played in his present circumstance.

"If you stay in Homicide long enough," she said, "there's going to be one you can't bring to the mat."

House shook his head. "I know. Look, let's enjoy some lunch, then ask me anything you want."

The waiter mercifully cleared their salad plates. He was followed by two others, who placed their steaks in front of them simultaneously. The side dishes were arranged with care, then they left them alone to eat.

The small talk continued as they ate. It was clear why House had made a request to eat before they dove into the heart of the meeting. Johnny knew he wanted to live a bit more in the pleasant past before awakening the demons that haunted him.

They passed the next thirty minutes talking about current patrol cars versus the cars House had driven as a rookie. Next they spent some time talking department politics, and Johnny had to admit that he was intrigued to learn more about the people at the helm of the Lawler PD, including the practical jokes they played as young officers. As the last of the steak disappeared, they were discussing the worst murderers Lawler had ever put away and the difference that modern forensic techniques could have made in those cases.

All three declined dessert, and House and Holly ordered coffee. Johnny ordered his usual green tea and took the expected grief from House.

"Till, what the hell is that stuff? We had an IA sergeant when I was in that unit who would interview prospective recruits with a dozen donuts on his desk. He would ask them if they wanted a donut, and they invariably said, 'No thanks.' He would look at them and smile, asking them if they really wanted to be police officers. It was classic and really got them to loosen up."

"Try it," Johnny said. "It won't kill you."

"That's the problem," House replied. "It won't kill you quickly, and you'll have to look at that green stuff in the cup while you drink it! I'll stick to the high-test java, thank you very much. You, too, Holly?"

"You bet." Holly was still amazed how House was calling her by her first name and Johnny by his last. She figured he would have been able to rationalize it with clarity if she asked him, but she didn't really care.

"Okay, Till. Do you want me to start, or do you have some questions?"

"Your choice, House. I'd really like your overall take on the case. Anything will help me."

House took a sip of his coffee, then straightened the napkin in front of him after taking it off his lap and folding it. "Mike Dunlap was, by all accounts, an excellent law enforcement officer. Things were different then. You should know that no one wanted that job as a liaison in the schools. It was a real pain in the ass. The kids were okay, but the parents, the administrators . . . what a mess. The principals got a bright idea one year that the officers in the schools should check their weapons with the principal before they went in! Pure, unadulterated stupidity, and the idea went nowhere, but it did hit the news.

"Anyway, Dunlap was the perfect guy for the job. He loved kids and had no problem dealing with the politics. I guess he saw a higher purpose to the bullshit he had to cut through to get the job done. Mike was on the scene when a group of kids hit a tree one night and died. They were all under the influence. He worked that wreck and helped pull those bodies out of the car. His wife said it changed him, and he started speaking to kids the week before prom weekend. When the position came up doing public relations in the high schools, Mike was all over it. What a waste." He took another long sip of his coffee.

"So you knew him?" Johnny didn't have his notepad out. He wanted to keep the flow of conversation moving.

House finished his coffee and waved to the waiter for a refill. "Yeah, we crossed paths a few times. The department was smaller back then, about three hundred sworn." House looked at Holly in an effort to engage her. "How many are you up to now?"

"About seven hundred twenty-five at last count, and the chief is asking for more bodies," she replied.

"Damn! Little Lawler PD approaching the one thousand mark! Who would have thought? Anyway, Dunlap and I ran into each other from time to time. I think we may have worked a traffic detail together at the Light of the Star Church on the North Side once or twice. That was it. But that's why I picked up his case. I kind of felt like I owed it to him, you know? We weren't friends, but I'd like to think he would have tried to catch someone who murdered me."

Johnny let him finish. "It appears that the initial investigation was very thorough and an all-hands-on-deck deal."

"Damn straight. From the outset, everyone believed Dunlap was killed because he wore the uniform. Aside from the public fear that inspired everyone, we were all pretty pissed off and, let's say, more than a little bit motivated."

"Was there any indication that he knew his killer?" Holly jumped in.

"Not in the traditional sense. I mean, the killing was not particularly vicious like you would expect if it was personal, with thirty stab wounds or a dozen shots fired. You had to wonder, though, because most cops are on the alert, especially when they're in uniform. So it's possible that someone knew him enough to get close without a response from him. You know how that is, though. 'Officer, can you tell me how to get to Maple Street?' is enough for most cops to let people get close, especially with a guy like Dunlap, who really cared about people."

"Did you feel confident that all of the personal leads were tracked down? Any connections to his family and friends?" Johnny was sipping his tea. "I'm just trying to avoid plowing old ground that will never produce, especially old ground that will open old wounds."

"Good call, and very considerate of you." The waiter came by and freshened up the coffee at the table. Johnny received more hot water and a new tea bag. "To be perfectly frank about it, the initial investigation was a bit lacking in that regard. Oh, they cleared his wife, checked the household finances, that sort of thing, but they were really focused on a cop killing, not the killing of a guy who happened to be a cop. That changed though. After the leads dried up about six months after the killing, the major in Homicide at the time . . . I don't recall his name . . ."

"Quinn," Johnny chimed in. He wanted House to know that he knew the file. Johnny had done a spreadsheet on the manpower in place at the time of the killing, as well as any time that a detective started working the case again.

House laughed. "Porky Quinn. Nice guy. He was 'aerobically challenged' or 'under tall,' you might say. He was grandfathered in past the physical-fitness requirements. He was a good detective. Started with the force when he was about nineteen. His momma had to buy his gun and bullets for him. Had to be twenty-one then." House laughed again. "Too bad you missed him at the department. He was hysterical and exemplified the dark humor of the Homicide Unit."

"Should we talk to him?" Holly asked.

"It would be a pretty dull conversation. His heart gave out about a year after he retired. He's buried in Cleveland, Georgia, next to his parents. We sent a caravan of blue lights to his funeral. That little town never knew what hit it. I was the third car from the front." House looked into his coffee for a moment before he started speaking again.

"Anyway, Quinn was catching a lot of heat, and he was a tenacious SOB. He wanted the crime cleared on his watch, so word was he assigned three detectives to start from scratch and go over every possible motive. The feds were working the case, too, at that point. They got involved from the perspective of Dunlap being targeted because he wore the badge."

"Anything turn up?" Johnny asked.

"No. Remember that the Homicide Unit was smaller then, and it was harder to get assigned there. The detectives were top notch, and three of them, well, that's a bad day for any perp. Between them and the feds, who were trying to close their case, as well, the Dunlap family and friends got a thorough going over. No affairs, no recent changes in insurance policies, no grudges in the family, no neighborhood disputes, and no general psychos in the circle. It all came up empty. The feds had the ability to track several subversive groups and gangs that were always threatening to kill cops. All dead ends, though."

"What about perps who Dunlap arrested or kids at the school?"

"They covered that, too. Like most street cops, the majority of his arrests were traffic-related or misdemeanors. He made an occasional felony arrest for dope or a rare firearm on campus, as you would expect. He caught a bank robber after a chase shortly before he went to the school liaison position, but that's about it."

"I saw the news clipping in the file. Someone tracked down that perp and his family."

"Well, it was easy to find the perp. He hung himself before trial. They grilled his relatives along with a few of his felony family, past accomplices, and others. Nada. They either had alibis, which most of the time meant that they were in prison, or they lived out of state and had no idea either Dunlap or the perp was dead."

"What about the school connection?" Holly asked as she sipped her water.

"Dead ends. He never even had a difficult arrest during that time. The kids loved him, even when he had to get on them or take them in. As I said, he arrested several for dope, weapons, that kind of thing." House smiled. "He was especially funny when he found out a kid was truant. He was known to go to their houses and bring them to the school. Then he would walk them to class. He filled out the paperwork to charge them through the juvenile court, but they usually didn't do it twice."

"I'm surprised they opened the door for him at their houses."

"Well, if they weren't home, he knew where to find them. If they were, he had them convinced that federal law allowed the police to enter a house without a warrant to find a truant kid. One of a kind." House smiled.

"So," Johnny said, "if the roles were reversed, knowing what you know, where would you start?"

House thought about that. He took a sip of his coffee, looked at Holly, then back at Johnny. He put his cup down and stared into it for a minute. "Here's my gut. There's a connection that was fresh. Everyone just missed it, or there was no trail leading to it."

"Why do you think that?"

"People who are mad enough, crazy enough, or motivated enough to take on a uniformed cop are not going to miss an opportunity or wait for years to do it. They would take the first window they saw and do it. So, I guess that the connection to his killer was probably fresh—within a few months at the most before his death." House picked up his cup and drank the last of his coffee. He did not signal for a refill. It was clear the interview was over. "At least, I hope to God that's the case," he said, gesturing to Johnny then Holly with the cup.

"Why do you say that?" Holly said.

"Because if there isn't, then it was a true stranger-on-stranger crime. Whether it was random or planned, if Dunlap's murderer hasn't been caught and the killer was a stranger who picked Mike Dunlap out of chance, then he'll never be caught. I hate to say what I've been thinking for years, but that's the truth. So if I were you, Till, I'd look for connections that could have been missed. Remember that the forensics for electronics were pretty crude in those days. Dunlap had a pager, not a cell phone, and it did not have a large memory. If I remember correctly, the last three or four pages were from his wife, one of the school administrators, the department, and a pay phone at the school. We tracked all of them."

"What was the last one?" Holly was ready to try to put something together.

"The pager showed the number from the pay phone and a code: #3400 930. I memorized it, wrote it down, and struggled with it for years. No one was ever able to make any sense of it. I'm still running it through my head, though."

"Any surveillance video of the school pay phone?" Holly looked hopeful.

"Not in those days, my dear. Surveillance inside the schools was taboo! The only cameras were mounted outside to catch burglars. It wasn't until the schools started getting sued for not breaking up fights that the principals gave the green light to putting them inside."

There were no more words spoken at the table. The waiter brought the check upon House's signal, and House gave him a corporate credit card.

"Thanks for the lunch," Holly said.

"Yep. It was a very nice treat, and you're right. It's a change from fast food," Johnny added.

House just nodded. "Nice of you to say, but my guess is neither of you eats a lot of fast food. Too fit. Holly here doesn't even use cream or artificial sweeteners, just one packet of raw sugar. And you, Mr. Green Tea, I'm guessing you don't spend a lot of time waiting at drive-thru windows."

Holly and Johnny smiled. They all got up and started walking toward the door. As they exited out of the front door, House stopped. He looked at both of them. "Did you ever let anyone down, Till?"

"I don't think so. At least, I hope not."

House put his sunglasses on as the valet drove up in his car. "I wish I could say the same. You catch the bastard who killed Dunlap. Not because it's your job or to save face for pulling a tough one from the cold case room. You catch him because Dunlap deserved that. Call me when you do. I want to be there to watch him die."

House shook their hands, got into his car, and drove away.

As Holly and Johnny watched House leave the lot, they were silent for a moment. Johnny spoke first. "Wow. That's real pain, the kind that keeps you up at night."

Holly nodded. "We keep talking about how these retired guys have time to think about new angles and leads. I guess the worst part is, they have all that time to think and no ability to do anything about it."

They walked to Johnny's car and got in. As Johnny started out of the lot, he looked down at the GPS. "What do you have the rest of the day?"

Holly looked out the passenger window. "Make a few calls, meet up with a robbery victim who found a picture of the necklace the bastard pulled off her neck at gunpoint, and look over a case file. I have a probable cause hearing coming up."

"Sounds like a lovely afternoon."

"You?" Holly was looking at Johnny now.

"Looking through some notes. I'm meeting with Captain Little about the Dunlap case. I thought he left some info out of the case file about a student named Melanie Rast. At first, it pissed me off that her name wasn't in the file and made me wonder what else was missing. Worth cleared it up. It was in the confidential notes on the computer." Johnny made a point to make sure those notes were pointed out to the next detective who pulled a cold case.

Holly smiled. "My guess is Little was a detective then, but remember, he's not anymore. He's a handful. Be careful."

Johnny nodded while slowing for a person moving a tractor from one farm to another. The smell of diesel fuel and manure passed through the car. "I'm bringing Worth with me."

"Good idea."

Johnny smiled. "I get the impression that his offer of assistance was more of an order than a suggestion, but it works for me. I've got to get as much information about this girl as I can. Even the notes in the confidential file are sparse. It may be something new to track down, although Worth said they explored the inappropriate relationship angle in the past."

"Lettieri said the student killer angle was not explored fully. I get the idea that he'd be all over that." She thought for a second. "What makes you so hot on it?"

"She disappeared off the map a few days after Dunlap died, but no one put that together. Her name came up in the first days after his death, and they focused on other suspects. Looking back now, I can see how strange it is and definitely worth a look."

Holly nodded. "New eyes, new perspective."

"Yep. Let's just hope it's not another dead end."

CHAPTER 15

J ohnny pulled into the parking lot of Molly's fifteen minutes early. The sun was coming up and the sky was beautiful. He loved an early drive in, filled with time to think without avoiding people commuting to work in massive packs of cars that moved to their own rhythm and at their own pace like a wild school of enormous fish. Sunrises were magical in police work. Often, you were alone or surrounded by the quiet as the world woke up. Everything was peaceful. An old cop Johnny once met said, "Sunrises are your time on morning watch. The bad guys have finally gone to bed, the hellraisers have gone to find something to eat, and the only people you see around you are the good folks going to work!" *Maybe he was onto something.*

Johnny let the captain pull in, park, and find a seat in the restaurant. As long as he wouldn't be late, he wanted Captain Herman Little to have his choice of tables and seats. He would likely be in uniform and want to face the door. A little control at the outset might get him relaxed. *No idea how he's going to react to my questions.*

He watched as Captain Herman Little did as he expected, getting a table in the back corner and sitting to face the door. On the way in, he spoke with every server and shouted to the cook through the pass-through. This was his turf. *Worth knew exactly what he was doing.*

Johnny got out and walked across the parking lot. It was eight minutes to seven. As he walked to the door, Major Bill Worth stepped from a car parked at the southwest corner and held the door open for him.

"Good instincts, Till." He motioned to the door. "After you." Bill Worth was smiling.

As the two men approached Herman Little, he stood up next to the booth. He was a slim black man about six feet, three inches tall. He looked sharp in the uniform. Johnny noticed that he was wearing body armor and a backup weapon on his ankle. *Taking uniform patrol seriously. That's a refreshing sign.*

"Major, good morning!" Little held out his hand to Bill Worth.

"Good morning, Captain," Worth said while shaking Little's hand. "Thanks for taking the time to meet with us. You still prefer mornings?"

"Yep. Lunches take too much time. My pleasure."

"This is Detective Johnny Till. He's one of mine in Homicide."

Johnny leaned forward and extended his hand to Little, who shook it with a firm grip. "Pleasure, Till. Great work on that Emerson hit-and-run case. What kind of human being leaves a kid to die?"

"Thank you, sir. I'm flattered that you remember that."

The three men sat down. "Well, it was hard not to miss it. The story was in the paper for a week."

"True," Johnny said. "They couldn't get enough of that story."

Little leaned in and whispered to both men, "That's because deep down, they don't want to believe that people like Laymen exist. You see, catching him makes them—and a lot of other people—recognize that they need cops. That makes them uncomfortable."

Johnny nodded. "We hunt the evil you pretend doesn't exist."

"Damn right." Little was nodding his head when the waitress came over.

She was a short woman in her late sixties. One look, and Johnny could tell life had not been kind to her. "Well, how is it I have three great-looking cops in my section this morning?" She put a cup of coffee and a glass of water in front of Little. *Worth was right. This is his usual place.*

"Rochelle," Little spoke, "this is Major Bill Worth and Detective Johnny Till, two of Lawler PD's finest. Smart cops. Homicide detectives."

"Well, I'm too old to have done anything, so they must be here for a great breakfast! Two more coffees?"

"Coffee for me," Worth said.

"Any chance you have green tea?" Johnny asked.

"Clearly, you're the young one! Yes, darling. We do. Believe it or not, we even have gluten-free pancakes, turkey bacon, and tofu for lunch." She winked at Little. "Gotta keep up with the times!" She stood there poised and ready to write their orders. "I know you haven't seen the menus, but I know cops are always in a hurry, so . . ."

They ordered, and she was off in a hurry. She returned about two minutes later with a cup of coffee, hot water, and two bags of green tea. Then she left so they could talk.

"Green tea, Till?" Captain Little furrowed his brow

when he spoke, and Johnny got the impression the question would have been less formal without the major there.

Icebreaker. Excellent. "I just never really liked coffee," Johnny responded.

"Bill, how did this man make it this far in police work without drinking coffee?" asked Little. Worth smiled and started drinking. Little raised his coffee cup as Johnny started steeping his tea. "More power to you. I've had so much coffee, I can't even tell you if I like it anymore. It's just part of my routine."

"So what's new on the South Side, Herman?" Worth asked.

True to his word, Little winced as he drank the hot coffee, but never missed a beat. Johnny smiled a bit. "Same old thing. Gangs are the number-one problem. Felony crimes, drug dealing, and still recruiting kids from middle schools."

"Sickening. Some of those kids don't have a chance." Worth shook his head.

"Well, I'm using the resources I have. I put a uniform at every apartment complex every morning where I know the gangs recruit. I figure if we can keep the kids from being truant, and keep the gang members away from them on the bus stops, we'll make a dent in it. We do the same thing in the afternoon. Some of my folks follow the buses when they are close to the schools. It's amazing how many kids walk off the bus and directly into the schools when the folks in blue are watching."

"Good use of resources, if you ask me." Worth was clearly impressed with the program.

"Feels like fingers in the dam, Bill," said Little. "Once they get to school, we have to rely on the school resource officers and the teachers. Our officers do their jobs, but some of the teachers don't even want them there."

"Hard to fight that," Johnny jumped in.

"Oh, but I do, Detective." *Not "Johnny" yet.* "I have my patrol officers dropping in unexpectedly all the time. They come for breakfast and lunch and have been known to play a pickup game of basketball or soccer with the kids at recess. Some of the parents have complained, but it's my job to take the heat. If we focus on making a difference with them now, maybe they won't be in the backs of patrol cars later."

"And the cop haters?" Worth asked, smiling.

"I gave up trying to appease them long ago. Of course, in a way, it's different for me as a black officer. Let's just be honest. The worst they can do is call me an Uncle Tom, but they can't call me a racist. I have to use my race sometimes to keep our programs going. Sad, in a way."

"Agreed. Sounds like your heart is still in the right place. Always was," Worth said, a reminder to Johnny to tread lightly.

The food arrived, and the three of them began eating.

"So I appreciate your intel and help with the armed robbery we had last week, Bill," Little said. "We were able to use it to take the perp down outside his house. A serial armed robber arrested without a shot being fired." He took a bite of his French toast and looked at Johnny. "Why didn't that make the papers?"

"Social media is free, Captain. Post it." Johnny felt it was appropriate to jump into the conversation.

"True, Till. We need to do much more of that. Problem is, we're usually on the way to the next call, or on the South Side, the next armed robbery." Little thought for a moment. "You're right. That's still fresh news. I'll call that reporter who covered your hit-and-run case, Banks."

"Here." Johnny took out his cell phone. "I'll send you his cell and office number. Done."

Without looking at his phone, Little put his right elbow on the table. "Already have my cell number, I see." He stared at Johnny.

"I might have been late for breakfast if I was called out last night, Captain. I wanted to have the number with me." *Let's see if he buys that. Not likely. He's suspicious.*

"Well played, Till. Now, what does Homicide want to chat about?" He was more serious, but not angry.

Bill Worth stepped on Johnny's foot and spoke. "Herman, Till is new to Homicide, as you probably read in that news article on the hit-and-run. He's sharp, and I've been impressed with his work. When I turned him loose in the cold case room, he pulled a red file—the Dunlap case. I tried to talk him out of it, but he would have none of it. He's gone after it like a dog with a bone. I'm having to watch his overtime to make certain he gets some sleep. I encouraged him to interview everyone who was involved with the case. Hell, he's even scheduling an interview with me." Worth looked at Johnny, then back at Little.

"I bet you're looking forward to that." Little smiled a bit and looked directly at Johnny, but it was clear he was talking to Worth.

"You were one of the original detectives, so he's getting around to you. I thought I should be here for protocol given your rank, and besides," Worth took another bite of his waffle, "I miss eating at Molly's."

The tension at the table lowered somewhat, and the three men went back to eating. After Rochelle refreshed the two coffees, she walked away.

"Hard life." Johnny said.

"How'd you pick that up?" Little was poised to listen intently.

Worth was quiet now, pretending to be more interested in his waffle than anything else. Johnny recognized the opening. "Her nose is crooked and has obviously been broken at least once, along with three fingers. They stood apart from the others that were straight, so it was not from arthritis. She's limping, but it's hard to tell if that's from the same abuse or being on her feet all day."

Little looked at Johnny. "Could've been a car wreck."

"Possible, sir, but not likely. She's right-handed, and all of the broken fingers are on her right hand. Abusers typically grab the dominant hand to keep their victim from fighting back. When she poured the refills, I saw what looks like a through-and-through stab wound to the bottom of her right arm—large entry on the palmar aspect of her forearm with a smaller corresponding wound on the dorsal side. Likely a defensive wound." Johnny took a sip of water and went back to eating. He finished his eggs, then spoke again as Little stared at him. "All that in her life and she's still smiling. I'm always amazed at the resilience of people."

Worth looked up and saw Little nodding his head. "Johnny, I've been coming here for years, and I've known Rochelle for over twenty. I met her when I shot and killed her husband when I responded to a domestic call." He paused a moment and took a sip of water. "I'd been there many times when he'd beaten her up, but he was always gone. That night, I found him on top of her, stabbing her with a butcher knife." He looked up and watched Rochelle speaking with a couple who recently sat down. "I can still taste the blood. There was so much of it, that metallic taste was in the air." Little smiled faintly. "She nearly died in my arms that night. I was a sergeant, and that bastard nearly killed me, two of my officers, and Rochelle. I was able to sidestep him and get the shots off. He landed at my feet and stabbed me in the shin as he landed on the floor, dead."

Worth jumped in. "I remember that. Lettieri and Bastin caught that case." He lifted his coffee cup. "If it weren't for you, we would've buried Rochelle and two cops that night."

"Too true. He moved faster than anything I'd ever seen, and I boxed for years, Johnny. Truth is, when I'm here I can't get the memories of that night truly out of my head."

"Why here then?" Johnny looked at Little, who returned his gaze.

"Because Rochelle is proof that I made a difference on one night, on one call. That keeps me grounded. It also helps me remember what my officers face every day."

The three men sat silently for a few minutes.

Johnny broke the silence. "Captain, I know your time is tight, and you appear to be a bottom-line guy. I spoke with Violet Sanders this week. I was at West Lawler High School gathering some pictures, and she pulled me into her office."

Little sat back in his chair. "Okay, Johnny. Let's have it. Just ask."

"Did she tell you that Dunlap was having an inappropriate relationship with Melanie Renee Rast?"

Focused, Little replied, "Yes, she did, Detective Till. Yes, she did, and I left it out of the file for a specific reason."

"Sir?"

"Because it was *bullshit*." Little's eyes were fixed, his lips pursed, and the vein on his forehead protruding. He caught his anger, paused, and looked down. Then, clearly trying to control his temper, he continued, "Dunlap was my friend and a damn good cop. He asked to be assigned to the schools. At that time, it was a shit detail, basically took you out of the promotion ladder."

"Why?" Johnny asked.

"Not a lot of arrests in the schools back then. We were still able to keep the wolves outside the gate. So a few years in the school and your stats went to shit."

"So why ask for that assignment?"

"Well, not everyone can go from Traffic to Homicide," snapped Little, before catching Worth's hard stare. The small exchange, barely perceptible to anyone else at Molly's, was evidence of why Worth needed to be at that table. "That was a cheap shot, Johnny. I apologize, truly. You didn't deserve that." Little sat back and rubbed his neck with his right hand. "Okay. Here it is. I thought Sanders was nuts. Still do. She was always calling us on leads that never panned out. You know the 'reliable informant' you learned about in the academy? Well, she was just the opposite. The woman should've spent her time in the library writing fiction. She has quite the imagination. However, you know what they say: Crazy doesn't mean stupid. So I took a solid week to check it out. I spoke with Dunlap's friends, Rast's friends, everyone I could. I even spoke with Dunlap's wife about it, and that sucked. Turns out she knew the girl's name."

"Melanie Rast?" Johnny asked.

"Yep. She and Mike went to Melanie's mother's funeral, and it was a thin crowd. Even the school only sent a few folks. The funeral took place during school hours. So it was the Dunlaps, a few administrators, Melanie, and a friend with her friend's parents, and that was about it. Sad case."

"Did you ever speak with Melanie Rast?"

"Sure did. She got pissed when I asked about her relationship with Dunlap. She told me when her mom killed herself, she became a leper at school, and she wasn't popular to start with. Mike was the only one who spoke with her. You see, he knew about the suicide and reached out to her. She ran away a few times but was generally a good kid. Couldn't blame her for trying to escape that environment—drunk, abusive mother with equally charming boyfriends."

"Where did you interview her?"

Little thought about it for a minute. "Anna Dunlap set it up. Melanie was at a friend's house. Dunlap's death shook her up, and she hadn't been back to school. She couldn't give me much. She was a mess. Told me she lost the only adult guy who acted like a father. Then she shut down and wouldn't talk at all. I got the impression that she knew something, and I even tried to get someone at the school to reach out to her. No luck. Anna Dunlap tried, as well, but she was in the wind."

"She never came back to school," Johnny concluded.

"Figures. Nothing to come back to." Little shook his head. "I knew she wasn't the shooter, so at that point, I moved onto other leads. It's hard for you to imagine the absolute shitstorm this was. We were chasing leads night and day."

"I've learned that from a lot of people, Captain. No judgment from anyone at this table," Johnny said as Worth nodded. "How did you rule her out as the shooter?"

"Too short. The trajectory of the shots was level. Mike was a tall guy, over six feet. Melanie barely scraped five feet even."

Damn good police work. Impressive, Johnny thought. "So, why not put it into the file?"

Little looked at Worth then at Johnny. "Should have. I should have, but I was trying to protect three people: Anna Dunlap from having to answer questions, Melanie Rast from being hounded by people, and the memory of my friend, Mike Dunlap." He took a deep breath and let it out. "If you're here to tell me I missed a link to his killer or hamstrung the investigation since then, just come out with it and I'll have to live with that."

"I haven't found anything that links her, Captain."

"Yet."

Johnny nodded his head. "It may be a rabbit down a hole, but everyone else in that file is available except for a couple of ancillary folks who are dead. Melanie Rast should be alive based upon her age, but she vanished from the grid."

Little was listening intently now. "When?"

"As you now know, she never went back to school, but she also never renewed her DL. It expired on her eighteenth birthday. What eighteen-year-old doesn't renew? I can't find anything on her in any database."

"She was on a track to live a hard life. Did you try the prison system or," he hesitated, "or the obits?"

"Yes, sir. Nothing. She just disappeared."

Little nodded, then he looked at Worth. "Bill, do you remember that underground group that the department investigated for making kids disappear from abusive situations? 'Light' something."

Worth looked up at the ceiling for a minute. "The Way and the Light."

"That's it." Little slapped the table and looked at Johnny. "Okay. Put yourself in that environment twenty years ago before the internet, before the advocacy groups were fully formed, and before there was a true recognition of what cops knew about domestic and sexual-assault victims."

"Which was?"

"They needed resources. Finally, now people have listened to us, but we were screaming it back then."

Johnny nodded and took out his notepad.

Little didn't slow down. "Anyway, it was a great thought, but the program was run by a couple of nuts. They hated the police, hid victims and witnesses, one of them went to jail for obstruction, and the other did about a month in jail for refusing to disclose the location of an abused child. The judge finally let her out when she gave up the information." Little paused to take a drink of water. "Anyway, that led some folks at the DA's office to put their own victim-witness programs together and shut that group down." He waved to Rochelle, who took the plates and freshened his coffee. When she walked away, he continued. "There was no oversight, no board of directors, no attorneys involved. Those two women were rogues. There's no telling what they did."

"Do you think Melanie was taken in by The Way and the Light?"

"'Taken in' is a generous term. I'm a deacon in my church, Johnny, and I always resented The Way and the Light's efforts to hijack John 8:12. 'I am the light of the world. Whoever follows me will never walk in darkness but will have the light of life.' I cuss a good bit, Johnny, but I know my Bible. These clowns used the Bible to dupe kids and DV victims into running from the resources that were available. There were rumors that the adults had opportunities for a better life, but what would they do with kids? We could never prove anything, but all theories were on the table, even selling them to illegal adoptions. Anyway, if Melanie Renee Rast disappeared before her eighteenth birthday, they may have been involved."

"Where would you start, Captain?" Johnny asked, although he knew exactly what to do and where to go. Worth knew it, too.

Little sat up a bit straighter. "Hospital and school records. Look for next of kin and emergency contacts. You can take a young girl out of the community, but she will reach out to someone. Check with her friend and the family she stayed with, as well. Melanie would be about thirty-seven now. Be forewarned, Till. These folks will protect her to the death. They've probably had their heads filled with all sorts of lies by The Way and the Light."

"What about the two folks who ran the group?"

"As they said in *Casablanca*, 'I'm afraid the conversation would be a bit one-sided,'" Little said. "Both dead . . . murder-suicide, and the last one to die torched their house. No records. Crazy bitches. Maybe they thought they were doing the right thing. Anyway, God will judge them, not me." Little took out a twenty and put it on the table. Johnny reached for his wallet. "Save it, Johnny. She'll never bring a bill."

"Her boss okay with that?" Worth asked, looking at Rochelle as she exchanged laughs with another customer.

"She owns the place. She used to bring me bills marked 'paid in full' in her handwriting but got tired of watching me walk out of here wiping my eyes. Now I just hide the money on the table. I know she donates it, so it's a little game we play."

"So . . ." Johnny paused. "Rochelle owns Molly's Restaurant?"

"You don't mess with the name. Molly's has been here for more than fifty years. Rochelle bought it from Molly when she retired." He sighed. "A true success story."

Johnny put his wallet away. He reached across the table and shook Little's hand. "It's an honor, Captain, and I'm sorry you lost your friend."

Little put his head down, then looked up and thanked Johnny. His eyes were glassy. "Thanks, Johnny. You find who killed him, you let me know. I want to see the wrath of God visited upon him when they put the needle in his arm."

"Count on it, sir."

As the three men walked out, Little stopped to speak with Rochelle. Worth and Johnny continued to their cars.

"Let's meet back at the office. I've got a stop to make," Worth said, nodding his head toward the restaurant. "You handled that like a seasoned detective. Well done." With that, he was gone.

Johnny got into his car and drove to his office. He had three grand jury subpoenas to prepare: one for school records, one for medical records, and one to the Bureau of Vital Statistics. At least they would afford some level of protection from public disclosure until he knew what he had.

CHAPTER 16

Johnny typed up the subpoenas then called his new best friend in the Lawler DA's office, Ana Liss. Fortunately, she was in her office and not in court—a rare moment.

"ADA Liss, can I help you?"

"Ana, Johnny Till. How are you doing?"

"Excellent, *Detective*. You?" Her emphasis on "detective" was a private joke. They had planned to keep that promotion quiet to lull the defense attorney into the trap he fell in at trial. It had worked like a charm. "To what do I owe this gracious call, Mr. Homicide? Do you long for another fatality wreck to prosecute with me?"

"I'm sure there will be others. There are a few that may not plea out."

"Doubtful. Stakes are too high with the new statutory penalties. What's up?" Liss asked.

"I need three grand jury subpoenas for records. Can you help? It's time sensitive and a very important case."

"I'm intrigued. Can you draft them and come up to my office?"

"Already drafted," Johnny answered.

"Email the drafts so I can look them over while you're on your way."

"I'd rather not. That would make them subject to the Open Records Act."

"They are sensitive." She sighed. "Okay. I'll bring my section leader in on this to make it go smoothly. The grand jury is in session today until four, so we have plenty of time."

"Great. See you in ten."

Johnny hung up the phone and went by Sergeant Rostavic's office to let him know where he was headed. When Rostavic heard the subpoenas were on the Dunlap case, he offered to drive Johnny and drop him off so he wouldn't have to park. He wanted to hear about the progress and the potential for new information.

An hour later, Johnny took the subpoenas to the chief of the Lawler County School Police to avoid any repeat inquiries from the West Lawler High School staff, the repository of records for the Lawler Medical Center, and the Bureau of Vital Statistics. He went there last, hoping they could perform a search right then and provide the documents. He expected the other two entities would have to retrieve the records from storage or sit someone at a computer to search. He was right. He walked out of the Bureau of Vital Statistics with a thick envelope.

Sergeant Rostavic, who graciously acted as Johnny's chauffer, got the full report and was up to speed. When Johnny emerged from the Bureau of Vital Statistics, Rostavic picked him up and drove directly to a parking lot so they could see what they had.

As Johnny broke the seal, Vinnie Rostavic cringed.

"Relax, Sarge," Johnny said. "I specified we needed three copies of everything in the grand jury subpoena. I squared it with the DA that one certified copy was for Homicide."

"Good thinking."

"I had to do that in traffic wreck cases. If I didn't, I'd wait weeks for the DA to present the records back to the grand jury while my leads went cold."

Rostavic nodded.

Johnny opened a smaller envelope and started to read. "Hot damn! We got her!" He handed the pages to Rostavic as he finished reading them. When he looked over, his sergeant was wide-eyed and grinning as Johnny read from the report. "On December 9, 1998, about a month after Dunlap was killed and the day after her eighteenth birthday, Melanie Renee Rast legally changed her name to Maureen Roberts."

"Why didn't your search find the public notice that the court has to file in the paper?" Rostavic asked.

"Turns out the legislature passed a statute allowing a person to bypass that process if they could convince a judge that any such filing would put the person in danger. So The Way and the Light folks probably hired an attorney to help Melanie petition a judge for an order."

They finished reading the documents, then Johnny put them back into the envelope. "Let's get back to the office, Sarge."

"What about the other documents?" Rostavic asked.

"This was the royal flush! The others would only be necessary if this didn't pan out. This is also a much quicker way to find her. The other records are about her old life. This should take me right to her . . . with a lot less reading."

About twenty minutes later, they pulled into the parking lot of headquarters. Johnny looked at Vinnie Rostavic for a second, like he was waiting for permission to get out of the car or for some words of guidance.

"Stop looking at my ugly mug and go!" Rostavic exclaimed. With that bit of encouragement, Johnny practically ran into the building.

After entering the unit, he knocked on Major Worth's office door. He was inside discussing a case with Holly and Lieutenant Biggers. "Sorry to interrupt, Major," Johnny said as he peeked into the room. "I found her!"

"Rast?"

"The one and only. Going to run her now." Johnny went to his desk and put in his password to get to the NCIC database. He looked up and realized Sergeant Rostavic, Lieutenant Biggers, Major Worth, and Detective Forrester were standing behind him in his cubicle. Rostavic was filling them in as Johnny typed.

"What address did she use on the petition?" Biggers asked.

Vinnie Rostavic answered, "We figure it was either her mother's house or a fake address to further hide the trail."

We. That made Johnny feel good. *No one in Homicide solves anything alone.*

"What do you think, Johnny? Where do you think she went?" Biggers asked as Johnny pressed the enter key and waited with everyone else.

"She had no one to go to and nowhere to run. My guess is she never left Lawler, or if she did, she's still close by." As he spoke, the return began to fill the screen.

"Holy crap. Here all along," Holly said, staring at the screen.

"Which means she saw all the news articles, the news shows, and the pleas for information. If she is involved or has information, she must have a damn good reason for staying quiet." Vinnie Rostavic had some contempt in his voice. Johnny figured he earned it and cut him some slack.

MAUREEN ROBERTS DOB 12/10/71
4873 REDDINGTON WAY
COLTRANE, GEORGIA, 30339
5' 00" 124 POUNDS
HAIR: BLONDE
EYES: HAZEL
LICENSE RESTRICTIONS: CORRECTIVE LENSES

Major Bill Worth was leaning on the top of Johnny's cubicle. He stood up straight, made eye contact with everyone, then spoke. "Let's hit this hard, but from a distance. Holly, get on another terminal and find everything you can about her: work, social media, married, kids, professional licenses, anything. We may only get one shot at speaking with her. Like Vinnie said, she had a good reason to stay quiet, or at least thought she did."

Vinnie spoke to Johnny as he continued to type. "Three runaway events, correct?"

"Yes, sir."

"Okay. They usually didn't fingerprint juveniles on runaways then, but I'm going to try to get any prints we have from Juvenile. We may need them to prove who she is, if she denies it."

"Good point. She may very likely deny it," Worth said, his wheels spinning. "Bring a fingerprint scanner with you when you go. She likely has prints on file for something—a pistol permit, pouring license, anything. Let's lock this down." He paused. "Everyone in the unit, in front of Till's desk right now!"

Worth was well-respected and rarely had to give anyone an order. Johnny heard a dozen desk chairs move at
once, and everyone from detectives to crime-scene techs
to administrative staff gathered around. Once they were
assembled, Worth spoke quietly and with authority.

"We have a new lead in the Dunlap case—the first in
more than a decade. We have no idea where it will lead,
if anywhere. The murder of Officer Michael Dunlap hit
this department like a ton of bricks, and the fact that it
has remained a cold case has been, in some ways, just as
hard to live with. The worst thing you can give a victim
is false hope. Every cop in this building is, as far as I'm
concerned, a victim of Dunlap's murder. I'm going to
personally speak with everyone assigned to this unit. I
want nothing leaked or discussed about this outside of
this office. Understood?"

The chorus of "Yes, sir" was nearly simultaneous.
Johnny barely heard it. He knew that Ana Liss used a
case pending before the grand jury as the basis for the
subpoenas to keep anyone involved in responding in the
dark. It was a calculated risk, as Johnny's efforts to find
Melanie Renee Rast, now Maureen Roberts, would never
result in a challenge to the prosecution of Dunlap's killer.
As Little said, Rast definitely didn't shoot Dunlap.

CHAPTER 17

T hirty minutes later, Holly, Johnny, Vinnie, Biggers, and Worth met again in Worth's office. "Okay," Worth said, "what do we have?"

Holly spoke first. "Maureen Roberts is a registered nurse working on a telemetry project. She works from her home, essentially, monitoring patients who need to check in with their doctors on a regular basis. The company uses videoconferencing to allow them to bill insurance, Medicare, and the like. Troubled pregnancies, homebound, severe diabetics, those types of patients. The company is called TeleDoc. It's located in Michigan. Everyone is virtual. They don't even have a home office."

"Smart," Worth said. "Keeps her from running into any old classmates. A change of hair color and a pair of glasses, and no one would know her through a camera lens. So, we know she's smart. Where did she go to school?"

"Courtesy of the United States Army. Finished her GED after basic training at Fort Benning, then did her core classes online. The army stationed her in San Antonio at Brooke Army Medical Center. She attended the University of Texas for two years and finished her nursing degree. When she got out of the army after six years, she came back to Lawler County."

"Vinnie? Any prints?"

"Fortunately for us, our girl was not happy about going back home. Can't say I blame her, but she punched a corrections officer at the youth detention center when she was arrested. They didn't charge her with the assault because she broke down, begging to stay there. They did print her though. We can also get her prints from the army, but that would take a lot of red tape."

"Those databases won't intersect with our fingerprint reader, anyway." Worth paused. "Bring the fingerprint reader. She doesn't know what's in the database. Bring a fingerprint tech, as well, to get a clean set, if she balks. Just keep the tech around the corner."

"Social media?"

Holly looked at her notes. "Nada, boss. She's still staying well below the radar."

"Johnny? Anything on your end?" Worth asked.

"I found the nursing license, and her prints will be on file from that, but as you said, not likely with NCIC."

"I have a friend at the licensing board for MDs and RNs. She's helped me track down a couple of less-than-cooperative healthcare providers in the past. I think she'll spot us a set of records, especially for this case. Between the set from youth detention and the nursing board, our tech should be able to match up a good set, if necessary." Worth looked at Johnny. "Anything else?"

"Yep. She never married, but she has a daughter." He looked at his notes. "Meredith Brittany Roberts, age sixteen. I also have pictures of Maureen and her daughter from the DMV. Her daughter has a Facebook page and an Instagram handle, but—and this is hard to believe—she doesn't post much."

"Maybe her mom keeps a tight leash on her," Holly chimed in.

"Makes sense." Worth nodded. "Can't keep kids off of that stuff. Where does Meredith attend school?"

"She's away at a boarding school in North Georgia." Johnny checked his notes. "Sacred Cross."

"Costs a good bit, but well-trained nurses make good coin." Worth leaned back in his chair and put his hands behind his head. "Okay, what's your play, Johnny?"

Johnny thought a second. "Holly, what shift does she work?"

Holly checked her notes. "I called on a dummy line and feigned a desire to have her specifically as a nurse monitoring my mother. She rotates, but she has enough seniority to be on day shift most of the time." Holly looked on another page of her notes. "7:00 a.m. to 7:00 p.m. Off days rotate, as well. She is currently working Tuesday through Friday."

Johnny nodded. "Okay, we need to catch her when she's fresh and finished with her shift. She'll likely balk about speaking with us if she has patients counting on her. Normally, a twelve-hour shift would wipe her out, but let's hope that's the case. I don't want to wait for Saturday and find out she's heading out of town to see a friend." He turned toward Worth. "We'll do some surveillance and knock on her door this evening at ten till seven. Less chance of her being gone to work out or eat dinner. She'll still be on or near the phone and inside the house. Her shift will be over soon after that, so she'll have no excuses as to why she can't speak with us."

"And if she refuses to speak?" Holly asked the question everyone had on their minds.

Johnny looked at the group, then back at Holly. "My gut says she will cooperate. Running is hard. I never caught a fugitive who didn't fall asleep when they were finally caught. She's done nothing wrong, but I can only guess that she's tired of running, as well."

"That depends upon whom or what she is running from," Holly chimed in. Johnny nodded.

Worth looked at the group of seasoned detectives in his office. They were looking for endorsement from him as a leader. "Sounds like that's our plan. Bring Beaker from Crime Scene. He just came back from a fingerprint analysis class I sent him to. It costs the department a fortune and got him a free trip to New Orleans, so it's time for him to earn his keep." Everyone chuckled. "He's up for anything to help the team, as you know. He's also good with people, putting them at ease."

Beaker was a slim, extremely well-educated crime-scene tech with a degree in chemistry. He loved working with law enforcement and was a dedicated professional. He was also a dead ringer for Beaker on *The Muppet Show*. Jim Henson would have been proud to look at him—life imitating art.

Vinnie was looking at Worth. "Major, do you want all four of us on this?"

"Yes." Worth looked around. "I'll take the heat for the OT or I'll pay it myself. I'm about to brief Chief Porter. I'm sure she'll approve whatever we need."

"Good," Vinnie said. "I don't want to let this one go, and I want to be there to support Till and Forrester if they need anything."

Worth nodded. "I also asked Millie Roth, the DA

herself, to attend the meeting with the chief. If you need a quick warrant, subpoena, or even a material witness proceeding, I don't want any delays."

"Before we go, I want to thank everyone here for the support," Johnny said. "I'm the FNG. So I know this wouldn't happen without y'all."

They all nodded. "Just stay the course, Fido. Don't give up that bone." Worth smiled at Johnny and put his hands back behind his head.

CHAPTER 18

T he address 4873 Reddington Way was a simple, two-story, three-and-two home in the most vanilla of Lawler's suburbs. Like most of the subdivisions, this one was built in sections using plans that varied little. New owners had their choice of a few building plans and construction. The idea was to prevent the houses from looking like they emerged from a copy machine, and the effort was somewhat successful. It was the perfect place to hide in the open.

Johnny, Holly, and Vinnie sat in a surveillance van on the corner. Through the back window, they could see the woman now known as Maureen Roberts sitting at a desk with a headset on. Her computer screen displayed the face of an elderly man with almost pasty skin. Roberts was looking up to a camera as she spoke. A green light on the camera advised the call was active.

"We can wait until the green light goes out close to seven. That will mean the calls are over," Johnny said, trying to soak in every detail of the room and the process. When the green light turned red, he looked at his watch. "That's three calls I witnessed with an average of twelve minutes."

"Maybe the max is fifteen. You know, some sort of billing guideline." Holly was sitting at a computer still looking for more information.

"Well, we have another hour to establish the pattern. When does Beaker arrive, Sarge?" Johnny never took his eyes off the binoculars that were fixed into the periscope of the van.

"He's due to arrive at 5:45," Vinnie said. "I had him drive to Atlanta to pick up the prints from the nursing board. You should've seen him when I told him about the operation. He was like a kid at Christmas."

"He's a good one. I'm glad he'll be with us. He's helped me print many subjects and victims alike. He can charm anyone, and it's hard to get prints when they're uncooperative." Holly was still typing while she spoke. "Hey, Johnny, the phone company records we got on her won't help much. She's on the phone so much, it would take weeks to make sense of any patterns beyond her work calls. Sorry."

"No problem, Holly. Just keep sending the positive mojo through the window into that house. We need a co-operative witness."

"She's alone, right?" Holly asked.

Johnny did another quick scan of the house, looking into every window. "No other movement or lights anywhere else in the house. I did notice that she has the alarm on. She must have the motion detectors bypassed or be able to activate the alarm from the panel I can see in the home office. She's concerned about someone coming to visit."

The next hour passed slowly. Aside from the occasional quip or joke, the group remained quiet. Vinnie took notes, and Johnny maintained surveillance. Maureen Roberts' car was in the garage, so it wasn't visible, but the state tag office provided the information on the two vehicles registered to her. The purchase of one of them coincided with her daughter's sixteenth birthday, but Johnny figured it was likely in the garage if she was at boarding school.

Beaker went out on the radio to advise he was at location Zulu Niner, the designation given to the operation to prevent anyone in the media from getting nosy, and at the same time, heading off any 911 calls about the van.

Everything is in place, Johnny thought. *Let's just hope she'll speak with us.*

CHAPTER 19

At 6:45, the green light on the camera sitting on top of Maureen Roberts' computer screen turned red, and for the first time in three hours, she took off her headset.

"Go time," Johnny said.

Vinnie stayed with the van maintaining surveillance while Holly and Johnny got out and climbed into Holly's car, which was parked a half block away. Holly activated the microphone on her phone, and they drove to the front of Maureen Roberts' home. They pulled into the driveway to prevent her from leaving, then got out quickly.

As Holly walked close to Johnny, she tapped him on the shoulder. "All you, unless you need me." The plan was to have Johnny's questions distract Maureen so she forgot about Holly and the likelihood of a recording.

Johnny and Holly stood to the sides of the door and rang the bell. The police knock was not the best play here, at least at the outset. It took a few seconds, but the porch light came on. As they were trained, Holly and Johnny moved farther apart. In the doorframe, above the doorbell, Johnny saw the camera.

"Who is it?" Maureen's voice was stern but shaky.

"Police, Ms. Roberts. We have a few questions."

"Hold your credentials up to the camera above the door."

Two cameras, Johnny thought. *She probably thought the one in the doorframe would go unnoticed.*

Johnny and Holly took out their badges and IDs, then showed both to the camera above the door.

"What do you want, Till and Forrester?"

Using our names, trying to get some semblance of control. Scared to death. This will not be easy. Johnny lowered his voice. "Ms. Roberts, we're just here to ask some questions. We don't have any bad news." He paused. *Time to use some leverage.* "I'm telling you the truth. You can call 911 and verify who we are." When Johnny didn't hear the door unlock, he spoke again. "Ms. Roberts, I promise. Meredith is fine. We just want to ask you some questions."

A minute later, the lock turned on the deadbolt, the chain came off, and the door opened. Melanie Rast—now Maureen Roberts—had changed very little in the past twenty years. Her eyes were set hard on Johnny. "You've got some nerve mentioning my daughter. I'm texting her now."

"I didn't mean to upset you, Ms. Roberts. I just wanted to take that off the table in case you thought we were here to deliver bad news."

Roberts was texting quickly, and after a minute, she put her phone down. Holly and Johnny both saw the nine-millimeter Beretta 92FS sitting next to the door. She had obviously had it in her hand until she saw their identification.

"May we speak with you, Ms. Roberts? It won't take along."

Reluctantly, she waved them into the kitchen. She left the Beretta at the door. Normally, Johnny or Holly would've secured it, but there were two of them, and they needed to gain her trust quickly. Taking control of her firearm was not the way to do that.

Johnny and Holly sat down when asked to do so. However, Roberts took a few minutes to sit. She was standing with her arms crossed, staring at them. Finally, she sat at the head of the table and looked right at Johnny. Johnny and Holly pushed their business cards in front of her.

"You have a few minutes, that's all. I have patients to care for. I'm a telenurse, and my patients need me."

Johnny looked at her. "We don't want to take any more of your time than is necessary. We'll get you back to your patients as quickly as we can." *No need to tell her what we know about her schedule. Let her feel like's she's in control . . . for now.*

Roberts nodded. "Okay. You're here. I'm listening. What questions do you want to ask me? That crazy kid down the street get arrested again?"

"No, ma'am," Johnny said softly. "None of your neighbors know we're here. We have specific questions for you." He paused and leaned forward. "We believe you can help us."

"I stay out of trouble. I served my country. My daughter goes to school away from here, as you obviously know. So how could I possibly help the Lawler Police Department?"

"We're trying to locate a person who may have information about a crime, a very serious crime, that happened a long time ago."

Johnny watched as Roberts began shaking. She

noticed it, too, and grabbed her own hands to try to stop it. "Who are you looking for?"

Johnny watched her face. "We need desperately to speak with Melanie Renee Rast." He saw the tears well up in her eyes, and she audibly caught her breath. Roberts looked down at the table, then at the ceiling, trying to avoid looking at either Johnny or Holly. "She's not in any trouble, Ms. Roberts," Johnny said. "In fact, we believe she's probably scared, and if I were her, I would be, as well. I want her to know that she is safe, that anything she says and knows may help us catch a killer, and she doesn't need to be afraid anymore."

The tears were running down her face uncontrollably now, but she was holding in the sobs for the moment. She opened her mouth to speak, but nothing came out. Johnny took out her current driver's license picture and put it on the table. As she looked at it, he pulled out her picture from her nursing license application, then her first driver's license picture taken at sixteen years old. She broke down then.

Johnny and Holly said nothing for at least five minutes while she wept. Holly stood and retrieved some tissues from the table next to the television. She handed the box to Roberts, who wiped her eyes. After she caught her breath enough to speak, she took the picture of Melanie Renee Rast in her hands. "I haven't seen this picture for so many years. My mom had me when she was about this age. We looked so much alike . . . until the alcohol stole that, too." She wiped her eyes again and took a deep breath. "I'm Melanie Rast, Detective Till."

CHAPTER 20

O ver the next two hours, Holly and Johnny heard the complete story of what happened to Melanie Rast— how The Way and the Light had hired an attorney for her, got her a new name, and helped her enlist in the army. "It was a great place to hide. New name, moving around, the security of living on the base. No one could find me."

"Why did you come back to Lawler?" Johnny asked.

"The simple answer is I got tired of running. I took precautions to protect my daughter through boarding school, stayed off the radar of anyone I knew before, got a job 'out of state' for all practical purposes, and life has been good. I have a good life, Detective Till. I don't need a lot of excitement." She put her head in her hands as her elbows rested on the table. "I've had enough for a lifetime."

"I know, Ms. Roberts," Johnny said. "I lost my dad when I was young, too."

Roberts shook her head. "You never really get past it, do you?" It was more of a statement than a question.

"No. I guess you never do." Johnny's voice cracked.

"Okay. Now that you both have ruined my makeup,

and you obviously know I have no patients waiting for me because no one has called, what questions do you have for Melanie Rast?" Maureen Roberts smiled a bit.

This will be harder than anything so far. "Ms. Roberts, I'm a homicide detective. Detective Forrester and I both work in that unit. Each detective works a lot of horrible crimes, and each also works an old case that has remained unsolved. The case I'm working involves the murder of a police officer in 1998. His name was—"

"Mike Dunlap." Tears began streaming down Roberts' cheeks again. "He was my friend. He cared about me when it seemed no one else did."

"We believe you may have some information that will help us solve his murder and bring the killer to justice."

Roberts wiped her cheeks, then pulled another tissue from the box. She hardly even noticed Holly anymore. "I can't imagine how I can help. I spoke with a detective shortly after Mike died."

"I know. Detective Little. He's a captain now. He remembers speaking with you. He said you were overcome with grief, and I can hardly imagine the pain you had inside you at that time. Officer Dunlap was murdered about two months after your mother died. But," Johnny leaned forward again, "Captain Little believes there was more that you were afraid to tell him. He didn't want to push you then, and after that . . ."

"After that, I was gone." Roberts nodded her head. "He's right. I'll tell you what I know, but you have to protect me and my daughter. I don't care if it's been twenty years. He will find me. He said he would never stop looking for me if I ever said a word."

"Who, Ms. Roberts? Who told you that?"

"When I ran away from home, there were men who

tried to pick me up, you know. They thought, I guess, that I was a prostitute. Some nights I just wandered the streets when I ran off. One night, a guy tried to pick me up. He said he had a place I could stay with other girls from around here. He said he took good care of them and paid them well to do what I was probably doing for a few bucks. Well, I busted him in the nose with a roll of quarters I kept in my hand when I was walking, and I ran down an alley."

"Did you get away from him, Ms. Roberts?" Johnny asked.

"Please, call me Maureen. I probably won't even answer to Melanie anymore." She took a drink of the water Holly had poured for her, then continued. "I thought I did, but he showed up at the football game the night Mike was killed. He caught me in a dark area where I was watching the game." She caught her breath deep in her chest. "He put a knife to my throat and told me to give him my coat and hat. He said if I didn't, they would find me Monday morning under the bleachers after the cats and racoons ate my face. His eyes were so scary, and he was still sporting a black eye from where I had hit him. So I got out of my coat and hat and gave them to him. He kept asking me, 'Who did you tell?' over and over. I guess he was worried that I told the cops about him trying to pick me up, or worse—about the other girls he had. He said he was watching me at school and saw me talking with Mike. I shook my head and told him I didn't tell anyone. I was so scared."

"What happened next?"

"I was set to meet Mike that night to tell him that someone was keeping young girls as prostitutes." She wiped her eyes again. "He didn't know all that. He just knew I needed to speak with him, and he told me I could tell him anything. So I started walking to meet him, and that's when I heard the gunshots. They were so loud! I ran to where we were set to meet, and I saw him lying there in a puddle of blood . . . so I ran."

"Did you tell anyone?"

"No, I was too scared. Then the guy showed up again two days later, right before I spoke with Detective Little. I was staying with a neighbor. He told me if I ever told anyone about him, he would kill me, my neighbor, her daughter, and Mike's wife." She paused. "He even knew her name—Anna Dunlap. That was it. I got out of there as soon as I could, and The Way and the Light people helped me disappear."

Holly and Johnny were both stunned by what they had heard, but it made sense. Dunlap had been expecting someone to meet him. The coat and hat had let the killer get close.

"Was this man alone, Maureen?" Johnny asked.

"I never saw anyone with him."

"Can you describe him? Would you recognize him if you saw him again?"

"Listen to me," Maureen said sternly. "Why do you think I work from home and keep that Beretta handy? I would recognize him, and I'll kill him on the spot if I ever see him again."

"What about the truck he was driving when you met him? Do you remember the tag number?" Johnny didn't expect that she could provide anything helpful about either from so long ago, especially while under stress.

"Sorry. It was just a truck." Roberts seemed disappointed that she could not help.

She couldn't describe the truck or provide the tag. It's a long shot, but I need to ask. "Maureen, think hard. Do you remember if he used a name when he introduced himself?"

"Only one name. I don't know if it was his first or last name, but it was weird. 'Mang' or something like that."

Holly and Johnny looked at each other. "Was he a white man? Did he have an accent?"

"He was taller than I am, but really skinny, so he was able to get into my coat. Asian guy about six feet. That's why I couldn't tell what his name was, plus I was scared."

"Are you saying he had an accent? Was he hard to understand?"

"Not real hard, but yeah. His accent was thick." She paused. "I never misunderstood his threats, though. They were real clear."

"We can get you somewhere safe, Maureen. Would you meet with one of our sketch artists tonight?"

She took a deep breath. "I guess I need to help you find him, now that you know who I am. If you can find me, he can, too." She picked up her cell phone. "I have about a week and a half of vacation time. I'll take it, so maybe I can return to a normal life when this is over."

As Maureen made her call, Holly called Vinnie and asked him to pull the van into the driveway. Then she called the Homicide Unit and told them to have a sketch artist on the way to meet them. It would be a long night. Her next call would be to the local PD near Meredith's school. If this guy was still out there, he could get to Maureen easier than killing a cop.

CHAPTER 21

s Johnny rode back to the Homicide Unit with Holly driving and Maureen Roberts in the back seat, he couldn't shake the feeling that Roberts might be in danger. She was sure certain of it. He'd learned not to second-guess people who know more about things than you do.

Johnny took out his phone and sent a text to Lieutenant Dan Paschal. Till here. I have a lead in the Dunlap case. Can you meet me in Homicide in fifteen minutes?

The response took all of a minute: C U there.

Next, Johnny called Major Worth. "We're on the way, sir. Yes, she's with us."

Worth had not said a word other than to state his name. He instantly knew Johnny couldn't talk. "Good work. Bring her in the sally port near the 911 center. The media never looks there. I'm on my way." He paused. "Anything solid on Dunlap?"

"Yes, sir. We'll be there in about fifteen minutes."

Worth hung up, but Johnny kept speaking to Maureen, describing security details, safe houses, and other points that were going through his head. Maureen needed to hear it. She had to know that Johnny would protect her and her daughter.

Finally, Johnny sent a text to Beaker and Vinnie: Look sharp. Let's trust her instincts for now. She's concerned. We should be, too. BTW we'll print her just in case, but it's her.

Holly turned down a side street near headquarters that was a crescent road. It was a great way to lose a tail and expose reporters who were trailing homicide detectives. Holly made the turn, navigated the crescent, then turned back onto the main road a block away from headquarters. "We're good. No one behind us."

The words helped Maureen relax.

Holly pulled into the sally port, and Vinnie pulled the van in to block the driveway. Maureen saw what they were doing, and it made her feel much better. Johnny opened the door to the back and helped Maureen out.

Major Worth was holding the door to the building open and waved Maureen to him. The door closed behind her, and Johnny and Maureen walked quickly, following Major Worth. She saw a women's restroom and ran in, holding her hand over her mouth. Outside, Johnny and Worth could hear her retching.

"Did she deny it was her?" Worth asked, standing with Johnny in the hallway.

"No. I convinced her we knew, so it was worthless to try to deny it. We're going to get her prints, anyway."

"Good call."

Maureen emerged from the restroom looking very pale. She was wiping her face with a cold towel.

"You can lie down in my office, if that will help," Worth said, his hand on her left shoulder as she walked. He wanted to know if she was about to fall.

"No. Believe it or not, I feel better now. This is a lot for me. Some cold water would be nice."

"We have some in the unit." Worth made it a point not to use the word *homicide* with her. She could freeze up at any moment and decide not to cooperate. She was a wild card in a stacked deck. They had waited too long to get a break in this case.

When the three of them arrived in the Homicide Unit, the sketch artist, Laura Marin, stood up. Johnny nodded to her and waved his hand down. She sat and waited patiently. They took Maureen to the conference room, not an interview room. They wanted her to feel comfortable. After a half glass of cold water, Johnny asked her if she was willing to meet with a forensic sketch artist. She agreed, and Johnny waved Laura in. Then he excused himself. He'd learned that Laura worked better without interruptions, and she was very good.

As Johnny stepped out, he saw Lieutenant Dan Paschal talking with Worth. When he saw Johnny, he waved him over. Paschal was dressed in a pair of jeans, a skull cap, biker boots, a T-shirt, and a biker vest. On the back was a three-part patch that read SILENT GUARDIANS ALABAMA.

"Making new friends?" Johnny smiled.

"Not as many as you, Johnny," Paschal replied. "What do you have?"

"We have a woman who may have met Dunlap's killer. She's with a sketch artist now."

"Where has she been?"

"Long story, Lieutenant. We may need your help, though."

"Anything we can do."

"She says this same guy tried to pick her up when she

was a runaway. Told her he had a lot of young girls like her that he took care of. He said he'd pay her money and keep her safe from the street."

"What did she do?" Paschal asked.

"Sounds like she broke his nose," Johnny replied.

Paschal smiled. "I think I like her already." He paused. "What do you have on him without the sketch?"

"Tall, slim, Asian male with a heavy accent. Probably good with a knife. He threatened her with one when he stole her hat and coat. He was able to get into it, and she was pretty petite. She also says he found her a day or two after Dunlap's murder and threatened her, the family she was living with, and Dunlap's wife."

"He knew Dunlap's wife?"

"By name, but that might have been in the paper. What struck me is, if he did kill Dunlap, he had a big pair to hang around. Something must've been keeping him here. The place was crawling with state, local, and federal cops."

Paschal nodded. "Very strange. I'll need to get to the office and get started with our analysts. We had computer files then, but a lot of the intel was kept in files. They've been scanned now, but it's not easy to search. Let me know when you have the sketch."

Johnny began walking to his cubicle to download the audio from the interview with Maureen Roberts in case he needed it for a warrant.

"Till!" Johnny turned and saw Paschal walking toward him. "Johnny, push hard, but stay objective. You'll need everything you can get on this case. Don't place all your hope on a sketch based on an eyewitness account from twenty years ago."

"Understood. She was a victim."

"All the same, this needs to be a solid case. Verify everything she says . . . twice."

"Roger that."

"One more thing, Johnny."

"Sir?"

"You can always call me for help."

Johnny nodded, and Paschal walked out of the unit.

CHAPTER 22

T hirty minutes later, Laura emerged with her sketch pad. She pointed Maureen to the ladies' room, then walked into Johnny's cubicle. Holly and Worth saw her come out and walked over to see what she had. Vinnie left his office, trailing the others.

"She's good. Very detailed," Laura said as she opened her sketch pad. Johnny had seen some sketches that looked almost cartoonish, but this one did not. It looked realistic and damn near like a photograph.

"Any hesitation?" Johnny asked.

"None at all. She started out telling me the typical stuff I have to pull out, like the shape of the face, the distance between the eyes, and the point of the chin. I think this guy was burned into her memory. It's one of the clearest interactions I've had with a witness, period. Let me get a photo of the sketch, and then you can have it. Then we can use the facial recognition software in the Intelligence Unit to see what we can find."

Johnny took the sketch and put it on the wall of his cubicle. He took a few photographs of it, as did Holly, Worth, and Vinnie. As they looked at it, Laura emailed the photo she took with her camera to the Intelligence

Unit. Then she picked up her cell phone and let the analyst know it was on the way.

As Maureen started to walk back to the conference room, Johnny took the glass of water she was using and offered to refill it. After she sat down, he thanked her and asked her to be patient. Then he walked out and handed the glass to Beaker to start printing it immediately. Johnny got another glass from the break room and filled it with water. After he gave it to Maureen, he walked back to his cubicle.

He looked at Worth, Holly, and Vinnie. "Well, Beaker will confirm in a few minutes, but I believe that is Melanie Rast."

* * *

The call from the Intelligence Unit came ten minutes later while the group was listening to the recording of Johnny and Holly's meeting with Maureen. The facial recognition software was hit and miss, but when it got a hit, it was strong. The analyst told Laura that Lieutenant Paschal was coming down with the results and a line-up array of photos for the witness.

A few minutes later, Paschal flew into the unit, out of breath. "She's still here. Tell me she's still here!"

Johnny answered, "Yes, sir. She's in the conference room. We're running her prints from a water glass to double check her identity. I also sent a text to Captain Little. He interviewed her shortly after Dunlap's murder. He's on his way now."

"Excellent. Well," he looked at everyone gathered around Johnny's cubicle, "we need to verify her sketch and recollection with a photo array."

"You got a hit on the facial recognition?" Worth asked, looking directly at Paschal.

"Yes, sir, but we need to verify it. This was a short look at a suspect twenty years ago. Let me guess, bad lighting every time she saw him?"

"All but one. His last threat was during the daylight," Johnny confirmed.

Paschal nodded. "Good. All the same, here are the photos I want you to use, Johnny."

"Which is the hit?"

"Not a chance. We're keeping this double blind. Neither one of you will know. Just walk her through it," Paschal looked at Holly, "with a witness and on video, if possible."

"We have video and audio in that room," Worth said. "I have to turn it on from my office. Stand by." Worth walked away, then came back a few minutes later. "Good to go."

Johnny and Holly took the photographs and walked into the conference room.

"You doing okay, Maureen? Need anything?" Holly asked.

"No, Detectives. You have both been more than kind." Her eyes swelled again. "I just keep wondering if I had been braver, if you would've caught him by now, or if I had done something different, Mike would be alive now."

"You were a seventeen-year-old kid, Maureen. You were brave. That's why you're here." Johnny put the photos down on the table. "I know you did the sketch, but I have several photos for you to look at. Please tell me if you can pick out the man who threatened your life and took your jacket and hat the night Officer Michael Dunlap was murdered."

As Johnny spread out the photographs, Maureen gasped.

"Do you see him, Maureen?" Holly asked, putting her

hand on Maureen's shoulder. "It's okay. You're safe. Meredith is safe. It's also okay if you don't see him."

"That's him," Maureen Roberts said as she pointed to the photo, put her hand over the face, and looked away. Johnny turned the photo over and had her initial the photograph. Then Johnny wrote the date and time on the back. He signed it and passed it to Holly to sign. Next Johnny put the photo back into the array and took a picture of the complete assembly of pictures.

"Are you certain, Maureen?" Holly asked.

"One hundred percent. I can almost smell his foul breath when I look at the picture."

"Okay, Maureen. Sit tight. We'll be right back," Johnny said and opened the door.

Holly and Johnny walked into Worth's office, where Vinnie, Worth, and Paschal were watching live.

"Holy crap! I've never seen a victim that certain. She was trembling when she saw his picture. Who is this guy?" Holly said, shaking her head.

"Learning who he is will be the easiest part. That picture is from Interpol. That's Phillip Meng," Paschal said, looking at the picture as he spoke.

"She told us the guy used the name Mang, but his accent was hard to understand," Holly explained.

"The sketch hit on Meng as well through facial recognition, but I had to be sure." Paschal was visibly excited.

Worth, sitting behind his desk, was unaccustomed to seeing Paschal this animated. "Who is he, Paschal?" As he started to speak, Captain Herman Little rushed into Worth's office.

He took one look at the screen and turned to Johnny. "Well, I'm buying lunch for you, Till. That," he said, pointing at the screen, "is Melanie Rast.

CHAPTER 23

C aptain Little was nearly out of breath. He had clearly run from the parking lot to get to the Homicide Unit in order to put his eyes on the girl he knew as Melanie Rast. He was so focused, he hardly acknowledged anyone else in Worth's office.

"Thanks for coming over so quickly, Captain," Johnny said.

"Least I could do. Your comments at breakfast hit me hard. You have to understand. We were so focused on a killer that I guess we overlooked the school kids." He then looked at the other folks in the room and nodded to Major Worth.

"Very true, Herman." Worth was providing absolution as much as confirmation. "We're keeping this under wraps in case it turns out to be a dead end. There are too many folks that don't deserve to be disappointed."

Little nodded his head. "No argument there." He stood there a moment, then looked at Paschal and back at Johnny. It was clear that something big was going on. "Till, I really appreciate the call. I'm going to step away." He paused and extended his hand to Johnny. "The case is clearly in good hands." With that, he walked out of the unit and drove back to his house.

A few minutes passed as they all took account of the magnitude of how big any news about Dunlap's killer would be. Paschal broke the silence: "Major, Phillip Meng is a ghost, for all practical purposes. He's been wanted by American law enforcement for at least ten years, and by European and Chinese authorities for longer than that."

"What's his deal?" Holly asked, hanging on every word.

"In simple terms, he's a salesman: guns, women, mercenaries, drugs, you name it. He'll broker deals and profit from them."

"Murder on his list of priors?" Johnny asked while writing in his notebook.

"Not officially, but he is rumored to eliminate problems in his own field of influence rather than contracting out. Interpol lists him as wanted for questioning in three homicides. In each case, they were either former associates or people who got in the way of deals."

"Any murders for hire? Dunlap's murder was clean . . . professional, but quick." Johnny was thinking back to a theory one of the original detectives documented in the case file.

"Sales are sales. Given the ruthless way he does business, I don't think you can rule out a murder if the price was right."

"Why Dunlap?" Worth asked. He was on his feet now, tapping a pencil on his desk.

"Johnny," Paschal continued, "I imagine the detectives did a deep dive into Dunlap's finances as part of the investigation."

"At least three times. It looks like they went back to that well when everything else came up short."

Paschal was thinking. "Any suspicious deposits or accounts would have triggered them to look further. No . . . it may be something as simple as Dunlap getting in Meng's way."

"What if Meng was following Melanie and saw she was close to Dunlap?" Holly asked, looking at Johnny. "I mean, she said she spent a lot of time speaking with Dunlap, especially after she ran away."

"The high school campuses were much more open then. He could've damn near walked in on the pretense of doing maintenance or delivering lunch to a student as a parent," Vinnie said, thinking through the theory.

"But how did he know Dunlap would be at the football game?" Holly chimed in.

"Because he always was." Johnny went back to his notes. "Violet Sanders said Dunlap was always hanging around the dances, games—any event, even after hours. If Meng was on the campus at a football game, he would have seen Dunlap there. We know he was there that night, because he took Melanie's coat and hat. He must've marked where Dunlap was and decided to use her coat and hat to get close to him."

"A football game on a Friday night would have been a great way to hide in the open," Worth said, still tapping his pencil, although the tempo increased. Something was bothering him, but he wanted to let his crew work through this.

"So he was concerned that Dunlap would bring the hammer down on his operation running girls if Melanie spoke with him. That's why he asked her up front before he stole her coat and hat. But," Holly paused, "why not just kill Melanie?"

"Maybe he thought she could be turned and put into his stable," Vinnie said, "or maybe he didn't think she was a real threat but was convinced Dunlap would find out eventually because he saw them together a lot." Vinnie looked at Johnny, who was running the scenarios through his head.

"Melanie broke Meng's nose. He knew he'd never get her into his stable without a fight, which he didn't want," Johnny said. "So he scares her, makes certain she knows he's watching her, then, in one step, insures that she will not talk and takes out the only person she probably would tell if given the chance. He knew she was a runaway. That's how he met her."

Worth cleared his throat. Everyone looked at him and stopped speaking. "All viable theories, but we have nothing to tie Meng to the murder of Officer Mike Dunlap. No gun, no eyewitness, no forensic evidence. If Meng were here right now, all Johnny could do was interview him and try for a confession."

The fact that Worth still saw this as Johnny's case, even though it had taken on a new, broader life, was comforting to Johnny. It was also a bit unnerving.

Paschal's shaking head caught everyone's attention. "You get Meng in an interview room, he will say absolutely nothing," he said. "You need to find another way. He's been detained a few times by German, Irish, and Chinese officials. His silence is the only reason he is still around. If they got a confession out of him for some of the crimes he's accused of, he'd have been dead a long time ago."

"Do we know if he's still alive?" Worth asked. "After all, being whacked in his line of business and with the company he keeps is an occupational hazard."

"Everything we have right now, Major, indicates he's still alive. I'm putting out some inquiries to see if anyone knows if he's in the States," Paschal said.

"Great. Thanks, Lieutenant." Johnny's voice betrayed the true optimism he held.

"Don't get your hopes up, Johnny. If he is here, he's probably not using his real name. If he is outside the United States, assuming you can find him, it will be difficult to get him back." Paschal was trying to be realistic without sounding like a pessimist.

"Let's hope for the best." Worth put down his pencil and started giving assignments. "Johnny, you get a list of Meng's aliases and keep running them every way you can. Holly, check your DEA contacts. See if Meng is currently on their radar. He could be selling drugs now. Do the same with the FBI and ATF. Sales are sales. Vinnie, see if any BOLOs of abductions from that time period match Meng. The area Maureen mentioned was a no-man's-land for runaways back then. If he was abducting and selling girls, someone may have described him to our detectives or beat units. Maybe someone tracked down some information on him that might help us now."

Paschal asked Worth, "Can you authorize protective custody? Whether or not Meng is in the country, she is too critical a witness to risk her getting a case of the rabbit. Her daughter is in boarding school, and usually tuition is paid up front. So if she decides her daughter is safe through the end of the school year, she could get gone pretty easily."

"Johnny?" Worth asked.

"Agreed, Major. The DA would definitely get us a material witness warrant in a heartbeat, if we need it."

"Let's try to do it voluntarily." Worth looked at Paschal. "Take her with you tonight and keep me and Till posted on where she is and how she's doing. We'll handle it in-house for forty-eight hours, then get the US Marshals involved if we need to keep her in custody longer than that."

"I've also got some contacts out of state to stash her safely. Just let me know," Paschal said, then picked up his phone and called two of his undercover agents to get them to the Homicide Unit.

"Anything else, Detective Till?" Worth asked, smiling at Johnny.

"Sure, Major. Let's shake the trees and see if Meng falls out. Sounds like that won't be easy."

"Exactly." Worth picked up his phone to brief Chief Porter. "And it never is. Be patient. It could take a while." He looked at Paschal, who was taking notes and shaking his head. "Am I missing something, Danny?"

Paschal instantly looked up. His time in the police department and the military instilled in him a need to be intentional and blunt with bad news. "Major, assuming he is alive, assuming he is in the United States, and assuming we can find him," he looked around at Johnny and Holly, "all big ifs. You're right. He's a professional. You'll need something tangible and rock solid to nail him for Mike Dunlap's murder. A guy like Meng doesn't make mistakes. If he killed Dunlap, you're probably right about the theory of tying up a loose end. But," he paused, "he would've planned it from soup to nuts, including his exit, avoiding any evidence that would link him later, and the incredible heat the murder of a cop would bring. He could've been caught by sheer accident from the overwhelming police presence in the area in the days and weeks after Dunlap's murder."

"But he wasn't," Johnny said. He also glanced at Worth, who looked frustrated to come close to finding the man who killed Dunlap only to possibly see the opportunity vanish. "You're telling us to be meticulous," Johnny said to Paschal.

"Meticulous and careful. The number of people who have killed a cop and not been caught quickly is extremely small, an elite fraternity. He didn't escape and avoid us for this long because he's stupid. Add to the fact that if you start on a lead and his bosses find out he's wanted, he may be dead before you even put your eyes on him. You're going to need solid evidence, timing, and—"

"Luck." Detectives often joked about it, but when the word came from Worth's mouth, it put a chill in the air. He looked at the detectives who respected him and smiled. "We're due some luck in this one. Now go find his ass and the evidence that will put him in the chair."

"Roger that," Johnny said, "on both counts."

Bill Worth watched Johnny walk toward the door. "Till, hold up a minute." Johnny stopped and let everyone exit Major Worth's office. When they were alone, Worth motioned to him to walk out a door behind Worth's desk. "I want to show you something."

They went through the door into a staircase and started climbing. Two floors later, they reached a hatch marked ROOF ACCESS: AUTHORIZED PERSONNEL ONLY. A short ladder led to the hatch. Worth started climbing the ladder, then looked back at Johnny. "You're authorized. Come on."

Johnny climbed the ladder as Worth opened the hatch, which creaked in staunch objection to his efforts. The men walked out onto the roof, and Johnny followed

Worth to the north side that looked out upon green space, some buildings, and a lot of houses. Looking north, they could see the red flashing lights on the radio tower on top of Kennesaw Mountain, and turning south, the bright lights of the city seemed to drown out the stars.

As they looked out, both were quiet. Worth spoke first. "I come up here every once in a while. I can point to about twenty homicide locations by memory." He paused and looked at Johnny. "Where do you think the next five will be?"

"No idea. If I knew, I'd do something to try to prevent them," Johnny answered.

"Exactly, but you can't prevent all of them, and there's no way to predict where the next one will be any more than you can predict how they will be killed, why, or the names of the perpetrators. That, Johnny, is the reality of a homicide detective's life. We don't pick the crimes we investigate or the circumstances that led to people's deaths. As to the next five, we may solve all in a day, or you and I may be looking at the site of the next cold case—the next whodunit that frustrates homicide detectives at Lawlor PD for fifty years," Worth continued.

"If that's the case, that doesn't mean those detectives didn't work hard, weren't smart, or didn't have the tools needed to solve them. There are simply more reasons for murder, more ways to kill, and more stories and ways to cover it up than there are homicide detectives." Johnny was still looking out. "Catching murderers makes the headlines, Johnny, but the job is hunting killers. Sometimes, people do get away with murder."

"Seems like a big job, especially in Dunlap's case. I just

hope I'm up to it." Johnny ran his hands over his face and sighed.

"I could see that the weight of this case is getting to you." Worth looked Johnny in the eyes. "That's normal. Every case will do that. If I had a second thought about your determination and abilities, I'd have Biggers and Rostavic taking over as lead, and you'd be running errands for them."

Johnny nodded. "There's a lot riding on this case for the department, Anna Dunlap, Maureen Roberts . . ."

"And you?" Worth smiled and put his hand on Johnny's shoulder. "Have some faith in Johnny Till. We do."

Johnny nodded and looked out into the darkness for a moment more before he turned to follow Worth back to the hatch.

CHAPTER 24

T he next day, Holly walked into the office and found Johnny at his desk. "I'm early. You're just insane! How long have you been here . . . or have you left since we spoke with Paschal?"

Johnny smiled but didn't look up. "I went home, but I was working there, too."

"Meng?"

"Damn right. Paschal wasn't kidding. This guy is like a dust storm. When he is active, he's deadly, and when he's not, he's in the wind without a single fucking trace."

"Got anyone else on it?" Holly asked.

"Not on my end. I was encouraged to let Paschal work his magic with what Worth called 'other resources,' so I'm sticking to my own efforts."

"Good plan. Paschal is one of the best. Rumor is, he has ties in every federal agency, even the ones that don't exist." Holly smiled.

"I'll take help from any source to bring this one home." Johnny looked at the murder board. "I can't wait to put this case down."

Holly picked up her backpack from the half wall of Johnny's cubicle. "You know, somehow I believe you have the smarts to get it done." Johnny looked up at her. "You've certainly moved the needle farther than anyone else," she said. Johnny sat a bit taller in his chair. The reality of her statement hit him for the first time.

Eager to change the subject, and concerned he was turning red, he spoke up as he moved his eyes back to his computer screen. "Still on to come with me this morning?"

"Yep. I'll meet you in the parking lot. I need to check on something before we go."

"Alone?" Johnny asked.

"It's just a subpoena for surveillance video on a homicide I picked up. Thanks, though."

"See you then." With that, Johnny was back in the database he was searching. Holly walked to her desk and got her day started.

* * *

At five minutes to ten, Holly was parking in front of headquarters when Johnny came out and got into her car. "Where to now?" Holly asked, looking at her watch.

"Gotta knock out the hardest interview we'll have in this case."

"Damn. How did she take your call?"

"Anna Dunlap is the polite woman I expected. Let's just hope she's patient, as well," Johnny said.

Holly and Johnny drove the twelve miles out of town to pick up the interstate. As they headed south on I-75 toward the river, Johnny punched the street address into the GPS in Holly's car.

"What did she say when you called her?"

"Well," Johnny said, "she was much more gracious

than I expected. She interrupted me after I introduced myself and asked me if I'd checked out Dunlap's cold case file. When I said I had, she just told me to come by and ask her whatever I wanted. It was sad, really. She seemed to be just going through the motions."

"Has everyone who checked out Dunlap's file met with her?" Holly glanced over at Johnny.

"Not all, but most. Some were focused on associations, others on finances. I bet those were tough questions."

"No doubt," Holly agreed.

"I don't blame them, though. As time's passed, the theories have grown broader. Somehow, I got the impression that she's learned not to take it personally. I'm pretty sure she was looked at a few times as a potential suspect," Johnny said.

"As a cop's wife, she probably expected that."

"She had a strong alibi that no one was able to break. Go ten miles on Forsyth Street, then a left onto Rackland Avenue." Johnny paused. "You haven't told me anything about your current cold case."

"Compared to yours, it's vanilla. Prostitute found dead near a dive bar. No ID, no jewelry, no tats. All we have is a partial set of teeth."

"Partial set. Interesting. No fingerprints?"

"Not on file. Strange for a prostitute, I know. Anyway, she was found dead and the case went cold. I keep hoping one day I can tell her family what happened to her."

"Yep. At least that's something."

"Gotta be better than wondering for the rest of your life," Holly said.

"Not so sure," Johnny replied. "There is hope in not knowing."

"And a lot of pain." Holly made the turn onto Rackland and another onto Westwind Court. She pulled into the driveway of Anna Dunlap's house and asked, "Is this where they lived together, or is it a new place?"

"Same one. She's never left. Three years ago, one of the detectives who picked up the case said he found Dunlap's clothes and uniforms still hanging in the closets."

"Wow. Can't imagine." Holly shook her head.

They walked to the front door and stood in front of it. They knew she would look prior to opening the door. Standing off to the side as usual would appear rude to a cop's widow.

She smiled at them as she opened the door. "Please, come in, Detective Till."

"Johnny. This is my partner, Holly Forrester."

"Holly." The detective extended her hand, and Anna Dunlap shook it.

"Welcome, both of you. Please come into the kitchen. I brewed some fresh iced tea. I hope you'll have some," Anna offered.

"That would be great," Holly replied with a smile.

They sat at the table, and Anna poured three glasses of tea. Then she put out a plate of cookies. She sat down, looked at the table in front of her, then spoke in a calm, even tone. "Johnny, Holly, I know this is hard for both of you. Let me help by saying that I believe all of the hard questions have been asked. 'Was Mike having an affair?' 'Did you two argue that day?' 'Was I thinking of leaving?' I've heard it all. So don't be embarrassed or hesitant. The three of us have one common goal: to find out who murdered my husband on November 4, 1998, and bring them to a courtroom to stand trial."

"I truly appreciate that, Mrs. Dunlap," Johnny said with a slight smile.

"Anna. I insist."

"Okay, Anna."

Anna looked at Johnny. Her big, brown eyes and slim face bore the weight of pain, worry, and on some level, fear. Despite the support of a grieving department and a grateful community, she still faced many days and nights alone.

I can only imagine how it is to know that his killer is still out there, Johnny thought. *Some burdens break people slowly, like sand pouring into a sack on their backs one grain at a time. At some point, they get used to it . . . until they collapse under the weight.*

"Anna," Johnny began, "I pulled Mike's case to work on."

Anna smiled. "A cold case on the murder of a cop. You're a brave man, Johnny."

Johnny smiled a little and said, "I'm going through the case, reorganizing the information, and using some of the more modern tools we have today that were not available back then. My goal is to solve it, but—"

"But if you can't, you want to give someone else a better shot at doing so," Anna interrupted. "Good plan. And admirable, if you ask me." She took a sip of her tea. "So many detectives took up this case. First, they were mainly Mike's friends in the department. Then it was a string of guys about to retire who were looking for one last chance to solve 'the big one.' As the years passed and we became a cold case, I was frankly just surprised when someone new picked up the case."

"We" became a cold case. Interesting. Johnny took a sip of tea and watched Anna do the same. *I guess she has earned the right to be a bit cynical.*

Holly let some time pass before she spoke. "It's clear that you've never lost hope, Anna. That's comforting to me."

Anna looked at Holly and smiled. "Sometimes, hope is all you have as a cop's wife. Hope that he will come home every day, hope that we'll make ends meet at the end of the month, hope that he'll decide to do something else." She looked up to the ceiling. "All I have now is hope that you'll catch the son of a bitch who murdered my husband." She took a moment and wiped her eyes. "I'm sorry. The anger comes out sometimes. I try to keep it out of the equation, but between grief and anger . . ."

"Tough choice," Holly responded.

Anna chuckled. "I guess anger helps you work out and grief makes you want to stay on the couch!" Johnny and Holly smiled. "Maybe I should write a book and use that as the title."

Anna took a cookie off the plate and broke it in half. She never took a bite. As she stared at it, Johnny started again. "Anna, time is a funny thing. Some people think that memory only fades with time. I disagree. I think sometimes, time can help us forget the things that aren't important, and all that remains are the good memories and the key facts and details that we've decided to hang on to."

Anna Dunlap picked up her head and stared at Johnny. After an uncomfortable pause, she spoke, and Johnny saw a tear run down her right cheek. "You've lost someone—someone close to you—like I did, unexpectedly."

Holly looked at her partner, who did not break Anna's gaze. She saw something on his face she'd never seen before: vulnerability. She wondered if she should break the silence, rescue him. In any other victim interview, she would have stepped in and put an end to it. Yet this was not just any victim interview. Holly had been holding back her tears for the past fifteen minutes.

Johnny finally broke from Anna's gaze and looked down. "My dad. We got a visit from an army chaplain and a member of his US Special Forces Command. They came to my school with my mom. I was called to the principal's office, and they told me he was never coming home."

The silence at the table was both deafening and healing. They simply drank their tea and passed the box of tissues. When the time was right, Johnny leaned forward. "Anna, I'm not going to push you or ask you to rehash what you've told people in the past. I've been through the file. I just want you to tell me those things that are still stuck in your mind, the thoughts and concerns that will not go away."

"I'll do it, Johnny, I will. But put everything you have into this. I don't know how many times I can meet with a new set of detectives about this case. So promise me that."

"You have my word, Anna."

CHAPTER 25

Holly and Johnny drove back to Lawler PD quietly. Neither of them spoke for about fifteen minutes, which was very unusual. Finally, as they got through the city traffic and onto the four-lane highway, Holly broke the silence.

"I keep wondering what we can do to dive back into the hours and days before Dunlap died with a different perspective. It's not going to be easy. That was a long time ago. Missing the first forty-eight hours is a bitch."

Johnny was shaking his head. "There really is no way to do it. At least, not in the traditional sense. We can't trace his steps or line up the people who spoke with him and watch their body language. Too much time has passed. Besides, some damn good detectives did that already. No. We've got to find a way to use the tools we have that they did not."

"Good luck with that." Holly waved her hand. "The pager thing is a dead end. We had a few dealers still using them when I worked in Narcs. They thought it was old school and would keep us from tracking them. They didn't know we could get a duplicate with a warrant and receive all the same numbers. The retro feel wore off of the trend when we busted a few, but the pagers were a pain in the ass. It was much harder to triangulate a location from the calls, and they weren't supported by a lot of technology. Compared to our cell phones, they were like two cans connected with string. Very simple technology."

"I'm thinking something different that might let us take advantage of the time that has passed."

Holly turned to Johnny. "Okay, you've got me interested."

"The evidence from the Dunlap case is sealed. I looked through the file and no one ever combed the clothes looking for trace DNA, fibers, or hair samples that didn't match Dunlap's."

"It may be preserved, but those clothes have been handled a lot—the first officers at the scene, the paramedics, firefighters, a bunch of folks. There were pretty rudimentary protocols in place then. You don't think someone has checked for DNA on this case yet? Not likely."

"I know, but the crime lab is always coming up with better ways to sample or test the samples we have. Like any technology, it increases exponentially once it's available. As for the people who handled the evidence, we can or should be able to exclude all of them. I know some of them may be out of the business or retired, but at least we can track them down."

Holly was quietly considering the possibility when Johnny started up again.

"Think about this. Whose DNA would you expect to find on Dunlap's uniform? Not as a whole, but in parts that not everyone would touch."

"You mean, like, away from his sleeves?" Holly asked.

"Right. People might brush by him in the hallways,

but the top of his collar, the middle of his chest, those areas would be reserved for more personal contact."

"They also would be touched by every EMT who got to the scene," she thought out loud.

"The back of his uniform is not likely to give us anything because he fell onto it and was lying on the ground. There's no telling what was on the ground that night. That's why they didn't vacuum the scene."

"What about the other side of the equation?"

"You've lost me, Holly."

"What about Dunlap's efforts to reach others that night and the days prior? House has a point that it only takes a little effort to get close to a cop, but I keep thinking about the relationship House said Dunlap had with the kids. He went to their houses, brought them back to school, and House said if they weren't home, Dunlap knew where to find them."

Johnny was quiet, his mind reflecting on House's words. "Okay, so if you're a school resource officer with the ability to find kids who are truant but not home, how do you keep track of their usual hideouts?"

"Kids probably tell you. You might also rely on parents, an occasional teacher in the know, and maybe on the Intelligence Unit at the PD."

"What about a database? Do you think he had one?" Johnny asked.

"I'm sure they checked his computer," Holly replied, "especially the second time through, as House said."

"Dunlap seemed like an old-school guy to me. The pager was issued to him. I saw that in the file. He didn't have his own, even though a lot of guys did back then."

"What are you thinking, a notebook?"

"The department issued them back then, including

diaries and calendars. Some of the guys in Homicide still use them. I watched Worth walk around with one open on a scene last week," Johnny observed.

"The major came out on a scene?" She smiled.

"Yeah. It was the officer-involved shooting with the deputy from the Lawler Sheriff's Office last week. The deputy showed up at a house to serve a misdemeanor theft warrant, and his knock on the door interrupted a drug deal. Two perps ran, and one fired twice through the front door. I guess he didn't know the deputy was standing to the side of the door. His last mistake was opening the door to finish off the deputy."

"Why didn't you call me, if you worked it?" Holly looked at Johnny. She was clearly upset that she missed out on something.

"I didn't. I responded because I was close, and so did Worth. Vinnie and Lieutenant Biggers caught it. Worth stuck around long enough to meet with the sheriff and decide who was working what."

Holly thought for a moment. "Sounds like you know the file pretty well. Did they find a notebook in Dunlap's personal property?"

"One on his person and several in his patrol car. I remember they went through them, but I need to review the file to see what they found and what they tracked down."

"You mean you don't have it memorized?" Holly smiled.

"Not hardly, but thanks for the vote of confidence. I do know just where to go, though. I'll hit it as soon as I get back to the office."

They drove for a few more minutes and were close to the office when they heard a call go out on the radio.

"Any unit in the area of Warren Road and Fisher Parkway, we have a silent alarm at the Community City Bank. A customer in the parking lot called 911 reporting three men entering the bank wearing brown clothing, ball caps, and sunglasses. He reported one of them was armed."

Holly grabbed the microphone. "825 and 830, we are about two away and responding. Advise uniform units we are in plain clothes."

"Roger, 825. Stand by for updates." The radio lit up with other units broadcasting their response times and locations. It was clear that Holly and Johnny were the closest by several minutes.

Johnny never hit the siren to avoid creating a hostage situation. He remembered what the instructors in the academy told him: "Get them out of the building if at all possible." As Johnny turned the corner behind the bank, he and Holly got out. Holly spoke into her portable radio and advised they were on the scene.

They put on their body armor and Johnny grabbed his patrol rifle. He handed Holly the shotgun, and they started walking across the parking lot toward the rear of the bank, using the cars in the parking lot as cover and concealment. The bank was an outparcel in a shopping center with a grocery store as an anchor. As they passed people walking in the parking lot, they told them to leave. A few of them asked the question that every street cop has been asked when running toward a scene with a gun out: "Is something going on?"

They heard the radio even though they had the volume down as low as possible. "825 and 830, be advised we have a witness in the parking lot at the front of the bank on the line. He advises that the suspects are about to come out of the bank. All three are armed—two with long guns and one with a handgun."

Holly spoke into her portable, "Which side of the bank, and does he see a vehicle waiting for them?"

"Stand by." The radio was silent for a moment, then came back to life as Holly and Johnny were about fifteen yards from the bank. They were behind an unoccupied pickup truck with a full view of the two southern corners of the building. "The witness advises that the suspects are walking south toward the back of the bank. He does not see a vehicle related to them."

Johnny took up a position kneeling behind the front driver's corner of the truck. Holly was behind him, leaning over the hood but still behind the engine. Johnny whispered, "The only car I see is that blue sedan, but I don't see anyone behind the wheel."

Holly stared at the car. "Look at the tailpipe. It's running." The car was parked parallel to the side of the bank in a legal parking spot. "You hear the description, Johnny. They're pros."

"Roger that." As he spoke, they saw the three men walking almost casually toward the running sedan. As they approached, Johnny heard three uniform patrol units announce they were on the scene on the north side of the bank. While Johnny was concerned about a crossfire, he was also acutely aware that he and Holly were likely all that stood between the bad guys and an escape. Dangerous men on the move were deadly. He also saw that the building behind the robbers' vehicle was solid brick, no windows. He heard Holly giving out the description of the sedan and the suspects. When she was done, Johnny spoke quickly: "You ready?"

"Go!"

"POLICE! DROP YOUR WEAPONS!" They both shouted loudly from their positions behind the truck. The three robbers stopped and looked around, trying to determine where the voices came from. Although they were both concealed, the pickup truck was the only vehicle close to them that the robbers could not see both sides of. The lead robber, closest to the driver's door of the sedan, leveled his rifle and started shooting. The other two took cover behind the sedan and scanned for other cops.

The cops on the other side of the building yelled, "Shots fired!" into their radios as they worked to maneuver behind the bank. One officer ducked behind the wheel of his patrol car and pulled it up to block the exit at the south side of the building. The robbers were likely trapped. He then bailed out of the driver's door as two of the robbers began shooting at the marked unit. Johnny and Holly took advantage of the redirected fire and put their heads up.

As Johnny took aim, the movement of the robbers seemed to slow to a crawl. He felt himself pull the trigger, but only heard the sound of his heart pounding. He moved the rifle to stay on target but was puzzled by the lack of noise when he pulled the trigger.

Is something wrong with this gun?

As he focused, his peripheral vision caught brass being ejected from the rifle. It seemed to spin and dance in the air, as if gravity had no effect. Still, his heart boomed in his ears like a huge bass drum to the exclusion of every other sound.

Johnny's first three shots hit the robber closest to the front of the sedan in the chest. The rounds made him stumble back against the wall, but he still held his rifle and began to raise it again. Johnny fired three more times, and the robber fell to the ground.

Holly had directed her fire to the second robber, who was shooting at the patrol car. She shot three times, and the first round of buckshot penetrated both windows in the rear of the sedan. A few of the pellets struck the robber, who did not react. The second and third blast caught him straight in the chest, and he doubled up, but he kept firing.

"Body armor!" Holly yelled.

Johnny took a bead on the side of the head of the second robber as he tried to crouch down behind the engine of the sedan and then fired. The round struck the robber in the temple, painting a grotesque pattern on the white brick of the bank wall. The blood seemed to spray for minutes instead of a fraction of a second, and Johnny found himself thinking that blood spatter would be on the news that night and on the wall forever.

As the second robber fell, the third began firing and running toward the front door of the bank. Holly fired at him, knowing the brick wall would provide a safe back stop for the pellets. She aimed low, trying to take his legs out from under him. *No body armor on your legs, asshole,* she thought.

Johnny tried to get a clear sight picture on the third robber but couldn't do so from in front of the truck. He elected to keep covering the two suspects on the ground. Johnny yelled to the officer on the other side of the patrol car, who was about twenty feet away, "Can you see him? Is he down?"

The officer did not respond, and Johnny feared the worst.

The first pattern of pellets hit the third suspect, but he barely slowed. As Holly prepared to fire the last round from the shotgun, the suspect started to approach the front of the bank. That's when Holly heard a volley of rounds, at least eight. As the robber stopped in midstride, she heard a final shot and watched the back of the robber's head blow away. He fell to the ground. A man in plain clothes approached the robber and kicked his gun away. Then, he took a position at the corner of the bank, using the wall for cover.

"Three suspects down!" Johnny yelled.

Holly advised radio to send EMS and asked all officers on the scene to check in with radio. A patrol sergeant approached the south side of the bank with a rifle in his hands and ran in a low crouch toward the patrol car blocking the south-side exit that was riddled with bullet holes. He crouched down out of the sight of Johnny and began yelling into his radio, "Officer down! Send EMS to the south entrance! CPR in progress!"

As Johnny watched, a group of four uniformed officers approached the downed officer and provided cover as he was dragged to another patrol car that pulled up with the back door open. The sergeant pulled the injured officer on top of himself and lay back in the back seat of the patrol car. The car quickly took off toward the south entrance to the shopping center.

Then the four patrol officers began to advance on the two downed suspects. They handcuffed them and announced when they were both in custody and that the car was cleared. As soon as they did, Holly saw two uniformed officers approach the front corner of the bank and handcuff the third suspect. The man in plain clothes holstered his weapon as the officers took the third suspect into custody.

Holly and Johnny came out from behind the truck and checked themselves for injuries. Johnny had some cuts on his face from flying glass, likely from the headlight of the truck. Fortunately, he was wearing sunglasses that protected his eyes. Holly was uninjured.

Holly spoke into her portable. "Radio, confirm with the bank that the interior is secure."

"Stand by, 825." As Holly and Johnny walked toward the front of the bank, the radio came to life again. "825, be advised that all personnel inside the bank are secure and safe. Password received from bank security. All units, the bank is safe to enter."

"Clear. Send a crime-scene unit and notify the chain of command. Several officers involved in the gunfight with the suspects. We will need units to close off the shopping center and canvass for witnesses and any injuries. Suspects were shooting toward the parking lot when they engaged us."

"825, do you have eyes on the witness who called 911? We lost contact. Is he okay?"

"Stand by, radio." Holly approached the man who shot and killed the third suspect. He was wearing street clothes and was staring at the now-handcuffed third suspect, who was obviously dead. "Are you okay?"

The man was shaking. Holly had to walk up and touch his arm to get him to respond. When she touched him, he jumped and looked at her. Holly had seen that look before. It was sheer terror.

"Are you okay? I'm Detective Holly Forrester. What agency do you work for?"

The man finally seemed to focus on her. "I'm not a cop. I'm okay, I guess." He paused and took a deep breath. "There were people in the parking lot. A woman with two kids was in a minivan next to me. If he got past me, he could have carjacked them."

"It's okay. You're safe now." Holly looked at the front

of the bank and saw a woman hugging two small children. They were standing beside a minivan parked next to a small pickup truck. "Is that your blue pickup?"

"Yes, ma'am. I was going to go into the bank when I saw the robbers go in. I called 911 and gave the operator information. I figured I could just stay in my truck and wait. I never figured they'd start shooting at y'all." The man was weak in the knees.

"Are you okay?"

Then he looked at Holly. "Oh, my God. I killed him."

Holly put her right hand on his left shoulder. "Come on. Let's go sit on the tailgate of your truck and wait. There's no need for you to stand here." She stood in front of the man to block his view of the dead robber.

Johnny walked up as Holly moved the man away. He took note of where the man was standing and walked toward him. "You probably saved some lives, sir."

The man stared at Johnny, barely registering the words. Suddenly, the man responded, "Are you okay? You're bleeding! I've got a first-aid kit in my truck."

Johnny had wiped away the blood from his face but underestimated how much a facial wound will bleed. He wiped his face again. "It's okay. I'll get one of the EMTs to take a look at it when they can."

"Is your officer okay?" The man spoke softly as Holly lowered the gate of his truck so he could sit.

Holly and Johnny looked at each other. Neither one of them wanted to answer. Finally, Holly spoke. It appeared she was gaining a rapport with the man. "They're getting him to the hospital. Hopefully, he'll be okay. Are you hurt?"

Just then, it occurred to the man that he might have been shot and killed. "I guess so. Do you see any blood on me? I mean, I'm so flipped out right now, I can barely feel anything. I guess I don't feel like I'm injured."

Holly took a minute or two to look at his head and scan down. She did not see anything except some white dust on his chest.

"Don't wipe it away, but you have some brick dust on your chest. We'll get someone to photograph it."

"Brick dust? From where? How?"

Johnny looked at the man's chest. "It's from the corner of the building. I saw a few nicks in the wall when I walked up."

"You mean he was shooting at me?" The man's eyes got big.

"Well, he was shooting, but he may have been trying to keep other cops away from the front of the building so he could jack someone and get a car." Johnny looked at Holly. She knew that he was signaling her to take over.

"What's your name?" Holly asked.

"Jake Moretta. My real name is John Kenneth, but everyone knows me as Jake."

"Is there anyone you want to call, Jake? A family member, a pastor, a lawyer?"

"A lawyer? Do I need one? He was trying to kill all of you!"

Holly pointed at Johnny, who had walked a few feet away and was talking on his phone. "He's calling our police lawyers. It's okay. You did nothing wrong. In fact, you probably saved a lot of lives. If he got into a car, there would have been a chase and more gunfire. If he got to that woman and her children, they never would've lived through it." She paused. "You stopped him. As long as you legally own the gun, you're fine."

"Yes, ma'am. I've got a concealed-weapon license. I

never thought I'd have to shoot anyone." Jake looked down and started to tear up.

Holly put her hand on his shoulder again. "No one ever does, Jake. I'm glad you were armed and willing to help. It's okay. Just let your emotions come out."

Jake had started to breathe in short breaths. "How are you so calm?"

Holly smiled. "Don't confuse training and experience for calm. I'm about to shake myself to pieces. I just don't want to do it in front of everyone."

As they sat there, the woman near the minivan walked up. "I'm Rose Herndon. I saw everything. I was afraid to leave and made my kids lie down on the floor of the van. Are you okay? Is he okay?"

Holly patted Jake's shoulder. "He'll be okay." It was a bit of a lie. Holly knew Jake Moretta would never be the same. "We'll need to get your name and information. I don't have a notepad with me, but one of the detectives will speak with you. Can you stay here for a bit?" Holly also knew that while Rose believed that she saw everything, and did see a lot of important events, she could not have seen anything that occurred on the south side of the bank.

"Of course. Can I speak with him?" she said as she pointed to Jake. Rose walked closer to Jake. She reached out and touched his left hand as her eyes filled with tears. She tried to speak, but nothing came out. She took a deep breath, then tried again. "You are a very brave man. You saved my children. I can never repay you for what you did. Thank you." Jake stood, and she tucked under his arm for a hug.

Johnny was on the phone with Major Worth, who was on the way to the scene. Johnny also called Joe Amorini, an attorney for the Fraternal Order of Police, for him and for Holly. He'd carried Amorini's card in his wallet for years. He called him once before when a suspect accused him of stealing money from his wallet. When the suspect was proven to be lying, Amorini successfully sued him for slander on Johnny's behalf. Johnny never forgot the dedication he showed. This would be a long scene, and per protocol, the shooting would be presented to a grand jury. Johnny hated that he had to think about a lawyer right now, but that was the reality of policing.

Johnny's conversation with Worth was short. As expected, Worth wanted to confirm that he and Holly were okay and if any other officers were injured. Johnny explained about the one officer who was down, and Worth promised to try to get an update.

As Johnny walked back to Holly and Jake, Rose walked to Johnny and told him he was bleeding. A lieutenant walked up to Johnny and told him to have a seat on the gate of the pickup truck. He then called for and waved to a paramedic unit that was parked on the curb to the south side of the bank. Two paramedics came up and started to examine Johnny. There were several pieces of glass embedded in his skin; a few were deep.

"You'll have to get to the ER. Can you drive yourself, or do you want us to take you?"

"Not in my car," Johnny said. "It will be inside the crime-scene tape. When my major gets here, he'll have someone run me down there. Can you put something on it for now?"

"Sure." The paramedic dug around in his bag and made a dressing and bandage for Johnny's forehead and cheek. He then had Johnny sign a treatment sheet and refusal of transport. As he was finishing up, Worth pulled to the curb. He was a commanding presence and showed no signs of stress. Johnny knew he had the respect of a lot of Lawler PD troops, and he understood why in that moment.

When Worth hung up his phone, he was approached by a patrol captain and lieutenant and briefed about the situation. He then took command and gave several instructions. Johnny heard him address both of them by their first names.

Worth approached them and for the first time looked concerned as he saw the bandages on Johnny's face. "You both okay?"

"Yes, sir," Holly answered. "Johnny caught some glass, but thank God we're both okay."

Johnny looked at Worth. "It looks worse than it is."

"I hope so," Worth answered. "Glass?"

"From the headlight, most likely. I was crouched behind the front of an old pickup truck. How's our officer?"

Worth didn't respond. He looked at Jake Moretta and extended his hand. "I'm Major Bill Worth with the Lawler Police. You must be Moretta."

Jake put out his hand. "Yes, sir."

"I've heard some preliminary information, and the captain on the scene reviewed the 911 recordings and the security footage from the front and side of the bank. Thank you for protecting my officers."

Jake was shocked. He really wasn't sure what to expect, but a thank-you from law enforcement was not high on his list. "I did what any of you would have done for me and my family, sir." Jake was quiet. "Am I going to be taken into custody?"

"Not a chance, Jake, but someone will be taking your weapon. Please understand that's routine. It's evidence.

We'll get it checked for ballistics, and I'll push as hard as I can to get the state folks to return it to you ASAP."

"I appreciate it. This is my competition gun."

"IPSC?" Worth asked, curious about the type of competition.

"IDPA," Jake responded, but he seemed a bit shocked. "I like the focus on 'real world' self-defense shooting."

Johnny and Holly had not missed the fact that Worth ignored their question about the downed officer. They took the hint, and without speaking a word understood that this was not the time to follow up.

"Please excuse us, Jake, but I need to borrow Detectives Forrester and Till for a moment." He waved, and Vinnie Rostavic came over. "Jake, this is Sergeant Vladimir Rostavic."

"Vinnie," he said as he extended his hand to Jake. "Can I get you some water or a cup of coffee?"

"Water would be great. I feel like I swallowed a bucket of sand."

"You got it. Stand by." Vinnie walked to a bank security officer who had arrived a few moments before. The man spoke with Vinnie, then went into the bank. Vinnie then walked back to Jake as Worth was speaking.

"Jake, Vinnie will be staying with you. We do not leave people alone after they're involved in a shooting. It's for a couple of reasons, one of which is chain of evidence. So Vinnie will be with you and can get you anything you need. We have pastors and counselors we can call through the police department, and Vinnie can arrange that. If you need some time alone or if you have an attorney who arrives, Vinnie will give you some space, but he will be with you until you are released by the special agents with the state." Jake nodded as the bank security officer walked up to them with a handful of cold water bottles. "Did I miss anything, Vinnie?"

"No, Bill. You did a great job." Vinnie was smiling. He had worked with Worth for many years. The two of them instantly took cues from each other to avoid rank around Jake to keep him from feeling uncomfortable. "I'll take care of him."

Worth, Holly, and Johnny shook hands with Jake and then walked toward Worth's car. As they spoke, they saw the Lawler PD command vehicle pull into the parking lot behind the bank. It was a large RV that had been seized from a drug dealer. A sign on the back advertised that fact. When they got to Worth's car out of earshot of anyone, Worth asked if they were still doing okay.

"My ears have started ringing," Johnny said.

"That's a good sign," Holly said. "After my first shooting, it took a while to even hear the ringing."

Johnny had no idea Holly had been involved in a shooting, and it appeared she had been involved in more than one.

"From what I understand, both of you did some good work and definitely kept these jokers from getting away."

"Yes, sir," Johnny said. "Any one of us would have done the same thing. The real hero is Jake. I had no clear shot when that guy ran, and Holly had hit him several times with buckshot."

"My last safe shot at him was with the bank as a backstop. Once he crossed in front, I would have been forced to leave cover to go after him. I think Jake stopped him from carjacking that woman and her kids, or someone else."

"That's what everyone says, and a quick peek the

bank video backs it up. All the uniform patrol units were on the back and south side of the bank. The perps weren't able to get in the front door. A well-trained manager locked the door as soon as they left."

"That took some guts," Johnny volunteered.

"I'll bet she's been robbed before," Holly said.

"I'll put money on it, Holly," Worth said. "Now, about the downed officer. His name is Joe Turner. He's a master patrol officer with twenty-five years in. I was speaking with the chief as I drove up. She's at the hospital. Apparently, Turner took a round in the neck from one of the perps. It was a high-velocity round. He went into shock and probably suffered a cardiac arrhythmia. When they got him out of the line of fire, one of the patrol officers retrieved an automatic defibrillator from the pharmacy in the strip center behind the bank. They brought him back, and he's breathing on his own. He's lost a lot of blood, but he's got a bunch of folks ready to donate if the Red Cross runs out."

"How did the officer know there was an AED in the pharmacy? Lucky guess, or does he shop there?" Johnny asked.

"Well, when they got him out of the line of fire, the officers put him on the parking lot and started CPR again. One of the pharmacists came running out of the building in a low crouch waving the AED. I spoke with Sergeant Sam Alexander. He said the pharmacist thought they were under fire but ran out anyway. She hooked up the AED while they continued chest compressions and then fired it up. Turner came back a few minutes later and was conscious when the ambulance took him to the hospital."

"Sometimes the planets line up," Johnny said, shaking

his head. "I want to shake that pharmacist's hand. That's pretty strong."

"She's still pretty freaked out. Army corpsman, three deployments. Told Alexander that's the first time she's run into the line of fire without body armor."

"Thank God she did," Holly added. "It's easy to forget the folks around us. Today, they saved the day."

"Will Turner make it?" Johnny was hoping for an answer that wouldn't crush both him and Holly.

"It's too early to tell. The bullet missed his spine, but sounds like it did a lot of nerve damage." Worth saw both of their faces sink when he told them. "I'll keep you updated as I get information. Have your lawyers arrived? We're not going to discuss the shooting until they do."

"He should be here in a few. I called Amorini."

Worth smiled. "Good choice. Not his first time at the rodeo."

"Any civilians injured?" Johnny was almost afraid to ask.

"Surprisingly, no. Those idiots were spraying y'all down pretty heavy, and Lord knows where they landed, but right now it looks like no other casualties." Worth was thinking. "Here's the deal. The state agents are going to want to talk with you, but that's your choice, as you know. Our Internal Affairs folks will take their time. They'll probably introduce themselves and put you on paid leave for a few days. Take as long as you need. Right now, I'm going to have one of the uniforms drive you to the hospital." He looked at Holly. "*Both* of you."

"I'm good, sir. I can stay here."

"I think you should have your left leg checked."

Holly looked at her left leg and saw blood on the outside flowing down into her shoe. It was a small wound that seemed to have stopped bleeding almost entirely. "I didn't even notice it."

"Adrenaline. Probably a skip from the pavement or a secondary impact from a round through the truck. I know you've been through this before, Holly. I worked both of them, but no shooting is ever like another. Take your time. You both have my cell if you need to chat. Remember to use the chaplains and peer counselors. That's what they're there for. Anything else?" Worth asked.

"When the attorney gets here—" Johnny said, and Worth cut him off.

"I'll send him to the hospital. I know Joe, and he'll want to see the scene before he speaks with you. Now go before I have to order you." Worth smiled. "You both did some great work today. I'm proud and honored to work with both of you. You'll probably run into the chief at the hospital. I've never seen one of us at the hospital when she wasn't there to check on them."

Holly and Johnny thanked him. A detective Johnny never met drove them from the parking lot, and they saw the machine in full run. The press was staged in the north corner of the parking lot, the public information officers were milling around the command vehicle, and the crime-scene techs had started taking pictures. The entire parking lot was a homicide scene as they worked to account for every round fired; they all had to land someplace. Johnny thought about the words of an instructor in a homicide class he took: *Bullets don't care a lick about crime-scene tape.* That was true today.

As they drove away, Johnny could not believe the number of police cars he saw. From the state patrol to two sheriff's offices and several city agencies, they all came running to help. The knowledge that they would run toward danger and that he would do the same for them touched Johnny. Strangers united by an oath—that's something that many people would never understand.

As they arrived at the hospital, Johnny saw the other part of the machine. There was a line of media trucks and cars at the back of the hospital with hospital security working to stage them in a confined area. There was also a whole passel of police cars from a bunch of jurisdictions. The enormity of the event, and the fact that the intense scrutiny those minutes of his life would receive struck him. Johnny hoped the process would not overshadow the fact that a street cop was inside fighting to stay alive.

CHAPTER 26

J ohnny and Holly were at the hospital for hours. They were both examined, and the doctors ran them through a CT scan to ensure their cuts didn't contain embedded objects—either bullet fragments or secondary objects like glass. Holly's worst injury was caused by a bullet fragment that likely skipped off the pavement. It was flat and extremely sharp. The state investigators took it for evidence.

A plastic surgeon was called in to remove the glass from Johnny's face. He didn't insist on it, but the emergency room doctor did. "The slivers are on the curves of your face. They will scar. I'd feel better getting a good plastic surgeon on it."

Johnny didn't argue.

He was lying in the hospital bed while the plastic surgeon was finishing up when Holly and Worth came into the room. Johnny had a drape over his face, but he heard three voices. "Joe? Is that you?"

"Yes, Detective. Congrats on the promotion, by the way. I appreciate the call." Joe Amorini spoke to the doctor, who was sewing the last of five incisions. "Will he still be able to model for *GQ*?"

The surgeon laughed. "Well, my work is good, but I can only do the best with what I have to work with."

Everyone laughed while Worth put a chair next to Johnny's bed for Holly to sit next to Johnny's bed. Her leg had been stitched up, but he imagined it was throbbing a bit.

When the surgeon was finished, the nurse removed the drape. The surgeon spoke with Johnny about the care for the incisions and the sutures, then shook his hand. "Remember what I said, Detective. Anytime, anywhere."

"Yes, ma'am. Thank you for coming in."

They all watched the surgeon leave the room.

"What's that about?" Worth was looking at the bandages on Johnny's face.

"Her brother is a cop in Atlanta. She told me these types of cuts can take a while to heal and may require some topical revisions. She said she's available to help, no cost, and always available to talk."

"That's refreshing to see," Amorini said. He looked at Johnny and Holly. "Have you both been released? We should talk. I left the scene a few minutes ago." He then turned to Major Worth. "Thank you, Major, for the professional courtesies." The two men shook hands.

Worth nodded to Holly and Johnny. He knew they needed some privacy to speak with their attorney. "I'll be out of your hair in a few. You two need anything?"

Holly and Johnny both shook their heads.

"Before you go to find a quiet place to chat, the chief would like to speak with you. Stand by one."

Worth left and reappeared less than five minutes later with Chief Karen Porter. She was a fit-looking woman in her early fifties. She had been chief of the Lawler County Police Department for five years and was with the FBI and two other agencies before that. As a chief, she was well-respected as one of the first women to serve on the SWAT team of the sheriff's office she worked with just before she started with the FBI. She was no-nonsense, practical, and plainspoken. She was also a homicide detective at one time and treated that unit with the care it deserved.

When she walked in, she was very respectful of the circumstances. Both detectives were wearing surgical scrubs, as their street clothes were taken as evidence. Johnny's face was pretty swollen, but the detectives looked better than she hoped, given the description of what they endured at the scene.

"Detectives, counselor. The major tells me you're both okay. Our prayers have been answered. Is there anything you need? Any questions I can answer for you?"

"How's Turner, Chief?" Holly was direct and spoke quickly. Johnny was about to ask the same thing.

"He's in critical condition with a wound to the neck. Lots of damage, and he's still in surgery, but fortunately, his spine was not severed. Detective Till, I reviewed the surveillance footage from the bank. Your shot prevented the perp from finishing off Turner. They tell me the dash camera and body-camera footage are even more clear."

"Is he in surgery still?" Holly was surprised.

"Yes, and he will be for several more hours. There is a team of neurosurgeons working to put him back together."

"I pray they're the best," Joe Amorini chimed in.

"I'd like to think so." She smiled. "One is my brother."

"We'd like to see his wife and family before we leave." Johnny realized that he spoke for Holly without any input from her. She was nodding when he looked at her.

"I understand. Major Worth, please ask hospital security to take all of you to the surgical waiting room via the staff elevators. The media is all over the hospital, and I want these detectives to have some down time."

"Yes, ma'am. Will do."

"There is one thing I need to tell you." She looked around as Worth closed the door to the tiny room. "You may want to sit down." She waited until both detectives sat, Johnny on the bed and Holly on a chair. Joe Amorini was listening intently. "You have counsel, so while I will answer any questions I can, I advise you not to make any statements after you hear what I have to say. Understood?"

They both nodded. Johnny looked at his major, who had his head down.

The chief continued, "There were three suspects. It appears they make up the same crew that has robbed at least a dozen banks in the five-county area in the past eighteen months. The FBI compared their height and weight on the bank surveillance footage, and they're pretty certain they are the same folks. In one of the holdups, there was a fourth robber, but there have been three on every other occasion."

The detectives nodded. "You didn't shut the door to tell us that, Chief." Holly's voice was even and flat, but respectful.

The chief sighed. "The group has been identified as part of a local gang—the Robber Barons. I guess they think the name is cool." *There is no easy way to say this*, Porter thought.

"One of the deceased males was fifteen years old." The words seemed to linger in the air. "It wasn't a gang initiation. At least, the FBI doesn't think so. These guys were funding operations, and the robbers were trained."

No one in the room spoke. *Fifteen. Unbelievable.* Johnny heard the words resonate in his mind.

Major Worth spoke first and broke the silence. His face was fixed and his eyes narrow. He was looking at Holly and Johnny like they were the only people in the room. "Any one of them would've killed you in a heartbeat and driven off. It's entirely possible the fifteen-year-old shot Officer Turner and was planning to finish him off—"

"When I shot him," Johnny interrupted. He paused, and no one in the room said a word. "I shot a kid."

Bill Worth and the chief simultaneously put their hands on Johnny's shoulders. Holly leaned over from her chair and wrapped her hand around Johnny's forearm. "There's nothing easy about this, Johnny. The chief will give you all the time you need," Worth reassured him.

"Absolutely." There was a long pause and the chief stepped back. "Anything else?" Holly and Johnny shook their heads. The chief looked at Amorini. "Nothing? Not even from you?" She smiled.

"I have nothing to add, except to say that you and all of your officers are in our thoughts and prayers, as always."

"Thanks, Joe. That's a first from an attorney—nothing to say." She smiled. "In all candor, Detectives, there were a dozen people in that bank, four people in the parking lot, and countless others in the shopping center who will go home tonight thanks to your quick, decisive actions. You reflect the highest standards not only of the Lawler PD, but of American law enforcement. I know you're going through a lot. I've been there. But don't lose sight of the great work you did. This department and the community owe you a debt of gratitude for standing in the gap." She reached into her jacket. "Here is my card with my personal cell. Call me if you need anything."

They both thanked the chief, and she turned to leave.

"One more thing, Till. Looks like I made the right decision to move you to Homicide." She turned and left the room.

Major Worth motioned to the door. "Are you ready to check on Turner's family?"

Johnny and Holly stood and walked through the door. As they walked through the busy emergency department, they watched the nurses and doctors looking at them. Most smiled and nodded; a couple scowled. That's when Johnny realized that the deceased robbers had come to the same hospital. The doctors and nurses knew the police had shot and killed a teenager. Joe Amorini saw the effect of the scowls on his clients. "Focus on the positive. The others made their judgments with little or no information. They don't deserve your concern."

The director of hospital security, Preston Marshall, met them at the back of the emergency department and began leading them down the trauma hall that was closed to the public. They arrived at an elevator marked TRAUMA STAFF ONLY and waited for the car to arrive. While they were waiting, Marshall looked at them. "I spent twenty-five years on the job in New York City. Glad we get to keep you guys."

Holly nodded. Johnny shook his hand.

As the elevator reached the second floor, they turned right toward the trauma waiting room. Next to the large room filled with people was a smaller room designated FAMILY CONSULTATION. A uniformed Lawler officer stood outside. He nodded at them as they arrived. Then he stood to the side and allowed them to enter.

Inside was standing room only. Uniformed officers, detectives, and people in plain clothes that Johnny expected were family members were holding each other and speaking quietly. There were only four chairs in the room. Elise and Maggie Turner, Joe's wife and daughter, were seated.

As Holly and Johnny walked into the room, Preston Marshall shook Major Worth's hand, said something Johnny couldn't hear, then left. Everyone in the room stopped speaking and looked at them. The silence was nearly uncomfortable. It was broken by Elise Turner's words as she stood and put her arms around them. She had been told of their role at the bank and the injuries they suffered. When they walked in wearing surgical scrubs and she saw the bandages on Johnny's face, she knew instantly who they were.

"Thank you," she managed to get out. "Thank you for saving my husband." Her words brought everyone in the room to tears. It seemed like she held them forever. When she let go, she wiped her eyes.

Johnny and Holly were fighting to keep their emotions under control as Elise introduced them to her daughter, her parents, and Joe's parents. They all shook hands with or hugged Holly and Johnny, who finally lost the battle. Tears rolled down their cheeks as they hugged Turner's family.

Holding her mother's hand, Maggie Turner stepped up to them. "Don't cry. He'll be okay. My dad is the strongest cop in the world. He'll come home to us. He always does." Johnny hoped to hell she was right.

Holly and Johnny spent the rest of the afternoon and early evening meeting with Joe Amorini and receiving letters advising they were on administrative leave with pay. The interviews with the state investigators were voluntary, of course, as they were conducting a criminal investigation. However, the interviews with Internal Affairs investigators were mandatory, pursuant to the Garrity decision. They had to answer those questions, but their truthful responses were inadmissible against them in any criminal case.

Joe Amorini discussed the process. They all agreed to give statements to the criminal investigators and then to the Internal Affairs Unit. It would be a week or two before the process was complete, including the psychological assessment to determine if they were ready to return to duty, and a firearms-qualification session.

During this time, the leads in the Dunlap case would be getting colder. "I've still got some of the Dunlap files at my house," Johnny told Holly.

"Understood. I'm going to smuggle some home from my cases. I'll go nuts sitting at home for more than a couple of days. I can't stay home for a day with the flu without going out of my mind." She looked at him. "Are you going to talk to someone about the shooting? I mean, the age of the perp?"

"Probably. Worth is right. He would've killed any one of us and not blinked. It's just that you think of bad guys as just that—big, bad men. Shooting and killing a kid . . . that's not something I prepared for."

Joe Amorini heard them talking. When they finished, he put his hands on their shoulders. "This is tough, and I won't pretend to know everything you are going through. I'll just say this: Everyone would rather be talking to you than about you. Enough said on that."

Joe Amorini watched them get into a detective car to

be driven home. He knew it would be a long road. He also knew that they were lucky to be alive, like the hundred or so other cops he'd represented after shootings. If the media would just focus on the violence the robbers unleashed and not the age of one of their gang, the case would be out of the headlines soon.

What are the odds of that? he nearly said out loud as he got into his car. He made a mental note to call Johnny Till tomorrow after he got some rest. Most of the time, a text was all it took to ensure his client was okay.

CHAPTER 27

T hat night, Johnny lay in bed staring at the ceiling. Sleep came in small sprints filled with rapid flashes of memories. It was like a movie playing in the front of his mind that he couldn't turn off.

In his dreams, when he did sleep, the outcome at the bank was different. At times Holly was dead, Turner was dead, Johnny was shot, or the bad guys got away because the bullets bounced off of them. Each time he awoke, he was in a cold sweat. When finally asleep, he recalled in his dreams what his conscious mind had not allowed him to remember: the sound of the bullets hitting the truck he used for cover and the asphalt around him. He also re-membered the screams of Turner and the officers who worked to save him.

Joe Amorini had cautioned him to avoid alcohol, and he declined the pain meds the doc offered. So he was on his own. When he gave up on sleep he did a hundred push-ups and as many pull-ups as he could. For some reason, he checked his phone. He had texts from Holly, the chief, and Bill Worth.

The chief and Worth were checking on him. Holly's text was simple and short: The first night is the

hardest. It gets better. Call if you need
to talk.

It was odd, but it helped to know that she was there. Johnny also came to a realization in that moment. He had told his mother that he was okay, and she knew not to ask too many questions. That was great. She would support him no matter what. He realized, though, that he had no one close to him. Four years of college failed to help him land a serious prospect for marriage, and his work life kept him too busy to date or too intolerant of the negative opinions of cops on the lips of many single women in the community.

Can't be single forever.

Johnny took a hot shower and lay back down on his bed. Time to try to get some sleep. His eyes closed as the nightmares started again, and his eyes shot open after a bullet ripped through the woman at the van standing next to her children.

I hope they're right. This could get old. Guess I'll just wait for daylight.

The next few hours saw the struggle between stamina and fatigue. The daylight brought an end to the dreams, but not the reality of having taken two lives.

CHAPTER 28

T hree days after the shooting, Johnny was up at 6:00 a.m. and out to the gym. After a long workout on weights and resistance training, he jumped in the hot tub at the gym, then went home.

When he arrived home, Johnny saw the newspaper in his driveway. When he picked up the paper and opened it, he felt like his feet had been nailed to the floor.

POLICE ADMIT COP KILLED TEEN
DURING ROBBERY

The headline was above the fold of the paper. The story described the information as a hot tip freshly extracted from the police department, like details on the Watergate burglary from Deep Throat. In reality, the information was part of a press release yesterday afternoon, along with Johnny and Holly's names and work history in the department. The public-information officer, Karl Rowls, called Johnny to warn him it was coming and advise they had no choice under the new statute passed last year.

"Sorry, Johnny. We must release details within forty-eight hours now."

"Understood, Karl. Not your fault." Johnny paused. "How bad is it out there? I haven't been watching the news."

Karl paused and breathed out a long breath. "Bad. It'll blow over, though. The woman y'all saved has been very vocal and jumped in a reporter's shit when he asked her on camera if the shooting of the robbers was 'necessary.' Too bad you didn't see that. It was epic. They nearly missed the blanking-out of her words during the live broadcast. She let them have it. I have it on my computer when you're ready to see it."

"She was pretty vocal at the scene. That doesn't surprise me."

"They've been hounding the civilian shooter pretty badly. He's called up here asking for protection for his house. He took some time to get away, but a group of protesters showed up at his place and his neighbors called him."

"What are they protesting?"

"The fact that they have nothing else to do, I guess. They found some social media pictures of him at shooting competitions and are painting him as some sort of trained assassin. Stupid. We identified several as paid protestors. The beat units that responded took two to jail for possession of Molotov cocktails. Crazy shit."

"Indeed." Johnny thought for a moment about the pressure Jake Moretta was under with that crap. "I feel for him. I have a lot of support from the department. He's out there alone."

"We offered him access to a peer counselor. He spoke with him. I'm not sure, but I think one of the department chaplains also reached out to him. He'll be okay, Johnny. There are a lot of people coming out of the woodwork to support him."

"That's good to hear."

"They're also pretty vocal about supporting you and Holly, as well."

Johnny paused. The thought of strangers defending him made him tear up. "Thanks for letting me know, Karl."

"No problem, Johnny. I've been there. Just lay low, and let the magic of the news cycle be your friend."

"Something tells me you've got a plan."

"Well, as luck would have it, Officer Turner is able to speak! He and his family have agreed to do a short press conference with the chief and his surgeons at the hospital. My phone's been going nonstop with requests for an exclusive on Turner."

"The timing of this press conference?"

"Purely coincidental, Detective Till. It has nothing to do with the article on the front page of the *Lawler Monitor* this morning, if that's what you're asking."

Johnny could almost hear the smile in his voice. Johnny was quiet for a while. Rowls did not rush him. "Thanks for that."

"Thank Turner when you see him. He insisted on it. He heard about the controversy brewing about the robber's age and reached out to me via text demanding to make a statement."

"How's he doing?"

"Strong as an ox with a long recovery to go." There was a long pause. "He asked me to give you a message."

"Great. I haven't gone to see him because I was afraid the media was still all over the hospital."

"Good call. They are and have been."

"What's the message?" Johnny asked.

"It's short. He can only speak in small phrases. He

said, and this is a quote, 'Thank Till for another day with my wife and kids.'"

Johnny couldn't speak. The silence on the phone was expected. After a full minute, Rowls spoke again. "I'm happy to sneak you in to see him any time you want. The director of security is a good friend. We can put you in scrubs or a maintenance outfit, get you in and out the employee entrance and elevators. Let me know."

"Will do, Karl. Thanks."

"Just doing my job, brother. Just like you." Rowls heard nothing. "Call any time, Johnny." Then he hung up.

Johnny turned his attention to the newspaper again and saw the article was written by none other than Sands Banks. As Johnny read the article, he realized it was pretty evenly balanced and was not a hit piece on Johnny or the department. The story covered the life of the robber, his purported gang ties, and the arrest of three high-level gang leaders for conspiracy in connection with the bank robbery and death of the three robbers. He also stated—three times—that the young robber was wearing a ski mask.

All in all, not as bad as the title. But the title flashes to everyone who walks past a newsstand or newspaper vending machine.

Johnny picked up his cell phone, fought the voice in his head that told him to put it down, then sent Sands a text: Thanks for getting the truth out.

The reply was quick: That's my job. Care to do an interview?

Can't.

Understood.

That title, though.

Copy editors, not me. You okay?

Will be.

Off the record?

A reporter asking me to go off the record? ROTFL!

Quite the switch in roles.

Yep. Sure.

My mom was in that bank, Till. If they didn't come out like y'all let them, or were allowed to run back in, she would have been a hostage or gone now.

Johnny thought about Sands' words. *He must have known the manager locked the door when the robbers left. He also knew the glass door wouldn't have stopped them from getting back in. Interesting words for a guy who covers the police beat . . . "gone now."*

Johnny typed a response. Glad she's okay.

Let me know if you change your mind about an interview.

You looking for an exclusive?

You bet your ass! All those hit-and-run cases I helped you solve . . . LOL!

I forgot about those. You bet, but don't hold your breath.

I won't. I know the department policy. I have a copy on my computer. Stay well.

You, too.

CHAPTER 29

ohnny had just put his phone down when he heard a car pull up in his driveway. A quick peek out the window confirmed it was not a van full of protesters, but it wasn't a police car, either. Johnny watched the car as the driver took a while to get out. The windows were tinted, far more than allowed by law, and Johnny started thinking about killing a gang member a few days before. As he was about to grab a pistol, the car door opened and Lieutenant Dan Paschal got out. He was wearing jeans and a windbreaker with cowboy boots.

Man, I hope to work in that unit one day.

He watched as Paschal walked up to his door and rang the bell. Johnny opened it and invited him in. The two men sat at the kitchen table, and Johnny got Paschal a glass of water.

"So, official business or a social visit?"

Paschal smiled. "A little bit of both, I guess. My car is less noticeable than a sedan with black-walled tires, and the chief asked me to check on you."

Johnny sat down and took a sip of his shake. "I'm glad you did."

"I'm also one of the department's peer counselors.

Anything you say to me stays confidential, understood?"

"Absolutely. I appreciate the visit." Johnny picked up the paper and handed it to him. "You see this yet?"

"Yep. I expected that. Anything to sell papers." Paschal put the paper down. "Don't let it make you second-guess what you did. Fifteen or fifty-nine, he was trying to kill you and anyone else who got into his way. He damn near succeeded with Turner."

"I understand. That part I get. It's the rest that's tough."

"What's that?"

Johnny sat forward in his chair. "What led him to that bank, and the fact that he'll never do the things you and I look forward to."

"Like?"

"Like walking along a lake, watching a damn Super Bowl game, getting married." Johnny got quiet and bowed his head.

"As for what led him there, a lot of really bad choices. As for the rest, I've been married five times. It's not all it's cracked up to be."

Johnny's head shot up. "Five times?"

"Yep. I stopped after that."

"Good call." Johnny smiled. "You suck at it." The two men laughed.

"The evidence would seem to support that theory." He paused. "What else is eating at you, Johnny?"

"I heard he didn't have a lot of opportunities in his life. He grew up without a father, and—"

Paschal cut him off. "So did you."

Johnny nodded. "I guess I wish he took a different path and never showed up at that bank."

"I bet right now you wish you never showed up at the bank."

Johnny sat up straight in his chair. "Never once. If it wasn't me, it would've been another cop, or Holly could've been alone."

Paschal nodded. "So what you're saying is that your choices brought you to the bank that day. Sound familiar?"

Johnny nodded. "Doesn't make it any easier."

Paschal took a sip of water. "I've been a cop and a soldier for more than twenty years. I've been in some pretty fierce firefights, and they're all different. However, there is one common denominator in all of them."

"You're alive?"

"Damn right, and sometimes I wonder why, too." He paused. "But there's something else, as well, Johnny. You need to get right with the fact that you were there at that moment, that precise moment, to make a difference. Sometimes it's hard to understand what the difference is, but in your case, it's easy."

"Really? I'd love to hear your thoughts."

"You saved lives, prevented deaths, and fulfilled your oath of office."

Johnny nodded his head. "I guess that's true."

"Time will help, but don't think you'll ever forget what happened. Just accept it as a part of your life story. In time, it will not be in the forefront of your mind every day."

Johnny sat with Paschal for a while. Their conversation drifted to and from the shooting, but Paschal never made Johnny feel like he was on a schedule. When the conversation slowed to a natural, long pause, Paschal got up and headed toward the door, then he left. As Johnny watched him drive off, he thought about what he said. *I don't think it will get any easier, but Paschal's right. The difference we made is the fact that the victims lived to tell the tale. I guess that must be enough.*

CHAPTER 30

H annah's fog began to slowly lift. Her eyes were still cloudy when the dank smell of sweat and stale air permeated her nose. Deep inside her mind, the confusion was giving way to fear.

Where am I? Am I alone again, like in the hotel? I'm not moving anymore. When did they take us out of the truck?

Slowly, Hannah moved her left leg. She realized that she could move a leg or foot and still pretend she was out of it. Opening her eyes, on the other hand, was danger-ous—and painful, as she learned.

No weight on me this time. No one on top of me. Sheets . . . it feels like sheets.

As Hannah started to try to make sense of her sur-roundings, she heard a soft, calm voice. It struck her deep in her heart. The only voices she had heard since the bar were the shouts of her captors or the whimpers and screams of the girls around her.

Is this a new trick to get us to let our guards down? Am I just dreaming?

As Hannah thought and fought back the panic, she be-gan to understand the words being whispered into her left ear.

"Drink. It's okay. It's not from them."

I can't trust anyone, but she doesn't sound like them. Hannah had heard the voices of several women throughout her ordeal who were helping her captors. They were often more harsh than the men who ordered them around. *This voice, though . . . it's like a child.*

"Drink. Here, watch me."

Hannah opened her eyes slowly and watched as a small-framed young girl brought a ceramic cup to her lips. She took a long sip, then again put the cup to Hannah's lips. An almost surrealistic calm came over Hannah. The calm of being close to a child reminded her of the time she spent babysitting in her neighborhood. She searched the girl's face, looking for signs that she was being tricked again, but saw none. All she saw, despite the smile, was pain—pain and fear.

"Drink. It's okay," the young girl said again.

Hannah moved her lips, and the girl tipped the cup to allow her to receive some of the cool water.

"Go slow. It's easier if you go slow."

Hannah felt her throat reject the rapid flood of moisture. It was a change from the extreme thirst and dryness she'd felt since riding in the dark cargo hold of the truck. She looked at the girl and thought, *Still no sign of a trick or evil intent.*

As Hannah stared, the girl spoke again. "Drink more." Her voice dropped into a lower whisper. "I know how to get more water that doesn't taste bad or make you sleep. Drink this, and I'll get you more."

Hannah's throat adjusted to the moisture, and she drank deeply. Her empty stomach lit up as the cool water seemed to go straight down to the bottom of her belly. When the water was gone, she again looked at the girl, who now had a wide smile. She patted Hannah's head. "I'll be back in a second." She returned a minute or two later, looked at Hannah, again took a sip of the cup of water, then handed it to Hannah, who was sitting up now. Hannah drank deeply. Then the two of them sat up, looking at each other.

"I get the water from the back of the toilet, in the big tank thing. That's the only water that doesn't taste bad or make me sleepy."

Hannah nodded.

"I'm Britt. Are you Hannah?"

Hearing her name for the first time in a long while made Hannah cry. She nodded her head.

"It's okay." Britt put her hand on Hannah's face and wiped away a tear. "They really don't hurt us here, unless you do bad things. If you do what they say, you'll go home soon. They all say we will."

Hannah looked into the eyes of Britt and saw the unmistakable signs of innocent hope and faith in a better future, which just made her cry harder. Hannah ran her hand through Britt's long brown hair. It was surprisingly clean. "You have pretty hair. Do you brush it a lot?"

Britt sat up a little taller. "Yes! Mr. Robert bought me a nice brush. He comes to see me a lot. That's what I call him. I don't really know his name." She looked at Hannah, who was crying steadily now. "Will you brush my hair, Hannah?" When Hannah nodded, Britt disappeared. She returned a few minutes later, running like a child at the fair racing her friends to the Ferris wheel. She handed Hannah a large brush with coarse, plastic bristles. "Here." Hannah watched as Britt turned around and faced away from her. She was sitting up straight with her hands in her lap. While she waited for

Hannah to begin, she turned her head to the right. "When you're done, I'll brush yours."

Hannah got up to her knees and began brushing Britt's hair. The tears began to slow, and she soaked in the comfort that came from being with a child. "Britt, how long have you been here?"

Britt answered without turning around. She moved a bit as Hannah worked through a small tangle on the right side of her head. "I don't know. I guess a while. I saw a Christmas tree out the window once, so I guess about a year, because I was with my family on Christmas vacation when the men took me and brought me here."

"Where were you when the men took you?" Hannah realized she had begun speaking like Britt, like a child.

"We were on the highway and stopped at a place to eat. We were driving to see my Nana in Florida." Her voice was soft, low, and so matter of fact that it struck Hannah by surprise.

Hannah continued to brush Britt's hair and speak softly to her. They spoke about Britt's school, her friends, and her brother. Finally, Hannah was convinced that Britt had no idea what had happened to her. She had just accepted her surroundings as a new normal. She was a tiny person who had no way to fight, so she just did what she was told.

As Hannah finished brushing Britt's hair, they looked like two girls at a sleepover talking about boys or the politics surrounding a Sadie Hawkins dance. Hannah asked the question she had tried to avoid for the half hour or so they had been together. "Britt?"

"Yes?"

"How old are you?"

"Twelve."

Hannah put her arms around Britt's shoulders and hugged her tightly. Hannah's tears turned to sobs now.

Britt put her little hands on Hannah's. "I know you're older than me, but will you be my friend?"

Hannah couldn't stop crying, but she took a deep breath, looked at the dark plastic covering the windows of the bedroom, and whispered into Britt's right ear, "Yes, sweetheart. I will be your friend."

CHAPTER 31

Hannah was led to a couch in a large room by one of the older women who seemed to always be watching the girls. She sat down, trying to shake the fog from the last meal she ate. As much as she tried to avoid the food, and Britt taught her how to avoid the drinks, she eventually got hungry and gave in.

The room was filled with girls and women. Some were younger than Hannah—Britt's age—and some looked ten years older, their eyes sunken in, faces thin, and their bare legs looking barely strong enough to hold them up.

One of the older women who constantly gave orders started to speak to someone. "Time for a detour? I've got orders to give you thirty minutes with the one of your choice."

A man standing close to Hannah spoke first, causing her blood to run cold. Although she'd never seen his face before, she recognized his voice from the warehouse when she first came out of the truck. "I'll pass, unless you have an Asian."

"I've got you. Oral or straight sex only, no anal. Take her." The woman pointed to a girl about sixteen who was sitting on the floor. She seemed barely able to hold her head up.

"Fine with me."

"How about you, tough guy? Want some pussy for the road?"

Another man, larger than the first, spoke. "Damn right! I want the one who just came in." He was staring at Hannah. "She was in one of my shipments." Hannah's blood ran cold.

"No way. Not the new girls. They bring a higher price." She paused. "Pick one of these." She waved her arm around the room where twelve women were sitting, watching him. Several were barely conscious from the heroin.

"Nothing younger?"

"Not for free, tough guy. That'll cost you."

"How come he gets a young one?"

"Benefits of being the boss's favorite." She smiled.

"Fuck you, then. They're all worn out."

"Suit yourself."

The man went outside to wait in the truck while his partner pulled a short Asian girl to her feet. "Where?"

"Right here, or in that room." She pointed. "Remember, no anal, or you'll have to deal with the management."

"Got it."

The girl was barely able to stand. He half carried her into the next room.

The older woman walked toward Hannah. She stood at the edge of the couch, leaned over, and looked into Hannah's eyes. "You awake, honey?"

Hannah nodded her head. She looked around and was filled with fear.

"Listen closely. Do what I say, when I say, and you'll be fine. You'll get used to it. Fuck up, and you'll get the beating of your life." The woman put her hand under Hannah's chin. "It'd be a shame to break this pretty face. Look at her." The woman pointed to a young woman of about nineteen. Her right eye was black and blue, and her nose was flat. "She didn't listen. Understand?"

Hannah nodded. The words "break" and "face" brought terror into her heart and she started to shake. It was the kind of language she heard in a violent movie. Her mind brought up an image of a girl in her high school who went through the windshield of a car when her drunk mother hit a car head on. The months of bandages, sipping her meals, the stitches, and the scars that never faded.

"Now go through that door and get a shower. There's some food in the kitchen. We have company coming over in about an hour. You'll be the star of the show." The woman's smile was sickening.

The hot water failed to stop or even slow her shaking. For the first time, her guts and determination were not enough to keep her from losing it.

As Hannah finished her shower, she looked for an avenue of escape. Unfortunately, two of the girls from the room followed her and watched her every move. They watched her as she used the bathroom, showered, and they handed her some clothes to put on. They consisted of a miniskirt and a cropped top. Then, they led her to the kitchen and got Hannah some food. When she finished the snacks they provided, they gave her a bottle of water. Hannah was so thirsty. She took the time to look around the room. *Two windows with bars . . . no go. No other doors. Focus and take your time. Be ready when the opportunity is there.*

Hannah took a big gulp of the water and instantly knew her mistake. *No! No! Not again.* The effect was not as strong as the last time, and Hannah felt somewhat conscious. Her thoughts were scattered and fragmented. She remembered walking and meeting someone. It was like being on autopilot. She remembered being told to put her head into his lap, the hand of the older woman holding her hair tight enough to hurt and keep her from falling asleep and seeing a gold D tattoo on his thigh.

The rest of the night was a blur.

CHAPTER 32

"**N**o, it's no trouble at all. Just have them check in with us when they arrive." Major Worth was speaking into the phone. He stopped and appeared to be listening. He saw Johnny at the door and waved him in, gesturing to a seat in front of the desk. He then turned his attention back to the phone. "I understand, but you don't know this joker. He may be a witness in your case, but he's a suspect in three unsolved homicides in two neighboring counties. He knows us and wants to keep us happy, even though it's common knowledge we're after his ass."

Johnny looked around the office. He had been staring at the murder board before he came in: three new cases, all caught by other detectives. As the new guy, he would've had at least one of them.

Worth continued after a long pause. "Yep. We'll send two folks with you. He's a bad man who carefully considers every move. When you make the notification, he just might make the mistake we've been waiting for." Worth paused for a while and took a sip of coffee. "Okay, call when you're about thirty minutes out. Bye."

As the major hung up the phone, Johnny spoke first.

"Out-of-town cops delivering bad news to one of our more upstanding citizens?" It was his first day back in since the shooting at the bank. He was looking forward to jumping back into the mix.

Worth laughed. "Local gangbanger and enforcer named Edward Rawlings, a.k.a. 'Heavy D.' Went freelance about eight years ago whacking anyone with a price on his head. Our Gang Unit knows him well, and we've interviewed him several times. He claims he is retired and always brings an attorney with him. Walker and Polk County Homicide folks are convinced he's responsible for at least three spots in the morgue, but they've never been able to pin anything on him. If it's him, he's methodical and patient. That's a bad combination for us in a murder perp."

"He's a witness?"

"Yep. Seems that his cousin in South Carolina met an untimely end when a convenience store owner decided not to go gentle into that good night. The cousin . . ." He rattled a paper on his desk. "The cousin goes by the name of Micro. His real name is Ernest Rand. Likes to rob and beat cashiers. When he tried to force the store owner and a female cashier into the back for some assault and probably a rape, the store owner *carpe diem*ed and lit up Micro with a .45."

"Praise the Lord and pass the ammunition!"

"Absolutely!" Worth agreed. "Well, the Carolina folks want to chat with our local guy, as Mr. Heavy D and Micro exchanged several texts and calls before Micro left this earth. I'm sure they were exchanging recipes and Bible passages, but they want to speak with him. Waste of time, most likely, as he probably won't talk to anyone about it. But he might retaliate or tip his hand in anger."

Johnny was sitting on the edge of his seat. He was itching to work on something. He enjoyed working out for two hours a day and catching up on his sleep, but after he binge-watched Netflix for a few days, he was craving something to do.

Worth locked eyes with him. It was obvious he was studying his face. "Hardly any scars. Just get the stitches out?"

"Yesterday afternoon. Hurt like a bitch, too. However, the doc did a great job. She said the lines at the closure points and the holes from the sutures will fade with a little vitamin E and time."

Worth nodded his head. "She's right." He sat back in his chair and put his hands behind his head. "And if she's wrong, chicks dig scars." Worth smiled. Johnny knew the close examination had little to do with any potential external scarring. "How are you doing, Johnny? Getting some sleep?"

"Yep. The first two nights were a bit tough, then I think I just crashed." He paused. "The first two nights, I just kept playing it over in my head. When I did sleep, the endings were varied . . . and not all that pleasant."

"Normal aftermath." Worth sipped his coffee. "Your brain was still in survival mode for the first two sleep cycles and was then trying to sort out what happened." He paused, then sat forward again. "I've seen the preliminary report and the videos. Textbook job in a horrible situation." He scanned Johnny's face. "I just hope I would perform that well under that type of pressure."

"That means a lot, sir, but with all due respect, your opinion doesn't matter," said Johnny. "Does the DA agree? How about the media?"

Worth took in a deep breath, then let it out. "You're new to Homicide. Here's a little inside baseball. No one comes back after a shooting until the DA gives a preliminary opinion clearing the officer. That's not to say that she won't convene a grand jury or do a more formal inquiry, but in a case like this, with a dozen or more witnesses, several angles of video, and shots fired and landing in officers, her initial opinion has plenty of foundation."

Johnny nodded. "Great to hear. And the media?"

"They have a job to do, Johnny. Often our procedures complicate that job. They do not have access to the same information we do—at least, not yet. But once they do, they will either drop it or acknowledge that you did the right thing." Worth leaned back in his chair. "As to the small percentage of folks who hate cops, always will, and have never seen a justified shooting in their lives, welcome to their list."

Johnny just sat back and said nothing. Then he looked up. "Well, I'm ready to jump back in." He put a smile on his face to let his boss know he was done speaking about it.

"And I'm guessing you didn't spend a minute looking at the Dunlap file while you were out." Worth smiled.

Johnny smiled and nodded.

"Let me guess. Still chasing Meng?"

"Darndest thing I've ever seen, Major. That guy pops up, then disappears like a damn prairie dog, and his tunnels don't seem to make any sense—at least, not to me right now."

"You just haven't seen it yet. The good thing is, you are not alone. Johnny, I've had more witnesses, victims, CIs, and perps found by our Intelligence Unit than I can count. Keep at it, but have faith in Paschal. Truth is, I wouldn't want him looking for my ass." He winked at Johnny.

"Me either. I get the sense I'd be dead before I saw him." Johnny took the opportunity to change the subject. "Anyway, that was all hypothetical. I was on 'admin leave.' I'm just looking forward to a fun interview with this perp-slash-grieving-relative."

"Glad you think so, because you'll be joining them. I'm keeping you on days for a while until we finish your training. That way, the first homicide you work will be with a seasoned partner, like Holly or someone else if she's off or in court. Night watch folks usually work the deaths on their own, at least initially. There's a lot of pressure, especially with an impatient patrol supervisor." Worth wrote a note. "These two detectives should arrive around eleven. Take them over to see Lieutenant Ramirez in Gangs first. He can get you the most recent address for Heavy D and let you know the latest scoop on his activities. Be sure to write up what you find. We don't have an active homicide case on him, but we'll pass on whatever we find to the folks in Walker and Polk."

"Why not have the Walker and Polk folks tag along with the Carolina detectives?"

"Good thought, but Heavy D won't talk if they're around. He clams up and wouldn't yell for help if his momma's house was on fire. Like I said, he's pretty smart."

"Sounds like a prince."

"That's how he gets away with working for hire. All of the gangs know he'll never squeal them out. Wire yourself up, and get anything you can on tape. Word is, he was close to his cousin, and he may slip up. I'll ask the

Gang Unit to watch him for a few days after they make the notification. We'll see if he increases his calls or decides to take a leisurely trip to the South Carolina Low Country."

"Will do. Maybe we'll get something out of it." Johnny took the piece of paper with the names and cell numbers of the detectives.

"Just be certain you don't get an IA investigation out of it. This guy is cool, calculating, and smart. He's also a cold-blooded killer. Watch your ass around him, Johnny. Keep your guard up."

"Yes, sir. Thanks for the heads-up."

As Johnny walked out of the office, he heard Worth speak. "Welcome back, Till." Johnny looked back to see Worth looking down and already working on a report.

CHAPTER 33

T he Homicide Unit was busy already with quite a few detectives at their desks. Manny Lopero was still there after working morning watch. He was passing off information on a fatal stabbing he worked in Zone 6. He closed the case quite easily when the perpetrator was found dead around the block from the bar where the stabbing took place. The wound looked self-inflicted, but Manny wasn't sure. He was briefing Sergeant Rostavic as they decided who would attend the autopsy that morning.

Johnny settled into his desk with a fresh cup of tea. He had barely logged in when a line of folks, from detectives to crime-scene techs to secretaries, came by to welcome him back. One of them brought him a copy of the *Lawler Monitor* from three days ago.

"You're famous, Till!" She was an older woman in her late sixties, slightly built, with dark, dyed hair always worn in a bun. Joy was a bit like the surrogate grandmother for the detectives and had been with the department for forty years. She had a picture of herself when she started and was quite the looker in her late twenties. Her story was well-known in the county. She married a

Lawler deputy after a year or two, and the two seemed destined to be happy. After the deputy was struck and killed by a drunk driver while directing traffic at a car wreck, she moved to Homicide and had been there ever since. Her two children were grown and out. It seemed Johnny Till was her latest adopted son.

"We all get our fifteen minutes," Johnny said as Joy smiled at him. The headline was short and powerful.

FIFTEEN YEARS TO SERVE IS ALL I CAN GIVE YOU

The quote was from Judge Mandy Whitlow from her sentencing of Randy Laymen for his role in the death of Sadie Emerson. Apparently, Laymen chose to lash out at the judge after she announced the sentence and read the conditions. He was also quoted, "You're punishing me because I wouldn't plead guilty!" Judge Whitlow responded that she was punishing him for stealing the life of an innocent little girl who was robbed of her chance to live her life and grow old.

A large section of the article printed Sadie's poem that Rhonda Emerson read during her impact statement. They were the words of a child with the wisdom of the ages.

"My Town":
My town is my home for me and my friends.
I like to see them again and again.
Mr. Harris at school makes us follow the rules.
Ms. Robinson makes spelling seem cool.
I like seeing Raven, McKenzie, and Jack.
They make me laugh on the bus while we ride in the back.
Mr. Rodney's real nice as he bags up our food.

Mom says he's special. He is to me, too.
In school we learn about places all around.
But I like living here, in my little town.

"Thanks, Joy. It was quite a show. I was there."

"I thought you were on admin leave?"

"I was. I cleared it with the major, and the judge let me sneak in the side door of the court at the request of Ana Liss. I wouldn't have missed it for anything."

Joy nodded. "Any other drama the paper left out?"

"Just the usual nonsense. A couple of defense attorneys were being interviewed just outside the courthouse about how horrible it was that Laymen would spend time in prison instead of a treatment facility. They also called fifteen years a 'death sentence' for Laymen." Johnny shook his head. "I did get to see Sadie's parents again."

Joy pulled her hands to her chest and her face fell. "I cannot imagine." There was a long pause. Neither she nor Johnny said a word. When she spoke, her voice cracked. "They'll never be the same, Johnny. It will never make sense to them."

Johnny got up and gave Joy a hug. A couple of detectives walked by on their way from the coffee machine and just smiled. Joy giving or getting hugs from, as she called them, "her detectives" was not unusual.

In typical fashion, she pulled herself together and wiped her eyes. "I bet they think you hung the moon!"

"Yeah, I guess they do." Johnny was standing in front of his desk and grabbed his tea. "They both knew about the shooting at the bank, obviously, and saw the news. Ana Liss brought them back to meet with me in a private conference room near the judge's chambers."

"Interesting. What was their take on it?"

"Well, they're pretty straightforward and generous. They offered to hire an attorney for me if I needed one." Johnny looked up at Joy. "That really got me, you know. They just watched a man argue about the sentence he received for killing their daughter, and they were thinking about my well-being." He took another sip of tea. He looked up at Joy. "It makes me want to be a better person, you know."

Joy smiled and touched his hand. "You already are." Then she walked back to her office.

CHAPTER 34

While Johnny truly appreciated the kind words and support, he really wanted to get back to work. The well-wishing stopped after about half an hour, and Johnny was able to settle in.

"Has the major heard from the Carolina detectives yet?" Holly asked. She had just walked in and still had her gym bag in her left hand. This was her second day back after the shooting.

"Yep. He stopped me as I came in. They'll be here in time for lunch. We'll grab a bite, then see if Mr. Heavy D can fit us into his schedule."

"Have you dealt with him?" Holly inquired.

"I haven't as yet had the pleasure." Johnny spoke with a highbrow accent while picking up his cup. He held his pinky out for effect.

Holly laughed out loud. "Oh, it is an experience. We always put a Tac unit on notice when we head to his place, just to be safe. They'll be in the area if we need them. Nice accent. You're a natural smartass. You'll fit in well here. Let's call the Carolina guys and have them meet us. Any food preferences?"

"I'm easy. Anything from sushi to spareribs is fine."

Holly leaned forward to pick up the phone on Johnny's desk. "You mind?"

"Not at all." Johnny saw the true beauty in her face. She was a striking woman. He could only imagine how much she had to put up with from perps on the street while in uniform and now in Homicide. As a guy, he always had an element of anonymity about him. A female officer always had to put up with guff, often from coworkers. One look at Holly, however, and it was obvious that she did not play those games. Johnny was glad to work with her, as he always made it a point to treat all officers the same, irrespective of their gender. Because of that, he had great friendships with several female officers. He suspected Holly had heard about him from one of them, and that was fine with him.

"Okay. We'll meet you at HQ and drive over in separate cars." She paused. "You have the address? Good. You're about five out. We'll meet you in the parking lot. We're hungry, as well."

"Sounds like they're around the corner."

"Yep. Now for the hardest part of being a detective."

"Explaining the intel we have on Heavy D to folks who don't know him?"

"Nope! Getting four homicide detectives to decide where to eat lunch!" She winked at him. "I need to get something off my desk. It's a folder about Heavy D. I'll meet you at the back door. Can you sign us out on the board?"

Johnny looked over at the board. Every unit had one. It was an informal way to track officers when they were out of the office. It also served as a way to check in on them and know their location if, as his old lieutenant liked to say, "the excrement strikes the revolving air-circulation device."

Johnny looked down at the red binders on his desk. He expected this, but for the first time, he had to stop working the cold case to move onto an active investigation. Such was the frustration of cold cases. He locked the file back in the cabinet, then picked up his portable radio and his jacket. He walked toward the back door and the whiteboard with the names of all members of the Homicide Unit. He heard Holly coming up behind him as he moved the magnets for both of them to OUT and wrote LUNCH and INTERVIEW, then the address of Heavy D's house.

"I was coming to give you the address. Have you been there?"

"No, but I spent about thirty minutes going through his file in the computer when I got in."

Holly looked at his hands. He wasn't holding anything. She made a note that he'd memorized the address. They walked out the back door to the stairs.

"Your car or mine?" she asked.

"Just got mine. Let's break it in."

As they walked, Holly whispered to him, "You doing okay?"

"Yep. It took a while, but in the end, I'm just glad we're alive. Hear anything about Turner?"

"Surgery went well. He's starting rehab at the hospital. They say he'll have some deficits, but he'll be able to walk and use his arms."

"He's lucky."

"We're all lucky, Johnny. Those assholes could've killed all of us, and then some."

They did not speak again as they walked to the parking lot.

They were standing in the parking lot when a brand-new car rumbled in. The car was royal blue and had tinted windows that were definitely darker than legally allowed. As the car pulled into a parking space, they both saw the South Carolina tag. The car stopped, and the two detectives got out. As they walked toward Holly and Johnny, she whispered to him, "Well, at least they know how to arrive in style!"

As the two men approached, Johnny stuck out his hand. "Johnny Till. This is Holly Forrester."

The older detective was a black male in his midfifties. He was slightly built, but fit. He shook hands with both of them. "Ralph Fishman. Friends call me Red. This is my partner, Fred Cavert. He has a nickname, but I'll let him tell you."

Detective Cavert shook hands with both of them as he and Red laughed out loud. "We've been on the road too long," Cavert said. "Besides, it's tough traveling with an old man. He probably just forgot my nickname!" Cavert started laughing again, and Holly and Johnny joined them.

Red spoke up when his laughter subsided. "I imagine you have food in this town. We're starving!"

Johnny spoke up first. "Just about anything you want. Name it."

"Cavert is partial to burgers. That works for me."

"Got it. It's on the way. Follow us," Johnny offered.

The two cars left the parking lot and arrived a few minutes later at the Bull Pen. It was a local place well-known to cops in the area. The owner, Mitchell Vickers, was a huge supporter of law enforcement, and the food was incredibly fresh. They parked in front and walked in.

Vickers greeted them immediately from his regular post in front of the bar. "Come in, come in! How's our county's finest today?" Normally any cop would hate to be identified like this, but the place was full of uniforms, from city cops to state patrol.

"Life is great, Mitch!" Johnny moved forward and shook his hand.

"No more uniform for you, my friend! Homicide, huh?"

Johnny was surprised in a way, but Mitch always seemed to know when folks moved around. He made it his business to treat every customer like family. "Well, I guess they had enough of me in hit-and-run. Threw me out the door!"

"Not what I hear!" Mitch turned to Holly and gave her a hug. "How's Wonder Woman today?"

"Great, Mitch. Mitch, these are two homicide guys from out of state, Fishman and Cavert."

Mitch shook their hands, saying, "Welcome, welcome! Make yourselves at home." As much as Mitch seemed to talk too much, Johnny noticed that he never asked the detectives where they were from. He had an uncanny way of knowing when to keep quiet. "How about a place upstairs, so you can talk?" He looked down at the file in Holly's hand.

The four detectives followed him upstairs as he grabbed menus. He led them to a table in the back of the restaurant with six chairs around it. "This will give you room to spread out. I'll try to seat anyone else downstairs. Enjoy!"

They sat down, and Holly started talking first. "So what's with the fine ride? If that's standard issue in your department, I'm putting in an application!"

Red spoke up. "We borrowed it from our narcs. We figured we would be able to do a drive-by look-see to make certain Mr. Heavy—or is it Mr. D.?—is home before we knock."

"Good idea," she replied. It was obvious that Holly was impressed with their forethought. "He never quite rolls out the red carpet for us. Maybe it's something we've said, asking about homicides and such. In fact, we have a Tac unit on standby. I'll let them know when we approach." She grabbed her water and took a sip. "So spill it. How do you get 'Red' as a nickname? I'm sure it's a good story."

Johnny piped in, "And what was cracking you both up earlier?"

The two men looked at each other and started laughing again. Then Cavert spoke. He was a tall white guy in his early to midthirties with a lot of hair on his head that was barely cut to regulation. Johnny suspected he was a pretty good detective to get by with it.

"So my grandfather here is driving, and you'd think that the young guy would be the one to get into trouble with a car like that. But no! He's hauling ass down every road we hit! He's revving the engine at red lights, challenging everything to race . . . I mean, it was comical! So we pull up to a red light getting ready to get back on the interstate after a pit stop, and we are next to a gorgeous car! The thing is jet black, blacked-out windows with a performance package. So, numb nuts here revs the engine and waits. Nothing. He does it again, nothing. When the light turns, he hits it hard and pulls away. Well, the other car pulls in behind us and lights us up! It was a local cop surfing for street racers! He comes up to the car, and we're both laughing! As he approaches, Red hits the blues and our car lights up like a Christmas tree! That cop had a great sense of humor. We stayed on the side of the road laughing and cutting up for about ten minutes before he remembered he had backup staging on the interstate in anticipation of a chase. Of course, the tag on our car comes back 'not on file,' but I'm sure they'll send a notice to our chief that someone ran it."

"That's going to be a fun conversation," Holly piped up in between wiping the tears out of her eyes from laughing.

"Not really," Red explained. "He's a car freak. He knows I'd get in trouble driving that car. We went to the academy together."

The waitress came by to take their orders and drop an appetizer of onion rings. "On the house, per Mitch. Enjoy!"

They ordered their food and Johnny grabbed one of the largest and best onion rings he'd ever tasted. "You can feel your blood slowing down with every bite, but it's some of the best food anywhere!"

Red and Cavert each grabbed one and bit down. "Awesome!" Cavert said.

Red looked at Holly. "So you want to know why they call me Red? Well, it's not because of my hair!" He ran his hand across a smooth, bald head and chuckled. "You see, I love to fish, and redfish are huge on the coast of Carolina. Well, one morning I was running late and caught a homicide on the way in. I usually shower at the office when I fish early, and I barely had time to change out of my fishing clothes into my detecting clothes! I jumped into an unmarked with my partner at the time, and we headed to the call. It was a good call, and we chased the perp for about thirty-six hours until we locked him up. It was a great case. One of those that you either solve in the first few days or not at all, you know. The perp was literally at an ATM getting out all the money he could when we found him. He was getting ready to beat feet!" Red grabbed another onion ring. "Anyway, I had pulled into the parking lot of Homicide around 0700 and didn't get back into my car until 0400 two days later."

"Don't tell me," Johnny chimed in. Holly figured it out and put her hand over her mouth.

"Let's just say it was August in coastal South Carolina, and I had the most aromatic car in the entire department, complete with a ten-pound sunbaked redfish!" All four of them winced. "It was not as bad as you'd think," Red said, then grabbed another onion ring. He leaned forward for effect. "It was worse!"

As they finished laughing, the waitress brought their burgers. Johnny was amazed at how the four of them got along. He was not surprised, though. Cops generally share a common bond, and service in some units comes with a lot of mutual respect. SWAT, Motors, Narcs, and Homicide were known for it. It was comforting. Every good homicide detective knows their role, and it was good to know Johnny had been accepted into the family.

As they ate, Holly looked around, then pulled out her file. She lowered her voice and spoke to Red and Cavert. "How much do you know about Mr. Heavy D?"

"We know he's a player in the homicide-for-hire rings. His cousin was a lowlife. He was a suspect in several strong-arm robberies of people from eight to eighty. No one was surprised when he was shot by the store clerk. They all knew him and were on high alert when he was in the area."

"So what connection do you think Heavy D has to your dead perp?" Holly was asking the questions now. Johnny sat back and watched.

"We're not really sure, but our dead guy was not smart enough to plan anything on his own. We know he communicated with his cousin Heavy a lot recently and just before the robbery, so that gives us a reason to chat with the young man." Red smiled when Cavert finished.

Holly started again. "Heavy D," she emphasized the D, "he is bad news, and he never travels alone. Our Gang Unit hasn't figured out yet why he operates with relative impunity, but we know he always has a stack of goons around him. Like I said before, we always put our street-level Tac folks on alert when we go speak with him, just like today."

Cavert seemed to focus on that information. "You have a full-time Tac unit?"

"Yep," Holly answered. "They mostly work traffic in high-crime areas, look for fugitives, and handle high-risk warrants. We use them on a standby basis in cases like this. They'll be in unmarked cars about a block away."

"What type of interactions have you had with Heavy D personally?" Cavert asked.

"Well, I've interviewed him a few times about neighborhood events. He can talk in circles for hours, but that's fine. I've got hours of tape and video on him showing his weaknesses and tells. It'll come in handy one day."

Red looked at Johnny. "How about you?"

Johnny smiled. "You guys are lucky! Today you get to work with the world's newest homicide detective. I started a few weeks ago, but today's my first day back."

"An exotic vacation, I hope." Red was smiling.

Holly answered when she saw Johnny pick up his glass and take a long drink of water. "We were both on admin leave. Shooting at a bank."

"Community City Bank?" He seemed surprised.

"That's the one," Johnny answered.

"We heard about that in South Carolina. It made the national news. Y'all were the shooters?"

Holly spoke as Johnny grabbed the last onion ring. He clearly didn't want to speak about it anymore. "That's us. It was pretty intense."

"Damn good police work, if you ask me," Cavert said. When Johnny looked up, Cavert locked eyes with him. "I've been there. It gets easier. Glad we get to keep y'all."

Johnny nodded.

"I'm buying your lunch!" Red said. He then looked directly at Johnny. "It's an honorable mission in a great profession. Always be proud of what we do in Homicide." And there it was: confirmation of what Johnny had heard. He had joined a cohesive group. To him, it meant that he had to be at his best every day.

"Here's a folder on Heavy D. He's got quite the colorful past. There are two pictures, one for each of you. He makes no effort to change his appearance. He will have security, as expected. They will be armed and carrying openly. There are few of them I know to be convicted felons, and we never let that slide. If they are felons and packing, they leave with us when we're through." Holly was very matter of fact, and her smile was gone.

"Sounds like we should expect trouble," Red whispered.

Holly responded quickly. "We always expect trouble anytime he's involved, but it is typically less than you think. He does not move a muscle when one of his crew is going to jail. That's one of the reasons we're convinced he's connected to more than just the local gangs. He knows not to get involved."

"Why do the perps go quietly?" Red responded.

"He pays them well, and they have protection in the prison system. Their families get a stipend while they are in, and unfortunately, they're not in for very long."

"Quite a system," Cavert said and picked up his sweet tea.

Holly smiled. "He also knows from experience that we'll bring the world down on him if he puts his hands on one of us." Red nodded to her. "Take a look through the file, and let us know when you're done. We'll meet up with Tac and get them set on our radio frequency, as well as on our body bug."

"High-tech, huh?" Red smiled.

"Low, really," Holly countered. "We have a number we can call that turns our cell phones into one-way microphones. It works really well, as long as the signal is clear. I spent five years UC with the feds. Now they have some cool toys!"

Johnny made a note to ask her about that work later. He had had no idea.

A few minutes later, they left the restaurant having experienced another one of Mitch's deep discounts. On the way out, he gave his trademark comforting words: "Be safe and God bless!" It was reassuring in a couple of ways. First, it was genuine, and second, it was always good to know that citizens were pulling for the police. Asking God to have a hand in it, well, Johnny always thought that was a good idea.

CHAPTER 35

H olly, Johnny, Red, and Cavert met with the Tac units in the parking lot of the courthouse around the corner. The Tac commander was Brian Hancock. He was a stocky man in his midfifties and solid. Hancock had been on SWAT for more than twenty years and had a great reputation in the department and the surrounding counties. If things went bad, you wanted him on your side.

Hancock met everyone. He knew Holly from previous work with Homicide. He was jovial until it came to outlining the operational details. Then he was all business. He outlined the location of his eight Tac officers, who would be in four cars. They would all be listening to the body bug. The last thing he did was provide the "go word" that signaled they were in trouble. Then he programmed the portable radios of the Carolina officers to the local frequency and asked for any questions. Hearing none, they all drove toward the home of Mr. Heavy D.

As they drove to the house, Johnny could tell Holly was focused. He was relieved when she started to speak.

"Well, you're about to learn the first thing about Homicide."

"What's that?"

"Once you're in the unit, no one really wants to see you coming. Families know you're there to deliver bad news, line officers know they're going to be stuck holding a crime scene while you work, and perps know you're sniffing around or about to snatch someone up," Holly explained.

"That's awesome."

"Yep. One of the many perks of the job! The Tac guys will break off on the next block. Let Red and Cavert do a drive-by to look for Heavy's car." She picked up her portable radio and keyed the mic.

"Red, we'll pull off at the curb and let you do a drive-by. Come around the block and get behind us when you're through." Holly's voice was flat and even.

"Does he stay on the porch?" Red asked. "How will we know for sure that he's there?"

"Look for his security. If they're on the porch, his majesty is in residence," Holly answered.

"Roger that."

Johnny pulled to the curb and let Red and Cavert pass. "Hope this goes smoothly," Johnny said to Holly.

"His choice, Johnny. It's always their choice," she said. "There's something about his connection to South Carolina that has me on edge. I wonder if he was getting intel for a hit from his cousin."

"As good a theory as any. We should check, all kidding aside, to make certain there were no upcoming family events that a defense attorney could use to explain his contact."

"Good idea." Holly was impressed that he was thinking that far ahead. "So what's it like bringing one of those DUI homicides to trial? Tough?"

"Damn, it's hard. The families of the perp always bring up their great history in the community. Their coworkers testify about their great work ethic, and the defense attorneys are very good. They have a lot to work with, too. There's more case law about DUIs than the murder statute, because more people fight them in the appellate courts. So the defense attorneys have a lot of ammunition to try to suppress the evidence, fight the science, and put stumbling blocks in front of the prosecutors. That's why only a few of the DAs want to mess with them."

"Makes sense, but I had no idea. I went from the street to Narcs. Must've been my charming personality," Holly deadpanned.

Johnny smiled. "There's one other obstacle with every jury trial. Most of the time, the family members and coworkers are right. The perp is a good person with a bad problem with alcohol or drugs. It's not like bringing a gangbanger or jealous husband to trial for a murder. The jury will often sympathize with the defendant in a DUI homicide. They have been known to acquit them of the more serious charges."

"That would really piss me off."

"For me, I make the best case I can, then try to live with what the courts and juries do. That's where my control ends. A very wise investigator told me that just before I started with the department. I just want the families and other survivors to know that I did everything I could do. That, and that somebody gave a damn."

"Amen to that." She looked in the sideview mirror. "Here they come."

The car pulled behind them, but no one got out. That

would have attracted too much attention. The radio keyed up. It was Red. "There's about four guys on the front porch. Shirts are untucked. My guess is, they're packing. They eyed us when we drove by, probably waiting for the window to roll down for a real drive-by. From the looks of that neighborhood, it wouldn't be the first one."

Holly responded, "You are correct. Heavenly Acres it is not. If the security is on the porch, he's probably there. He keeps his car in the garage, so we can't go by that. I say let's go. Agreed?"

"Yep. We're right behind you."

Johnny pulled the car away from the curb and onto the street. Holly turned on her phone and spoke into it, letting the Tac folks know they were heading in. Down the street, a car flashed its lights. Everyone was on board.

"Johnny, I know you've been on the street a while, but watch your ass. We take zero crap from these guys. It's the only way we can be effective. Don't let the lack of a uniform intimidate you." She reached forward and knocked on his chest. She felt his body armor and the shock plate. She smiled. "Good boy. We are gonna get along just fine." She paused for a minute as Johnny started to turn left down the street. "Just in case you were wondering, I'm also wearing mine." She paused. "And *no*, you cannot check."

They both laughed.

"I guess I'll have to take your word for it. No need to spend time in Internal Affairs to prove a point!"

They pulled up in front of the house and blocked the driveway. At first, the guys on the front porch started to move forward, and one of them began to pull up his shirt. However, he stopped quickly and let it fall when he saw Holly hold her badge out the passenger window in her left hand.

"Good morning, guys!" she said as she smiled. "Great day for a visit, don't you agree?"

All four detectives got out quickly and walked to the front door. It was obvious that the security on the front porch had no idea how to handle this. They were prepared for an assault from the street or someone rushing the house, but four detectives crazy enough to walk up to the front door? That was not covered in their training manual. So, as Holly expected, they just stood there as she knocked on the door. As she predicted, once someone heard a knock, they assumed that the security on the porch had cleared them to enter. A member of Heavy D's security team opened the door and stepped back so whoever was there could enter.

Holly stepped in, and the other three detectives followed her. Mr. Heavy D was sitting in a recliner in the living room. He sat forward at first to get a look at her badge, then sat back with a smile on his face.

"Heavy D! Long time, no talk." Holly looked him dead in the eye. No fear.

He answered casually while waving his security away, telling them to turn around and put their backs to the detectives. He also told them to put their hands on top of their heads. "Detective Forrester! It's been a long time. Welcome to my home. You can see my boys have their backs to you, so they present no threat. Please don't nut up and shoot them. Good help is hard to find these days . . . especially after you took a few of them with you the last time you were here."

"We sure did, Heavy. Who knows? Maybe a couple more will take a ride today. They look like their pants are a little heavy, and Scooter over there has a gang tattoo and inmate ink on his right hand. You sure he's not a convicted felon? Maybe I should check."

"No need to go through all that. You tell me who you want to check, and they'll cooperate. You know how I roll, always cooperative with the local po-po—excuse me, police *officers*." His emphasis on "officers" was not meant as a compliment. "My apologies." Then, the large grin. "Should I call my attorney now or wait until later?"

"We need to talk, and you need to answer some questions. You know the drill," Holly said.

Heavy D stood and pulled up his shirt to show his waistband. "You have my consent and my cooperation. Besides, you've been on camera since you drove up, so there's nothing to hide here." He allowed Johnny to pat him down. Johnny then looked at him. "Of course, check the recliner and anything within my reach. I'm on probation, you know. I always cooperate." Johnny checked the recliner and found nothing. He motioned for Heavy D to sit back down, and he did. "Now to what do I owe this honored visit and all this attention?"

Red needed no further prompting. "We're here to chat about your cousin, Ernest Rand."

Johnny and Holly watched the men standing around the room while the two Carolina detectives took over.

"Ernie, yeah, he's like my little bro. Is he in some sort of trouble, Detective . . . what was your name?"

"Fishman. Not anymore." Red looked directly at Heavy D, showing neither fear nor respect.

Heavy D started to clench his jaw, then smiled. "It's great to hear that he turned his life around! He was heading down a bad path, and I had been talking with him, trying to get him to give up his old thug ways. So many bad influences in society these days."

"When was the last time you spoke with him?" Red asked.

"I guess a few days ago. Is he in lockup? I can't afford to bail him out. I mean, look at my modest living quarters."

Red smiled. "Looks like you've got it fixed up real nice. My guess is you have experience decorating small spaces." Holly and Johnny nearly started laughing at that one. Cavert just smiled.

"I'm sure I don't know what you mean. Is Ernest in trouble? Can I help?"

"Not unless you can raise the dead." Red waited for the reaction. Heavy D was grabbing the arms of the chair. "Don't bullshit me, Edward. You know he's in the morgue in South Carolina."

The use of his given name seemed to torque Heavy D even more than Red's assertive presence. There was a flash of anger, more like rage, then the smile emerged again. "I seem to recall my momma saying something about a death in the family. I'm sad to learn it was him."

Red softened his face intentionally. "So you weren't aware of his death prior to me telling you?"

"No, sir."

"Well, let me apologize. My condolences for your loss."

Heavy D seemed to study Red's face for a minute. "There's no Fishman assigned to Homicide in the Lawler PD. So where do you work?" The fact that he knew this was disconcerting, but none of the detectives even flinched.

"Detective Cavert and I are from South Carolina, Ballard County. We're investigating his death. We came here to notify his close cousin, Edward. Now I'm glad we came. It would have been terrible to pass such bad and unexpected news over the telephone."

Heavy D knew they were messing with him. He also knew he was on thin ice. He already lied to them once about not knowing he was dead. *Stupid mistake*, he thought. He had to admit to the calls, as he figured they had his cousin's cell phone.

"You don't exactly look upset. I thought you two were close, like *brothers*," Cavert added.

"Well, Detective, I also know the reality of the street. Even though I tried to get him to give up the life, I recognize that he made his choices. Robbing people is a good way to get dead, especially with all these citizens packing."

Red smiled. *Second mistake*, Red thought. Red had not told him who shot his cousin.

Cavert took over while Heavy D was trying to figure out why his new friend Detective Fishman was smiling. "So what was his street name?"

"Just because he was in the life, doesn't mean he had a street name."

Holly laughed and said, "Li'l man, how's your big brother? Is he done with that stint I put him in for?"

One of the men facing away with his hands up responded, "He's okay. Not ready to send you any Christmas cards, though. He's making it."

Holly looked at Heavy D. "You were saying?" Johnny had to put his hand over his mouth to keep from laughing.

Heavy D forced another smile. "I don't know. I think it was Mikey or something."

That's number three, Red thought. He and Cavert knew that Heavy D's texts referenced Ernest as "Micro."

Red stared at Heavy D and spoke to Johnny. "Do you have that item we discussed?"

Johnny turned and handed Heavy D a search warrant for the premises. Heavy D looked at it and read that they were looking for a cell phone with a specific number assigned and a specific serial number and brand.

"I'd like to call my lawyer," Heavy D said.

Cavert spoke up. "I'd like a Porsche, but I don't have one."

Holly spoke loudly and in a strong tone. "Gentlemen, we are executing a search warrant. As you are in this house, you are subject to search. If any of you decide to leave, which would be very rude, you will be quickly apprehended and charged with obstructing an official investigation. Now I know some of you may be thinking that you outnumber us. First, I can even the odds before you get a chance to turn around. Second, there are, as you expect, more waiting outside. So keep your hands on your heads."

One guy behind Heavy D started sprinting toward the door. However, he had to pass Holly on the way. She put her knee up while turning sideways in his direction and stopped him cold. He went down hard, and she had him handcuffed before he could react. Johnny took up a position at the door with his gun drawn. Holly pulled a weapon from the man's waistband and put it in the back of her pants.

She was not even out of breath. "Now, Maurice, I thought you were smarter than that." In between gasps for air, the man on the ground tried to speak. "Not only did I lock you up for robbery last year, you're still on probation for possession, and that means you cannot be in possession of a gun."

"Yes, ma'am."

Heavy D shook his head. "I tell them to treat officers with respect, but sometimes they don't listen." Again, he smiled at Holly.

Holly leaned down to Maurice again. "It also means you cannot associate with known felons." She smiled at Heavy D.

"What you gonna do, take all of us in?" It was a voice from a big guy who stood across the room from the rest of the group. Johnny estimated that his arms were eighteen inches around. He had a tattoo on his right bicep that read CEO-MURDAVILLE. He was turning toward the detectives. Just then the door opened, and Hancock and his team came in dressed out in full SWAT gear.

Hancock moved quickly into the gap between the detectives and the putative chief executive. He picked the big guy up off his feet as he moved, like he was a child, and put him against the wall, handcuffing him. "I imagine you have a permit for this?" Hancock pulled a small-framed semiautomatic from the man's waistband. As Hancock looked at it, he smiled. "I guess you also bought it at a scratch-and-dent sale. The serial number is gone."

"I got nothing to say," he responded.

Hancock called for a beat unit to bring a paddy wagon to the residence.

The sight of the rest of the Tac team, complete with M4 rifles, poured a bucket of water on the intentions of Heavy D's crew. They disarmed everyone after they were on the floor, making a point to intentionally treat Heavy D better than the rest of the folks in the house. A uniformed car arrived and then a paddy wagon. They ran everyone's name and date of birth. Of the ten "security" men, eight were prohibited from possessing a weapon either because they were felons or due to the status of their cases in the criminal justice system. Some were on probation and prohibited from possessing firearms, or the rest were on pretrial release with the same restriction. The remaining two were a mystery. One was completely clean for all intents and purposes, other than the fact that he was in the house with known felons. The last one could not be identified. That was problematic. Hancock called for a portable fingerprint scanner.

The detectives removed the batteries of all the cell phones, checking for the one listed on the search warrant. During the arrests of the eight, several pills, joints, and bags of drugs were found. The detectives checked Heavy D's phone, but it did not match.

"So, no match, I guess. What are you going to do?" Heavy D was smiling.

Red smiled at him. "Oh, no. You can have this one. We'll just keep looking until we find the one we need."

Now that the Tac team was present, Johnny started looking for the other cell phone. He went into a bedroom and opened a nightstand. In the nightstand were three things: Heavy D's wallet, a cell phone, and an ounce of cocaine.

"Bingo," Johnny said, and he walked back to the room. He checked the serial number and announced they had the correct cell phone. At that point, all searching stopped. Johnny went up to Holly and asked her how she wanted to proceed. They both knew that in order to search for drugs, they needed a separate search warrant, because they had found the phone listed on the warrant.

She whispered to Hancock, who just shook his head.

He stepped outside and got on his cell phone. Holly walked close to Heavy D. "And I thought you were smart, my friend. Leaving your wallet and phone next to your stash? Very dumb."

Heavy D was mad—very mad—and his face was getting red. The smile was gone.

One of the Tac guys, who looked like he had his own zip code, walked close to Heavy D. He looked straight at him and pushed his M4 behind his back on the sling. "You know what's worse than getting busted with an eight ball of coke?" Heavy D didn't answer. "Getting a case of the stupids and trying to resist arrest. There's only one way to play this, boss. Turn around and put your hands behind your back. You're under arrest."

The look on Heavy D's face was clear. No more poker face. He wanted to hurt someone. He looked straight at Holly and tried to stare her down. She did not miss a beat. "You feelin' froggy? Go ahead and jump. I'll tell him to wait outside!" she said, pointing at the SWAT officer.

Heavy D swallowed and took a deep breath, then out came the smile. "Not at all, Officer. I believe this is a mistake, but you'll get no resistance from me." Then he put his hands on his head, stood up, turned around, and slowly put his hands behind his back. He was handcuffed quickly and brought outside to a patrol car to be kept away from everyone else.

At that point, Hancock came back in. "Intelligence will be here within a half hour with a search warrant. They'll bring a K9 with them. Looks like a good day at the office!"

Holly laughed. "Yep. Someone is not going to be happy. I smelled the fresh weed when I came in. It's almost raw. My guess is, you'll find a hydroponic system in the basement. Thanks for crashing the party."

"No problem," Hancock answered. "When I heard the others talking back and the scuffle, we decided to come in. It's tough with you. Your voice never wavers."

Holly smiled. Johnny and the other detectives saw it. She answered in a half laugh. "These punks are nothing. I guess I did too much time on wires doing buys. It takes a lot to get me to flinch."

"That's a good thing," Hancock said. "We got it from here. We'll keep it locked down until the search warrant gets here. Take who you want, and leave the rest. I'll make sure they find a home. Looks like the easiest route is to call probation and pretrial release."

Red and Cavert shook the hands of the Tac officers and thanked them. Johnny did, too. Holly just gave a broad thanks to all of them and patted Hancock on the back as she walked out. The mutual respect was obvious. It was clear they'd been in hairier situations than this in the past.

The detectives told the uniformed officer to bring Heavy D back to the Homicide Unit and wait for them. Johnny and Red headed to the magistrate to secure a search warrant for the phone they seized, and Holly and Cavert followed the uniformed car. It was going to be a long day.

CHAPTER 36

J ohnny was looking forward to a ride and chat with Red. He was a seasoned detective and had played Heavy D well. It was impressive.

"So how did you decide to play to his ego?" Johnny was hoping the question wouldn't sound silly.

Red responded after a few minutes. "What makes you think I was playing to his ego?"

"Well, you stopped the nice banter Holly started, you called him by his given name in front of his crew, and you let him lie to you."

"How could you tell he was lying?"

"His voice went up. You never told him that his cousin was shot by a store owner, but he knew it anyway. I'm not sure how, but you had proof he called his cousin 'Micro.'"

Red smiled. "Not bad for a rookie homicide detective! All of the text messages are between two numbers, but he calls him Micro twice. Three lies in ten minutes. He's nervous about something. From what y'all have said, he's usually pretty cool. Now he's got three counts of a felony for lying to officers during an investigation. I'm assuming that's a crime in this state."

"Indeed. I'm assuming you want to wait to charge him."

"Yep. I want to interview him about those text messages on Micro's phone. See if we can get some information to piece together about any connections to South Carolina's growing gang problem."

Johnny smiled. "Ever notice how every city and state has a *growing* gang problem and not an *actual* gang problem?"

"I have. If people treated ants the same way they treat gangs, there'd be enough to carry all of us away!" Red laughed at his own joke. "You've got some good instincts. What brought you to Homicide?"

"Where else can I track down killers? I've always wanted to do it."

"For a new guy, you've got good instincts. I have to have a local with me. Do you want to sit in when I have a chat with Mr. Heavy D?"

"Sounds like a great opportunity. Can I interject something?" Johnny asked.

"Any time. If you're gonna get good in Homicide, you'd better learn to listen to people. I'm sure you could teach me something. What ya got?"

"Let's secure the search warrant for the cell phone, then get someone at the PD to start analyzing it. Let's look for photos of him with Micro, as I'm assuming you have a picture of him."

"I do. What else?"

"Let's ask for any photos or evidence of Heavy D being in South Carolina, making calls to South Carolina, GPS history, or any ties to any crimes committed there. In addition, we can look for information related to drug sales and other criminal activity, especially after finding his cell with a bunch of coke! What a goober."

"I like it. Go on."

"Okay. We go back to Homicide and tell him we will be with him in a bit. His curiosity will prevent him from calling his lawyer. I'll wait until you leave and tell him I think this South Carolina stuff is stupid, and I want to get home to get to a movie with my girlfriend. I'll tell him to just answer the questions about his cousin so we can all go home. That will give our technical guys the time to execute the search warrant on the phone. It shouldn't take more than an hour."

"Who has the phone?" Red was writing a note on his pad.

"I gave it to Holly. As soon as I get the search warrant, I'll email the warrant to her. She'll take it to the IT guys so they can start while we're on the way back. By the time I speak with his highness, Heavy D, we'll be about thirty minutes away from having all the answers."

Red nodded. "Good plan. How come you can't take the warrant electronically via video?"

"Our chief magistrate has a bug up his butt about search warrants and wants all officers to appear in person. It's not required by any law, but he's the judge."

"I hear that," Red said and smiled. He looked out the window for a moment, then spoke again. "You've got a lot of experience with interrogations and phones for a guy who just started in Homicide."

"Well, I came from a fatality hit-and-run unit. You'd be surprised how much people text their friends when they plow into a pedestrian then leave the scene." Johnny looked over at Red and smiled.

"I'll bet. Did you like it over there? I actually loved traffic when I was on the street."

"It was great, but I was ready for a change. You get

tired of dealing with the same motivations and causes for every crime."

"Do tell." Red was looking at Johnny now.

"Impatience and stupidity. People were either too busy to pay attention to the road or too stupid to stop drinking." Johnny's face flushed red. Although he tried to stop the anger, sometimes it came through.

"Interesting observation. We get involved in traffic homicides on occasion. They're not easy." Red paused. "You should do well in Homicide. Besides, I bet you know how to work those damn computers to spit stuff out, as well!"

"I do okay on them. It's a great way to find people and to break alibis, Red." Johnny pulled into the Magistrate Court building. "By the way, we're going in a back door. No need to check your weapon."

"That's a switch."

"Yeah. They had an active shooter wannabe in the neighboring county who never got off a shot. He was taken down by a county police officer with the backup weapon that he wasn't supposed to be carrying. After that, everyone decided to stop the charade and let officers carry in the building. From what I hear, the judges are fine with it."

"They should be." Red laughed. "More than half of the ones I've spoken with are carrying on the bench."

"The funny part was the officer who saved the day toted three days for violation of policy," Johnny complained.

"That was stupid." Johnny heard the disgust in Red's voice. "They should've given him a medal."

"They did, and a local car dealership gave him an award that came with an honorarium."

"Let me guess. The total of three days' pay?" Red leaned toward Johnny.

"And not a penny more." Johnny winked.

Johnny swiped his access card, and the two men walked up a flight of stairs to a door marked MAGISTRATE JUDGE. Johnny knocked and heard the judge tell them to come in. About twenty minutes later, they were walking back to the car and Johnny's phone rang.

"Till. Yep. Did you get the warrant I emailed you? Okay. How long? Great. See you in about twenty minutes."

"Was that Holly?"

"No, our IT guy, Detective Nat Franetti. He's the best. Has a master's degree in computer science and has taken about every class you can find. The local FBI office uses him occasionally for their federal cases. He'll find those texts, even if Heavy D tried to erase them."

"What happens in Vegas stays on your phone, huh?" Red asked.

"Very true."

They were back at Homicide in about ten minutes, faster than expected. Johnny went into the unit and found the major speaking with Holly behind a closed door. He then went to the interrogation room and made certain the audio and video were working. Then he showed Red where to stand to watch and listen. He went in to speak with the man of the hour.

Heavy D was sitting in a chair, handcuffed below the table. He appeared to be sleeping, but Johnny saw that his chest was rising and falling pretty quickly. He thought that was odd. When Johnny said something, Heavy D picked up his head and smiled. That amazing smile—no doubt an instruction from a defense attorney to keep him from saying something stupid.

"Good afternoon. I'm Detective Till. We met earlier."

"Actually, we did not. You were in my home and did not tell me your name. I find that impolite." His smile extended.

"An oversight on my part. I was just there watching the show. You've been waiting a while, and I apologize. I've been running around in a car with one of those South Carolina guys listening to all their nonsense about a case they have. Well, I've got my own cases to worry about."

Heavy D just looked at him.

"Look, I don't know about this thing with your cousin, and I don't give a shit. I was asked to babysit these guys while they're here. That's all I'm gonna do, but it's getting old. You don't want to be here, and I've got a date tonight. So I'm working on getting both of us out of this room at a reasonable time and definitely before dinner. Just give me about thirty minutes, and I'll be back. We'll let him ask his questions, we'll both be done, and he'll be headed back home. Sound good to you?"

Heavy D was not new to this rodeo. He stared at Johnny and tried to size him up. He was really having trouble. So he tried to get inside his head and make him let his guard down. "I've never met you. The other detective, the good-looking one, I've met her before. The other guys are not from here, but you, where'd you come from?"

"Traffic Unit. I'm a traffic cop, dude. In fact, today is my first day in Homicide. Can you believe it? This is the greatest! No more working outside, no more writing tickets! What a waste. I've been looking to get off the street for a long time. They had an opening, and I took it!"

"So that's why you're more interested in getting laid than making an arrest."

"Damn right! I have no idea how long I can ride this gravy train, but this place is awesome! If I get good at it, they'll put me on morning watch working overnight by myself! That would cut into my sack time." Johnny winked at Heavy D, who laughed. "So here's the deal. Just work with this guy, and let's go home. He's got nothing on you about a death in another state. Just humor him and let me meet that blonde for dinner. Sound good?"

Heavy D smiled at him. It was a different smile than before. This one seemed genuine. Johnny walked out, again telling Heavy D it would just be a few minutes. When he walked into the hall outside the interview room, Red and Cavert were smiling and holding out their hands for a fist bump. Johnny smiled and went to his desk to check on the progress on Heavy D's phone. On the way, he passed Holly as she came out of the major's office. "You in a sling?"

Holly smiled. "No. I just need to fill out a use-of-force on the perp I cuffed before I go home. I knew he surprised me, but I didn't realize that I hit him that hard. Apparently, he's at the hospital speaking with a surgeon. He may have a hernia and internal bleeding from a bruised spleen."

"I thought he was coming at you, and I was pretty sure he was armed. I don't think you did anything wrong."

"Thanks, neither does anyone else. I'll fill out the report. I planned to, anyway. I've seen this before, though.

The guys who get a mark from any contact with a female officer think they can scream brutality. After all, a woman would have to be crazy or acting out of anger to leave a mark. It's bullshit, but it's the truth."

"It was impressive, though. You put him down pretty quickly," Johnny said.

"When my dad heard me say in high school that I wanted to be a cop, he enrolled me in martial arts classes. It was fun, and sometimes I was the only girl. It was a great way to meet guys, if you didn't mind getting sweaty and bruised with them."

"I'll keep that in mind. Did they field-test the coke we found with his phone?"

"Yep. The narcs said it was cocaine and very high quality. Mr. Heavy D is going away for quite a while, but we'll keep that quiet for a bit. How's the phone look-see coming?"

"I'm calling Franetti now." Johnny reached his desk and picked up his phone. He grabbed a pad on his desk and listened to the phone ring. The unit secretary picked up the phone and told Johnny that Detective Franetti was on his way down to Homicide. "He should be there in a few."

"Trouble?" Holly asked.

"Not sure. Nat is on his way down. Francine in the unit said he was excited. He should be here any minute."

"Great. I'll get Red and Cavert," Holly offered.

Nat Franetti used his access card to enter the Homicide Unit about five minutes later, and he was with his captain, Dan Morse. They were both extremely excited about something. Both of them were veteran detectives who made the decision to use their computer skills to catch bad guys from behind their desks. Johnny always admired them for that. They rarely got the thrill of placing cuffs on the bad guys. They were usually assisting with the casework of other investigators and detectives. They had both received a wall of awards, and Johnny felt the department was lucky to have them.

The meeting took place in the conference room in Homicide. In addition to Johnny, Holly, Red, and Cavert, Major Worth was there. Johnny also saw Captain Ken Roscoe come in. He was the commander of the Sex Crimes Unit, which included the Crimes Against Children Unit and the Sex-Trafficking Unit. Everyone was introduced, and Johnny knew things were about to get real. Franetti put a thumb drive into the laptop on the desk, and the screen showed the case number, the search-warrant number, and Heavy D's real name.

"Okay. You guys hit the jackpot! What do you know about this guy, Heavy D?" Franetti was a slight guy, but not what you would expect in a guy this into computers. He was a seasoned cop and detective who just happened to spend a lot of time in the gym and running marathons when he wasn't behind a computer.

Holly spoke up. "He's a suspect in several homicides, has ties to a gangbanger in South Carolina, and is a reported hit guy and problem solver for some local gangs. He's done a few short stints in prison, but nothing too long."

Captain Roscoe piped in. "Were the drugs a surprise to you?"

"No," Holly said. "I imagine he smokes and snorts like any other jackass we chase."

"How about girls? Any rumors of him running girls?" Franetti could barely sit still.

"Aside from the odd hooker that hung around his crew, nothing that we know of."

"Well, today is Christmas! I found all of the texts you were looking for. That was easy. He tried to erase a few of the more pertinent ones. From what Till told me, I can tell you he was directing operations in Carolina. He and his buddy Micro were thick as thieves. Micro didn't do much without checking with him first. The communications stopped the day Micro died, so Heavy D must have known he was gone. Not a single call, text, or email to him after that night about an hour after Micro was shot." He looked directly at Red and Cavert.

Major Worth spoke up. "Sounds like there's more than that, Nat."

"Oh, yeah! We found a bunch of pictures of him doing drugs. Just name them—coke, meth, weed, even shooting something up in his groin, of all places! I'll have trouble getting those pics out of my mind."

"He's on probation," Holly chimed in. "He's gotta meet with a probation officer, so he can't go in there with track marks. Not sure how he's passing the piss tests."

"Well, no one is going to find the marks there. But here's the motherload. We found a bunch of photos of him getting oral sex from girls, and they looked pretty young. There were only a few in the recent photos, and he tried to delete the rest. Useless, of course, but an A for effort."

Ken Roscoe sat forward in his chair. "How young were the girls?"

"Well, Captain, I had that same question in my mind. I can show you the pictures if you need to see them, but all of you would have to sign the log."

"I'll pass, unless we need to," Red volunteered.

"Sorry, boss, but you're going to want to see them to put this guy away. Captain Roscoe, I thought at least one of the girls looked familiar from a sex-trafficking BOLO you sent around. So I recovered all of the photos on the phone. Then I used a new facial-recognition software I am beta-testing with the FBI and US Marshals, and voila!"

Franetti hit a combination of keys, and photos of missing girls came up. They ranged in age from nine to sixteen. All were on posters for girls believed to be involved in sex trafficking. The group stared at the seventy-five posters on the screen. No one said a word.

Captain Roscoe picked up his phone and dialed a number. He spoke into the phone and told someone to get to the Homicide conference room ASAP. He also called Brian Hancock and told him to hold the scene pending another search warrant. When he finished, he told Franetti to continue.

"Keep in mind, these are the girls I could identify. There are at least fifty more. I believe he stopped using that phone about a week ago because it was acting up. Even though he tried to delete the photos, the memory in his phone was toast. It was probably acting up a lot. That's why he had a different phone on him when Johnny patted him down."

"Are all of the girls performing sex acts, Nat?" Roscoe asked.

"Yes, sir. All of them on Heavy D, and some of them are in various stages of undress."

"How do you know it's Heavy D's *equipment*?" Red asked what everyone in the room wanted to know.

"Well, that's where the drugs bite him on the nuts, so to speak! Remember I said he was injecting the drugs into his groin? Well, he has a tattoo high on the inside of his left thigh. It's a letter D in gold with bags of money inside. Pretty weird, but hey, I'm not a tat guy. I checked the Lawler Sheriff's Office and asked my buddy to send me a list and photos of Heavy D's tats. It's him, no doubt. We've got at least one hundred counts of forced oral sodomy, aggravated child molestation, and false imprisonment, and that's before we find his home computer. I'll bet there's hundreds of these pictures. In my experience, these guys keep the pics to get off on later. Some of them even trade the pics." He looked around the room. "Your tough guy hitman is a pedophile. Who knew?"

Major Worth spoke up. "Good work, Nat, as always! Anything else?"

"Yes, Major. We've got a bunch of pics of him posing with firearms that I can date after his first felony conviction, but that is the least of his worries now. Each act with a minor is a mandatory minimum of fifteen years, and that's if you don't take him federal and let the FBI charge him. They have so many aggravators and multipliers, he's looking at several hundred years. I also found about two hundred pictures of young girls, about the same age range, in various stages of undress. This guy is a pedophile from the get-go. He'll never see the light of day." He started tapping keys and pulled up a picture. "There's something y'all should see."

The group focused on the picture. "Hannah Trover? Who is she?" Worth was focused on the picture and the information on the missing-persons poster.

"The hits just keep on coming. She's eighteen. Disappeared from a bar in Daytona Beach, Florida. Her dad is a cop in Chicago." The room was quiet. "We haven't notified him that we found her picture. The timing of that call is up to y'all."

No one spoke for a few minutes as they studied her picture. She was a beautiful girl with dark skin and light-green eyes. In the picture, she was smiling. Johnny wondered what she was doing at that moment, if she was still even alive.

The door opened and two detectives from Sex Crimes came in. Captain Roscoe introduced them as Sergeants Stacy Krebs and Laura Bennett from Crimes Against Children and Sex Trafficking, respectively. Captain Roscoe brought them up to speed and told them to secure a search warrant for Heavy D's computers, car, and house. They left with a promise of a follow-up briefing when Captain Roscoe left the meeting.

Captain Roscoe looked at Nat for a minute, then spoke up. "Okay, Nat. I agree, great job, as always. How long will it take you to process his computer once we get it you?"

"You know how much I hate these guys, Captain. Get it to me by 1800, and you'll have the results by midnight, 0800 tomorrow at the latest. I'm not expecting a lot of security, but there are a lot of encryption programs commercially available now. I may have to go 'black hat' on 'em."

"Great. Captain Morse, I'll approve the overtime on your unit. I want this guy shut down, and I want any leads on where we can find these girls. Do you have anything now?"

"As you know, Captain," Nat spoke up, "we've been able to find some of these girls using the data imprinted on the photographs when they are taken. I did a quick search on a few of them, and it appears that the location and GPS tags were either not captured or were removed. It's also possible that the photos were taken with another camera and sent to the phone we searched. I can find out, but I need more time to do that. There's one other, more disturbing possibility. The pictures could have been taken in a safe room."

Nat looked around and could see no one was familiar with the term. "It's a relatively new thing being seen in bigger drug operations. The perps line the walls of a room with anything to stop a signal—tinfoil, concrete, steel—to prevent narcs from transmitting while in the room. Of course, the phone would still take pictures, but without a signal from anywhere, there would not be any information to imprint on the pictures."

Captain Roscoe then spoke up. "Why is that so disturbing to you? These idiots have been working to disrupt our communications for years."

Nat looked around at the room. "We've just started seeing these types of rooms at the big cartel level. They're expensive to build, especially in flop houses and transient locations. I checked around, and no one has seen one in connection with a sex-trafficking case. If these bastards have figured that out, they've gone to a whole new level of sophistication. It's going to be harder to catch them. As you know, we've saved a couple of girls when they called 911 on the john's phone. This would put an end to that."

Nat punched a couple of keys and brought up a search screen. "Captain, as you know, I don't like to lose. We've been beta-testing a bunch of software, as I stated earlier. You may not know this, but all social media is connected one way or the other. So if you post a picture on one social media site, it goes into this huge pool. So after I got clear pics of the girls, I ran a sort of offline search of their faces on all forms of social media and the internet as a whole. I found recent sites with their pictures that were verified by the facial-recognition software. I have someone going through those sites right now trying to ID the locations, and frankly, we could use more help. Of course, the best way to find them is to get Mr. Heavy D in there to fess up."

"That won't be easy," Holly said. "Once he believes he's going to prison, he'll shut up. I've interviewed him before."

Major Worth was sitting and thinking. Finally, he spoke up. "Detectives Fishman and Cavert, how much do you need out of Heavy D to answer your questions and broaden the investigation to monopolize on what Detective Franetti found about Heavy D's ties to South Carolina?"

Red and Cavert conferred for a moment. Then Red answered. "It seems like the evidence on the phone is enough to broaden our investigation. However, we want to chat with him to confront him with the texts and calls. I need to know if he is an accessory to the robbery that led to his cousin's death. That won't take me long."

"Johnny, do you have charges on him now, aside from the drugs and the items on his phone?"

"Yes, Major. He lied to us three times in his house during a voluntary interview."

"Okay. Here's what we'll do. Ken, jump in any time and give me your thoughts. We'll let Fishman and Cavert get what they need. Johnny, you go in with one of them and help out. Be the fly on the wall as much as you can. Add any lies he tells to the charges. Holly, you go secure the arrest warrant on the false statements and obstruction charges. Once we have him locked down on those charges, we'll show him the screenshots from his phone.

Hopefully, that will be enough for him to want to make a deal and give up the location of the girls."

"He's been in prison before, Major." Holly was sitting forward in her chair. "He's not afraid. For crying out loud, he's a damn celebrity in the joint."

Major Worth smiled and leaned toward her over the table. "He was when he was a hitman and gangbanger. He's going to do the hardest time of his life as a child molester. He's got nowhere to hide, and he'll know that. He may be dead if he makes bond. Yep, that's the best leverage we have. Ken, you have your guys join Johnny once he lays out the photos. He'll be pretty vulnerable at that point. Maybe you'll be able to get him to help himself."

"Good strategy, Major. I agree." Captain Roscoe was red-faced and obviously looking forward to finding those girls.

"Okay. Let's keep the momentum on this," Worth said. "We'll start the interviews in fifteen minutes. I'll get the chief on the line and brief her. Then she and I will call the DA." He looked around the room. "Folks, this is excellent work! Well done!" It was a trademark of Worth's. If you worked with him, you always knew where you stood.

Johnny got up and walked toward the door with Red. They had some work to do to prepare, and they had to stay on schedule. Heavy D hadn't asked for his lawyer yet, although they were certain someone had called him on his behalf.

While Red went to the restroom, Johnny stepped to the side before he entered the briefing room. He took out his phone and gathered his thoughts. While it was a close call as to protocol, sometimes it's easier to apologize than ask for permission. He had seen the information on the BOLO for Hannah Trover and thought he might be able to get some information, something very fresh, that would help with Heavy D.

He walked into a closet reserved for office supplies, and in the company of boxes of binder clips, stacks of notepads, and rolls of paper towels, he placed a call.

"Lieutenant Maxwell Trover, please."

"This is Trover."

Johnny had obviously reached his cell number. *Makes sense. Any cop would know to give a twenty-four-hour number.*

"Lieutenant, I'm Detective Johnny Till with the Lawler County Police Department." Johnny's voice left him for a second.

The pause prompted Trover to respond. "What can I do for you, Till?"

"I'm calling about a missing-person report on—"

"Did you find Hannah?" Trover blurted out.

Shit. What do I tell him? "Not yet, sir, but we're tracking a lead on her." Silence on the phone. "When was the last time you heard anything about or from her?"

Trover cleared his throat. Johnny imagined that he was having a hard time speaking. "The last we heard was when she disappeared."

"No ransom or threats?"

"None. Till, I've been a cop for over twenty years. I wish they demanded money. I'd have her back by now, whatever it took. The lack of demands makes me fear the worst. I . . ." His voice fell apart and Johnny heard people around him speaking.

"I'll let you know as soon as we have something concrete. I promise."

About a minute later, Trover came back onto the phone. "Till, where the hell is Lawler County?"

"Georgia, sir."

"You can give me an update in person."

Johnny tried to respond, but the line was dead.

CHAPTER 37

Afew a quick huddle about their game plan, Red and Johnny entered the interview room. Heavy D made a big point of acting like he was asleep. Red was in charge and let Heavy D know it immediately.

"Rise and shine, sleeping beauty!" He then pounded the table. Heavy D had been leaning back in the chair, and he sat up slowly.

"So tell us about your boy Ernest. Who did he run with in this thug life you were working to get him out of?"

"Well, Detective, they're in another state, so I'm afraid I can't help you." The smile emerged again.

"You said you don't know his street name, right?"

"Yes, sir. That's a part of his life I did not want to acknowledge or encourage."

"Then how come you refer to him as Micro in these text messages?" Red put the text messages on the table. Heavy D read them carefully. He was still smiling. Red made a big deal of putting them into evidence bags, even though they were copies of what Detective Franetti gave them.

Some people make the mistake of believing that calloused criminals are uneducated or stupid. Nothing could be further from the truth in the case of Mr. Heavy D. He had graduated from high school and was accepted to every state school he applied to. He started college and attended just long enough to learn what he needed to know about the opposition, just like a business-school analysis. Except in his case, he got a two-year degree in criminal justice. He was a force to be reckoned with, just as Holly had told them. Unfortunately for him, Holly also told them about all of his weaknesses based upon the interview tapes she had.

When he was finished reading, Heavy D leaned back and smiled. "You know, I guess there's some kind of misunderstanding. I've called Ernest Micro since we were kids. Was that his street name?"

Red just smiled. "Very good, Edward. Not smart, but good. We've spoken to your mom while you were cooling off in here. Strange, but she never heard of the name Micro. So tell me, is your momma a liar?"

Heavy D's whole countenance changed. This was not an act now. This was deep. *Holly was right*, Johnny thought. *He hates when people bring up or involve his family.*

"You're bullshittin' me. You never spoke with my mother."

"Well, let's see, Edward. Does this number look familiar?" Red turned around his own cell phone to show Heavy D the number on his recent calls list. Thanks to Franetti, the thirty-second call appeared to last twenty minutes. *Ah, the wonders of technology.* "Any other lies you want to tell, or can we get down to business?" Red sat back down in his chair and opened a folder without waiting for an answer.

Heavy D was still fuming, but he answered some questions. He claimed he did not know anything about

Micro's activities in South Carolina. He was stone-walling, running out of options. Red had to start making progress quickly before he called for his attorney.

"So who told you Micro was greased by a store owner during a robbery?"

"You did, dumbass."

"No, no. I asked you if you knew he was dead, and you volunteered that information. I have that entire conversation on tape. Do you care to hear it?"

Heavy D was thinking. He did not like this, but still couldn't figure out how they could touch him for a robbery in South Carolina. "I don't need to hear it. I guess I misunderstood you."

Red started laughing. "Misunderstood something I didn't say? How long do you think it's going to take for one of those goobers we arrested out of your house to rat you out to keep his sorry ass out of prison?"

"Not my crew. They ain't no damn rats!" Heavy D hissed.

"Because you take care of them on the inside? Well, I doubt you'll be able to take care of yourself on the inside."

Heavy D's face changed. He tried to look smug, but he was getting worried. He'd underestimated the old detective. He'd missed something. "What the hell are you talking about? You got nothing on me."

"Not true, Edward. You see, you told three lies to detectives during our interview at your house. You lied about Micro's street name, you lied about knowing he was dead, and you lied about knowing how he died. That's three felonies in this state, not to mention the coke we found."

"That's bullshit! I didn't have possession. You guys don't even have a decent equal-access case. Anyone could have put that coke in that drawer." He was clearly getting concerned.

"Anyone? And it just happened to land in a drawer next to your wallet and cell phone, next to your bed? You're slipping, my friend." Red leaned forward until he was about six inches away from Heavy D's face. "I never said it was in a drawer."

Heavy D tried to stand. He looked at Johnny and yelled, "Get this asshole out of my face! You said it would be a few simple questions, and now he's threatening to pin four felonies on me? Fuck both of you!"

Johnny took over, as they had planned. "He can't charge you with anything in this state. All the Georgia charges are up to me. Just answer his questions about South Carolina, and you and I will discuss some information that might make me forget about the coke and everything else."

Heavy D seemed to weigh the prospect. Then he spoke in a clear tone through his now-famous smile. "Detectives, I would like to help you, but I believe the tone of this meeting has become hostile. So I request to speak with my lawyer before I answer any further questions."

Red was impressed. He'd interviewed a lot of criminals in his time, but none of them played to the camera and audio as well as Mr. Heavy D.

"No problem, sir." Johnny picked up the handset on the phone sitting on the small table. "I'm happy to call him for you. Just give me the number."

"Bullshit. I'll call him."

Johnny smiled. "Now that would be dumb. If you call him in this room, anything you say will be recorded. I'll put him on speaker and tell him where you are, what interview room you're in, and ask him for his ETA."

Heavy D looked at Johnny sideways. "What's your deal, man?"

"No deal here, partner," Johnny said. "I know the law, and I'm not going to risk my career screwing up. You want a lawyer? That's fine with me." He then looked at Heavy D. "What's the number?"

Heavy D gave him the number, and Johnny dialed it with the phone on speaker. It was his lawyer's cell phone.

"Rappin," he answered. It was Walter Rappin, one of the best attorneys in the state, and a man known to be as gracious as he was vigorous.

"Mr. Rappin, this is Lawler County Detective Till. I have you on speaker in interrogation room five in the Homicide Unit. Mr. Heavy D—excuse me, Edward Rawlings—requested that I contact you. He is requesting your presence before we ask him any more questions."

There was a pause on the phone, likely for Rappin to comprehend what he was hearing. "Well, Detective, I truly appreciate your call. We have not spoken in a while. Is my client able to hear, as well?"

"Oh, yes, sir. He's sitting right here. However, I don't recommend that you speak with him privately, as this line could be taped."

"Very kind of you, Detective Till. Edward, I'll be there in about ten minutes. Do not answer any questions until I arrive. Do you understand?"

"Yes, Walter." Heavy D's voice was flat, like a schoolboy who knew he was in trouble.

"Detective Till, please refrain from asking my client any questions until I arrive. I will try to avoid any undue delay."

"Of course, Mr. Rappin. I appreciate your courtesy."

Rappin hung up.

The three men sat there, saying nothing. The silence was too much for Heavy D. "I told you gentlemen, my lawyer would be en route without delay and will be able to appropriately advise me regarding any further questioning."

"Great," Red said. "Sounds like a nice guy! I look forward to meeting him."

Johnny reached into the folder he had on the floor. Heavy D was trying to see what he had in his hands. "Since we cannot ask you any more questions, I thought I would give you some photos to look at. Maybe when Mr. Rappin gets here, you could help us with some missing-person cases."

Heavy D said nothing, and Johnny spread out five of the missing-person posters Franetti had given him. Heavy D looked at them and studied each one. "Yeah, I don't know them."

Johnny spoke up. "I didn't ask you if you did! In fact, I didn't ask you any questions at all. I'm just trying to save time for Mr. Rappin. After all, you pay him by the hour."

"Yeah, but like I said, I don't know them, so I'm afraid I can't help you gentlemen."

Johnny took out another folder. "You know, sometimes these posters are hard to go by. I mean, people change, and girls, you know, they're always changing their makeup and their hairstyles. See if these photos help." Johnny then laid out five photos of the same girls taken from Heavy D's cell phone. He positioned them directly above the posters. Then, as Heavy D was starting to hyperventilate, Johnny put one more piece of paper on the table above the pictures. Each piece of paper had the age of the girl in the photo. Red looked at Heavy D's forehead. He was sweating.

The two detectives got up and left the photos in the room. "We'll wait outside until your lawyer gets here, Edward." Red was smiling. The two men walked out the door. Outside, they shook hands.

Major Worth walked into the hall. "How long do you think it will take?"

"Less than three minutes, if you ask me," Johnny said. They watched as Heavy D reached his one free hand up to turn the phone around. Then he pushed the speaker button and dialed a number. He was pretty fast for a guy chained to a desk.

At the same time, the phone rang in the house where Johnny met Heavy D a few hours earlier. It rang until someone picked up. The phone was answered by the recently identified Ronnie Barnes. He was the only guy from the house who was not in the county lockup. "Yo."

"Who is this?" Heavy D whispered.

"It's Punch. Is that you, Heavy? Where you at?"

"Yeah, it's me, dumbass. I'm in Lawler Homicide waiting on my lawyer. Listen, you gotta do something for me."

"Of course. Name it, bro."

"Take down this number: 01-277-478-5564. It's an international number. Call them and tell whoever answers I said to burn it all! You got that?"

"Yeah. I got it."

"One other thing. There's a laptop computer under the floor in my closet. Pull up the carpet, and you'll see that the boards come up. Take it out and throw that bitch in the river right now. Got it?"

"Will do. Hang tough, bro. They can't crack you!"

"Damn straight." Heavy D hung up the phone and sat back. He was smiling again.

On the other end of the phone stood Heavy D's soldier, ready to obey. On any normal day, he'd have started dialing the number by now. However, today was not any normal day. Sitting to his left and his right, sharing a phone extension that was plugged into a splitter in the jack and through a recorder, were Sergeants Krebs and Bennett. They smiled as the soldier hung up.

Punch looked down, then swiveled between the two detectives. "We have a deal, right? I'm out of the state by midnight, just like you promised."

"Yes," Krebs said, "quit your whining." She looked to the chair by the television. "Does that still work for you?"

A tall man with a blue raid jacket with FBI on the front left side spoke up. "Cool your heels. We'll get you out of here. First, we've got to find a laptop, and you've got a call to make."

The FBI agent and Sergeant Krebs walked to the bedroom with Heavy D's soldier between them. Sergeant Bennett was already on her phone working with Homeland Security to locate that number.

CHAPTER 38

T rue to his word, Walter Rappin arrived promptly, as expected. He was a short, stocky man with a full head of salt-and-pepper hair. His face was smooth and tan. He was in very good shape and looked far less stressed at this point than his client.

Johnny had gotten to know Rappin three years before when he defended a physician. She had been on her way home from a holiday party when she ran a red light and killed four people in a van. Ironically, they were all extremely intoxicated, but their driver was not. They took the time to have a designated driver, only to lose their lives to an intoxicated emergency room doctor. Rappin tried every way he could to explain why she had walked away from the scene and was found in a nearby restaurant. However, Johnny had interviewed everyone she saw and who spoke with her that night. His case was airtight. It was sealed with the surveillance video from a nearby business that showed how she had gotten out of her car, looked into the van, then walked away.

The jury in that case had an obvious predilection to sympathy for her, as well as a belief in her innocence. However, the evidence was overwhelming, despite the inability of the van driver to identify her. Even the story of how she had turned to alcohol to ease the pain of the carnage she saw during her nights in the ER was not enough.

In the end, a tearful jury had returned a verdict of guilty on all counts. The judge had sentenced her to seventy-five years in prison. Johnny had never forgotten the look on her face when she left the courtroom. He spoke about it often to high school students the week before prom. He also had never forgotten the professionalism of her lawyer who, after the jury was out, his client had left with the deputies, and her family had left the courtroom, had walked over to Johnny and shaken his hand. He had also shaken the hands of the two prosecutors.

"Officer Till, I want to congratulate you and the state's attorneys on your work," he had said.

Johnny was a bit taken back. "I thought you would've been less than happy with me."

"On the contrary, Officer. These prosecutors will tell you that my role as a defense attorney is to test the strength of the state's evidence and safeguard the constitutional rights of my clients. While the process may be adversarial, the people involved need not be adversaries. I respect anyone who is dedicated to getting the truth, even if that truth does not help my client." He had then turned to one of the prosecutors. "I'll see you next week in front of Judge Wister." They had nodded to each other, and Rappin left the courtroom.

Johnny had never forgotten that exchange, and ever since, he always gave a firm and friendly handshake to Walter Rappin. It was well-known among all of the cops in the area that if you had a weak case, you were in for a tough cross-examination, and if you had a great case, you'd better know the facts, but either way, Walter Rappin treated everyone with respect.

"Detective Till, good to see you again." Rappin offered a hand to Johnny. "Congratulations on the promotion! I can say I'm not surprised."

"Good to see you, too, Mr. Rappin. Thanks for getting here so quickly."

"Well, it was obvious from the tenor of my client's voice and your call to me directly that there was some urgency to the matter. May we speak for a moment before I see my client?"

"Sure. Let me introduce you to a couple of people first. This is my partner, Holly Forrester, and these are two homicide detectives from Ballard County, South Carolina, Detectives Fishman and Cavert."

Everyone shook hands.

"It's good to see you again, Detective Forrester. I believe we have a case together now . . . let me see . . . last name is Marlow, I believe," Rappin said.

Holly was clearly on her guard but replied in a pleasant manner. "Ronald Marlow, yes, sir. You've got your work cut out for you with him."

"Sadly, Detective, that is more the rule than the exception." Rappin smiled at her. "So based upon his location, I'm guessing Edward did not run a stop sign."

Red chuckled, and Johnny spoke up. "No, sir, more than just a stop sign. His cousin, Ernest Rand, also known as Micro, was shot and killed in Ballard County by a storekeeper during a robbery. It seems there was a great deal of communication between Edward and Ernest that ceased immediately after Micro was dead. However, when we met with Edward earlier, he denied material facts about the case that he clearly knew."

"I'm assuming this was a voluntary interaction with my client. Where did it take place?"

"In his living room. We knocked, and he invited us in." Holly smiled.

Rappin sighed. "I have no doubt that he did. He probably also gave you consent to search. It is amazing what enlightenment an associate's degree in criminal justice can provide."

Johnny smiled. "He probably would have if we asked, but we had a search warrant for a cell phone."

"Did you locate it?"

"Yes, in a drawer in his nightstand next to his wallet and an eight ball of cocaine."

Rappin smiled and shook his head. "Well, as you know, it will be difficult for me to advise him to incriminate himself any more than he may have done already. In addition, he has an aversion to police stations, and will likely ask me to get him a bond as soon as possible. Knowing you, Detective Till, there's more to this story. I imagine you have some *incentive* for me to encourage him to cooperate."

Red looked at Rappin. He was amazed by his demeanor and his candor. Despite his best efforts, Red was really starting to like the guy.

"Indeed, there is. Detectives Fishman and Cavert need to know whether this was a clumsy robbery, or if there was more to it. As to incentive, let's just go back into the interview room. We'll show you what we have, and you can make a decision as to whether or not it is in Edward's best interests to assist."

"Fair enough. Lead on," Rappin offered.

As Johnny walked toward the interview room, Rappin picked up his cell phone. He called his office and told them he would not be back in the office until tomorrow morning. As he was hanging up the phone, Red and Johnny looked at each other. Red nearly laughed.

As they entered the room, Rappin spoke with Heavy D. "Edward, I came as quickly as I could."

"Get me out of this place, Mr. Rappin! These guys are tripping! They're trying to pin all sorts of bullshit on me!"

Walter Rappin looked at the posters, the photographs, and the cards with the ages of the girls and took in the situation with a quick glance. He looked up at Heavy D and patted him on the arm as he took a seat next to him on the same side of the table. "Let's just listen, Edward, and hear what they have to say. Perhaps you can help these detectives. As I've told you before, listening is more important than talking." With these last words, the stare Rappin gave Heavy D was more akin to a parent giving the "nuclear look" to a toddler.

Heavy D was silent, looking down, and no longer smiling.

Johnny began the conversation. "I'll assume that your client will stick to his earlier statement that he does not know any of these girls?"

"If that's what he said."

Heavy D leaned over and whispered into Rappin's ear. Rappin closed his eyes briefly before speaking, no doubt to absorb the vulgar description of the girls or the motivation of the detectives.

"Well, that's unfortunate." Red shook his head while staring at Heavy D.

Johnny took a pen and pointed to the tattoo on the inner-left thigh of the person receiving oral sex in the photos. "Does that look familiar, Edward?" Johnny's use of his given name was a marked change in their interactions, and Heavy D knew it. Johnny added a certain lilt to his voice as he said it.

"Lots of guys got tattoos, Jack." The words came out of Heavy D's mouth before Rappin could stop him.

Rappin put his hand on Heavy D's wrist and squeezed. "We are listening right now, Edward." Rappin then removed his hand and looked at Johnny. "Do you have some reason to believe that these pictures portray my client? And, may I ask you where you procured these photographs?"

Johnny put a photo on the table with the stamp of the Lawler County Sheriff's Office. "This is one of the many tattoos on Edward's body that was photographed two years ago when he was arrested as a suspect in a rape. The DA declined to prosecute the rape when the victim left the state and refused to cooperate. Alana Garcia was her name."

"I read about that in the paper," Rappin said as he smiled coyly at Johnny knowing that Johnny realized that any police investigations involving Heavy D also involved his lawyer. Rappin looked at Heavy D, who was staring blankly at the newly introduced photograph. He was caught, and he had no one to blame but himself. "May I inquire about the origin of these photographs on the table? If you told me, I missed it."

"They were on your client's cell phone, along with others containing the same subject matter. All totaled, we found about two hundred photos of young girls in various stages of undress."

Rappin was silent, and it was obvious that he was thinking hard. "Naturally, you had a search warrant for the phone?"

Johnny looked at Heavy D. "Of course. I went out of my way to preserve Edward's constitutional rights."

Heavy D was unable to sit still. He knew this was bad—very bad. He leaned forward and started to speak, when Rappin put his right hand on his left shoulder. "We are still listening, Edward. Remember, just listen."

Red spoke up. "So as you can see, there are ample incentives for your client to assist us in South Carolina."

Rappin was still thinking. His wheels were turning. He sat up in his chair and smiled. "Detective Till, I believe it would be appropriate for me to speak with my client. I understand that you have no obligation to do so, but I would like to know if there is any other evidence, especially of this nature," He pointed and waved at the photos on the table. "Of course, any information you can provide would assist me in properly advising my client."

Red sat back in his chair with his arms folded. *This guy is smooth! No wonder juries like him.*

Johnny produced a small digital recorder and hit the play button. Heavy D's conversation with his soldier regarding the laptop and the mysterious international number played loudly. Heavy D was shaking with rage. "That was a private call! No way you had time to get a wiretap!"

"Shut up, Edward!" Rappin was losing his patience.

"You will recall that we told you and your client that the phone line was monitored and taped when we called you," Johnny said to Rappin.

Rappin just nodded his head. After a moment, Johnny looked straight at Heavy D and stared into his eyes. "We have the laptop and a search warrant for it. Our IT guys are tearing it apart now. We'll know more in a few hours, but if what we found on this phone is any indication of what we'll find on his laptop, there'll be a new chomo in the state system. You know that term, Edward? Chomo, short for child molester?" He paused. "Of course, we could speak to the feds and have the US Attorney's Office handle it. It makes no difference to us." Johnny leaned forward. "But it will make a difference to Edward here. Mandatory sentences per picture and sex act. That's a lot of time in prison as everyone's bitch."

Heavy D could stand it no longer. He came unglued and started screaming. Rappin was unable to control him. Johnny didn't move away and continued to lock eyes with Heavy D. Then Red and Johnny stood up, and Red opened the door. "Mr. Rappin, we'll turn off the audio when we leave to give you some time to speak with and advise your client. Will that be sufficient to give you privacy?"

"Yes, Detective Fishman. That will do. Very kind of you."

Johnny marked the audio and video before he left the interview room by stating the time and date and advising the recording would be paused to allow counsel to confer with his client. Then Johnny and Red stepped into the hall, and Holly witnessed Johnny pausing the recordings. Major Worth and Captain Roscoe were in the hall.

"Let's give them some time to chat," Roscoe said. "I want to get away from this door to speak with you."

Johnny spoke up. "Yes, sir, but I want to get a uniformed officer to stand by the door. This guy is coming unglued."

"Way ahead of you, Johnny," Worth said. He stepped around and opened another interview room. A uniformed officer was inside and stepped out. Major Worth gave him some instructions and advised they would be in the conference room if he needed anything and to let them know when the attorney was finished with his client.

The detectives walked into the conference room and sat down. Major Worth pulled the conference phone toward him and dialed the number for Detective Franetti.

"Franetti."

"Nat, Major Worth. I've got you on speaker. Captain Roscoe is here with all the detectives you met earlier. Any update?"

"Sure. I've cracked his password, and I've already made a ghost copy of the drive. I'm searching it right now. That will take a while, but I can tell we're going to find a bunch of stuff! I always do an initial inventory of the computer and take screenshots just to ensure I know what's there and avoid any wiping programs. His photo and video folders are filled with pics. Also, he's got a lot of contacts for a guy in his business. Usually they only have a couple and keep most of the stuff on their phones. This guy is more like a businessman. It's kind of surprising."

"Any international numbers?" Roscoe said.

"Hang on. Do you have a specific country code you are looking for?"

"Yes, 01. Start with that."

"Stand by one. Yep. There is one. It's associated with contact labeled 'Honri la Fille.' Does that name mean anything?"

Holly spoke up. "Not likely. *La fille* means little girl. It helps, but not the way we need."

Worth spoke again. "See if you find anything that will help us triangulate his location at any time in the past thirty days. Also, go back to his cell phone and check his numbers in the history. See if there is any location he visited or called from more than others. He's been there a lot lately, so if he's had that laptop and phone for a while, it should be easy to find."

"Roger that, Major. Hold on a second. You gave me an idea." The line was silent for a few minutes, and the only sound was the rapid clicking of computer keys. "Yep. Here's the operating software dates. He's only had the laptop for about eight months. Now he could have archived older pics and videos, and some of these could be downloaded from the net."

"Downloaded from the net," Cavert said in disgust. "Sick bastards travel in packs."

"No doubt," replied Red.

"Captain, I also went back to the download from his phone. You were right. There are a high number of calls to a phone with a 01 international number, but he was in the metro area when he called. In addition, that number called him several times while he was here," Nat said.

"Any ideas on where the call was going?" Roscoe was taking notes.

"Well, sir, I checked, and 01 is the country code for the Virgin Islands and the United States. But I don't think that's relevant."

"What do you mean?"

"Captain, I think those calls were made to and from an international number, but then routed to a cell or land-line in the United States."

Holly's ears perked up. "We heard the drug cartels were working on that technology, but it was too sketchy. That was a few years ago, though."

"Holly, I thought that was you. I went to a briefing last month with . . . um, an agency with a local office. They believe that technology has been perfected," Nat explained.

"Is it expensive?" Roscoe said.

"Sure, but they have a lot to lose. Wiretaps on foreign numbers are harder to obtain, and there's a question about whether or not you need a federal FISA warrant if the calls are between or from foreign numbers based in the United States. That requires a lot of paperwork and a special hearing. So if they can use this method, they would effectively shut all local, state, and a lot of federal investigations down."

Johnny's head was spinning a mile a minute. He looked at Roscoe. "Captain, this is a problem. I know we've got a great hand to play and an opportunity to find these girls—every one of them. However, the longer Heavy D stays in that interview room, the better the chance that his buddies are going to start to wonder where he is. It appears that he frequents these locations a lot. If they get nervous because he misses an appointment or something, they'll disappear . . . probably with the girls."

"Or worse," Holly added.

Captain Roscoe was thinking, as well. This was a real possibility and part of what made these sex traffickers so hard to catch. "I agree, Johnny. We need to get this into overdrive. At the same time, there's no way he's going to get a significant deal. He's going away for a long time. Let's get the DA on the line and find out how they want to play this. The FBI is already involved, and we can coordinate the US Attorney's involvement. In fact, they're probably waiting on a call from us already. The good news is, the DA and the AUSA have been playing well in the sandbox on these cases lately. Major? This case started in your unit."

"Let's get Franetti down here with whatever he has right now," Worth said. "Captain, you call the DA and the AUSA. Let's get them down here. You've got the strongest ties with the feds on this. You should make the call. I'm going to call the chief when we get done and give her an update."

Roscoe picked up his phone and started texting. He was setting up a priority conference call with the AUSA and the DA through his office.

Johnny asked Franetti to come down to the Homicide office. He was thinking about the way to bring the most weight onto Heavy D's shoulders in the shortest amount of time. When he got off the phone, he looked at Major Worth. "He's on his way, sir. Five minutes. I think I've got this figured out."

Major Worth leaned forward. "Okay, let's hear it."

CHAPTER 39

"Okay," Johnny said, "the trouble with these guys is they know more of what they've done than we ever do, even after we catch them. Let's use that. Let's show him what we have to sweat him, then use the intel the captain has on sex trafficking in the area to give him the impression we're closing in on the local operation. If he thinks he's the only one to know that the entire metro and state operation is about to fall, he may try to strike a deal."

Captain Roscoe was nodding. "What about that Jane Doe y'all were working that we believe was tied to sex trafficking? She's still unidentified, right?"

Holly spoke up. "Yep, unfortunately. That's my case. It's been a tough case from the get-go."

"I'm betting that he's seen so many of those girls that he can't remember all of them. I'm also certain the lighting isn't the best in these places. If his laptop is filled with pictures, it's because he wants trophies. If we give her a name, tell him we know where she's been working, and tell him there's a picture of her on his laptop, that will get his pulse up."

"I like it," Holly said, "and for all we know, she *is* on

his laptop, or he has visited her. I'll get her picture and see if Franetti found any pics that look like her."

As she left, Franetti came into the conference room with a laptop and an external drive. He set everything down on the desk and plugged in his laptop. When he finished booting up his computer, he looked up and realized everyone in the room was staring at him.

"God, I only have to worry about a gun, handcuffs, and a radio!" Red said. The room erupted in laughter.

Even Franetti laughed and turned a bit red-faced. "I love what I do, Red, but it requires a shit-ton of gear!"

"Anything so far, Nat?" Major Worth was still smiling. "We have a plan to turn the heat up on him, and we need everything we can get. Time is of the essence."

"Yes, sir. In short, this guy is into underaged girls and sex trafficking up to his eyeballs. I identified a lot more girls, and based upon my call with Till, I think I've found a pattern of his travels related to his visits with the girls."

"Did he keep a regular schedule?" Roscoe asked.

"Not regular, but I'd be willing to testify to a pattern. Mornings only, between 1000 hours and noon or in the afternoons between 1400 and 1700 hours. I also saw that Mondays and Thursdays are his preferred appointments."

"What is this based upon?" asked Worth.

"Well, sir, it was not easy. However, I triangulated his calls for about a week, figuring this guy, like everyone else, is probably on the phone all the time. When I found some patterns, I plugged in known addresses we expected him to frequent and created a program to rule them out. The computer still gathers the info, and I can put that together later for court, but there's no need to focus on places we don't suspect to be involved. In all the cases I've worked, I've never seen these kids brought to a person's house—too dangerous. Hotels, yes, but house calls are extremely rare. The visits take place in a secure environment. That's one of the reasons why it's so hard to get a UC inside with video or a wire."

"What did you rule out?" Johnny was listening intently. He was fascinated with the speed with which Franetti worked. As he spoke, Holly came back into the conference room.

"Well, on a long shot, I figured three places were out: his house, his momma's house, and his parole officer's building. Those seemed to be fair game to exclude."

Cavert piped in, "Let's hope so."

Franetti began again. "So when I let the program work on the locations we had in his phone, and not all of his calls have a location, I found three spots that he frequented. One is a diner where, as we know from previous cases, he does business. Too public for this, though, and we've checked the backgrounds of the owners ten ways 'til Sunday. They're clean. Another is the nightclub on Pratt in the Industrial District, Eclipse. While it's possible he could meet someone there occasionally, it would be pretty risky due to the amount of people. Some of these girls can be made up to maybe look eighteen, but no way the security would let them into a twenty-one-and-over club. Oh, I ruled out his workout place as well, as he only goes there early in the morning, and he looks like he does work out a lot, so he must be doing something legit there. That leaves this one area."

Franetti turned on a projector and put a map onto the screen. The section of the map showed an upper-middle-class neighborhood on the southeast side of the county. It was a decent place to live and had relatively little crime.

Johnny spoke up. "Not a bad area, but the residents there are more likely to keep to themselves. They are also gone a lot during the day. Mostly blue-collar workers with two-income families. The midmorning and early afternoon time slot might be popular there. Not a lot of folks to track who comes and goes."

Cavert studied the map. "Do you know that area well, Johnny?"

"Pretty well. It was my first precinct assignment out of the academy. We weren't in that neighborhood much, though. Occasional car break-in, stuff like that."

"Can you enlarge the map a bit?" Cavert was seeing something Johnny was missing. Franetti enlarged the map, then looked at Cavert, who started pointing. "There, in the bottom part of the map. There's an interstate entrance and exit within a half mile. There's also immediate access to a four-lane controlled-access highway."

"What am I missing?" Captain Roscoe was looking at Cavert, getting frustrated.

"Well, sir, we have a lot of drug houses in our county that get shipments from the boat docks. The dopers have gotten smart about where they put their safe houses. They've learned that it's hard for the cops to block off entrances to major arteries, like interstates and controlled-access highways, so that makes it harder to create a perimeter and execute a search warrant. The proximity to those roads also makes it easier for them to do their deals while making it harder for us to do surveillance on cars as they approach and leave."

Captain Roscoe made some notes, then looked up. "Were any of these houses running kids?"

"No, but smuggling is smuggling, I figure," Cavert

said. The group took a moment to take that in as Franetti started typing furiously.

"That's not a bad theory." Franetti nodded as he typed. "My program did not give me a specific house, and I figure Heavy D doesn't call as he arrives. He probably calls within a block or two to let them know he is coming. But if you're right, the house will be on a two-way street. That would be harder for marked units to block." Franetti put the map back into position and highlighted a block of Durango Way.

"Why that block?" Holly sounded amazed.

Franetti used a laser pointer to circle a spot on the map. "That street is two-way, the house faces that street, the interstate is to the north, and the controlled-access four-lane is in the opposite direction."

"Two escape routes," Red said softly.

"And two ways to bring customers and girls in to avoid arousing suspicion," Franetti said. "Also, this is an older part of the county, so the lot sizes on these houses are a bit bigger. The houses on Durango go through to the street behind them." He looked at the map for a few seconds. "Bellemeade Street—it's one-way north, but in a pinch, they would have a way to get out on another street."

"It's been a while since I worked down there, but do any of the houses have attached garages that go to Bellemeade?" Captain Roscoe was looking at the map and also responding to a text.

"Stand by," Franetti said. Then he switched to a satellite view of the same area. He scanned the street on his laptop while everyone else stared at the screen. "There are three. The addresses are 191, 207, and 265."

"Why this particular block, Nat?" Major Worth was still skeptical.

"Yeah, we got sidetracked." He picked up a laser pointer and highlighted some areas on the screen. "This section of the area is within three blocks of ninety percent of Heavy D's calls during the time periods we discussed. If he was calling when he was a couple of minutes away to make certain there were no police in the area and the girls were ready for him," he paused, "and he was using different routes to approach, this is the pattern we would expect."

"That's a few ifs, Nat, but I can't argue with the logic," Worth said.

Roscoe put down his phone. He was still looking at the map when he spoke. "Detective Franetti, I'm not sure how your mind works, and quite frankly it scares me that I may figure that out one day, but," he paused and stared at a puzzled Franetti, "you're a damned genius! I just got a text from Sergeant Bennett. She's on the scene of the search warrant. She's working with the FBI and Homeland Security. They searched their databases for the international number we have and got a hit to a guy on an Interpol watch list. They knew he was in the United States, but as they told Sergeant Bennett, they 'sort of lost track of him' after he left Kennedy Airport a few months ago. As crazy as it sounds, for some reason he kept his cell phone active. They expect he uses burner phones for the majority of his work. There must be a reason he's using that number."

"Has he ever run girls?" Holly was leaning forward. She was now planning her approach to the area in her mind. It was built into her from years of undercover work.

Roscoe spoke quickly to answer her question. "Yes, and that's why Interpol is tracking him."

"Or *trying* to track him." Red sighed.

Roscoe continued, "The FBI is getting a warrant to track that phone. Between Heavy D's use of that phone and the Interpol hit, they won't have any trouble. From there, we'll know if he's still here. As to the connection to the house, Franetti, one of our guy's cousins lives in the US. His name is Checkonski. He is legit on the surface, but the FBI agent working with Bennett said they've been watching him for a while. See if he owns any property in that area."

Franetti was already typing. "Roger that, sir. Stand by one." In about three minutes, Franetti threw his arms up in the air. "Gotcha, you son of a bitch!" He pushed some additional keys and the screen changed. Up on the screen was a tax-assessor listing in the name of Andrei Checkonski. "He's also on the water bill, the cable bill, the phone bill . . ."

"We get the point, Nat." Worth was holding up his hand. "191 Durango Way."

"What's our next move, Major?" Johnny was halfway out of his chair.

"Not sure if a judge will think we have enough yet. We can't hit that house without a bit more probable cause, but I also want to get the layout. We'll need a Tac team, and those girls will be in danger. If Nat is right, they're sophisticated and will be prepared. I'm not sure if that means they will fight, kill the girls, take hostages, or what they'll do, but I want more intel into the layout of the house. That's where you come in, Johnny."

"Me, sir?"

"Yep. You and Red are about to make Heavy D lose about twenty pounds of sweat."

"That's not the only way he's gonna drop weight when we tell him that address!" Red laughed. So did everyone else.

"You're probably right. Maybe you should bring him a change of underwear," Roscoe chimed in.

Major Worth started again. "With this address, we're taking away another one of his bargaining chips, and he's running out of them. He and his lawyer know he'd better start turning into a concerned citizen soon, or he'll lose all of his leverage toward a plea bargain."

Roscoe looked at Worth. "Bill, we're not going to be waiting long. Once the feds get that warrant, we will be ready to move, especially if our cooperative suspect provides the remaining details we need. Let's go to your office and get the Tac commander on the phone. We'll also need to brief the chief."

The Homicide secretary knocked, then came into the conference room. "Major, there's two attorneys here from the US Attorney's Office and one from the Lawler DA's office. Should I show them in?"

"Yes, Charlotte. That'll be great." He then turned to Johnny and Red. "The captain and I will be in my office. Bring the legal eagles up to speed and see how they want to handle any requests for immunity, leniency, for-giveness, or whatever the hell else this pedophile asshole will be asking for. I think the time is right to chat with them before you go back in."

"Got it," Johnny said. "It's gonna get interesting between them. I hope we don't end up in a jurisdictional pissing contest."

"I doubt it," Roscoe said. "The joint task force has done very well working together on these issues. In fact, Sergeant Bennett had the cell numbers of the FBI and DHS agents on her phone. We routinely deal with these issues. Everyone is focused on saving these kids."

CHAPTER 40

T he door opened, and three attorneys walked into the conference room. The first was Ben Chambers. He was a tall, slim man with a full head of thick, gray hair. At six feet four inches, he forced everyone to look up. He was impeccably dressed, as was his trademark. He was also very formal, true to his military career. He'd retired from the United States Air Force Reserve two years earlier with the rank of brigadier general assigned to the Judge Advocate General Corps. His experience in the courtroom was legendary. He'd prosecuted hundreds of white-collar criminals during his twenty-five years with the United States Attorney's Office and was rumored to have been under FBI protection on several occasions.

Chambers introduced his coworker, Ann Cellestani. She was a woman in her late forties who was noticeably dressed down in a pair of blue jeans and a polo shirt. She was wearing a windbreaker that bore the seal of the United States Attorney's Office over the left breast and AUSA in bright-gold letters on the back. She looked around and spoke, apologizing for her casual dress, explaining that she was at a training class when she got the call. Johnny was encouraged that she felt it was important enough to come straight to the department without going home to change.

The third attorney needed no introduction to anyone in the room. Her name was Millicent Angela Roth. She was an Ivy League law graduate who came from one of the wealthiest law firms in the state. With any career path open to her as a young lawyer, she'd chosen prosecution. "Millie," as she was known, ran for district attorney at the age of thirty-three with eight years of experience and won by a landslide. Much to the dismay of her detractors, her success was not an anomaly, as predicted. Her first election was twenty-two years ago, and she showed no signs of slowing down. Her reputation as a hard-hitting and talented prosecutor kept her in the good graces of the public and the police, while her passion for fairness and alternative punishments made her popular with the judges and defense attorneys. Her efforts in so-called "alternative courts" for veterans, those addicted to alcohol and drugs, as well as the mentally ill, proved successful at every turn. She believed in justice, and when the case called for aggressive prosecution, she was a freight train in the courtroom. She was the perfect person to work on Mr. Heavy D's fears of never seeing daylight again.

After the pleasantries were exchanged, Franetti walked them through what he'd learned. After about twenty minutes, including briefings by Red and Johnny, they were up to speed. As they asked a few follow-up questions, the unit secretary knocked on the door again. "Mr. Rappin asked me to let you know he and his client are ready to speak with the detectives again."

Johnny smiled. "Please let Mr. Rappin know we'll be in

there in a few minutes." Then he looked at Red. "Show time."

Johnny knocked on the door to the interview room then opened the door. "Sorry to keep you waiting. I'm about to turn on the audio and video again. I just wanted to make certain you were aware of that."

"Of course, Detective Till. Thank you for the courtesy of the confirmation. My client and I have finished conferring," Rappin said.

Johnny nodded to Holly in the hallway, who turned on the recording devices as Red walked into the room. Johnny spoke up in the room to acknowledge openly that the video and audio recorders were running again. Then he stated the date and time for the record.

"So," Johnny spoke directly to Rappin while looking at Heavy D, "you wanted to speak with us?"

Heavy D was smiling again. Rappin spoke confidently, like a man about to wrap up a plea deal and be home in time for dinner. "My client is prepared to provide significantly helpful information to you and the district attorney in exchange for a reduced plea on the possible charges. So may I suggest that we speak with the district attorney by phone and make her aware of the situation?"

"Well, sir," Johnny started, "what type of significant information is your client willing to share? I mean, is it about drug dealers, gun runners, or some other type of crime?"

"I suppose that's a fair question, Detective Till. My client is prepared to provide information into a prolific sex-trafficking location within the county. I'm afraid that we need to secure some type of cooperation and assurances from the district attorney before we say anymore."

Red smiled back at Heavy D. In his mind, he was thinking about Micro's body lying on the street in South Carolina and the faces of the five store owners Micro robbed at gunpoint while Heavy D's cousin threatened to kill them. *No way you weren't involved. Payback is a bitch.*

Johnny never took his eyes off of Heavy D, as much as Rappin tried to draw his attention. However, Johnny wanted to watch Heavy D's smug smile disappear when he knew his bargaining chip and his best chance of avoiding a lifetime of forced sodomy and brutal beatings was gone. Johnny spoke in a casual manner. "If you mean 191 Durango Way, that's old news."

That's when it happened. Heavy D's smile was gone, and his jaw dropped. For the first time in his adult life, reality hit him, and he was genuinely scared. "How could you know anything, you punk? You're just lying! You don't have shit!" Heavy D spat out.

"Calm down, Edward!" Rappin said.

"I told you they were listening! This is bullshit! I'm gonna sue your asses for violating my attorney-client privilege."

"Edward!" Rappin grabbed his client's left shoulder and whispered into his left ear. "We never spoke the address. Remember? You wrote it down on my notepad, and I covered the words as you wrote. Now stop fucking around! Your ass is in this deep! You need to start listening to me."

As Rappin turned back toward Johnny, his face was flushed red. In all of the times Johnny saw him in court, he never saw him show that type of emotion. He thought of how lucky Heavy D was to have such a dedicated and talented attorney, and how stupid he was not to appreciate it or listen to his advice.

"Well, Detective Till, we still have other information

to share. I imagine you will be working to secure that residence and ensure the safety of the occupants and the officers effecting any arrests. True?"

"Very likely, Mr. Rappin. But I'm not certain that's enough to get him the deal he no doubt wants."

"Let's chat with the district attorney, if you don't mind. With all due respect, Detectives, this is her decision," Rappin offered respectfully.

The door opened and Millie Roth stepped in. "You're correct, Walter." She moved forward and shook his hand. "Let me introduce Ben Chambers and Ann Castellani with the United States Attorney's Office." Heavy D slumped in his chair and put his head back. "As these matters concern the United States Department of Justice, I believed it was best to get them involved up front."

As the three attorneys took their seats and took out their notes, Heavy D sat up straight in his chair. His face was set and far from the smile he displayed so many times in the past; this was more of a look of intense focus. It was a stunning change and took everyone by surprise.

"Edward, are you okay?" Rappin said.

"I'm fine, Walter. It's just that I've got something to say."

As everyone in the room looked at Heavy D intently, Rappin leaned to whisper in his ear again. "Edward, let me handle this. This is serious."

"Walter, this is not on you, it's on me. You've helped me a lot in the past, and I appreciate it. When those punks on Fourteenth wanted to rough you up because you weren't able to get their boy off, I stepped in. You're like an uncle to me, but it's time to stop the bullshit. I know what's gonna happen. The feds are gonna bullshit around, but at the end they're gonna put me away forever. As to the DA," he nodded to Roth, "she's gonna come after me with everything she's got. You're a great lawyer, Walter, the best, but I'm the only one who can get me out of this mess."

Rappin sat back. He looked at Edward. In the more than ten years that he had known him, he had never seen him this calm around police. Gone was the cocky, adolescent-like attitude. "Do you want me to stay, Edward?"

"Yes, Walter. I'll need your help after I say what I have to say. There will be details to work out, and I can't do that alone."

"Edward, I want to take one last opportunity to encourage you to discuss whatever you plan to say with me first." Rappin was somewhat in shock but doing his best to appear in control.

"No, Walter."

Ben Chambers spoke up. "Mr. Rawlings, you know this room is wired and everything you say is now being recorded and taped. You know that you have the right to confer with your lawyer, Mr. Rappin, right?"

Heavy D spoke in a normal and even tone. "Yes, sir. I understand all that. I also understand that I have a constitutional right to be silent, too. I signed one Miranda warning, and I'll sign another, if you want."

Chambers nodded to Johnny, who passed Heavy D another Miranda waiver. Heavy D signed it and was about to hand it back when Chambers spoke up. "Write down the time from the clock on the wall. Mr. Rappin, would you be kind enough to sign as a witness? Detective Till will be happy to do so, if you wish."

Walter Rappin turned the paper toward Johnny. "If you don't mind. I hate to be a stickler for details."

"Not at all," Chambers said. "Mr. Rawlings, you are correct about the magnitude of the crimes at issue. While we will take into account any information you provide, some things are beyond our control. On the flip side, should a federal agent or local officer be injured during the search that you correctly anticipate, I may be able to convince a federal judge that you failed to prevent those events. I doubt that would lead to any benefit during your sentencing."

"Relax. I know the deal. You're going to get your information. I need all the help with you feds that I can get, and I don't need to do anything that would get you pissed at me. But my one card to play here is bigger than any of you understand." He turned to look at the district attorney. "Ms. Roth is the person who will be able to help me the most."

"Really?" Millie said. "You know me that well?"

"Yeah. I've watched you. You don't give a rat's ass about anything when you set your mind to get someone. That's why I delivered the punk who carjacked your judge last year. I don't need that type of trouble."

Heavy D was referring to Marcus Riley, a crazy thug who carjacked a judge while high on meth. Riley was found in an alley beaten unconscious, tied to a fence with the judge's car keys in his pocket. Until that moment, no one knew how Riley came to be in the spot where the Lawler PD found him, based on an anonymous tip to the crime hotline.

While she was playing poker, Roth was having trouble not showing her hand. She let a bit of silence pass before she spoke. "Very kind of you, Mr. Rawlings, and quite out of character. You're not exactly the type of person who spends a great deal of time assisting local law enforcement."

"Well," Heavy D responded, "we all have our ways of

performing our civic duties." He smiled. "As to you, Detective Till," Heavy D looked up at Johnny, "you're gonna be a hero, too. You see, I'm gonna play all the cards I have to stay alive. But you, Ms. Roth, you're the key to keeping me safe. As the DA, you have pull with the feds. I want to be in a supermax, no contact with anyone, no chance of being raped or beat down. If I die, it will be on my terms, not when some young punks decide to take out a legend when I'm sixty."

"You're hardly a legend, Edward. You're a common criminal." Millie Roth's Southern accent made her comment almost seem polite.

"A criminal, yes, but common, no. You have no idea how many people I've whacked. Most of them you didn't even think about for a second. They were thugs, robbers, rapists who turned their backs on their brothers. They were dishonorable and deserved to die. You tell Worth he's gonna close a bunch of cases when I'm done. But first, I want that promise from you and the feds. Supermax, out of state, one hour out of my cell a day, and no contact with other inmates."

"You overestimate my pull with the Department of Justice, Edward," Roth offered.

"Well, start pulling harder. There are a bunch of girls—pretty, innocent girls—who are waiting to be rescued, and a bunch of cops are going to die if they don't hear what I have to tell them before they go in."

Chambers was whispering to Castellani. When they stopped, Chambers leaned toward Heavy D. "Let me save you the time, Mr. Rawlings. I have the authority to procure a solitary supermax cell for you for the rest of your life." He paused. "But I'm not going to sit here for another minute and get jerked around by you and your little 'I'm a badass' routine. I've watched much tougher men die." The words lingered in the air and created an eerie silence. "So you now know that I have the authority to get you what you want, but I'm gonna walk out of here in five minutes. I could put you away for over a hundred years if I let one of our interns try this case. In other words, impress me, or stop wasting my time."

His stare was intense. It was nothing Heavy D had ever seen from anyone in a suit. Even Walter Rappin was impressed. Although he had tried several federal cases, most involved drug trafficking or firearms charges. He heard a lot about Chambers, but only met him once at a fundraiser for fallen officers. Rappin always contributed.

Heavy D broke his stare at Chambers and looked back at Roth. His tone was calm and confident. "Mr. Chambers, you and Ms. Roth will both have something. I have information on crimes on the federal and state levels."

Chambers got up. "Goodbye, Mr. Rawlings."

As he grabbed the back of his chair to push it back in, Heavy D spoke. He never broke his stare at Roth. "I'm gonna give you a cop killer." The room was silent. "You'll never catch him without me. I know, because you haven't been able to catch him yet. It's been in all the papers."

Ever the one to keep the upper hand, Chambers raised his voice as he stood with his hands on the back of the chair. "Give me a name, or enjoy your stay in general population with a full dance card!"

Heavy D's eyes seemed to be glued to Roth. She wasn't backing down and was watching him. Heavy D spoke his next words with a practiced, slow over-enunciation. When he spoke the name, everyone was silent, even the detectives watching and listening behind the one-way glass. The chief and Bill Worth, who had just come back in from his call to the Tac unit, stood silent. In the interview room, Johnny Till seemed frozen as the name hung in the air. He knew it was a moment he would remember the rest of his life.

"Lawler Police Officer Michael Dunlap."

When the silence went on about a minute too long, Johnny spoke. He leaned forward and worked hard to keep his composure. He stood up and put his hands on the table to keep himself from sticking his finger in Heavy D's face.

"Let me tell you something, Edward. If you make me lose my patience with you, I'll make sure there's enough state time on you to watch you die a thousand times over. You were in middle school when he died. You don't know shit about that crime, and you're trying to jerk us around."

Everyone was staring at Johnny. Chambers was impressed.

Heavy D did not look away from Johnny, but he was clearly not the same smug character Johnny had met that afternoon. "Walter, what bank did we go to on Lambert about ten years ago?"

"First Security," Rappin responded evenly. "You got a safe deposit box and asked me to hold the key."

"Give them the key, Walter." Heavy D did not take his eyes off of Johnny. Perhaps it was an instinct learned from the street to always face a threat. Perhaps it was his last chance to be in charge of anything in his life.

Rappin was still. "Edward, are you sure?"

"Yes. You don't know what's in there. I made you sit outside in the lobby." Heavy D looked back to Johnny.

"In that box, you will find the two guns used to kill Officer Dunlap."

Johnny tapped Roth on her shoulder. He looked down at his pad and pulled back a piece of paper. On the page he wrote her a note: `Two guns used—that fact never released. Dunlap is my cold case.`

Roth acted like it was nothing and looked straight at Heavy D. Gone was the arrogance and confidence they all witnessed when they entered the room. He was now done playing games. He was clear the stakes were higher.

Johnny gathered his composure and focused on the interview. He sat down and flipped a couple of pages on his notepad, folding the prior pages over and underneath to ensure that Heavy D couldn't see the note he wrote to Roth. "I'm a pretty simple guy, Edward. You're a young criminal with an impressive history, but like I said, you were just about twelve years old when Dunlap was murdered. So how do you know anything about his murder, and how did you come to own anything connected with his murder?" Johnny was careful not to validate the number of guns used in the murder or the accuracy of any of Heavy D's information.

"You all think it's a game out there on the street. You're wrong. The guys I work with, my crew, and the people I do business with, they are not stupid. They're smart. They're also ruthless. So when I decided to freelance, I needed at least one person I could trust. My crew, the people you ran into at my house, they only stick around because I pay them a lot of money, and some of the bastards out there would sell their mothers to the DA or the feds for chickenfeed if they were in trouble."

"By freelance, you mean killing people for hire?" Johnny inquired.

"Yep. You see, every gang needs to keep their crews in line. They will beat down some punk who gets out of line, but they prefer to hire out a hit because it's messy. It also keeps the crews from getting out of control when they're told to just punish someone. You know, they understand that they can't turn a beatdown into a hit. Anyway, I figured there was good money in the freelance thing, so I decided to check it out. I'd already put down a couple of people, so it was no big deal."

"All right, Edward. I'm listening," Roth said. "But first, here's what we're going to do. I've got enough to get a search warrant for the safe deposit box, and I'm certain Mr. Rappin is going to cooperate and give us the box number and the key. To be safe, we'll get the warrant anyway. That will take a bit of time, though. So in the meantime, we're going to get a court reporter in here to have you give a statement under oath. We're going to talk about the house on Durango, the photos we have of you with the underage girls, and anything else you want to tell us, including the details about Officer Dunlap." Roth leaned forward. "And if you lie about the color of someone's T-shirt, I'll bury you in a jail cell for so long that by the time you get to a federal prison, you won't remember how to spell pedophile."

Roth continued, "Just remember, there are very few supermax cells in the Georgia Department of Corrections. It would take a lot to convince someone to let you occupy one just for your own protection." She paused and stared into Heavy D's eyes. "What is the name on the safe deposit box, and what is the number?"

"I had to use my real name, Edward Rawlings. Stupid

9/11 bullshit. I couldn't use a fake one without ID, and I didn't have time to wait. I had two hot guns in my backpack."

"The number?"

"Four-two-one."

Roth knew that as soon as she got the name and number out of him, one of the detectives listening in the other room would be leaving to get a search warrant for the safe deposit box. She was not going to risk having the evidence thrown out of court over some question of consent if Rappin gave them the key. No, this way was cleaner, and she liked it. They would get a forensic team to go with them when they opened the box.

What she didn't know was that Bill Worth was also sending a bomb tech to inspect the box before they opened it. After all, Heavy D was the worst type of criminal now: one with nothing to lose, playing the last card he had as part of a plan he had hatched years before.

"Okay," Roth began, "we'll have a court reporter here any moment."

"That seems quick," Rappin said. "Do you have one on speed dial?"

"No," she answered, again locking eyes with Heavy D. "I figured your client was smart enough to know when his goose is cooked and dressed. He knows he's got nowhere to go with me on one side and the feds on the other. He's also got the wild card of a bunch of gangbangers and sex traffickers who would put him in a box in a heartbeat just on general principle, and now he's been in custody for several hours. So I figured we were about to hear his best and last play—whatever that was. Let's hope for him he hasn't decided to bullshit me. A poker player with no cards always loses when someone calls their bluff."

"You got everything on tape. What's with the court reporter thing?" Heavy D seemed unsure of what was happening.

"Insurance, Edward," Roth said, smiling. "Electronics fail. And if you're telling the truth, we're gonna need this information for a lot of cases, because you will be testifying for the next ten years. No chances, no slack for you. That's the way I operate."

Heavy D's face contorted, and he nodded. He did not like the label and knew they left one out: snitch. "Makes sense. I don't give a rat's ass, anyway. I'll be dead on the street, and this is my only way to maybe stay alive in prison. Unless we can work out one of those witness-protection things with you feds."

"Let's hear what you have to say, Edward." Chambers was leaning forward now. "Those deals are on a put-up-or-shut-up basis. First, the information, and I mean *all* of it. Then *if* it pans out and we have bad guys lining up in our sights, then *maybe* we'll talk." Chambers was serious, but not as intense as Roth. He did not believe in even giving Heavy D the satisfaction of thinking he was considering a deal on the federal charges, but he was. There were thousands of girls being sold for sex around the world. If he could make a significant impact on that, he would recommend anything. But witness protection was approved at the top levels of the DOJ, and there was no way he would recommend anything until he was sure.

A few minutes later, a man came into the interview room and set up a stenotype. He had a laptop set up, as well, so they could read a rough draft of the transcript as he typed. Roth and Johnny stepped out while he set up.

They agreed that Johnny would ask the questions, and she and Chambers would listen, check the transcript, and chime in as necessary.

Johnny came in and sat down in front of Heavy D. He nodded to the court reporter, who asked Heavy D to raise his right hand. He administered the oath and poised his keys on the keyboard. Then the court reporter had everyone state and spell their names. Rappin got ready to take notes, and Johnny read the Miranda warning to Heavy D as the court reporter typed. Heavy D signed another Miranda waiver and sat back in his chair.

"So tell me about this mystery man and his two guns," Johnny began.

"I was in the lockup in Breven County about ten years ago, coolin' my heels, waiting for Walter here to work his magic and get me out. It was a bullshit charge, a couple of roaches, so I knew I'd be okay. Maybe pay a little fine. I also knew someone ratted me out. No excuse for that. Only one person had been in my car in the twenty-four hours before my arrest, so I knew it was him. The roaches had this special kind of paper, and I heard one of the cops talking about it when they were looking. It occurred to me that the guy had to go. He was in a gang affiliated with my crew but wasn't really a member. But I knew if I whacked him when I made bond, the cops would come straight to me. They're a pain in the ass, but they're not stupid. Hey, I'm kind of thirsty." He looked at Roth. "Can you get me a glass of water, pretty DA lady?"

Roth motioned toward the mirrored glass and then looked at him. "Coming up. Keep talking. I'm listening, but so far I'm not impressed. It sounds like a bunch of TV bullshit to me."

Heavy D smiled and looked at Johnny. "See what I

mean, man? Even when I'm trying to do the right thing, I can't get a break."

"Yep. You're positively persecuted, you poor thing." Johnny's voice was so sarcastic that Red nearly laughed. The door opened and a detective brought a paper cup with water to Johnny, who placed it on the table in front of Heavy D. "You were saying?"

"Yeah. So I was explaining my situation to a guy who had a similar problem. His girlfriend turned him in on a domestic violence charge, and he wasn't getting out soon enough to keep her from testifying. As we talked over the next few days, he told me he could help me using some guys from outside if I would help him when I got out. We both expected that I would be out in a few days. Of course, I smelled a setup. I'm not stupid. So I started asking around. I found out that the other prisoners were scared to death of this guy. I don't mean just the first-time punks who are afraid of their own shadows. I mean the seasoned guys, the pros. Hell, even the guards were afraid of him. That surprised me, because I'd never heard of him, and I know a lot of bad dudes."

Heavy D took a big drink of water, then put the cup down. He leaned back in his chair, took a deep breath in and out, then sat back up and started again. "I also got to thinking that I was probably not the only guy with this problem, you know? A rat can pop up anywhere, anytime. That was not my thing, though, whacking rats. Not to say that I hadn't dabbled in that line of work . . ."

Heavy D smiled and looked at a room full of people who were not amused, including his lawyer. He took another sip of water, then continued. "The next time I saw the guy, I asked him why he was asking me for help. He pulled me aside in the toilets, you know, where the guards can't video or audiotape. I thought right away, *This guy is pretty sharp.* Anyway, he tells me that he knows a bit about me, and he proceeds to list a few of my more major deals. He says he checked me out before coming into the lockup. When I asked him why he was checking on me, his answer made my blood go cold."

Heavy D looked down. Johnny read the discomfort on his face.

"What did he say, Edward?" Roth's callous tone made Heavy D's face scowl again.

"He told me he had a hit on me a month ago. Told me he did the background and all, and was set to kill me, but the guy refused to pay him the extra money he wanted based on my security. I thought he was full of crap, you know? Who was out to whack Heavy D? So I called him on it and asked him what he knew, and man, it freaked me out. He knew my address, my mom's address, the names of my crew, where I ate, my lady's name and address, all from his memory! It was scary. He also told me my habits. Again, he was right on. He could have taken me out any time if he wanted."

"Lucky you," Red said, keeping the pressure on Heavy D to keep talking.

"Yeah, lucky me. So he tells me that he never gets double-crossed and instead of killing me, he whacked the guy who refused to pay him! Just like that! When he told me the name of the guy who hired the hit, it made sense. It was a guy who tried to burn me on a meth deal. He showed up to the deal light, and I refused to buy any of it. Made me nervous. I guess he took it personally."

"Who took out the hit?" Johnny said.

"Little Beef. That was his street name. Son of a bitch was huge. I guess that was some kind of a joke." Heavy

D smiled. When he looked up, he saw the serious faces looking back at him. He instantly came back to the reality of where he was. "I think his real name was James or Jeffrey or something like that, because he had some ink on his arm with a name. Maybe it was his kid's name. Anyway, I knew Little Beef was a dead motherfucker, and no one on the street knew why. It was like the fucking CIA just took him out. One shot, back of the head, while he was walking to his car at a club. At the time, I just figured he shorted the wrong guy, like he tried to do to me. Not everyone is as forgiving as me."

He laughed for a second or two. Then he took some more water and started again. "I tell the guy thanks. I mean, I didn't know what else to say. Then I told him that we need people like him to keep the bangers in line. He tells me he's done with bangers, but that would be a good line of work for me. After all, I can move in those neighborhoods without attracting any suspicion, and every gang needs someone to settle the scores, kind of taking out the trash."

Johnny looked at Heavy D. "This guy was white?"

"Chinese or something like that, man. He was clean cut and tall for an Asian guy, though. He was right. Anyone would remember him in the hood, and he had no gang affiliation, so a lot of people wouldn't trust him."

As Heavy D finished, Johnny and Roth's cell phones buzzed with a text. It was from Major Worth. `Little Beef a.k.a. Jonathan Brind found dead, single GSW back of head in front of Shock and Awe. No leads or suspects.`

The information registered with Johnny, but it was the description of the mystery man as Asian that had his attention. He tried to form a picture of Meng's mugshot in his mind. *Easy, Johnny. Don't get ahead of yourself.*

"So how do I know you didn't whack Little Beef?" Johnny said, being careful not to give his real name. It was important right now to let Heavy D think he was in charge of the information he was providing.

"Good question, Detective, but check this out. I was under surveillance when he was shot. I seen the unmarked on my block, so I was staying home."

"You could have had him killed," Roth said.

"Not my style. Ask anyone, even your homicide detectives. Just because they can't pin them on me doesn't mean they don't know who I killed. I don't contract out. It's too messy. Always a risk some punk will try to turn on you or make a mess out of it and kill some innocent person on the street by mistake."

"Back to your Asian friend." Johnny spoke softly, trying to keep Heavy D on track and working hard not to betray the interest he had in this new player.

"We were in that toilet area for a while. I was kind of freaked out, you know. He tells me that I should be the guy to do it. Just stay with my crew but keep a lower profile. Get out of the drug business—I mean, personally out—and put the word out that I was available. He also said he would refer any new contracts to me, since he was done dealing with gangs. It sounded good to me, especially when some of these guys will pay big money to kill a rat, especially if he's talking to the feds." He looked at Chambers, who showed no change in his countenance.

"What's big money?" Roth spoke up, trying to get Heavy D focused solely on her again.

"Well, for a low-level punk, about five Gs. For a full-grown rat, fifty."

"You get paid in drugs?"

"No way! Cash is king, lady. Now if a crew had a pretty thing who wanted to come over and help show their appreciation, that was just a bonus. No, drugs make you and your crew crazy. All my guys were paid cash. That way, they didn't freak out and do stupid shit."

"So this guy agrees to help you set up shop just to get rid of his girlfriend?" Roth acted incredulous, but it was starting to make sense.

"Yeah. He was really pissed at her. They'd been together a long time. Also, he wasn't sure how much she knew. I guess he was afraid that she knew enough about the hits he was doing to turn him over. I didn't think so, though. I think he was just pissed off at her. He didn't say it, but she may have been stepping out on him, and he didn't seem like the forgiving kind of guy."

Heavy D drank the last of his water, then started again. "Now I'm not stupid. I told him before I helped him, I wanted insurance—something I could use against him if he double-crossed me. He thought about that a bit, then said he also wanted something. So I told him about a hit no one knows about, and I told him a few things the cops would never find. It was the only one where I didn't use a gun, so I figured that would be a big deal. He wanted the time and date, and then he stared at me. Crazy eyes, man. He told me he killed a cop and no one knew. I was quiet. That's some shit! You kill a cop, and the world starts looking for you. I knew he wasn't in jail for that, because he would've been in solitary."

"Then what happened?" Roth's tone was even.

"He told me that when I got out, that he wanted me to take care of his girlfriend and then get him a message. He would then put me in touch with a friend who would return the favor and kill the rat who put me in. I thought that wasn't a great plan, because I would be out when his girlfriend was done. He told me to take it or leave it. I said okay. I hate a rat, and I didn't know what other kind of damage he would do. So we exchanged names of the people we killed, he told me the name of his girlfriend, and we went our separate ways."

"When did you see him again? When did he give you the guns? You're boring me!" Chambers slapped the table when he spoke.

Heavy D seemed rattled for the first time and acted startled. He was clearly more afraid of the federal charges. "After I got out, I took care of his girlfriend. It was easy. She was an idiot. I made it look like a robbery behind the strip club where she worked. Anyway, I was sitting at home a couple of days later when this guy calls me, says I did a nice job and I should check the paper. I looked, and the rat was dead.

"Then, about a week later, the Asian guy himself comes up behind me in the parking lot of my gym. He scared the shit out of me! He tells me the deal is not done. He needs to know where the murder weapon was from the crime I told him about. He was looking pretty crazy, and I just told him. Then he hands me a backpack. I told him we were cool, but he said we both needed insurance. He told me to open the backpack later when no one was around, and that we would never see each other again. It was more of a threat than a promise. He said if he had a hit for me, I would get a call from him. That's it. I never saw him again."

"So what was in the backpack?" Roth was trying to keep him on track. She knew he could shut down at any point and demand something in writing. She needed to keep him talking.

"Two guns and a map."

"A map of what?" Johnny said.

"A map from Miami to a parking lot. I checked it out. It's the spot where the cop, Dunlap, was killed. I looked it all up on the internet. I also made sure I did *not* touch those damn guns. I didn't even check to see if they were loaded! I just put the whole backpack into the safe deposit box."

"Did he ever contact you?"

"A few times. Spooky shit. He would text a number or call me when I was out in public. I always got the feeling he was watching me when we spoke, but I never saw him again. He had a few hits for me—big ones. A couple were real hard, too. I always did them, and I always got paid cash. It showed up in a bag in weird places—my trash, my car, or I'd get a text telling me to go to a garbage container behind a strip mall somewhere. To tell you the truth, I never said no to him. I was afraid he'd kill me. He obviously could have had me anytime he wanted and already knew everything about me. I never knew where or when he'd show up."

"What name did you give him, Edward? Who did you kill? Who did you kill for him, and how? Details, Edward." Johnny was tapping his notepad as he spoke.

Rappin was just about resigned to the fact that he could not stop Heavy D, but he whispered to him. Heavy D just brushed him off. "Elaine Weeks. Crazy bitch. We went out a couple of times, and about a year later she tells someone I was a punk. It got back to me, and I got pissed. I caught her outside her apartment with a tire iron. Then I took her wallet to make it look like a robbery. I don't think anyone ever got tagged with it. I know they never came to speak to me. No one knew I was even around her."

"And the Asian's girlfriend?" Roth was poised with a pen in hand.

"April Lemonds. Pretty chick. Nice body. She danced at the Swan Club on Daniel. I went in there a few nights before, but not that night. They got cameras everywhere. She parked down the block and not in the fenced-in area for the rest of the dancers. I guess she felt like the Asian guy would find her in the fenced lot."

"How did you kill her?" Johnny was asking questions now. He knew that the detectives on the other side of the glass were researching as quickly as they could, and he needed to give them as much time as possible while keeping the information coming. The clock was ticking on Durango Way.

"I choked her out, then cut her from behind. A couple of deep stabs into her chest. She didn't make a lot of noise and didn't fight much. I took her purse, rings, and a nice gold watch."

"What did you do with the stuff?"

"Tossed them into the river, my friend. Too easy to trace if I tried to pawn it. It was tough to toss it, too. The watch was real high dollar. Looked like a Rolex or some shit. I could have gotten some bucks for it, but there was no messing with the guy. No way."

"What was the Asian's name?"

Heavy D sat back. He knew this was probably the last time he would have any control over anything. He decided to make them all wait a few more seconds before he told them. Finally, he put his hands behind his head and spoke. "Frederick Meng." He looked at Johnny and put up his hand. "Save the questions, just listen. Six-foot-two, about one-eighty-five. Black hair, dark eyes. He's got two tats that I saw. He has a crescent moon on his right shoulder with a blue star next to it. On his right forearm, he's got the head of a wolf with some crazy storm behind it. Nice ink, high dollar. Some accent, but he speaks English real well."

Johnny felt his blood run cold and his heart nearly stop. *This is it! This is the evidence we need to link Meng to Dunlap . . . if Heavy D isn't full of shit.*

Johnny stood up. He walked over to Heavy D. Leaning over the table from the side, he spoke like there was no one else in the room. "So Meng told you he killed a cop. Did he happen to tell you why?"

Heavy D knew he'd better tell the rest. There were no more cards to play, not really. "It was a hit. He was living in Florida and got a call."

"By who? Who wanted Dunlap dead?"

"He said it was a guy from Thailand who was running girls, but it was probably Meng himself. Running girls was new then, and Meng probably thought he could make a bunch of money. Dunlap worked in the schools. He was getting close to a kid at the school, you know. He started asking her a lot of questions, and Meng said the guy in Thailand started to get nervous when he found out."

"How did Meng get Dunlap to the spot where he killed him?" Johnny was careful not to describe or name the location.

"He told me they used the girl. She told Dunlap she would meet him and tell him the truth, but she was scared and he had to come alone."

"Why two guns?"

"The Asian said they wanted it to look like two people shot him. Throw off the cops. They figured they would have the cops looking for two guys, like a robbery gone bad."

"Who was the guy from Thailand?"

"He never told me. I wasn't surprised. I never tell anyone who orders a hit, and like I said, I figured it was Meng all along."

"What about the girl?"

"He said they sent her out of the country that night, but that was probably bullshit, too. My guess is, she was dead the next morning, and Meng probably killed her." Heavy D's face showed no emotion, speaking about her death like an insignificant fact in the story of the streets.

He doesn't know about Maureen, Johnny thought. *Makes sense. Meng wouldn't admit to leaving a loose end. Meng probably went by to kill her after Dunlap died, but couldn't do it without witnesses.*

The attorneys and detectives in the room were quiet. Even Rappin looked drained. After a couple of minutes, the DA motioned for someone to get Heavy D another cup of water. "Okay, Edward. We'll work on checking out these details. Now on to the house on Durango."

Heavy D's face changed. He sat back and slumped in his chair. His big play was over, and now he was just another rat. "You gotta protect me from now on! As soon as I leave this room, that crazy Asian can find me!"

Roth was emotionless. If Heavy D was looking for sympathy, he was shopping in the wrong aisle. Her eyes narrowed. "Durango, Edward."

Heavy D looked around, then looked at Roth. "What do you need to know?"

"First, you can convince me you have some current information about Durango. When was the last time you were there?"

"A few days ago."

Johnny reached into his folio and pulled out the

missing person BOLO on Hannah Trover. He folded the paper to conceal everything but Hannah's picture. Then he held it up to Heavy D. "Ever see her there?"

Heavy D leaned forward and took a second before he answered. "Her hair is different, but yeah. I saw her there. She was available that day."

"Available, but not your type?"

Heavy D leaned forward, and the contempt of the arrogant criminal was back on his face. *Fuck it. It doesn't matter now.* "She was too old for me, Detective. I got a blow job from her once while I was waiting for someone younger, but from that angle, it's hard to tell one bitch from another."

Johnny turned the BOLO toward one of the cameras and then toward the one-way mirror on the wall. Without missing a beat, he then put down the BOLO and handed Heavy D a notepad and pen. "I want a diagram of the house, a list of security you saw, and what they're carrying."

Heavy D picked up the pen and started drawing.

CHAPTER 41

Heavy D was still sitting in the interview room in the Homicide Unit hours later while detectives from Lawler PD and investigators from the Lawler Sheriff's Office and the Department of Corrections combed through records to verify or debunk Heavy D's story. Meanwhile, there was a meeting taking place in the command conference room. Chief Porter was sitting at the center of the table with five other commanders. The SWAT commander was giving a briefing on the plan SWAT developed to hit the house on Durango with a multijurisdictional entry team.

Seated around the table were agents from the local FBI office, as well as three high-ranking deputies from the United States Marshals Service, including the US Marshal over the Eleventh Federal Circuit. Millicent Roth was there, as well, along with Ben Chambers, Ann Castellani, and Lieutenant Dan Paschal. Captain Roscoe was watching intently and was sitting next to Sergeants Krebs and Bennett. They were in on the initial raid of Heavy D's house, so it only seemed fair for them to be here. It was an unwritten rule in law enforcement: If you got your teeth into the case, you would have a seat at the table when the main search went down.

Johnny and Holly were seated next to Major Worth, who was taking some notes but seemed more focused on taking in the big picture of the operation. There was no doubt that this was to be a big operation, and he would be the on-scene commander.

Mike Hancock was the third person to step to the whiteboard and interactive screen at the front of the room. First was Nat Franetti, who gave a rundown of the evidence they hoped to find. In an age of smartphones, memory sticks, and smart watches, it was important to ensure that the entry teams knew what an evidence stash looked like in case someone tried to destroy anything. Further, the detectives searching the house and property would need to know where to look and how such items could be disguised.

Next was Lieutenant Dan Paschal from the Intelligence Unit. He had photos of every member of Heavy D's crew, and showed a bunch of photos of Andrei Checkonski. They were old, for the most part, and a few were of bad quality and obviously taken with a telephoto lens. The clearest pictures were obviously enhanced photos to show what Checkonski would look like with a beard, moustache, glasses, or a shaved head. Fortunately, there was one good screenshot taken from the video at Kennedy Airport the last time Checkonski checked in through US Customs.

Johnny felt confident that they would recognize him if they saw him. If they got close enough, they would see a five-dot tattoo on the back of his right hand between his thumb and forefinger. The four dots on the outside stood for the four prison walls, and the one in the center stood for the inmate locked inside. Johnny had seen plenty of them on the street. "If you know how to read tats, you can do a virtual criminal history on a perp," Johnny recalled the immortal words of his field-training officer so many years ago.

If they captured Checkonski, the tattoo of a cross on his chest that started at the top of his sternum and ended at the top of his pelvis would be the key. Inside the cross were the words Потерянная душа. In Russian, they translated to "lost soul," a reference to Checkonski's life as an orphan. It all sounded good, but they had to find him first.

Mike Hancock was laying out a plan that would isolate the area first. This was tough, considering the location was selected for its proximity to two interstate highways and major side streets.

As Johnny watched Hancock describe the plan, he was amazed at both the simplicity and the tactics of it. Johnny leaned over to Major Worth. "He's in his element, isn't he?"

"He's one of the best in the Southeast, and maybe in the country. I stood next to him in a supermarket one time negotiating with a crazy bastard who took a bunch of hostages. It was just me and Hancock behind a body bunker. He told me to jump behind him if the shit turned south, but I know he'd have stepped in front of me in a heartbeat. I trust him completely."

That last comment meant a lot to Johnny. He'd seen Hancock work and knew of his reputation, but Worth was not easily impressed and did not tolerate fools well. In the time he'd gotten to know Worth, he'd never heard him say that about anyone.

Hancock was finishing up. "Okay. So the diversion on the interstate should buy us enough time to get the traffic stopped from inside the house. They've got surveillance cameras all over the house and in the trees, so they'll see the traffic stopping. My guess is, they'll tell everyone to stay put and wave off any customers by phone. We've been watching the house for several hours, and there are quite a few cars dropping people off. Our guess, based on our intel and the statement of our 'concerned citizen' cooling his heels in Homicide, is that there are about ten to twelve customers, eight or nine staff members, and anywhere from fifteen to twenty-two girls in the house. That's a lot of hands to watch, so let's all keep our heads on a swivel and out of our asses!"

The last comment drew a laugh from the group.

He continued, "After SWAT units clear the house and secure everyone, we have three canines who will sweep for explosives. If Franetti is right, these guys have access to explosives and love IEDs. They also have a reputation for destroying evidence and witnesses. After the bomb sweep is done, we'll give an all-clear for entry. One more thing. These girls don't know anything but the life they've been in for a lot of years. Many of them are drugged up at all times. Don't expect them to understand that you are there to save them."

He paused and made eye contact with everyone in the room. "And don't expect them all to be friendly. They can kill you, too. Any questions?" No one raised a hand. "We'll meet at the house in twenty-five minutes. Good hunting, folks. Make sure you come back for the debrief in one piece."

Everyone went to the parking lot, and Johnny and Holly stood at the back of Johnny's unmarked. "What do you think, Johnny?" Holly was putting on her body armor with heavy plates.

Johnny pulled on his body armor, inserted the plates,

then checked the chamber on his M4 rifle. "Well, Murphy's law nearly always controls, but we've put the pieces together. Let's hope it all falls into place."

Holly put her jump bag into Johnny's trunk, then put her rifle in, as well. Johnny put his rifle back into the case and got into the driver's side. Holly opened the door and got in. "It seems a bit too easy, if you ask me. These guys have probably had control of that house for years. The deed records don't show any recent sales." Holly shook her head. "They've got to have an exit strategy."

Johnny nodded his head. "Agreed. The SWAT folks will find it if the intel is not good enough."

As Johnny put the car into gear and pulled out of the space, Holly pulled her seatbelt across her body. "Yep. Sometimes, though, it's better to be lucky than good."

"I'll take a bucket of luck any day." Johnny smiled.

CHAPTER 42

J ohnny turned his car onto Cherokee Street and drove north to the interstate. He would get off two exits before the house and meet up in the parking deck of the Element Building, which housed the largest financial brokers in the Southeast. A retired Lawler cop worked security there and got clearance for them to use the two bottom levels of the deck. This would prevent a curious set of eyes from wondering why a bunch of dark sedans were staging up in the area.

As they approached the interstate, a set of yellow DOT trucks drove south on I-75, slowing traffic. As they approached the area near Durango, a city bus sputtered to a stop in the middle lane. Two older vehicles driven by plainclothes cops drove into the back of the bus and each other. Then, on cue, two other cars slid sideways in the lanes to the right and left, while two more cars T-boned them after skidding nearly to a stop. Prearranged ambulances, firetrucks, and marked police cars responded on cue to the collisions, and the entire interstate was blocked. The mother of all diversions was born. When the traffic stopped in all lanes, the DOT trucks pulled around the wrecks on the shoulders and turned off their yellow lights.

It only took a couple of smaller "incidents"—like a tractor trailer seemingly getting stuck while trying to turn left out of a side street, a tow truck helping a stranded motorist on the entrance ramp, and a city water truck occupied by FBI agents opening a manhole cover to make emergency repairs—to block the remaining roads. Once one interstate was blocked, the other would become impassable quickly, as would the larger side streets in the area. With ambulances and fire crews advised in advance of the road closures, all that was left to do was get the raid teams into place.

Below the ground, the FBI agents found the main power lines to the house and followed them to the area below Durango Way. They followed a map and soon were sitting under the target house. As they came to a stop and set up their listening devices, they saw the flashlights of the SWAT members assigned to the sewers.

Meanwhile, twelve armored personnel carriers rolled from a warehouse five blocks from the target house in that direction with Mike Hancock riding shotgun in the first vehicle. He was talking into the microphone mounted to his helmet. "Charlie One is rolling. Confirm all units in place."

An FBI agent in a helicopter keyed up his microphone. "Air three, roger. We have a full-fledged traffic cluster, sir. Glad I'm not in it."

"I'm clear. How about it, Cruiser One?" Hancock was talking with the lead FBI agent in charge of the logistics on the ground and under it.

"Ready for your arrival, Charlie One. EMS and fire are staged two blocks north."

"Got it," Hancock replied. "Okay, Bravo Two, are you in position?"

"Bravo Two is in position. Say the word, Charlie One."

"Charlie One to Bravo Three, time to turn the lights out. Charlie One to all units, going dark!"

A moment later, the entire block of 191 Durango Way went black as the power was shut down, along with the houses on the streets in front and behind the target house. The APCs rushed to the house with their headlights on to avoid collisions with a dog walker or anyone who was driving on the side streets. The vehicles pulled into position on Durango Way, and the doors opened. Fifty tactical officers approached with night-vision goggles available, but not yet in place. As they approached their designated targets and took their positions, they made entry and pulled down their night vision, pursuant to the no-knock warrants issued two hours prior by a magistrate who was fully briefed on the facts of the case. Her last words were "May God watch over you." She had no idea how prophetic those words would be.

There is an acceptable amount of chaos surrounding the service of any warrant. Much of it is by design and benefits the officers entering the unfamiliar buildings. The execution of a search warrant contains myriad unknowns and dangers. Even when an informant such as Heavy D supplies information, there is no way to be certain about hidden weapons, the number of people the teams will encounter, or the way the individuals inside will react when challenged. Every person challenged by a law enforcement officer makes a choice to react a certain way. Some seasoned criminals make no effort to comply with commands and instead attack the officer. While that's never a good idea, the results have the potential to be permanent for both the bad guy and the officers on the scene.

The first units breached the front door of 191 Durango quickly, even though the door was reinforced. The rear-entry team did the same, and both teams began sweeping the house. At both entrances, the officers took fire from the security team, who were placed mainly to prevent a robbery or eject unruly patrons. The officers leading the entry team took the rounds on the ballistic shields they carried. While the shield stopped the bullets, each one felt like the officer holding it was hit in the arm with a sledgehammer. The men shooting at them were hardened criminals with long histories of violent crime, but they were no match for professional SWAT operators.

The radio came to life after an uncomfortable silence. "Two perps down!"

As the units moved through, they secured several men using flexicuffs. They encountered young girls in each bedroom, and found that the bedrooms had been sectioned off to allow more than one bed to be used in relative privacy.

As they moved through the house, they could hear people moving, trying to avoid them. They also heard people speaking in several languages. Although most of the girls were scared and crying, some were yelling. In any language, it was obvious that those girls were not happy about the police presence. They were yelling warnings to someone.

One girl raised a small handgun at the officers. Fortunately, a SWAT operator was coming up to her side from a door in the hallway. Although she probably felt like a train hit her, she would live. The officers she pointed the gun at didn't fire for fear of hitting their teammate.

Hannah heard the gunfire and sat upright in her bed. She was weak and dehydrated, because she was trying to avoid being drugged again. Thanks to Britt, she learned to drink water only in the shower or from the tank on the back of the toilet.

Hannah looked around the small room and saw three other girls. They were all dressed in lingerie. She told them they had to hide, and two of them ran with her to the closet. When the third refused to come with them, Hannah and another girl dragged her there. She had just had a visit from two men and was heavily sedated.

"Not a sound! It may be the police, or it may be someone robbing the place. We'll stay here until we know it's safe," Hannah warned the girls.

In a few minutes, the main and upstairs levels of the house were secure, and the officers started clearing the basement. They found more makeshift bedrooms and more young girls. As the SWAT operators made their way through the house, the sheer number of partially clothed girls, some of whom were tied to beds, started taking a toll. They were law enforcement officers on a mission, but they were also husbands and fathers, wives and mothers. As difficult as it was, they kept moving, hoping that their efforts might bring hope for the girls they found.

In the basement, just ahead of the advancing SWAT teams, Checkonski ran to the east under the back door. He entered a closet and pushed hard on a panel in the back.

As the SWAT team entered that last room on his heels, they opened the door to the closet and found only a few clothes. The SWAT operator called for a K9 as he shined a flashlight on the walls of the closet. As he did so, he contacted Mike Hancock on the radio. "Unit 7412 to Charlie One."

"Go ahead."

"Charlie One, we've got a ferret. I need a K9 in the far bedroom at the east end of the basement."

"Roger." As he answered, a K9 unit with the Lawler County Sheriff's Office entered the front door of the house. She and her handler had been on standby outside to apprehend anyone who tried to run from the residence. The handler and his dog, Scout, ran into the house and down the stairs to the basement. At the bottom of the stairs, a SWAT officer radioed Unit 7412 that he was on the way and pointed toward the bedroom.

As they entered the bedroom, the K9 team began to work. "Find!" was the only command the handler gave Scout, who immediately began working to pick up a scent. The dog's breathing became audible, and she started making crossing patterns in the room before moving to the closet. Scout sniffed and explored the closet before pawing at the back panel vigorously.

"Pull her out!" the SWAT officer said. Then, he keyed up his microphone again. "Charlie One, we have confirmed we have a ferret." He tapped the wall, then spoke into his radio again. "7412 to 7414, I need breaching tools in the basement."

The handler pulled Scout from the closet and had her sit, waiting for the hidden door to be opened.

On the other side of the wall, a confident Checkonski was moving quickly but quietly through the damp tunnel he had prepared for this exact purpose. It reminded him of the tunnels he dug to escape from prisons in Russia and France. Compared to those paths to freedom, this was spacious. The smell of raw earth was not unfamiliar to him and no longer scared him as it once did. His first escape through a tunnel barely the width of his shoulders made his breathing labored, and his mind told him he was running out of air. Not tonight, though. Tonight, he was in a four-foot concrete pipe. No worries about the walls collapsing, water dripping on his head, or rats using a new path through the dirt. Tonight, the only minor inconvenience was not being able to stand up straight.

It was still amusing to him that the neighbors were easily convinced that the digging was no more than an effort to fix a broken septic system. They thought that the house next to Checkonski was occupied by a recluse. The lights came on at night, along with the television, and the vehicle in the driveway moved occasionally. Truth was, they were too busy with their own routines.

That was the benefit of being in the suburbs: everyone minded their own business. The other advantage was obvious. As long as he kept the girls under control and kept a low profile, he was able to operate inside the city, where businessmen and criminals alike could travel to the house, visit with his stable of women, and pay him as he wished. And pay they did, whether for more sex or to remain anonymous about the sex they had. The hidden cameras proved very lucrative and provided a great deal of private enjoyment for him.

The girls were another story altogether. It didn't take much to keep them quiet. When they first arrived, they were too scared or drugged to be a problem to anyone. After they adjusted to their new lifestyle, all it took was keeping them fed and giving them access to the drugs they wanted. After a year, they didn't know anything else. The key was to get them addicted quickly. The ones who didn't adjust and comply were sent overseas, and the threat of what was possible in those other houses was usually enough to keep even the tough ones under control.

Then there was the small percentage who bonded with their captors and visitors. They helped keep the others in line and were the ones he had to thank for having the time to escape into this tunnel. Their warnings provided him the precious seconds he needed, but even then, it was a close call—much closer than he wanted or expected.

As he made his way down the one hundred feet or so of the pipe, he could hear tapping at the entrance he left. He knew the door was reinforced, and it would take them a while to get through it. That would give him time to finish his arrangements in the tunnel and get up, out, and onto the street behind the house. *Cops . . . so predictable. They always come in the same way and park in front.*

He was surprised, though, when the lights went out. That was a new twist. Even the police in London and Berlin didn't do that. He figured someone just got a bit zealous and shut down the power. It didn't matter to him. By the time they turned the lights back on, he would be long gone.

Checkonski reached the turn in the tunnel and finished his preparations. Then he retrieved the bag he'd hidden containing cash, a couple of fake passports, two pistols with ammunition, sunglasses, a razor, and hair dye. In an hour, he would be just another person driving away from the city, looking nothing like any photo the police had of him. The money he'd wired overseas would allow him to live like a king.

As he pondered his next country of residence, he reached the ladder. He put the bag over his right shoulder and started to climb. He reached the top and flicked the latch to open the trap door in the floor of the residence next door to 191 Durango. He climbed out of the hole and contemplated closing it, as he'd done on his dry runs. He elected instead to keep it open as a private one-fingered salute to the cops who would eventually find it, if they survived the trip through the tunnel. He smiled as he contemplated the consequences of following him, and turned to walk out of the dark house. *Strange*, he thought. *They must have cut the lights here as well.*

He took two steps before the Axon Shockwave hit him. Twelve TASER cartridges struck him simultaneously. The SWAT team placed the device after the helicopter pilot saw something suspicious on the forward-looking infrared camera: a consistent heat signature leading from 191 Durango under the ground.

The SWAT commander ordered the use of the Shockwave in case some of the girls used the tunnel or Checkonski or his henchmen grabbed a girl to use as a hostage. The device worked well, and Checkonski was immobilized for five full seconds. At the initial shock, he dropped the gun in his right hand.

Using the sound of the TASER cartridges as a signal, the SWAT members moved in quickly. Although they would have handcuffed Checkonski while he was enjoying the effects of the TASER cartridges, the SWAT members had to stage up behind cover. Andrei Checkonski's body relaxed as the current stopped, and he was blinded by the intensity of the weapon lights on the M4 rifles pointed at him. When he heard the three United States Marshals yelling commands at him, he thought about running or reaching around to find the pistol. Then he heard one of them yell, "Put up your hands, Andrei, you're under arrest! Get down on the ground!"

The shock of hearing it was almost more threatening than the weapons pointed at him. *No one has called me that name in over ten years.* He looked on the ground using the light from the weapons, and located the pistol. His heart was pounding now as he contemplated his options. *Cops aren't like the Russian or Turkish military. They won't beat me, but the inmates . . . I'll be dead in any prison. Maybe I can take a couple with me.*

As he thought, he heard a soft voice from behind the lights: "Your choice, motherfucker." The words were so low and cold, they sent a chill through Checkonski. He caught a quick glimpse of the black shield the officers were behind. It was a choice he both feared and dreamed of his entire adult life. He portrayed himself as tough, strong, and an enforcer who beat people into submission. In reality, the people he beat were young girls and women. The few people he killed were brought to him tied up by the men he paid to do his dirty work.

In the movies, the American cops always said things like, "Don't do it," or told the bad guy to give up. *These guys want me to grab the gun, so they can kill me.*

As Checkonski slowly raised his hands up over his head, his body was slammed to the ground, and he heard his pistol skid across the floor. He felt someone fall hard on a knee across the back of his legs as his hands were pulled quickly behind his back. It all happened quickly in a well-rehearsed manner. His legs were shackled, as well. He was thoroughly searched, then he was hauled up onto his feet.

Checkonski smiled at his new captors. "I am a foreign national. I demand to be taken to the Russian embassy."

As he stood repeating the phrase, one of the US Marshals stood in front of him and moved close to his face. He stopped talking as he prepared to be beaten. The deputy marshal stood there for a second, then Checkonski saw the gloved hands remove the goggles, Kevlar helmet, and balaclava. Senior United States Marshal Sandra Dent looked at Checkonski through bright-blue eyes. She stared at him and studied his face.

"What do you want?" Checkonski's voice was flat.

"Three things, Andrei. First, I want to see what a coward looks like up close. Second, I know you'll never look this good again. You're going into general population. Third," she smiled, "I wanted you to know that a girl just knocked you down and handcuffed you, and there was nothing you could do about it."

The other five marshals laughed out loud.

Checkonski's face got red. He almost screamed, but held back. Marshal Dent never moved. "I demand to be taken to the Russian embassy at once." He spoke quietly, almost politely.

"Well, guys, I guess Mr. Child Rapist and Abductor hasn't heard the good news. Should we tell him now?"

A deep voice came from behind one of the masks. "Good a time as any."

Marshal Dent smiled. "The Russian embassy revoked your citizenship about two hours ago. It seems one of the Russian mobsters you blackmailed in your little house took offense." Checkonski's face fell. "Yep. It seems you are a man without a country, Andrei. Don't worry, though. The federal penitentiary is filled with people who love a good international experience. You will be very popular."

A few moments later, he was sitting in the back of a paddy wagon on his way to appear before a federal magistrate.

CHAPTER 43

A s the marshals announced that Checkonski was in custody, the SWAT operators breached the door at the entrance to the tunnel. As they looked down the pipe, they saw that the dim lighting did not provide a great deal of guidance for someone who didn't know the way.

As they prepared to enter the tunnel, Scout was poised to head in first. Her tail was wagging, and she exemplified the traits of a Belgian Malinois: work until they fall over. She climbed into the pipe with her handler and two SWAT operators, who acted as security. As they advanced slowly, Scout had her nose to the ground. About twenty-five feet into the tunnel, Scout stopped and started barking. When her handler tried to walk forward, she pushed him to the side of the wall while continuing to bark.

Just then, the radio came to life. It was one of the marshals at the other end of the tunnel. "ABORT! ABORT! All units exit the tunnel!"

Scout, her handler, and the two SWAT officers backed out toward the house. The marshals came onto the radio again. "Device found! Bring EOD to our location!"

Hours later, the bomb-disposal units from the Lawler PD and the FBI secured one hundred pounds of explosives in the tunnel. Checkonski's efforts to create a diversion to cover his escape failed, and all the officers and agents who entered the houses would return home to their families. Fortunately for everyone, Checkonski was handcuffed and unable to use his phone to trigger the device.

Five hours later, seven men who were Checkonski's customers were in custody, and fourteen girls were in a relief shelter for battered women. Translators on the language lines were working to determine the country of origin of the girls, even the ones who resisted efforts to help them. They had been captive so long; they were loyal to their captors, insisting that they would never provide any information.

* * *

Johnny and Holly had found four girls hiding in a closet. One was unconscious and was passed to the paramedics. Two spoke hardly any English and were shaking. Johnny guessed part of that was from withdrawals. They had a long road ahead of them. One girl reached out and latched on to Johnny. It was no surprise; Hannah grew up around uniforms and badges. Johnny held her. Then he took his raid jacket off and placed it around her, over the sheer material she was wearing.

As she hugged Johnny again, she started to sob. Johnny recognized her from the missing-person bulletin and the briefing. "It's okay, Hannah. You're safe now."

She squeezed Johnny tighter when she heard her name for the first time in weeks. "Thank you. Thank you. I knew someone would come for us." A moment later, she pushed back from Johnny quickly. "Britt! We've got to get Britt!" She was looking at Johnny, then Holly.

"Who is Britt?" Holly asked.

"She's one of the girls, but she's really young, like, twelve. She's so sweet."

"Where was she when the raid started?"

"They kept us in specific rooms. I think she's two rooms over from here, toward the back of the house."

Johnny and Holly passed the other girls off to paramedics, who covered them with blankets. Then they followed Hannah, who walked cautiously, looking around corners before she stepped.

"Hannah, it's okay," Holly said, placing a hand onto Hannah's shoulder. "No need to look out. The house is clear. You're safe now."

Hannah looked at her. "Sorry. They beat us if we moved around." She made the comment quickly without thinking about it, as the rules had become her way of life. The words hit Holly and Johnny like a hammer.

As Hannah led them to Britt's room, they saw two officers and a paramedic in the room at the bed. There was a small-framed girl on the bed. The paramedic was hooking her up to a defibrillator, and the officers were administering naloxone. The defibrillator sounded and the paramedic pushed everyone back. "Clear!" The shock caused Britt's body to jump, and the paramedic used a stethoscope to check her heart. "Nothing. Let's load and go, but I don't think she'll make it. That's four doses of naloxone."

The paramedic left the room, and one of the officers who was helping Britt walked up to Hannah, who was sobbing with her head down. "I'm so sorry." Hannah could see he was crying, as well. He dropped his head and wiped his eyes as he walked toward the door.

When Johnny put his arm around Hannah's shoulders, she collapsed into him. He held her up just as much as he held her to console her. In that moment, Johnny wasn't a cop; he was a person handed an impossible task: comfort a victim who would never be the same. Her words, barely audible over her sobs, would haunt Johnny for the rest of his life: "That could've been me. There were so many who died."

As one of the officers and two firefighters ran with Britt from the building, the halls of the house, the driveway, and the street leading to the ambulance were lined with officers and federal agents in raid jackets and SWAT gear. They stood silent, staring at the small, fragile girl on the stretcher while the mechanical device on her chest kept her heart pumping. The same officers and agents who minutes ago brought their training to bear to fulfill their oaths after putting on their brave faces were now holding their breath and fighting back their tears. The horrible waste of life, the loss of so much potential, and the stolen innocence of a child was too much for them to bear.

When the ambulance pulled away, they continued their work with few words, but the sniffles and barely audible prayers throughout the house and the yard could not be quelled. Their Kevlar vests could protect their hearts from the force of a bullet, but not from the horror that comes from the witnessing the suffering and death of a child.

Johnny brought Hannah out to an ambulance while Holly continued looking for victims inside the house. The search would be difficult, as the officers and agents expected the victims to hide. All they had known was fear for so long.

As EMTs gave Hannah a bottle of water, she spoke freely, though she was still groggy. Johnny pulled up his phone and scrolled through the database Franetti created. Then Johnny dialed a number he had recently saved in his phone.

"Hello?" The voice was tired, hollow, but had a faint sound of hope. "Till? Have anything? What do we know?" The background noises were different: louder, familiar.

That's the monorail at Hartsfield! He's in Atlanta! Johnny pulled in a deep breath that allowed him to get the words out. *There will be time for emotions later. This is not about me.* He had prepared for this call that he hoped would take place. He worked through it in his mind a hundred times. He planned to give details, answer questions, and get information, but his heart was speaking now. He only managed to say a few words before his voice failed him. "I'm here with Hannah, Lieutenant. She is alive, and she's coming home."

The voice on the other end of the phone went from flat to sobbing in a second. He must have been at work when Johnny first called and gone straight to the airport. *He told me I could update him in person.* Johnny passed the phone to Hannah's shaking hands.

"Daddy! I'm so sorry!"

Through powerful, heaving sobs, the kind that only come from the type of sadness that rocks the soul, Max Trover fought to speak. "It's okay, sweetheart. I'm on my way."

Barely able to speak, Hannah looked at Johnny as she spoke into the phone. "I don't even know where I am!"

"I do, Hannah, and nothing could keep me from you. I'm coming to take you home."

CHAPTER 44

Over the next few days, hopefully all of the girls would be identified and their names placed in a database. Families waiting for news of their missing daughters would finally learn they were alive. Then would come the long and arduous task of determining if it was safe for them to return to their home countries. For some, there would be no homecoming. Their captors and those who procured them into slavery would do anything to silence them and some of the victims would be ostracized and banished from their families. Many would likely receive asylum and temporary residence in the United States through the efforts of local and federal authorities. They would be asked to testify but could not be forced to do so.

As Johnny followed the progress of the crime-scene techs inside and outside of the house, he was fascinated by the complexity of the operation at 191 Durango Way. He stood with Holly as computers were removed from the house, along with hard drives, cameras, routers, and other electronic equipment. He also saw bags of drugs brought from the house. Most were used to keep the girls under control, while some were sold to customers.

"Makes you wonder how many of these houses there are in this county alone," Holly said in a flat tone.

"Not sure, but no way this is the only one." Johnny looked at the surrounding houses.

"Not to mention the entire US and other countries. It turns my stomach." Holly grimaced at the thoughts running through her mind.

Johnny glanced at his partner. "They'll follow any leads they can. Maybe they'll find a bunch more."

"I'd like to think you're right, but right now they're probably folding up shop and moving. I'll bet they have some sort of periodic check-in system. If someone doesn't check in on time, they start monitoring news stories. Once they hear about this raid, they'll scatter."

"That may be," Johnny said, "but they'll have Franetti on their asses!"

"I hope he tracks down every one of these mother-fuckers."

Holly and Johnny got into Johnny's car once the second truck was filled with evidence. There was nothing more for a homicide detective to do at that point. Johnny drove back to the office. They barely spoke a word. Some sights scar the mind.

CHAPTER 45

Johnny and Major Worth got off the plane in Miami and were met by two Miami-Dade homicide detectives. They showed their identification and were walked to two unmarked cars. They arrived at the Miami-Dade Homicide office and were introduced to the commander. They showed the commander their warrant and extradition writ. The local detectives verified the warrant through the National Crime Information Center, then obtained a fugitive warrant from a Florida judge. When it all checked out, they walked to a briefing room and met with the leader of Miami SWAT. He had a team of twelve SWAT officers assembled.

"We found your boy," the commander said. "Turns out our Intelligence folks have been monitoring him for a while, but never had enough on him for a warrant. How many people has he iced?"

Johnny spoke up. Even though Worth outranked him, it was an unwritten rule in Homicide: your case, your call. "Not sure, but he's probably been at it for more than twenty years."

"I understand he killed a cop?" The SWAT commander was reading the warrant.

"Yep. Michael Dunlap. His prints were on the inside

of a backpack where we found the guns he used. He also confessed to someone."

"Quite the criminal mastermind. Well, unless he fights the ride legally, he'll be back in your jurisdiction in twenty-four hours—*if* he plays nice with us."

"I wouldn't count on it."

"We can accommodate him in any scenario. Hopefully, he'll use the common sense God gave him and surrender. That's what we prefer, but I'm not taking any chances with a cop killer."

Several members of the SWAT team nodded.

A few minutes later, the plans were set and the units were en route to the house. A surveillance team had been in place for two days watching the small, three-bedroom house in a modest suburb of Miami proper. There were two cars in the driveway and only one person in the house. The units watched Frederick Meng come and go to the grocery store, a local bar, and a meeting that was likely in furtherance of his business, as it took place in a coffee shop frequented by known mobsters and owned by a Cuban refugee who was known to trade in drugs and girls. In fact, at the time, Meng was the only Asian in the building. It was convenient, as the Miami Intelligence Unit and the DEA had been working an undercover operation in the coffee shop for two years.

The house was at the end of a cul-de-sac, but there was a gravel path to the road in the neighborhood behind it. It led to some type of nature trail and green space. Johnny chuckled that none of the folks who raised money for the green space ever expected that a cop killer would find it an excellent escape route in the event of a police raid. *Then again*, he thought, *no one really knows who lives near them.*

The first units arrived quietly by trail bike, saturating the nature trail and green space, while the Miami park units closed the green space using signs that read CLOSED FOR MAINTENANCE. Until the story hit the press tomorrow, the people hoping for an afternoon run would just keep complaining to the officers on the scene and their local elected officials about the inefficiency of government and touting how they helped fund that park. It was amazing how everyone always believes they have everything figured out. When the story broke, they would change from complaining to bragging that they were practically there when it happened.

Once the units were in place behind the house, a group of four SWAT operators approached the house from the rear. They were careful to stay back beyond the field of view of the exterior cameras on the house until they were ready. They got into position, then gave a signal to the armored unit carrying ten SWAT members who would approach and enter the front of the house. As the officers approached the front of the house, the units at the back prepared for the worst.

The officers yelled loudly as they climbed the four steps to the porch, "POLICE WITH A WARRANT!" A moment later, one of the officers hit the door with a ram, expecting it to swing in. Instead, nothing happened. He hit it again with the same results. An officer ran up to the house with a large jack that was placed horizontally in the doorframe. The back door was also reinforced. As the officers worked the jack handle to spread the doorframes, a two-man observer unit watched the windows in the front of the house, looking for movement.

The units at the front door worked the doorframe away, then the first officer hit the door with the ram again.

This time, it gave way enough for them to enter after an officer threw a flash-bang device through the opening. As they entered the half-open door, the observer across the street announced that he saw movement in an upstairs window. The back door still held.

"All units, movement in the second story at the north end at the front of the house."

The units in the house and at the rear heard the announcement and braced for a firefight.

As the SWAT operators entered the house, the shots from inside started to ring out. High-caliber rifle rounds hit the shield-and-plate body armor of the first two officers. The response was both immediate and fierce. Meng, who was at the top of the stairs, retreated to a bedroom. Two officers pulled the officer who was shot from the house. He was stunned, but his body armor had stopped the rounds.

Officers approached the stairs in force, while others flooded in through the front door. They moved quickly and methodically from room to room, clearing them. In several rooms, they found long weapons positioned under windows. With each step, it became clear that Meng was prepared for a long fight. The threat of overwhelming force that so often ended these situations without a shot being fired wouldn't have the same effect here. It was now clear that he would fight to get away, or take out as many cops as he could before he died.

As the units cleared the rooms on the first floor at the north end of the house, the spotter again saw movement in the window upstairs. While Meng was crouched below the windowsill, the spotter saw the barrel of the rifle. A SWAT sniper across the street took up the slack on his trigger as he aimed below the window to where he estimated Meng would be crouched as a left-handed shooter. No detail was left out of the briefings. The bullet from the .338 Lapua penetrated the wall under the window in the front room and entered the chest of the shooter. The gun fell from his arms, and he was out of sight from the sniper and spotter.

"We have a subject down in the upstairs bedroom. We have no eyes on the subject! All units in the house, exit the rooms at the north end, first floor."

The SWAT officers moved to the stairs, having cleared the main level. One maintained cover on the basement door. Although they expected Meng to be alone, they were taking no chances.

A robot was brought up to the house and quickly sent upstairs. As it climbed the steps, the SWAT officers crept up the stairs. They found the bedroom door closed and learned quickly that it, too, was secured and reinforced. Meng had created a safe room. They used a breaching round from the robot to destroy the hinges and push the door down. The robot entered and searched the room while two SWAT officers cleared the other rooms.

Johnny watched the video screen as the robot camera panned the room. He and Worth were in a surveillance van. They had been watching the cameras on the helmets of the SWAT officers, but now turned their attention to the screen carrying only the feed from the robot.

As the robot turned the corner of the bed, Meng was on his side, breathing in short, labored breaths. As the robot approached, he raised a pistol and fired three times. When he realized that he was shooting at a machine, he turned his body with his last breaths and sprayed bullets toward the door. At the same time, three flash-bang grenades lobbed into the room in his direction. Most of the SWAT officers remained in place while one crawled low behind the doorframe to sight below the bed. He fired one shot at Meng, striking him in the forehead.

Michael Dunlap's killer was dead.

Johnny and Worth watched the robot video feed as it moved around the bed and focused on Meng's face. The .45 round provided signs of obvious death. Contrary to the thoughts of the cop haters, there was no rejoicing or high-fives, even among the SWAT team. They didn't win; they survived. They provided every opportunity for Meng to be taken into custody, but he made his choices. For the two officers who fired, there would be investigations and interviews, as well as downtime taking them away from the team. Fortunately, the city was large enough to have several SWAT team components. But if this team was called on during their absence, they would be weaker and more vulnerable.

Johnny got up and started walking toward the door of the large surveillance van. Worth looked at him. "You okay, Johnny?"

"Yep." Johnny pulled out his cell phone.

"Where are you headed?"

"There are some calls I promised to make."

Worth smiled, and Johnny turned toward the door. He opened the latch as he dialed the first number. Tony Tucci picked up the phone.

"We got him."

CHAPTER 46

Johnny and Holly pulled up to a house in the rural area of Lawler County. Two cars pulled up behind him. Lettieri drove Tucci in one car, and House arrived just behind them. As they got out, they gathered at the end of the driveway.

Lettieri spoke first. "So she knows we're coming?"

"Yes," Johnny replied.

"What did you tell her?" Tucci was focused on Johnny's response.

"I told her we had a break in the case. Told her I wanted to tell her in person."

Tucci nodded his head.

"How'd you keep the lid on the story in the media?" House was skeptical.

"Well," Johnny replied, "let's just say I have a friend, and I promised him an exclusive if he held the story for forty-eight hours. The rest of the media is still trying to figure out who Meng was, much less his connection to Georgia."

"That would do it." Tucci was looking at the house now.

"It's not gonna get done with us standing out here." Lettieri started walking up the driveway.

When they reached the front door, Holly and Johnny stood at the door, and Johnny rang the doorbell. The three retired detectives stood behind them.

Anna Dunlap walked to the door and looked out, then she opened it. Holly was amazed that she had a smile on her face. "Detective Till—excuse me, Johnny. Please come in." Then she saw the three detectives standing behind him. Her mouth came open, and her hands came to her face. Her face flushed as her eyes filled with tears. "You got him, didn't you?" Then she collapsed into Johnny's arms.

"We got him, Anna." He held her while she sobbed. Johnny looked up at the detectives with him. "We all got him."

Over the next two hours, Holly and Johnny told her everything—all the details she could take. She asked questions and broke down at some of the answers. They outlined the tremendous effort undertaken to find Michael Dunlap's killer.

The meeting was hard at times and unbearable at others. Johnny was struck with the privilege he had. After all these years, he got to tell her a story she never knew. Johnny told Anna that her husband gave his life trying to save a young girl he barely knew. She learned how the murder was nothing more than an effort to cover the tracks of an organized criminal enterprise. She also heard how difficult the case was to solve. He got to tell a victim that the person who killed an important person in her life was brought to justice. It was an honor every homicide detective cherished.

When the five detectives left, she hugged all of them. "I cannot wait to tell the kids, although I'm not sure how to do it."

Holly spoke up. "The department counselors and

chaplains are available to you and your family. Just say the word."

As they stood on the front porch running out of things to say, Anna Dunlap spoke softly as she looked at no one in particular. "So many years without answers. Maybe tonight will be different."

"Ma'am?" Johnny asked.

"Every night since Michael was murdered, I've prayed for answers." She took a deep breath. "Now I can just pray for peace."

The five detectives walked down the driveway toward their cars. They exchanged handshakes and hugs, and the three retired men took an opportunity to kid each other a few more times.

"Well, House. See you on the cover of *GQ* soon." Lettieri was laughing.

"Some of us set fashion trends, and others follow them," House responded.

"And some of us don't give a damn," Tucci stated flatly. That broke up the group.

Holly shook hands with the retired men and walked up to Tucci. "Anthony, can I call you to have lunch or breakfast and talk about old cases?"

"Well, of course, Holly. I just hope you won't be jealous when the waitresses hit on me." He smiled, and Holly hugged him.

Lettieri looked at House and motioned to his car. "Oh, yeah. Hang on." House went to his trunk and came back with a package. The three men walked close to each other, smiling.

Tucci spoke. "Detective Till, front and center!"

Johnny looked at Holly, who shrugged her shoulders. "Don't look at me. I have no idea what they're up to."

Johnny walked toward the men and stood up straight directly in front of Lettieri, who stood in the middle. Tucci took a piece of paper out of his pants pocket, unfolded it, and began to read. "Detective Till, you recently entered the ranks of an elite group of detectives. Around the world, in departments in every country, the detectives who work in the homicide division are revered, respected, and counted on to be the voices of the victims who can no longer speak. Even among our ranks, you have distinguished yourself. The three of us, who represent the 'old guard,' recognize your accomplishment in solving the murder of a law enforcement officer who was on duty protecting the citizens he swore to faithfully serve. We present to you this reminder of the past and the tradition that you carry on."

House passed the box to Holly. Johnny took it from her and shook their hands. Then he put the box down on the trunk of his unmarked car. "I'm speechless. This means a lot."

"You don't even know what it is! It could be a bag of crap." Lettieri started laughing, and House smacked the top of his head.

Johnny opened the box and pulled out a pair of George Carney–designed handcuffs from 1912, complete with a key. "Amazing!"

"Keep looking, Till." Tucci was standing back a bit, taking it all in.

A few seconds later, Johnny pulled an antique revolver from the box. It was a Colt Police Positive Special chambered for the .32-20 WCF cartridge. As Johnny looked over the gun, Holly leaned around his shoulder. Johnny looked up at the three men.

Tucci spoke first. "That's old school, Till."

"Like you young cops look at my flip phone!" Lettieri chimed in.

Tucci waved his hand at Lettieri. "Don't listen to this melon head! That, Johnny Till, is an authentic piece of law enforcement history. It takes a bottlenecked cartridge and was issued to cops around the turn of the 1900s. Very rare."

"A little reminder, Till." Lettieri had his arm over Tucci's shoulders. "Never forget where you came from and that you and Forrester are carrying out a long tradition in the world of homicide detectives."

"You've made my day, gentlemen. Thank you."

After another round of hugs and handshakes, the three cars left the front of Officer Michael Dunlap's house. Each car was filled with a sense of accomplishment and stories about the cases they worked and what lay ahead for them.

CHAPTER 47

As is often the case in the South, the spring came in tentatively with sunny, warm days running from the pattern of cold nights like an unruly child straying far from her parents in the grocery store. A nearly freezing morning could be followed by a consistent three days of comfortably sunny weather with mild nights. Today was one of the days Johnny loved: a mild night followed by a brilliant sunrise and clear skies. He went for a run in the morning, then got to his office early. He had an important duty to perform.

He had no set appointment, but Johnny felt it was one of the most important meetings of his career to date. Different from his typical sport coat and slacks, Johnny wore a suit today with a freshly pressed shirt and a new tie. He checked in at the office, then plugged the address into his GPS. The notation on his desk calendar read FOLLOW UP-DUNLAP.

He pulled out of the parking lot of headquarters and turned right toward the interstate. In a short thirty minutes, he reached his destination and parked his unmarked car. He was surprised to see two other unmarked cars just ahead of him. Standing next to them were Major

Bill Worth and Lieutenant Dan Paschal. Paschal, who normally wore jeans and a polo shirt, was also dressed in a suit. The two men watched Johnny walk up.

Johnny smiled and spoke to them. "You're either following me or getting ahead of me!"

All three men laughed. Johnny walked forward and shook their hands. "How did you know I'd be here?"

"The calendar entry was a dead giveaway, Johnny. Dunlap's case is closed. We boxed it up and sent it off to storage last week." Worth was smiling.

Johnny turned to Paschal. "Okay, I get how he knew, but you?"

Paschal put his left hand on Worth's right shoulder. "Let's just say a good intelligence lieutenant gathers information from any available source."

The men looked at each other for a moment, then Johnny spoke. "I came late to this. You guys were there that night. Maybe you should take the lead on this."

"Not a chance, Johnny," Worth said. "You earned this."

Johnny took a deep breath. "Okay, then. Let's go."

The three men walked off the paved road onto the rich, deep-green grass of the cemetery. They walked slowly to the top of a hill toward a set of headstones. As they approached, they slowed as the large headstone marking a family plot came into view.

"I remember this walk like it was yesterday." Paschal looked at Worth. "Remember the cold snap, Bill?"

"We were expecting snow!" Worth looked at Johnny, then back toward the headstones. "I remember the place was packed. The honor guard was to the right, if I remember correctly."

"Yep. They were awesome, Johnny. The twenty-one-gun-salute team was over the next hill, and the buglers played opposite each other from the right and left. You could see uniforms as far as you can see grass right now. It was amazing, and kids from the school stood everywhere with their parents." Paschal was gesturing as he spoke.

"It was an amazing display of respect," Worth said. He looked at Johnny differently than ever before. "Just like you being here today, Johnny."

Johnny looked at the two men. Then he turned to look at the headstone and read the inscribed family name, DUNLAP. All three walked to the grave marker with the name MICHAEL THOMAS DUNLAP engraved on it. Below the name were two dates, and below that a biblical inscription:

Blessed are the peacemakers,
for they shall be called the children of God.
Matthew 5:9

Johnny placed the flowers he'd brought in front and put his hands on the grave marker, letting them linger for a moment. Then he took a slip of paper from his pocket and put it on the top of the stone. He stepped back and gave a salute. "We got him, sir. May you rest in peace."

Worth and Paschal put their hands on the grave marker and closed their eyes in a silent prayer.

"Your dad would be proud of you, Johnny." Paschal patted Johnny on the back.

"Yes, sir. I believe he would."

"Come on. Let's get a bite of lunch at Ralphie's Dogs. It was one of Dunlap's favorites," Worth said with excitement in his voice. "Your steak will come later. A deal's a deal!"

"Great idea, Bill. Johnny, when we get there, remind me to tell you about the time Dunlap stopped a DUI driver who was completely naked!" Paschal was starting to laugh thinking about it.

Worth joined in, "I remember that night! It wasn't as crazy as the guy who broke into the Bells Ferry Country Store to steal all of the Twinkies because he heard on the news they weren't going to make 'em anymore!"

The three of them laughed. Johnny laughed, even though he wasn't there when it happened. It was that way with cops. They saw all sides and angles of human nature. They laughed because people did crazy things, and also because they had to laugh to get past the bad calls. Cops honor and revere their fallen heroes, then move on to the next day quietly, hoping and praying that another of their ranks will never fall in the line of duty. Such prayers are like the misguided hopes of a child. The fight to protect the innocent and keep evil from the door will always bring casualties.

For now, the three men carried on an ancient tradition in law enforcement. They toasted their fallen brother by reliving the good times, the crazy calls, and reminders that the day he died was only one day in the life of a man.

As the three men walked from the grave marker toward their cars, the sun's reflection off the top of the smooth granite was interrupted by a piece of faded white paper that read: HOMICIDE: OFFICER MICHAEL T. DUNLAP. Across the name was a red stamp with capital letters: COLD CASE: CLOSED.

AUTHOR'S NOTE

Human trafficking is a worldwide epidemic. The United States is neither immune nor off-limits to both the enslaving of young children—predominately girls—or their entry into sex slavery. The United States Department of Health and Human Services established a hotline to receive calls about human trafficking. In fiscal year 2017, the hotline received 62,835 calls from across the United States and US territories, identified 8,759 human-trafficking cases, and provided resources and referrals to 10,615 victims. The hotline also received information on 4,863 potential traffickers and 1,698 businesses facilitating human trafficking. More than 2,000 individuals who identified as victims of trafficking directly called the hotline seeking help.[1] As a criminal enterprise, logic dictates that these numbers barely scratch the surface of the true problem.

Sex trafficking cannot survive without the willing participation of people who seek out and pay for the services

---

[1] Office of the Under Secretary for Civilian Security, Department of State, 2018 Trafficking in Persons Report, p. 446, June 2018; https://www.state.gov/reports/2018-trafficking-in-persons.report/.

provided against the will of the victims. As a social issue, it is deeply tied to the illegal drug trade, the proliferation of gangs, illegal immigration, and a criminal justice system that fails to severely punish dangerous criminals and remove them from civilized society.

If you were shocked at what you read about human trafficking and sex slavery, please be motivated to act. Always remember that I have drastically reduced the actual descriptions of what happens to these victims. Through meetings with advocates who rescue victims, law enforcement officers who find victims and arrest their captors, and the prosecutors who strive to punish those responsible and destroy their networks, I have learned more than I care to think about. The true horror came when I heard stories from a dedicated undercover officer whose role was to buy children from the people who captured and enslaved them.

Any civilized society must work to protect its future and the most vulnerable of its citizens.

It's not our job to toughen our children up to face a cruel and heartless world. It's our job to raise children who will make the world a little less cruel and heartless.
—L. R. Knost

WHAT YOU CAN DO TO STOP HUMAN TRAFFICKING

Know the signs:
- Dressed inappropriately for the time or event
- Appears fearful, anxious, or nervous/paranoid
- Avoids eye contact
- Shows signs of sexual abuse
- Does not or is not allowed to speak for themselves
- Does not respond when asked questions
- Appears malnourished
- Has few or no personal possessions

GET HELP:
- Call 911
- Text HELP or INFO to BeFree (233733) for the National Human Trafficking Hotline (1-888-373-7888)
- Download the See Something, Send Something app

ABOUT THE AUTHOR

Lance J. LoRusso began his law enforcement career in 1988 and has been practicing law since 1999. His practice focuses on representing first responders including when they are injured on and off duty. To date, LoRusso has represented approximately eighty law enforcement officers involved in on-duty shootings or in-custody deaths. He regularly speaks to and instructs first responders from local, state, federal, and international agencies. His articles and blog posts have been featured in first-responder publications, including *SWAT*, and on websites such as Police One, Law Enforcement Today, and Officer Resource. His first book, *When Cops Kill: The Aftermath of a Critical Incident*, is referenced and used in law enforcement academies and criminal justice programs around the United States. His book *Blue News* addresses the intersection of law enforcement and media. His fiction book *Peacemaking* is a "Christian thriller" about a cop's walk with Christ, and *Parallax: Crime Tales* is an anthology of short stories. All of his books are available through www.lancelorussobooks.com and Amazon. The profits from his nonfiction books support first-responder charities.

OTHER BOOKS BY LANCE J. LORUSSO

The World-Class Rainmaker

When Cops Kill

Peacemaking

Blue News

Parallax

COMING SOON

Pursued